I0762270

THE CATALYST TRILOGY: BOOK 3

SOMETIMES OUR SEEDS CAN EVOLVE OUR DESTINIES

THE NESTLINGS

A NOVEL

SELIN SENOL-AKIN

The characters and events portrayed in this book are fictitious. Any similarity to real persons, living or dead, is coincidental and not intended by the author.

- Psychotherapy references were inspired by *Hallucinations* by Oliver Sacks *& It Didn't Start With You* by Mark Wolynn

ISBN: 978-1-7346563-6-7

PRINTED IN THE UNITED STATES OF AMERICA

Edited by: Kirsten McNeill

Dedicated first and foremost to my 'nestling' Dalya, for whom I've been flapping and extending my wings through the storms…

"Tend to your dream. Protect it as you would a fallen *nestling.* Until the day when it- and you- will fly."

JERRY SPINELLI

"…If I can…help one fainting robin unto his nest again, I shall not live in vain."

EMILY DICKINSON

CHAPTER 1

THE MARRIAGE

IS LIFE TRULY WHAT HAPPENS WHEN WE'RE BUSY MAKING OTHER plans? the groom mused, adjusting his black, silk bowtie. A wry smile played on his lips. *We haven't even said our vows yet, and I sound like a grumpy old man already.* Despite feeling utterly shocked still and rather unprepared—the groom had to admit he'd technically been cultivated for this day throughout his upbringing.

Groomed and doomed, he snickered to himself. Many around him had romanticized the concept of marriage as he was growing up, but the groom had witnessed more legal unions crumbling than remaining intact. Regardless, he had always figured that he would eventually fall into the societal trap and get married; he just never thought it'd happen like *this*.

Unexpectedly and excruciatingly, the groom thought, clicking his tongue against the roof of his mouth. *Too soon. Not right.*

The pregnancy. The lies. The secrets.

"Responsibility," the groom muttered under his breath. "I've got to do whatever is necessary."

"May I come in?" he heard the sultry voice call from the other side of the oak door.

"That depends, love," the groom said, fixing his collar and fidgeting with his cufflinks. "Are you in your bridal gown already? Because you know it's bad luck for the groom to see the bride before the wedding…"

"Oh, superstitious nonsense," his bride giggled. "Come on, I'm feeling ceremony jitters. I could really use your hug right about now. I'm coming in…"

A million thoughts raced through his mind at the stunning vision of his wife-to-be. Her hair was elegantly styled in a way he'd never seen on her before, and the off-white gown accentuated her rather slender waist, though the glimmer of a bump was undeniable. The groom approached her, pressing a soft kiss to her bare shoulder. He inhaled deeply the floral scent of the perfume clinging to her glistening skin.

"You look astonishing," he whispered, caressing his bride's neck, feeling the hairs on the back of her head stand erect- along with his own male organ.

"Thank you, baby," she whimpered, their lips meeting in a ravenous kiss. Their chemistry and acceptance of each other— it had to mean they were somehow 'meant to be', didn't it? If the groom even believed in such things, anyway.

What else could it have been, if not *kismet*? After everything they'd been through.

The crime. The groom would forever be haunted by what had happened. By how he had treated her. And, yet—she'd forgiven him. *No harm done, is there?* They could certainly put the past behind them and try to find happiness, couldn't they?

"Look at that…" his bride whispered, gazing at their reflection in the vanity table mirror.

"At what?" he asked, turning around to see her admiring gaze with a twinkle in her eye. He wrapped his arms around his bride's supple, cool skin from behind her, resting his chin on her shoulder. "Oh, *us*."

"That's right," she continued. "You and me. Who knew we'd make it to this point in time? I just hope that…nothing ruins it."

The groom nodded. It seemed his bride, too, had been having similar anxieties about everything.

"We're not supposed to talk about the past anymore, remember?" The groom grabbed his bride's torso and turned her toward him, his fingers lifting her chin closer to his own for another kiss. *Salty*. He was surprised to see her cheeks had suddenly become wet with tears.

"Hey, love. Look at me. Your make-up is going to smudge before the ceremony."

The bride's eyes were still closed as she hummed an indistinct tune.

"Baby, open your eyes and *look* at me!" the groom demanded, his voice tinged with urgency.

As soon as her pupils met his, the groom wished that they hadn't. Her gaze shot through him like a laser beam, fixed somewhere in the empty space behind them both, in the vicinity of the mirror. The groom, trembling now, couldn't bring himself to turn around to glimpse where she was staring.

A glimmer of orange light was burning bright as the reflection of a free-floating flame danced around her shiny eyes. Her skin had already become heated to his touch, causing the groom to pull his arms away.

The curse. Would it ever let them go?

CHAPTER 2

Toronto
2031

MALIN MAVERICK WAS CONTENT, ADMIRING HER SLENDER, satin-covered figure reflecting in the mirror. The corners of her candy-red lips curved upward. *This is the perfect prom dress*, she thought. *I just hope my mystery date agrees.*

Lucinda- her friend and classmate- had not too long ago come to her rescue from a recent bout of decision-making despair. "*Girl, as headstrong as I know you are, I refuse to let you attend this dance alone,"* she'd said. *"Bob told me he's got a friend from the neighborhood who's apparently seen you around. He's about our age and ruggedly handsome from his photo!"*

The guy in the photo had looked familiar to Malin. Almost like *déjà vu* of someone she'd met before, though she couldn't quite place when or where. *Those brown eyes.*

Each time she glanced at the handsome teenager's photo- now saved on her smartphone- her mind traveled to Norway, where she was born. *Could this guy be Norwegian or something?* Malin wondered. *Is that why I'm associating him with Norway?*

She closed her eyes, her thoughts traversing through time to the woods surrounding her childhood hometown of Sandnes. The family friend she came to call 'uncle' would lead her there, his golden retriever always in tow for her to play with. Malin loved that part.

"You can play out here with us anytime you want," he'd tell her. "Think of this as a secret haven."

"*Heaven?*" she remembered asking, smiling at her childhood naïveté.

"*Ha-ven,*" he'd enunciated, amused. "*It means- a refuge. A safe, comforting place. Like a treehouse or a secret hiding spot to play. Since your mom won't allow you to have a pet in the house, it can be your escape.*"

Malin clenched her fists, drawing a deep breath. She couldn't dare bring up Norway or those woods to her mother, though. The woman was already fragile, working hard to make a new life for them now. She certainly didn't want to trigger her mother's sensitivities.

I really need to be on Mom's good side this week, Malin thought as she tried to shrug off the past. *This prom dress I've reserved on layaway isn't going to buy itself!*

After a few photos in her terracotta-colored gown, Malin scrolled through her favorites, including selfies with her mother. The years had added subtle wrinkles in a most flattering way on her mother's face, especially around her smile lines. Kaitlin was always smiling for her daughter: even after her quick-lived bursts of emotional anger from time to time.

Malin would feel lucky if she could look as graceful as her mother when she herself was in her 40's. Her mother's thick and disheveled dark auburn hair, with several chunks of highlights thrown in over the years to frame her face, was graying at the roots- which added an unintentional, three-color look. Regardless, she insisted she was liking the 'natural' mode, stating it made her feel more 'authentic'.

Back to my big meeting with my handsome date tomorrow. Malin sighed, putting her regular jeans and sweatshirt back on as she got ready to return home. They'd agreed on a casual stroll to get to know each other a little before the dance. Even his name was enough to entice Malin. He sounded like a movie star. "Bo," Lucinda had told her. "Bo Du Feu."

§

Dear Ms. Ramsay

Congratulations on all your recent success with Ignite ©! On behalf of Dare Foods Canada, we'd like to propose a collaboration opportunity for the upcoming fiscal year.

Kaitlin stopped reading the rest of the letter, folding the printed sheet in half and inhaling the scent of the stationery. *Ms. Ramsay.* She shut her eyelids in reverie. Could I ever get used to my maiden name again?

"Mom, you've got another one," Malin called out as she treaded toward Kaitlin's slightly ajar bedroom door.

"Cool," Kaitlin shrugged, throwing a subtle smile in her daughter's direction. "How were classes today, sweetie?"

"Good, good," Malin responded, sneaking her head inside the room from behind the door. Her toothy grin revealed a subtle overbite. Kaitlin returned her smile, noticing a rectangular, ivory-colored envelope in her daughter's hand.

"I *may* have taken a little sneak peek at the mail today. You *do* always advise me to tell the truth, mom- that you'd get over it faster even if you get angry."

Malin's gold-streaked, chestnut brown hair fell across her almond-shaped and amber eyes. As always, she threw her head back to move the layers off of her visage; Kaitlin had worried it'd become a tic for Malin. Her daughter often seemed to have her silky, fine hair in her face, regardless of how many hair clips were fastened around her head.

Kaitlin beamed with pride as she nodded, often amused with her daughter's logical reasoning despite her antics. Many in their social circle told Kaitlin her daughter had taken after her rather than her father, yet she'd always seen Paul's face shape and smile- not to mention mannerisms- in Malin. *I hope she's inherited much better luck than both of us, that's for sure*, she thought with a groan.

"Here you go," Malin handed over the letter. "It's the twenty-first century, though, Mom! Why can't they just contact you online, anyway?"

Her eyes twinkled as she spoke, and her delicate features were accentuated further by a heart-shaped face that was leaner than her mother's angular one. Malin had grown into her features through the awkward preteen years, and Kaitlin couldn't believe her daughter had turned into a lovely young woman of almost eighteen already.

"I *do* provide the option of a post office box for snail mail on my blog, honey," Kaitlin said with a shrug, wiggling the envelope in her hands before stuffing it into her desk drawer.

"Hmm," Malin muttered, glancing at the framed wedding photo of her mother and father lingering around the shelf of books, seemingly placed as a bookend. A framed photo of herself as a baby held up a dozen or so books of random colors and sizes from the opposite end.

"Besides," Kaitlin went on, running her fingers with unevenly grown nails over some papers scattered around her desk. "I actually still get more e-mails than physical ones. But it has been nice collecting thankful family postcards from some of the snail-mail-preferring clients around the holidays, you know? I mean— classic ways can simply be sweeter."

"You sound like Dad, sometimes, Mom," Malin tilted her head with a mischievous grin. "Or the horror…," she added with an exaggerated gasp. "Even like *Grandma*!"

"Don't you dare *go there*, now!" Kaitlin scoffed with a laugh. Being compared to her overly critical and dramatic mother, Linda Ramsay, wasn't something Kaitlin welcomed beyond their physical likeness. Though she had come to accept her mother for who she is as she herself got older. Especially as she'd begun to come to terms with what had been plaguing their family. *Mom's simply done the best in the only way she learned how.*

"Maybe we should at least give them another PO Box address, don't you think?" Malin proposed in a serious tone. "This one's right by our place. Someone may figure out our residential address, and- you know- become like a crazy stalker, or something! Oh! And we can also…"

"I appreciate the suggestions, my smart cookie," Kaitlin interrupted with a smirk, swiveling her chair to fully face her daughter. Based on everything they'd been through over the years: Malin's sense of caution didn't surprise her in the slightest bit.

"And I'm used to your curiosities about my stuff by now, though it still doesn't make it right to open your mom's mail, eh, young lady? Anyway… is my princess ready for her big dance?"

"Only *you* can chastise me and then flatter me in the same sentence, Mom," Malin teased, rolling her eyes before quickly breaking out into a smile upon seeing the upset expression on her mother's face.

"Just playing! I *am* ready, yes! I mean, I think I am. I still have to break in those heels you gave me. Argh, I wish I could just wear sneakers- it's such a cute look under gowns, and I can dance better…"

"Malin…" Kaitlin raised a brow at her unconventional daughter.

"I know, I know," Malin rolled her eyes, adding a smile afterward. "*The prom is once in a lifetime*. Yes, yes. Thanks again for letting me borrow them!"

"You're welcome; hey, I'm just tickled we share the same shoe size now, honey," Kaitlin chuckled. Gone were the days when she'd feel comfortable walking in, or even have use for, the sparkling, Michael Kors platform sandals. "It's nice to share my barely-worn, *oldies but goodies* with my girl."

"Speaking of the prom, Mom," Malin started, biting her lower lip. "Has Uncle Aidan secured that limo yet? I promised Lucinda and Bob we'd get a better deal with him."

"Your uncle has been a bit *unreachable* again this week," Kaitlin muttered, shaking her head. Her 45-year-old brother, just two years her elder, had been living in New York City for quite some time now. He'd initially moved out there from Toronto in the diplomatic field, only to go on to pursue a job opportunity that eventually had him leading a booming car service company, with many contacts and branches throughout their native Canada. "But, of course, his texts have been promising *'the best'* upon "*…just a wee bit more…*," she enunciated in a masculine voice.

"*…patience, girls*!" Malin finished her mom's sentence, mimicking her uncle with a chuckle. "God, I love him. But when's he ever going to come down to earth? You'd think he would have learned by now with everything..."

"Probably *never*- unless those around him, including your grandmother, can stop idolizing him and justifying his reckless behaviors just because he's making the big bucks…." Kaitlin's voice trailed off. Her eyes stared blankly at her reflection in the mirror, focused more on the fading-beige wall behind her it also reflected, in addition to her own visage. *Some people never grow up.*

"Well, I idolize *you*," Malin walked up behind her mother, wrapping her arms around her with a hug. "You've been through so much, Mom, and yet you never failed to do the best for us."

Kaitlin took a deep breath, allowing herself to be enveloped in her daughter's embrace. "I did whatever was necessary for your ultimate, long-term well-being, my sweet."

"…And what ultimately was the best for everyone," her daughter added.

Was it? Kaitlin closed her eyes and swayed along with Malin. Fate was uncontrollable after a certain point. That much she'd learned by now. The events of the past decade flashed through her mind like a blur. How she'd never have thought things could have been able to get any stranger once she and her husband Paul had somehow managed to make it through his short stint in jail and survive the discovery of her closeness with those who'd framed him for murder.

Her mind drifted to 'The Group': a sexualized, quasi-spiritual cult of sorts that acted outwardly as an international paper-production business, doing local logging in the woods to distribute to mills and factories. How rattled Kaitlin had been upon discovering that the organization she'd initially thought she had come into contact with under 'coincidental' and professional circumstances had humans mixed with superhuman *jinns* as members! And that one of them in particular—a jinn named Finn Du Feu—had been assigned to seek her out on purpose.

How shaken her and Paul had become to inadvertently become gotten involved in their twisted and illogical sense of revenge, trying to excuse and cover up the murder committed by one of their own human members named Tan Kuvvet.

It turned out, however, that life would manage to surprise her in a plethora of novel ways every year since. Raising Malin had given her and Paul many beautiful memories- and for that she'd always be grateful. But it'd also brought up additional, painful triggers. Hauntings stemming from her own childhood.

"Oh, hey, Mom?" Malin calling out to her caused Kaitlin to shake the thoughts inside her mind along with her head. "I'm heading to the Eaton Centre. Let me know if you need anything."

Kaitlin smirked. *Good old, Malin.* "Where? Oh, right, right. You were going to show me a picture of you wearing that gown you'd liked, right?"

"Right," Malin retorted. "Yeah, I'll send you a picture of me wearing it. If you approve, I'll put it on layaway."

"Would you like me to come with you and see it in person, instead?"

"Oh, no, that's okay!" Malin insisted. "I don't want you to interrupt your work. I have a feeling you'll like it, anyway. Check your phone later for my text, Mom."

"Alright," Kaitlin responded. She raised an eyebrow, eyeing her daughter up and down. Would Malin truly be going shopping? Or would she be meeting some boy again?

Kaitlin sighed. She'd sworn to herself long ago to allow Malin to come to her when she felt ready with any dating situation, rather than snoop or assume too much. Unlike what she'd experienced with her own mother growing up. Besides, Malin wasn't exactly a child anymore.

"Just be careful, and please don't max out that credit card, again, though, sweety! Take it easy! Your father's just taken care of last month's balance."

"I know, I know," Malin winked at her, zipping the side of her athletic shoes.

"Oh, and I think I might take a nap while you're out, Mallie. I stayed up late on the computer. Take your keys just in case I'm in deep sleep."

"Okay, Mom… love you," Malin jiggled the keys latched onto a plethora of keychains from their travels.

"Drive safe!" Kaitlin stood still with her hands still lingering on the door she'd closed behind her daughter. How excited the girl was to be heading to the same mall Kaitlin herself had spent her youth shopping aimlessly, chatting with boys online through fake profiles with her childhood bestie, Sandy Burns-who'd been residing in New York City for a while, like her brother, in order to pursue a stage-acting career. They'd make the guys wait for them in front of certain stores- promising them a date- and then snicker from a distance before walking off.

Kaitlin giggled to herself. Had she always been a troublemaker? One time when Malin had pranked one of their neighbors for Halloween, her mother could be counted on to recollect the 'bad' from her childhood. *"Oh, Kaity, remember those summers by Balsam Lake? You used to knock on tourists' doors at all the surrounding chalets, and then run off! Just to amuse yourself! Knowing they'd open the door to find no one there. Be careful with Malin-she's becoming like you already."*

Had she really wanted Malin to become...*like her*? Kaitlin laughed aloud, plopping herself on the bed. Life could indeed be humorous at times. Paul had been the one to pressure them to have a child before she had felt ready maturity-wise, yet it was Kaitlin who'd ended up spending most of her time with their daughter. Happier so than she'd ever thought possible.

She extended her arms out on the smooth, un-creased left side of her bed. With a heavy sigh, she coiled back into her right corner. Curling her body up like a baby, Kaitlin brought herself to turn her back to the side of the bed empty now for so long. Her thoughts drifted back to Norway before dozing off. To everything that had transpired, catapulting her presence back in her hometown of Toronto again.

In a way, she was grateful to now be back in Canada, raising her teenager in the same town she herself had grown up in. The mother and daughter could relate with the same local gossip over some of the crazy local stores, and commiserate over the same perks and difficulties of the same neighborhood schools.

She'd repressed so much for so long. *Too long.* Malin had needed her mother to be strong, at least in appearance. In her solitude, Kaitlin finally allowed for the release of rolling tears that had long been hanging on to the corner of her eyes for dear life, the weight of the past decade bearing down on her.

CHAPTER 3

Sandnes
(present day)

KAITLIN MAVERICK WAS GRINNING EAR TO EAR, GIDDY AS A shelter puppy becoming adopted. Gazing outside her window at the late-summer sun glimmering through spruce tree branches, she closed her eyes and soaked in their rays tickling her face. The kitchen behind her smelled of inviting cinnamon, the aroma radiating a warmth not replicated by the Nordic chill outside fogging the glass.

Smiling, Kaitlin turned her attention back to the glittery, off-white envelope. She let out a yelp as she tore through the corners with anticipation, unfolding the letter inside.

"You can actually start using that envelope opener I got you any day now, you know?" teased Paul Maverick, her husband of nearly ten years. He was standing tall in a white undershirt that revealed firm, lean muscles, though the years, alongside of beer and late-night homesick poutine cravings, had softened and expanded his waistline. Leaning against the wall with a cup of coffee, his eyes flicked between her and his phone screen.

"It looks prettier staying put in my favorite coffee mug," Kaitlin retorted, sticking her tongue out at him once she'd made sure to catch his eye. Over the years, she had learned to chalk up Paul's snide remarks to his upbringing, as suggested to her by her therapist. *It's nothing personal,* she reminded herself.

"Oh, that's right," Paul feigned a thoughtful look, raising his forefinger up in the air. "I forgot about that huge, ostentatious Starbucks mug you use for decoration—and storage, apparently— rather than actual coffee."

"Well, that's what you get for insisting on a PO Box for me to keep in touch with my clients through physical mail," Kaitlin retorted without a flinch. She met Paul's eyes before adding a reassuring wink, ensuring his attention had drifted enough for her to focus back on her letter. *Pick your battles,* she reminded herself. Paul's low-grade teasing wasn't worth getting riled up over today.

"However I open the letters, Paulie, I do admit I get so excited to read this stuff now! It's become addictive!" Kaitlin cleared her throat and began to read the letter out loud.

Dear Mrs. Maverick,

Your ingenious cookies have transformed my marriage—and, in turn, our whole family dynamic! My husband is less stressed after work, which I love, and I feel less like a 'domesticated animal' or a 'disrespected 1950s housewife', as you wrote in one of your blogs about us modern women's fears. I'm less stressed with chores and child-rearing, feeling like an empowered woman in control of her life and accepting the benefits of staying home. I've left you a five-star review! Thank you for all you do!

With gratitude,
Lilian Clark

"Aww!" Kaitlin exclaimed, her eyes welling with happy tears. "Let me check the review page. Did you hear that, Paulie? I've received another one! This one says it's from Michigan, in the States."

Could the words of an encouraging follower and client be right? Kaitlin felt grateful for the dopamine rush of praise, especially after harsh reviews or slow sales. But even with positive feedback, a nagging doubt in the back of her mind questioned how long she could keep this momentum going.

Had her work really been able to shine some sort of light of on people's lives, whereas all she saw in the mirror and felt when alone with her thoughts was sometimes the opposite of the positivity they praised?

"Yes, I heard," Paul replied, munching on a cracker he'd picked up from a plastic container on the kitchen counter. "Charming. My wife's drug-cookies are all the rage across the pond, too!"

"Ha, ha," Kaitlin rolled her eyes with a sarcastic grin.

"See, babe?" Paul shrugged. "Physical mail lets us enjoy your fans' praises together!"

"Yes, all rather quite *charming*, indeed, babe," Kaitlin remarked, clicking the screen closed and shutting off her laptop. Sometimes, she suspected the PO box was his way of keeping 'The Group' from getting through to her online more secretly. She had, after all, changed her phone number since moving to their new place. *Paul just doesn't understand that keeping them away requires more than surveying my communication.*

"Actual mail is a physical keepsake, unlike e-mails that become deleted," Paul continued. "It *was* merely a suggestion, as you know. You can switch exclusively to e-mail anytime you want, *Madame Celebrity*."

"I didn't say anything, *Monsieur Old-School*," Kaitlin said with a shrug, her frustration evident. "I like keepsakes. All good."

She'd heard it all before. Her husband had been voicing his discomfort for years now with her entrepreneurial success of CBD-infused cookie sales, where a portion of the profits went to charity. She knew it'd been an unorthodox way to reach people with her writing while helping them with their personal lives and health, but Kaitlin enjoyed being able to make use of the *Marketing* background she'd acquired back in Canada.

Besides, Paul had 'suggested' a PO Box in *such* a tone- and so many times- that Kaitlin knew she'd never hear the end of it had she *not* followed through, and had chosen to solely use e-mail instead.

"You *did* always encourage me to get involved in baking more when we first got married, didn't you, babe?" Kaitlin watched as Paul shot her a polite, clenched-mouth smile and then proceeded to make himself comfortable in front of their television set. He didn't have to remind her with words that he'd meant for her to actually *do* the baking, and for guests in their home- not utilizing bakeries as business partners.

"After all," Kaitlin went on, shifting her gaze onto her fingernails as she fidgeted. "They are actually serving a purpose. The cookies help treat anxiety and depression, Paulie, not to mention chronic pain and inflammation. It's all particularly relevant in these lingering times of the pandemic! Come on, now!"

Her blog, *'Enthusiastic Musings of a Reluctant Housewife'*, had turned into an online success story in a matter of two years, and Kaitlin had relished putting their now nearly-eight-year-old daughter, Malin, into various school activities with her own earnings. She'd first started the blog to share book reviews and personal poetry, along with rants and raves about living in Norway as a foreigner.

Although the website had gradually begun to accumulate revenue through incorporating trending travel reviews that boosted advertisements, Kaitlin had felt she'd hit the jackpot when paid memberships *really* increased after a Norwegian singing sensation teamed up with her. She'd met 'Anine' at the gym in the nearby town of Stavanger, where she'd initially moved to as a newlywed to join her computer-whiz husband on his professional venture. She'd occasionally commuted back in order to keep in touch with the closest friend she'd made in Norway - Sibel Pak, keeping up bi-weekly workouts together until the Covid 19 pandemic restrictions closed the gyms for a good while.

Not knowing who the singer was, they'd commiserated side by side on the treadmills about sore muscles. Anine had praised her trips to Amsterdam and the 'magical cookies' there that also appeased physical pain along with low morale, and the rest was history. Kaitlin had caught the entrepreneurial bug, with various marketing ideas running through her head. She made contacts with a Dutch bakery through Anine, with cookie sales skyrocketing after the pop star later picked up on Kaitlin's personalized products in cooperation and promoted the cookies on her social media pages!

Kaitlin had long learned to repress her urge to fight back with Paul- especially regarding his disapproval of her 'free time' use as such. Calming her apprehension with mindfulness exercises and channeling stress into creative pursuits instead had become her lifeline in Norway, in addition to motherhood.

Stress.

The word lingered in Kaitlin's mind while she strutted toward their bedroom. Once inside the lavender-scented room, she threw herself on the king-sized mattress with a heavy sigh. Her mind traveled to the incident on the cliffs at Dalsnuten seven years ago. It was the last time- upon Kaitlin's insistence that the two of them stay apart as much as possible 'for the best for all parties involved'— that she had been embraced and kissed by *him*.

She smiled as the nickname she'd given him resounded inside her head. *Finn: the Jinn.* The visual of his bright green eyes in her memory reminded her of the mischievous, secret friendship of sorts that had formed between them. The mystery of it all managed to cyclically bring Kaitlin drama and heartbreak, yet also excitement to the mundane.

According to Sibel's Islamic beliefs- the jinn were living things mentioned in the Quran who existed in the same realm as humans while remaining invisible to most people. She'd divulged to Kaitlin that Finn and his kind were made of 'smokeless fire', allowing them the ability to travel and ascending speedily into the air, as well as transform themselves into animals and even forms resembling particular humans.

Kaitlin could still recall the day when she'd first heard of all those details. She'd outstretched her arms in front of her and wondered how in the world human flesh, in contrast to jinns, could be said to be made up of 'clay' and earth- though she could certainly attest to the 'heated' part about the makeup of Finn's existence.

She'd been taken aback by how open her mind had been to this new perspective. Back in her single life growing up in Toronto, Kaitlin would most certainly have laughed it off. She'd scoff that a friend was being 'ridiculous' to talk of such things, likening these 'jinns' to talk of ghouls or ghosts heard more frequently in the media. *If only things could be so simple,* Kaitlin thought.

The incident. That's what her therapist, Freya Olsdotter, had called it- what had happened to her on those cliffs seven years ago. During her post-partum period, Kaitlin had returned from some much-needed 'alone-time' hike in the nearby mountains. She hadn't begun driving yet, and had taken the bus out there when Malin was still very little and she and Paul had just moved to Sandnes. Her mother, Linda, had paid her first visit across the Atlantic to see the baby- overstaying her welcome to 'help' when Paul was thrown into jail!

Kaitlin shook her head, unnerved still by the memory of the injustice. Paul had been held several months at the time on bogus murder charges, thanks to the fabrication of the lead guru of 'The Group'- Lar Iktar. Blessedly, her husband had been released after a strong alibi came his way from a friend, as well as a confession from the actual murderer soon thereafter- voiced by cult-member Tan Kuvvet while committing suicide in front of the police. His self-sabotage had kept the shaken-up, remaining members of 'The Group' from continuing their antics.

Good riddance, Kaitlin thought, still simmering at the memory. *The Group* had managed to wreak havoc not just on her life but on Paul's as well. Her husband had confided in her about a jinn-like figure named Stig, who had appeared at his office to extract "evidence" from him—evidence that was later planted to implicate him in Linette's murder. Stig hadn't stopped there; he'd even shown up in Paul's jail cell, tormenting him and playing cruel games with his mind.

It had been an extra-challenging time, indeed- but her and Paul had somehow got through it. Alongside having faced the jail and jinn ordeal together, raising Malin had given the two of them a rare commonality that bonded them closer.

The incident. Kaitlin could never forget the look in Paul and her mother's eyes after her return from the hike. The looks of judgment from a second person in the house, in addition to Paul, glancing her up and down on a daily basis had only caused Kaitlin to hide within her shell further.

"Kaity...are you...alright?" Linda had ploddingly been shaking her head side to side. So, what if she'd just experienced a shocking occurrence during her hike, and couldn't shake it off for a good couple of hours when she'd returned home? Kaitlin had briefly glimpsed her disheveled appearance in the mirror by the shoe-racks upon her return home, but didn't care. Instead, she'd muttered something along the lines of — "I'm fine, *Maman,* just tired" —and had gone to lay next to her napping daughter.

Yes, Finn had appeared to her at those cliffs, but that wasn't unusual to Kaitlin by that point. He'd already gotten her accustomed to his way of doing that whenever she needed him and thought of him, bless his heart.

Finn. The jinn who had helped her during a dark moment on a steep edge at a high altitude. The simultaneous source of both scary enigma and enthralling excitement in her life who had somehow become a surprising and comforting confidant through the years.

The *friend*. Yes. Kaitlin had decided once and for all that that's what he was and would be to her. What else could he ever realistically be? Finn had looked straight into her eyes before the passionate kiss they'd shared on the cliff- the kiss which was still able to crimson Kaitlin's face with a mere thought to this day. *"Friendship on fire, Kaitlin,"* he had said. *"That's how some coin 'love'."*

What did Finn know about love, though? He was of a different world from her own and needed to simply know his place: as a good, secret *friend* to help them both deal with life, as far as she was concerned. He was her secret- not out of some inappropriate liaison between them, but rather due to his inhuman nature. *Others wouldn't understand.* Kaitlin often rationalized to herself. *They'd needlessly interfere.* The boundary she'd drawn around their special connection was for the best for both of them.

"God doesn't judge our improper thoughts and emotions, Kaitlin- as long as we can restrain our actions in accordance with them." Sibel's words echoing in Kaitlin's mind caused her to grin. *My little advisor*, she thought, giving her friend credit where it was due. Sibel wasn't meaning to preach to her- Kaitlin never got that sense, anyway. Instead, she helped entertain the millions of questions Kaitlin must have asked her Turkish friend once she'd realized that the new 'professional acquaintance' she'd made, seemingly randomly walking in the woods, was indeed a jinn! Sibel had first recognized the high possibility of him being as such from when Kaitlin had first revealed the strange details surrounding their initial meeting in the Stavanger woods, and his subsequent communications and appearances before her.

What time is it? Kaitlin took a deep breath and hugged her pillow tighter. She glanced at the alarm clock which read that it was about an hour until Malin would be back from school. She could afford a little nap, couldn't she? Paul could be heard shuffling around in the living room, and could welcome their daughter if Kaitlin couldn't wake up in time- though, bless her heart, her daughter's loud singing and calling out would likely awaken her in a heartbeat!

Kaitlin shuddered as the details of the *incident* that had materialized after Paul's return from jail occupied her thoughts while she attempted to doze off. Bigger than being pursued by a jinn in human form. Right when she'd thought it couldn't get any stranger, things had taken a turn for wilder than she could have ever imagined.

2014

DADDY? KAITLIN'S GAZE LOCKED ONTO THE DOLEFUL, DARK green eyes of the figure before her as she whimpered. These were the eyes of the man she hadn't seen since being told he'd left their family to be with another woman when Kaitlin was just a child. Could it really be? She'd just seen her father and heard his distinct voice! And Finn wasn't believing her! *Finn*. In all his limited visibility to most humans. He'd placed his hands on her shoulder and encouraged her to step back from the edge of the cliff, where she'd been lingering in her slightly-inebriated state. Kaitlin was still holding on to the butterflies in her stomach with the kiss he'd just given her, but the quivering inside her was quickly turning into fear. *I saw him, and I heard him. My father. He warned me not to fall.*

Finn had looked at Kaitlin with such concern in his eyes, as if *she* had been the odd one up there on the cliffs, and not him as the jinn! *Could his actions of concern really be out of pity?* Kaitlin questioned. She let out a groan.

"You need to rest," his voice was now soft, coaxing. "You can't take public transportation home now in this state. I'll take you

there faster. You just need to hold on tightly- wrap your arms around me, and trust me."

"It *was* him, Finn!" Kaitlin stammered, pointing to the spot where she'd seen him. "I saw my father- as clearly as day. I'm not crazy! I remember him distinctly."

Kaitlin took a step back and spun around in two circles, glancing every which way to see where he may have disappeared off to. What was he doing in Norway? For years, her father had been silent and off the radar in Canada somewhere with a new family, as far as she knew. Had he found out somehow that he'd become a grandfather, and wanted to pay a visit, too, like her mother? Whatever his reason was- she'd seen him, and heard him! It was her father! She was not suddenly going mad! Was she?

***Daddy?* Kaitlin turned in place to glimpse all around her, to no avail. Where had he gone? He'd better not have run out on her again! Vanishing without a trace like that! The least he could do was stay and introduce himself to her family, his granddaughter. And re-introduce himself to her.**

"You…remember him?" Finn muttered with a raised brow, his hands subtly graced Kaitlin's shoulders with a sizzle. "Okay. What did he look like? How old was he in appearance?"

Is he testing me?* Kaitlin thought in frustration. *I think I would know when I've heard and seen my own father.

"Look, I only want to know in case I see such a man around here, Kaitlin," Finn went on. "I don't mean to quiz or question you. It's just that- if he's run off somewhere, I'll find him for you. You know what I mean? That's all! Don't you worry."

***Oh, right.* It frustrated Kaitlin that she hadn't learned to control her thoughts around him. Though she had to admit- it did sometimes give her a little sense of comfort. Knowing Finn could read her most private thoughts, and still not have grown cold off her,**

gave her a strange sense of relief. Even if it was unsettling at times. *If I am going crazy, I guess he wouldn't judge. Would he?*

"Besides, you'd said it yourself- how you haven't seen him since you were a young girl. That he'd left you guys for another woman and later went to rehab, or something, before eventually losing touch for good? It's understandable if you were mistaken...."

"He was wearing the same gray t-shirt and jeans I recall from when I was, like, five years old, Finn," Kaitlin insisted in response, outreaching all five of her fingers on one hand before his face. "I remember how proud I'd felt. Being his daughter. We would go fishing, and he'd be so jovial and attentive with me— even more than with Aidan, my brother. The other kids would always look at us with envy. It was him, Finn! My father was standing right there! I'm telling you! He was just as I remember him vividly from our little trips to the lake. I was five years old, Finn! I was only five..."

Finn's expression softened, but there was something else behind his eyes, something unreadable. He stepped closer to her, taking her fingers gently in his hand, and kissed the tips of her fingers—wet with the tears she hadn't realized had started falling.

"That couldn't have actually happened, right, Kaitlin?" His voice was still calm, but there was an edge to it now, as if he were gently correcting her. "Let's think about this for a moment. If you're remembering your father from when you were five, how could he look the same now? Twenty years later? Same clothes? Same *everything*?"

Kaitlin wiped her tears, her heart heavy with confusion. He was right, wasn't he? *How could he* look the same? Time should have changed him. It had changed her, after all.

Finn smiled as he caressed her cheek. His touch was warm as always, even in the midst of near-freezing temperatures. *How can you manifest in human flesh so warm all the time?* Kaitlin was told

that his kind made up of fire energy would tire more to manifest into human forms than into animal ones. That God had apparently allowed them to do so, however, in order to be able to reach 'certain' humans in 'special circumstances'- the details of which weren't exactly explained to her too clearly.

She also remained confused as to how Finn's physical manifestation could remain ever fit and young, regardless of the spirit of his age in human years. When it came to human/jinn realms, Kaitlin could never feel too sure where the blurred line between dogmatic mandates widely believed to be ordained by God (whom she believed in as well) ended, and quasi-religious/nature-based philosophical blather preached by lowlifes like 'Lar Iktar' began.

Paul had ordered Iktar's bestselling book- 'Atlas for a Meaningful Life'- which also helped finance 'The Group' alongside the paper business that garnered clients. After checking it out: for the life of her, Kaitlin couldn't comprehend how this logically-speaking jinn-man before her could have fallen for the crap advocated by 'The Group'! And worse—that he'd somehow accepted being part of an organization that would allow for a murderer like Tan!

She'd often wonder through the years what had been in it for him, to become and actually remain a member—but Finn would often shut her questions out. He'd brush it off as something about feeling more welcomed in 'The Group' than with his own family, and had left it at that.

The guru's own name, too, was apparently fake! What a small world it was. To think that 'Lar' turned out to be some old friend of her husband's old boss in Quebec: John Walker. The two had apparently met in the Middle East as young men, back when 'Lar' had gone by the first name of 'Aresh'.

John Walker. The CEO who had fathered- out of wedlock with a mistress named Annika Peterson— a girl, Linette, who'd grow up to be a young woman that worked with Paul back in Canada before returning to her hometown of Trondheim.

You shouldn't have come back to Norway, Linette, **Kaitlin took a deep breath and closed her eyes.** ***You were just trying to get away from Tan—the man whom you met when you were both studying in Canada, and who then messed you up in your romantic relationship. I know. But he followed you! No one can outrun their troubles for too long. Wherever they go! He found you, and in all his possessiveness—murdered you!***

Kaitlin pressed her shut eyelid-muscles further as she inhaled, the air sharp in her lungs. ***You should have stayed in Canada, Linette. Maybe I should have, too.***

Her mind traveled to details Paul had provided her with. ***You should have stayed under the auspices of your father at that Montreal office. Maybe he could have protected you. Maybe you should have confided in your father.***

In her reverie, Kaitlin broke down in fuller sobs.

Father. **Why couldn't her own have remained in Kaitlin's life? Why did her father have to go? Why couldn't he have done whatever he seemingly needed to do to get away from her mother- if their love was indeed gone to warrant a divorce— but still not have left his kids, at least?**

And now? You appear back in my life now, Daddy—only to leave again? Why?

"Hey, Kaitlin!" She felt Finn's hands shake her shoulders on the elevated cliffs. Perhaps he truly had saved her life. She'd been standing so close to the edge. Too close.

"Snap back to the present, please," Finn had pleaded, pushing Kaitlin's feet farther from the edge of the sandy-colored

cliff. Kaitlin felt her body shudder with the jolt of wind swirling around her, blowing her long, dark auburn hair. She couldn't be too sure if the trembling had resulted from mother nature's strong gust of wind, or the jolt from Finn's supra-human, speedy approach toward her.

"I need you to go home to Malin," he insisted. "Go sniff her heavenly head, and not tell your mother or Paul about any of this. Just stay in the present, and take some time to rest. It'll be alright. Hang on to me, and I'll drop you home at lightning speed."

"Lightning speed?" To her surprise, her sobs turned to laughter. "Wait…wait. Are we going to, like, *fly*, or something, Finn?"

"Something like that," Finn joined her in laughter after initially shooting Kaitlin a look of concern. "Except- you won't be feeling a sensation of actually being elevated and flying there in real time, or anything of that kind. It'll be very quick. A teleportation, of sorts."

"I'm scared," her voice quavered.

"I'm just taking you home," Finn insisted. "You need rest."

Kaitlin hesitated. She didn't want to leave, not while so many questions remained unanswered. "What about—"

"No more questions," Finn interrupted gently. "Just trust me. Wrap your arms around me, and we'll get you home. Fast. You need to be with Malin. Hold on tightly to my waist. And remember. *Not a word.* They won't understand you. Just say you got tired on your hike. And go be in the present with Malin. She needs you, and you need her. Alright?

"Alright…" Kaitlin agreed with a grin, wrapping her arms around his rigid abs.

"Trust me," he insisted, before indeed transporting her in front of her apartment entrance. "It'll be worth it."

She closed her eyes and hugged his torso as tightly as she could. Entangled in each other's embrace, they spun one time- or so it seemed, as the whole thing became a blur. In a manner of what felt like mere seconds in human time, Kaitlin felt her feet lift off the mountainous ground and land on the gravel back in front of her building entrance. Her hands trembled slightly as she adjusted the collar of her coat, glancing all around to make sure no passerby had seen a woman seemingly appearing before them from thin air!

No one. Kaitlin exhaled a sigh of relief, as only a mother accompanying her child on a bicycle nearby was visible- and they both had their backs turned to her. *Oh, good.*

"Finn?" she called out, spinning slowly in a circle around herself. "I can go upstairs myself. Thank you. For everything today."

"Okay," Finn's voice echoed clear and crisp in her cloudy mind. *"You're welcome. It was worth it. Remember- you're always worth it."*

Kaitlin smiled into the empty space to her left. She could feel Finn's presence there, his warmth lingering in the air like a quiet echo. Even though he was no longer physically beside her, his energy was still tangible- a strange comfort in the midst of the uncertainty.

Dusting off her clothes, she smiled at the flowered-path decorating the green bushes to her and Paul's apartment complex, and walked up a short flight of stairs to enter their three-bedroom condo. Despite the North Sea view they'd enjoyed from their multi-floor and crowded apartment in Stavanger, this bigger place was as close to living in a private home as they were going to get— with the prices for those in Norwegian Kroner being what they were- and it radiated more coziness.

"*You're worth it,*" Finn had said. He would tell her that frequently, mostly with regards to the exhaustive energy it required

of him to manifest in human flesh-form, requiring time to recuperate afterward.

***Was* she really worth it? Was Kaitlin really deserving of any kind of genuine care and affection from another? Could she really trust Finn's words— when his various actions and words hadn't exactly been consistent with one another?**

How could she trust anyone with whom she'd felt so safe and cared for, yet who could also be capable of being involved in such a shady lifestyle? Someone part of a business luring clients on delusive pretenses, like her with the 'translation' services Finn had initially approached her with. A group allowing members to do things like implicate her husband in murder and throw him into jail. What if Paul's friend, Jeanette, hadn't provided the cops with a strong alibi? Would he still have been in jail?

***Jeanette.* Just thinking about her name made Kaitlin uneasy. Was there something more between Jeanette and Paul? Though the woman was married now, Kaitlin could never quite shake the suspicion. How well could she trust her own husband, let alone Finn?**

Enough!

Kaitlin forced her thoughts to halt before reaching for the keys in her mini, Coach cross-body bag. She took in a deep breath, her heart pounding with fear at the thought of how to act around her mother and Paul after everything that had just transpired. The image of her daughter's chubby cheeks flashing in her mind eased any apprehension, with longing taking over instead.

Kaitlin ran to the bathroom to splash water on her face and wash her hands before tiptoeing to Malin's room. She kneeled and sniffed her daughter's head, laying down on the guest bed adjacent to her crib.

***Mountain air.* The male voice she could have sworn was her father's, almost beckoning her to go to the cliffs. Her mind was still**

befuddled, and she had no idea what else it could have been. But she'd instinctively known it to be her father reaching out to her. Somehow. Someway.

Her mother had told them her father, Zachary, had a new family now and did not want to be bothered. Had he passed away or something, outside of her mother's knowledge? Was it his spirit trying to reach out to her? Or was her father alive- and merely trying to contact her with some sort of telepathic ability?

***"No actual spirit of the deceased can travel back to the realm of the living- or even to Heaven or Hell, before Judgement Day",* Sibel had claimed, after all. She had told her that what westerners tend to refer to as 'ghosts' were actually jinn, sometimes in disguise as human beings or even animals. Jinn would also apparently act as intermediaries between 'mediums' and 'the dead'; their longer-than-human lifespans, alongside their ability to traverse space rapidly due to a more elevated frequency than human beings, allowed the jinn to relay 'psychic' knowledge that had nothing to do with magical knowledge. Her friend had further divulged that such 'clairvoyant' collaborations were frowned upon by God, for both his human and jinn creations.**

Kaitlin had witnessed the jinn firsthand, but she wasn't too sure if she was similarly buying what she'd been told about ghosts and spirits after death not being really able to linger in the realm of the living. Perhaps there were some pieces of information— piece of the puzzle called the mystery of life—that Sibel herself wasn't privy to, either!

Even Finn not believing her was particularly shocking for Kaitlin. He'd told her that whoever she thought she'd seen wasn't one of his kind- and so that it couldn't have been a jinn. What else could it have been, then? Who else could it have been but her actual father, somehow? So many unanswered questions! So many

scrambled bits and pieces of thoughts were floating around her mind.

You're worth it. Finn's words echoed in her mind once more.

Yeah, right, Kaitlin mourned. He may have become a most curious sort of a jinn confidante for her through the years, but Finn was still a male! *I've apparently been replaced with Meredith—enough for Finn to have bloody reproduced with her, for goodness' sake!*

Bo. Kaitlin remembered the cream-colored Golden Retriever. Her puppy-gift for a brief time was also, apparently, their jinn offspring in canine form! Kaitlin couldn't forget Meredith's eyes before confessing as such to her in that damned forest, as Kaitlin had gone next to her then friend for comfort after the death of her lover- Tan.

It was no use living in some bittersweet, yet nostalgically-comforting land of possibilities. Reality: that was the land where she needed to reside. She had to be in the present- a present where her logical mind told Kaitlin that there was no justification for jealousy over a Finn-and-Meredith union. They were both jinn, and probably belonged together. Besides- Kaitlin herself was, after all, married, and with a child as well.

Practice mindfulness. Freya's words reverberated in her brain. Finn was with Meredith now—enough to reproduce some jinn offspring, Bo, who could transform into animal form like both of them could. Whether out of love, or mere 'platonic convenience and understanding', as Finn insisted- those three had become a jinn family. And Kaitlin had to focus on raising Malin with her husband in their own little, core family.

CHAPTER 4

THE SNAPPING OF PAUL'S FINGERS ACCOMPANIED HIS VOICE, cutting into Kaitlin's near stupor. "Nuts?" His throat-clearing was loud enough to shake her cognitively and somatically back into the present moment.

"What?" Kaitlin blinked, squinting at him as he waved a bag of pistachios in her face.

"Earth to wifey!" Paul grinned, his teasing tone cutting through her fog. "Want some?"

"Oh, no, thanks, babe," Kaitlin mumbled, rubbing her eyes as she jolted upright in bed. "What time is it? I've been napping for a while, haven't I? I didn't mean to. Is she here?"

"That's alright," Paul gave a casual shrug. "I mean, I found you in here, just staring at the ceiling. I figured you'd wanted to relax a bit before Malin's bus drops her off. She should be here any minute now."

"Oh..." Kaitlin's voice trailed off. Paul might have sounded nonchalant, but his eyes were asking the same question he never had to voice: *What's really going on?* She recognized the concern hidden behind his casual tone. He'd never been good at hiding his need for reassurance—almost as much as she struggled with hers.

Paul flopped down beside her on the bed, his weight shifting the mattress. "What's on your mind?"

Kaitlin hesitated, gathering her thoughts. She finally met his gaze, a half-smile playing on her lips. "Just thinking about how far I've come with this whole thing—the business, you know? And raising Malin too. You've got to give your wifey a little credit, right?"

Paul nodded and leaned over to kiss Kaitlin on her forehead. "I already do, babe. Consider it, you know- *tough love*, sometimes. I know you could branch out...*better*, let's say, than what some would view to be...*controversial* cookies. Not everyone approves of weed just because it's becoming more legalized worldwide."

"Well, thanks to *weed* customers- like our new friend *Lilian* from that letter- your wife's got an income," Kaitlin winked as she playfully punched Paul's shoulder. "Not to mention somewhat of a *life* herself while you go to work on most days, eh, babe?"

"A life mostly *online*..." Paul muttered under his breath.

"Paulie...," Kaitlin began in defense of her choices, but Paul cut her off adamantly, insistent.

"You could take Malin to more places when she has time off," he said, his voice turning a little more earnest. "Not just stay glued to your laptop while she watches shows or plays alone."

"May I remind you that I take her to her extracurricular classes?" Kaitlin's tone sharpened. "And by the way- she placed *second* in that piano competition!"

Paul rolled his eyes. "Oh, yes—how could I forget? Our daughter's award-winning rendition of *Mary Had a Little Lamb*, beating out the other kids' nursery rhymes."

"Paul!" Kaitlin placed her hands on her hips, her frustration rising. "What a terrible thing to say about our daughter, mocking her talent..."

"Babe, it's not our *daughter* that I'm mocking," her husband defended himself. "It's the *minimalist value* those classes have been providing so far! Speaking of which: did we really have to enroll her in that dance class, too?"

Paul groaned as he stood up from the bed and proceeded to stomp toward their living room. Kaitlin could see that his face had fallen as he darted a look at her across his shoulder. "Aren't we overdoing it a bit lately with *three* after-school activities a week now? She's only seven!"

"You know she needs this, Paulie," Kaitlin got up to follow behind him, her eyes cast down onto the faded carpet. "Art, music and dance: the social worker said those are the 'holy trinity' for our daughter based on her interests, remember? She needs to express herself. This is all to help her come out of her shell, since she hasn't really connected with much of the kids at her school or around the neighborhood."

"And whose fault is that?" Paul raised his brow. "You remain in your comfort zone, most of the time. And on the rare occasion you *do* socialize with other moms and their kids- such as seeing Sibel with her kids around- you see Malin *is* social. She *connects* with both Aylin and Hakan brilliantly- she's not shy at all when she plays with them!" He added a smile. "She gets that from me."

"Not this again..." Kaitlin placed her face in her hands. She despised it whenever he'd tried to make his reproaches sound like light, humorous remarks rather than jabs. "I'm literally, like, waiting for you to practically call me 'evil' or something for trying to carve a little life and space for myself in addition to raising her...*and you*, for that matter!"

"*You*...are the one raising your *old, aching* hubby?" Paul smirked lightly.

To Kaitlin's pleasant surprise, he remained silent afterwards; it was refreshing to observe her husband not starting one of his longer tirades again.

"Oh, lighten up," she decided to dismiss the indignant vibe that had arose between them. "With regards to stereotypical gender roles- we'd both be considered mid-life already, had we been living in more historic times..."

At 43 years old, Paul had become accustomed to frequently highlighting their age-gap dynamic. Many in their circle often thought he was around the same age, in fact, as his wife who was actually ten years his junior. It appeared to Kaitlin that his ego thrived on people paying him the compliment he almost expected each time he would refer to it. How unfair nature could be, Kaitlin would often think: aging being viewed by society to appear more charismatic for men than for women.

"I've got to marvel at the lucrative workings of my dear wife's imagination," Paul attempted a smile. "Look, I just want my girls to be happy. All I'm saying is: you haven't made much of an effort to expand your social circle here in Sandnes, hon. You're still stuck in Stavanger, it seems."

Was that a hint of suspicion she'd sensed, audible in Paul's tone? Kaitlin knew a part of him would always now associate Stavanger- where he'd discovered that his wife had hung out with 'The Group' in the woods-with *him*.

Finn.

But Kaitlin had also simply gotten used to her rising online success, with the coronavirus pandemic catalyzing many people to adjust their lifestyles to working remotely from home. That's all. Getting outside her comfort zone in order to fraternize with new social contacts simply wasn't as big a priority for Kaitlin as it once was. She remembered the women's non-profit organization she'd volunteered for when she first moved to Norway. At least that had led her to meeting Sibel. And thank God for that; she couldn't imagine her new life in Norway, not to mention getting through the *jinn* shocks, without her friend.

Finn's name flickered again in her mind. Kaitlin squeezed her eyes shut, fighting the intrusive thoughts.

Not now, Finn. Not while she was in the middle of an argument with Paul. The last thing she needed was him somehow getting involved in their domestic squabbles.

Kaitlin knew she had to control her thoughts about him unless she wanted to summon his attention on herself, particularly in moments like this- when she'd been arguing with Paul. In some mystical way, Finn would always know when she'd be in a place in her life most vulnerable to their connection.

It had almost become a game over the years- one where Kaitlin knew she was purposely being seduced. She would allow it, despite bouts of whining about him targeting her- complaints used mostly due to a sense of pride she would try to wear like a mask or a shield. He knew how to reel her in, and she didn't mind being his fish- as long as he didn't cook and eat her up alive. The excitement would always somehow feel worth the risks, and in time she'd grown to feel safer with him, albeit trusting him completely could never quite be in question.

Nonetheless, she'd been strong enough not to consciously summon him over the last several years- not to manifest in flesh, anyway. The therapy sessions her circle encouraged her to take did help her with regards to that, Kaitlin had to admit- alongside her keeping busy with activities for Malin and her own online work.

Paul continued, oblivious to the mental tug-of-war in her mind. "If we'd been in Montreal by now, Malin could've been playing with her cousins—she could have felt like part of a bigger family."

"Norway's been good to us," Kaitlin shot back, surprising herself. Paul raised an eyebrow at her tone, clearly not expecting such a sharp response. Despite how lonely she herself had felt when she'd first joined her then-new husband in Stavanger—where he'd found work as an Information Technology expert in the petroleum business- Kaitlin had grown to appreciate being in Europe.

Paul had since been offered opportunities back in Montreal- but Kaitlin had discouraged them. After all, she'd come to appreciate the healthy distance—as far as she was concerned— from Paul's toxically-clingy sisters and their children in Montreal. As well as from her own overbearing mother in Ontario!

"We've gotten through some crazy ordeals, but we did it together, Paulie," Kaitlin spoke softly. "Just you and me- and our daughter. Our *core family*. Here. We're doing it."

Paul's expression softened, and he kissed her forehead. "You're right," he murmured. "We've made it here. We've survived the darkest parts. I mean- the jinn, for God's sake!" His voice dropped to a whisper as his eyes darted around the room, as if expecting them to materialize at any moment.

Finn.

Kaitlin blinked and took a deep breath. This time, it wasn't her own thought of his name. After all, she'd also grown to recognize *his* mental call to her. Almost like a phone call, begging to be picked up. Whenever she'd welcome it and respond cognitively, he would talk to her through thoughts, and she'd respond. Such had become a very unorthodox way of keeping in touch between the two of them- akin to doing so through social media or text messages, albeit a supernatural one.

In time, Kaitlin had come to relish this as her secret world that no other human she knew was experiencing. It made Kaitlin feel *special*- and chosen, almost- to be going through such an experience. As long as Finn kept his word, and continued to respect her boundaries: she supposed there couldn't possibly be much harm in their friendship.

"*I just wanted to see how you girls are doing,"* Finn would tell her through her thoughts, whenever she'd be alone or laying down somewhere. *"Think of me as your jinn companion, and protector. How are you? How's Malin?"*

Not right now, Finn, Kaitlin mentally relayed to him. *Please get out of my head!*

"But that's all behind us now," Paul was continuing to explain himself. Luckily he seemingly hadn't noticed her distraction. Kaitlin shook her head and continued listening to him with a smile.

"You've made me the happiest man alive by giving me our

beautiful daughter. Thank you for sticking by your old man here."

"You're not *that* old," she ruffled his wavy, milk coffee-brown hair. It felt good to physically be able to touch her *husband*, and call him as such. He was, after all, her socially-accepted partner in life, despite their issues. *Social acceptance*. One less source of stress to worry about in an already arduous life.

"You've had to deal with too much, Kaitlin," Freya had told her. *"You've suffered through a minor nervous breakdown and panic attack during a lonely time, with back-to-back emotional triggers. Hallucinations with a sensory modality component attached to them- as you claim to have heard and seen your father- are not unusual..."*

"Hallucinations?" Kaitlin had interrupted, offended. She'd never even tried recreational drugs, and it wasn't like she'd relayed having seen outrageous things throughout her life. She had actually seen and heard her father on those cliffs, hadn't she? How could Freya- someone believing in her with regards to the supernatural vis-à-vis the jinn, not have a kinder understanding with regards to how she had experienced her father's presence?

"You're strong-willed, and you've managed to function outwardly. But there's so much you've had to swallow! So many layers you've grown over the decaying core of an onion that eventually surfaced. Outwardly, it appeared as if the layers were the real you, rather than artificial ones you've grown to adapt to, as if they were your own organically. It's all too much for any person to handle without any help."

"They couldn't break us," Paul continued, his voice low but steady. "They tried to mess with my head—sent me to jail, clouded your mind… tried to confuse you."

Kaitlin felt a familiar tension rise in her chest. She hated when the conversation veered back into those murky waters, especially the insinuations about Malin's paternity.

Finn.

Kaitlin blinked, pushing the thought aside. Her therapist's voice echoed in her mind. *You need to stay grounded, Kaitlin. You need to keep your family together.*

"Thanks for sticking with me through it all," Paul said, his voice sincere. He gave her a brief kiss before sitting back and studying her with concern. "But you're still in a daze today. Did you take your pill this morning?"

Kaitlin frowned, mentally scanning her morning routine. Had she? She didn't remember. Her therapist had prescribed escitalopram for her anxiety and mild OCD. Lately, the medication made her drowsy and gave her headaches. It wasn't ideal, but at least it kept the panic attacks at bay.

"I'm sure I did," she replied, though her uncertainty lingered.

Paul's skeptical look told her he wasn't convinced. "Tomorrow, I'm going to check in with you earlier, okay?" He raised an index finger, wagging it gently. "Make sure you're taking it with water, not caffeine this time."

"Aye, aye, captain," Kaitlin muttered, trying to keep the mood light as she reached for the remote. She clicked it on, switching to the local news channel in Norsk- *NRK Nyheter*- as opposed to the BBC channel in English the twosome usually preferred by default.

She shook the thoughts off her mind and sighed, smiling at Paul with a shrug. Working from home, so much had become so routine to Kaitlin that she would later realize sometimes she had done a little clean-up chore here or errand there without consciously being aware. Her memory indeed had been feeling slightly foggy lately. Yet Sandy—who'd been prescribed the same by their mutual therapist— swore by the meds, and so Kaitlin had continued to take them.

"Despite the controversy over the increased risk of myocarditis, advocates of the Moderna vaccine are still insisting on its efficacy with

the new variants," a handsome man with an angular jaw and rather bushy, light-blonde eyebrows was saying on the screen. *"Additional speculations that the virus itself may have been manmade in China, rather than spread naturally through animals, has further been alarming some."*

"The exact cause continues to remain known…Oh, sorry-I mean, *unknown*…" Kaitlin vocalized as the newscaster continued, correcting her translation into English. She silently patted herself on the back for the Norsk classes in which she'd managed to excel to the *Intermediate* level before taking a break, deciding that it'd be enough for the moment.

As the news droned on, Kaitlin's thoughts drifted. Her website work felt stable for now, but she often caught herself imagining a return to working in-person—perhaps once Malin was older. She cleared her throat and repeated the translated phrase once again, this time in the correct syntax. "The cause continues to remain unknown…."

"*Peh*," Paul scoffed, flipping through the last page of the newspaper. "I'm sure you were more right *before* your language correction, babe. I'm sure the cause *is* known, and the Americans *are* somehow involved in whatever caused it. Now they want to look like bloody heroes- advocating for some supposed remedy to their own ill!"

Kaitlin simply hummed a little sound in response, sipping on her second cup of hazelnut coffee, cradling the mug in her hands. Paul could oblige in conspiracy theories all he wanted, but they had both been recently fully vaccinated. It had become mandated for his regional meetings, which Kaitlin insisted on continuing to attend with him as they'd used to do when they'd first got married- albeit now with Malin on her lap. Despite his misgivings, Paul had caved into the vaccine along with Kaitlin- though they'd both agreed not to expose Malin to its strong, unsubstantiated-over-time contents just yet.

This needs a little bit more milk, Kaitlin thought with a disgusted look on her face, pacing toward the refrigerator. Her roaming eye got caught and lingered on the magnet calendar on the door before she opened it. '*M's Dance Recital'* was scribbled under September 16th for that following week. Right next to the shape of a heart she'd marked in red ink for the following day.

The little scribble mocked her from the fridge. *Mon Dieu!* Was it possible Paul hadn't even noticed their approaching anniversary? He was, after all, the kind of man who might notice a change in her hairstyle—but lately, even that felt rare. Making plans for just the two of them? Kaitlin couldn't even recall how long that had been. Her mind sought a memory to hang on to, mostly recalling jewelry or handbags arriving in the mail on her birthday or for the new year.

"You'd really feel special if I took you to some restaurant surrounded by heart stickers and buy you overpriced roses?" he'd asked last February, for instance. The memory of their Valentine's Day conversation sent a rush of pink hives crawling across her chest. "Surrounded by other couples falling for the same social scam? Come on, babe."

Kaitlin sighed and glanced at Paul out of the corner of her eye. He hadn't mentioned any plans. Had he forgotten their wedding date?

Calm down, Kaitlin. Three deep breaths in, exhale at the same slow rate.

Maybe Paul was just pretending to forget—part of an elaborate scheme for a surprise celebration. He should know by now she hated waiting, though- especially without so much as a hint that something special was in the works!

"You have what we call an 'anxious' style of attachment, Kaitlin," her therapist would likely say again if she brought it up to her now. *"Why do you think you need constant reassurance to feel loved?"*

Kaitlin let out an audible sigh and rinsed her forest-green mug in the sink. Whatever Paul's intentions were, one thing was certain: he could ignore things like her improved language skills all he wanted, but there'd be hell to pay if he dared to overlook their big, tenth wedding anniversary!

CHAPTER 5

Oslo

LAR IKTAR'S FOCUS SHIFTED AWAY FROM THE VIBRANT VIEW from the twentieth-floor view of The Group's corporate-headquarters suite, and onto himself. "Do I resemble George Clooney, Nora?" Stepping closer to the oval mirror adjacent to the loft's living room window that overlooked the bustling downtown capital, he was twisting his torso every which way to glance his reflection from different angles.

"I'm sorry?" Nora Berg stifled a chuckle, trying to maintain her composure. Professor Iktar's unexpected question almost caused her to spit out the mango juice she had just sipped on. It seemed that the tragic death seven years ago of one of her 'brother' members in The Group—Tan Kuvvet—wasn't the only thing troubling Master. Despite his insecurities, the salt-and-pepper hair atop his head was charismatic to her regardless of his 52 years on this earth, albeit a bit thinner than the way Nora remembered when she'd first met him.

"I was compared to him in Trondheim by those Azerbaijani clients during last week's meeting, my girl," Lar said, raising his chin while picking at his facial scruff. "I don't know. Perhaps I should let my hair and beard grow a little longer? It might make me look younger. What do you think?"

"You're even more handsome than the actor, Master," Nora reassured, giving Lar's shoulder a gentle squeeze as she trotted up next to him. She gazed at her own long, silky blonde mane staring back at her from the antiquated glass framed by rustic, hand-forged metal. "I'm telling you, Master: you only get better with age, like fine wine."

Lar took a puff of his cigar and sucked in his gut as he continued his self-scrutiny. "You flatter me, my beauty. But a good, long look at one's body reveals what good skincare and haircare can sometimes disguise."

He chuckled ruefully as his hands traveled down to his torso. "Stig's ab exercises haven't been doing me much good, I'm afraid. My metabolism has slowed, it seems. Can you believe I used to be able to down two whole falafel sandwiches without even a hint of bloating in my belly? Two! And now? I can barely pop a grape in my mouth without my stomach looking as if I'd had an entire turkey."

"Good health is more important than perfect abs, Master," Stig said with a chuckle, manifesting before them with a towel draped around his neck. "No need to compare your human body with mine. Have you been taking those herbal supplements I gave you? I read they're helpful to mankind."

"Oh, Stig's right, Master!" Nora chimed in eagerly, admiring her jinn-boyfriend's physique. How long had her jinn-lover been standing with them without manifesting in flesh form? To this day she could still never quite pinpoint or tell.

"I remember when I last saw my father- curcumin had worked wonders. My mom had said…"

"Nora!" Lar's voice cut through her musings, firm and unyielding. "We are like cats—royal, loyal, and ever-evolving. The past is dead. Leave it behind!"

"Yes, Master," Nora murmured, exchanging a quick glance with Stig before lowering her head. "I apologize."

Lar Iktar was the one to talk! The past wasn't so easily dismissed. It loomed like a shadow over Nora's thoughts, the memories sharp and unyielding. Her mother's disbelief…her brother's betrayal. Summoning all the courage she could muster up, Nora fought back tears that tended to well up whenever Lar mentioned the family she wasn't allowed to contact—in exchange for the life of luxury and affluence with 'The Group'.

Yes, her mother had hurt her by not believing her; by not standing up to her son when Nora had confided in her about her brother's harassment. But the woman loved her, hadn't she? Perhaps she regretted her actions by now. And her poor, ill father. He'd seen war, and was the withholding, silent type for as long as she could remember. Would he finally have missed her enough to express affection? If only Nora could be allowed to see them one more time to find out.

Stig wrapped a comforting arm around her, leading the two of them to take a seat down on the sofa. Nora felt grateful that her jinn lover could understand her thoughts. Lar Iktar— a fellow human like herself—luckily couldn't read minds like Stig could.

Though she loved 'The Group' as her new family, Nora couldn't help but question Lar's right to judge anyone for thinking about 'past lives'. Seven years had passed, but somehow Master could always be counted upon to bring just about any topic to her old groupmate, Tan! He could change his name, but not his thoughts, Nora supposed, recalling how she'd only found out more recently that Lar's birth name in his native, Emirati city of Dubai had been 'Aresh'. For seven whole years since Tan's suicide in the woods, she and the others had been enduring the faded exhilaration of Master Lar's aura.

Tan's increasing guilt over his murder of Linette Peterson at the time had led to his tragic end. According to what her cousin Anja from Stavanger had confided to Nora about her conversations with their late friend- he was also feeling trapped in an unsatisfactory relationship with Meredith Olsen, and unloved by Lar.

The past, Nora mourned, her eyes closed and head resting on Stig's firm chest whilst he scrolled through his cell phone messages.

Master Lar is the one to talk! He was even fixated still on his friend from the 1990's- some man named John Walker that turned out to be Linette's father! She could never forget how particularly distraught Master had been immediately after John's visit to Norway to inquire into her death seven winters ago.

"Master!" Nora had pleaded, stammering with desperation. *"The cops actually heard Tan confess to injecting that Linette woman. Don't you see? He did this to himself!"*

"It's no use, Nora," Lar had spoken softly. *"Thank you, though, for trying to make me feel better."*

"But it's the truth, Master!" Nora had pressed. *"And it also wasn't just the cyanide we provided to implicate Tan that freed Paul Maverick from jail. It was also that damned woman's alibi – Maverick's colleague named Jeanette or whatever. You can't keep blaming yourself. What's done is done!"*

"And who's gone is gone", Lar had mourned. He was rocking back and forth in his chair as he took in a deep breath and closed his wet eyes. "*I let Tan down, Nora! Maybe that's all I've ever done in this life...I've let everybody down. I'll never be a Socrates or a Nietzche! Maybe I've simply been deluding myself, and everyone around me in the process."*

Nora had shaken her head in disbelief. It was the first time she'd seen the man she'd come to respect, and obey, in tears like a little child.

"Paul Maverick managed to luck out of jail, Master, but his investigation was still ongoing. If Tan hadn't confessed all those things before sacrificing himself before the police in the woods, our involvement with the cyanide could still have been explained later on! Somehow, someway, we've always managed to help our fellow members. We do what we must to survive and thrive."

"Tan couldn't handle what he did to Linette," Lar uttered, eyes shut with repressed pain. *"He's blamed me for it. Who was I kidding?*

Tan couldn't ever love a man who, in his eyes, motivated him to murder someone he'd cared about."

"You've always said it, Master: death is a natural part of life, and Linette wouldn't have died if it wasn't her ordained time," Nora recalled responding to him as softly as she could. *"Somehow, someway- if God hadn't willed it, Tan's cyanide injection technically wouldn't have been successful that night of her passing."*

"He wasn't going to stay in jail long," Lar had muttered to the wall in front of his eyes. His dolorous voice was barely audible. *"I was going to get that Serdar kid involved- using him being a 'jealous roommate' as a motive. I wasn't going to allow my Tan to rot in jail! But he didn't know that. He was just supposed to stay there for a short time until everything became sorted out. That was the plan. Oh, I should have told him beforehand, Nora! I acted in haste. Jaan's return confused me! I panicked! I broke my own maxims. I left Tan alone. I caused him to do this to himself!"*

"It wasn't your fault." Nora had insisted, guiding him to the living room sofa and sitting beside him. *"Everything happens for a reason. We have to believe in our most basic maxim, Master."*

"Ah...if Jaan hadn't returned to my life at absolutely the worst time," Lar's voice had remained flat as he stared at the wallpaper. *"The cyanide was merely a small arrow for the cops in Tan's direction- just enough to satiate Jaan. It was to show him I wouldn't support someone who had murdered his daughter. I never meant for Tan to lose all hope and resort to...for him to actually..."*

"Hush now, Master, it's alright." Nora had comforted him, resting his head gently on her shoulder. *"We know all this already. It'll be alright."*

Lar had been inconsolable. *"I was going to free him... And him and I ... we were going to...we were supposed to..."*

His body was trembling, and Nora remembered wrapping her arms tighter around him. Was this the man who'd once stood so tall, proud and strong? Her rock, her savior, her mentor? Kneeling before her with tears running down his scruffy face, he was no different in that moment from a five-year-old boy crying over a broken toy.

"But you are right about one thing, Nora," he'd finally announced, clearing his throat seemingly in an attempt to regain his composure. *"Tan's death cannot be in vain. There must be a purpose for all of this, and I need to figure it out."*

Nora had nodded with a smile, remembering the day she'd first met Lar at that lecture back in Trondheim. He had quoted passages from the Quran- fusing religious text with his own convictions, and blending in influences from Sufism and Native American principles on the interaction of living things in nature. He'd just released his book, 'Atlas for the Meaningful Life', about his studies and own life epiphanies that would go on to become a regional bestseller.

"*Take that, mother*!" she would sometimes rebel in her mind. This was her new life. A new life that came with so much sacrifice, rules and restrictions. But a life of her own, nonetheless! A better life- where she was of service to a greater cause, and actually appreciated.

"*My friends, my family*," Lar had addressed the crowd during that momentous lecture before she'd been initiated into 'The Group'.

"*Who can we turn to when our families and those closest to us have turned their backs on us? We can only turn inward, and find Allah- or, whom the West refers to as 'God'. To a good and all-knowing Creator, who would never judge his own creations that don't hurt anyone but are consistently hurt by everyone around them. Constantly used and abused... with their good intentions becoming misconstrued and misused.*"

Tears had welled up in Nora's eyes whilst she looked around the lecture hall. In that moment, it'd felt as if this man before her just might have saved her life. And, in his own way- he had, indeed. Master Lar had become the loving parent she hadn't had, rescuing her from her brother's abuse and her mother's cold complacency.

She'd found warmth with 'The Group'- and a literal one with Stig, assigned to her there. Her cousin, Anja, in the Stavanger branch had never been quite in sync with her own assigned jinn, Bjorn. Nora felt extremely lucky that she and Stig had made a good match- despite having no choice in the matter, and despite their differences in form. Lar would encourage only jinn and human physical relations in 'The Group' in order to avoid breeding. He looked down on children as possibly hindering their organization's recruitment and business operations.

"I promised him yesterday, Nora," Lar had broken into Nora's thoughts on how much he'd changed since she'd first met him. *"I promised him I'd resolve to figure out the purpose of why his death had to happen in the grander scheme of things..."*

Nora could still remember her confusion that day. *"Yesterday? Oh! You mean- during your visit to the cemetery? Right, right. You never told us which one you went to, by the way, Master. Is Tan buried in Trondheim, next to Linette or something?"*

"What?" Lar had retorted with a jolt. *"Next to Linette? And, in that Christian cemetery? Are you crazy?"*

"I don't know, Master!" Nora had stammered. *"Maybe he had some last wish or something, written somewhere. In case he...Well, anyway- he was young, so...you're right, you're right. That'd be silly. What young person thinks about their death enough to leave post-mortem instructions? But then again- he did kill himself. So, he could have planned ahead and left notes on..."*

"Oh, stop the rambling nonsense, Nora!" Lar had dismissed, with a wave of his hand in the heavy air around them. *"Tan is a Muslim man. I made sure of a proper Islamic burial for him. Right here in Oslo, at the Gamblebyen Gravlund. He's here. He'll always be close to me."*

"Oh, yes, yes. Muslim. Yes, I suppose he was," Nora had uttered, facing the floor.

Flipping over her hair, Nora sighed deeply. When her eyes traveled back up from the floor, she noted that Master Lar had walked to his room without bothering to close his door. She shot Stig a look over her shoulder as she stood up, placing her forefinger before her lips to advise him to remain quiet. Inching her head closer to glimpse him sitting on his prayer mat, Nora quietly took a few steps backwards to give him his privacy.

She remembered how he'd similarly excused himself to his room to pray and linger alone after that depressing conversation they'd had seven years ago as well. His prayers had been less frequent back then; the years only seemed to lead him into making more conservative life choices. How much longer would it take him to get back into his groove-to throw those lavish parties for all of them again? Fun and games weren't why she'd signed up for 'The Group', yet they were certainly much-missed distractions from the phantoms of the past troubling her mind.

Nora stared at the floor, shaking her head. She had to remain hopeful that although nothing on earth remained the same, at least some more exciting bits and pieces from the past could be recreated somewhere along the line of life. For some comfort. And something to look forward to.

2014

PLACING THE MULTI-COLOR PRAYER BEADS BACK INTO THEIR cloth sack, Lar took a deep breath and closed his eyes. It'd been an arduous task to focus on his *Dhuhr* prayer that day. His heart sank at Nora's past tense usage to refer to Tan. How could Tan no longer be alive, and in his life? What motivation did

Lar now have left to go on? To persist with his mission and his writing, in this second chance of a life he'd created in Norway…where he could feel at one with nature, and at one with all kinds created by Allah? Could he throw caution to the wind? Could Lar Iktar indulge in the countless movies, books and social media posts that suggested taking advantage of his relative freedom in Norway— not to mention his position of wealth and power— and hook up with men through phone apps and bars?

He chuckled bitterly. After years of life experience, he had recognized his need for a connection. Some bloggers were calling it 'demisexual'—which he felt described him better than simply 'asexual' for abstaining from sex as an older adult. If it wasn't *true love*, it just wasn't doing it for him.

He'd also come to recognize in himself the belief that, if it wasn't a deep love— it wouldn't be worth disposing of his self-created shields to maintain his equilibrium. No matter how lonely he felt. He'd kept his desires to himself for so long. Doing so had become second nature to him over the years. He'd chosen, instead, to transform his lustful energies into his published works and a professional mission materialized through his disciples.

***Love.* He recalled that horrendous night after Tan's self-inflicted exit from this world, ending the life from his hard-earned, chiseled body—alongside any chances for the two of them to have a future. Lar had rushed to the morgue after Meredith called him in tears to share the details of what had just happened in the woods. He'd told the police he was the boy's relative, and they didn't question it much. And why would they? A murder suspect who'd just killed himself. It wasn't that much of a stretch, anyway. What other family would Tan have left? He hadn't kept in touch with his parents back in Turkey since joining 'The Group', and the *Politi*— the Norwegian authorities— didn't appear to know much about**

Islamic burial rituals.

"I need to take him to our mosque," Lar had sobbed, showing them a picture of himself with Tan. He had never been one for photographs—except for promotional material for 'The Group' or his books— but he was grateful to have taken some with Tan during their most recent New Year's celebration. How handsome Tan had looked in that photograph in his black suit, standing beside Lar with Nora on the other side.

Even in death, Tan's nude body appeared serene and beautiful, covered before him now in a white *kafan* cloth. It'd taken Lar all the strength he could muster to repress the bodily temptations he'd long forced himself to ignore, and not kiss Tan's chiseled, hairy chest. Wiping a tear from his eye, Lar had settled, instead, on taking one of Tan's lifeless hands: cold as ice, warmed now only with his lust. He took two of his fingers and placed them on his lips. A tear fell from his eye, tracing a path down Tan's lifeless skin. Lar instinctively licked it off, lost in fantasy of the plethora of physical and romantic possibilities that could have taken place between them.

"Your soul could not kiss mine in life," he whispered, gently pressing Tan's lifeless cold fingers on his lips and kissing them. "But you will always remain alive, young and beautiful inside me. I'm sorry that my love for you, and my desperation to keep you near me, has ultimately caused so much suffering."

If only, Lar thought, his heart heavy with sorrow. *Those must be the two most heartbreaking words in the English language*. As a fellow Muslim man, Lar understood the internal conflict Tan must have faced regarding his sexuality. He'd reminded him of his younger self in the Middle East- as Aresh Jahan- before becoming 'Lar Iktar' in Scandinavia.

Life was indeed ironic. Lar often found himself fueled by

memories of his first real lover and their stolen kisses and intimacy during a fateful summer in Dubai, on their internship as university students. How his 'Abdul Jaan Vaziri'—of half Lebanese and half Canadian descent— had changed his name, too. He'd become' John Walker', later fully living out the rest of his life as a straight-presenting man, after long-distance communication eventually dwindled between the two of them.

He had to be fair. Like Jaan, Tan hadn't exactly been out about his likely bisexuality either, Lar figured. Despite only sharing stolen glances and fleeting touches in the hallways, he and Tan hadn't even physically expressed anything. Yet Lar now realized that the special connection he and Tan had shared was beyond just mentor-and-disciple, and could even rival the more physical relationship he'd once had with Jaan. Love was love, and a connection was a connection- despite which form it took on in its expression.

Lar's mind drifted to his last conversation with his first lover following Tan's suicide. 'John' had left numerous voice messages, pleading to talk. Lar couldn't bring himself to answer the phone calls, feeling additionally betrayed by the shock of his *Abdul Jaan's* return after years of silence. The pain of losing Tan had caused him to feel that excruciating feeling of being abandoned once again.

"You shouldn't have protected a murderer in the first place, *Aresh Lar* bloody *Iktar!*" John's voice grew firmer as the messages went on, accusing him of shielding Tan from repercussions to pay for murdering his daughter.

***Yeah, right.* Lar would think, listening to such voice messages. If he hadn't had a guilty conscience to ease himself, why else would John be calling so much, trying to explain himself?**

"Please just pick up, Aresh. Let's discuss this face to face or live on the phone like two grown adults! Please just call me back. I

don't know why I have to pay for someone else's actions..."

His ears perked as the tone from the latest phone call indicated John's voice message was in the recording process. Lar couldn't take it anymore as he finally picked up the receiver.

"You're making *me* pay, Abe! Again!" Lar bellowed.

"Aresh!" John spoke, relieved. "How good to finally hear your voice. Look, can we just meet somewhere and..."

"You already abandoned me once," Lar wasn't going to let him have it without giving him a piece of his mind in its entirety. The memory of their brief reunion kiss caused Lar's body to tremble. He fought back the urge to release his tears, afraid they'd show in his voice.

"You ignored me for years, and then came back into my life when I'd finally begun to move on, and truly cared for another! Why did you show yourself to me? Now I'm abandoned... again.

"Oh, stop! I didn't abandon you- high and mighty, academic writer *Professor Iktar.* And I had no clue you'd cross my path in Norway on my search for my Linette..."

"It's Aresh *Jahan*, by the way," Lar deadpanned, interrupting John.

"What?"

"My real last name. My mother was of Persian descent. You knew me as Aresh Iktar. I was trying to fit into the Emirati culture. Heh! Youth..." he scoffed. "You never tried getting to know the real me, I suppose, let alone delve into anything with me beyond a summer fling."

"Alrighty, then, Aresh *Jahan*," John spoke after a brief silence. " Damn! What else *did* you lie to me about that summer, boy? And you're talking to me about not caring to know the real you- when you apparently didn't even *present* to me the real you!"

"Oh, please," Lar waved his hand dismissively before the

receiver. The sound of John's voice using the word 'boy' to once again refer to him now as a man in his middle age, just as he'd done so when they were both lovers as young men, excited him to the very core of his being. Regardless, Lar took a deep breath in and ignored his erection. "Look who's talking. You changed your name, too, *Vaziri!*"

"I only changed the spelling, since 'John' is easier for Canadians. And I just never used my middle name of 'Abdul' or 'Abe' much, that's all. Besides, 'Walker' was my birth father's *actual* last name— I didn't make anything up! You apparently went out of your way to go by two very different first and last names!"

"It was difficult for me in academia, okay?" Lar found himself chuckling with a more relaxed tone. Despite his anger, he needed to vent everything out and somehow that had always been easy to do with John. "After those September 11 attacks in the States, even my classmates and colleagues started looking at me funny..."

"But *Lar Iktar*?" John asked, stifling a laugh with his fist before his mouth. "Not exactly *Bob Smith*, or something common like that, come on, now."

"Well, I did first consider being called...*Larry*," Lar said in a lowered voice. He smiled, not knowing a similar smile became visible on the corners of John's mouth.

"Larry..." John deadpanned. "Sexy."

"Yes, yes- shut up!" Lar teased. His cheeks had reddened like a tomato. "I've been telling everyone I got 'Lar' from the root word for 'teacher'".

"Okay, professor," John responded, smiling. He continued after a momentary quiet lull between them. "Why can't you just ever have been fully yourself, *Aresh Jahan?*"

Lar's smile lingered in the wake of John's enunciation of his

entire name by birth. He cleared his head and shook it off. *No,* he told himself. Any possibility of a romantic reconciliation between himself and this cowardly man whom he'd once truly loved had perished along with poor, young Tan's life on earth.

"I just couldn't, okay?" He spoke softly into the phone. "I either didn't feel welcomed back in Dubai, or entirely safe here in Europe. Without some celebrity-sounding name to guise behind. Oh, I don't know. Not everyone has had it easy like you, with your daddy's money and business to take over. I come from a family of mere fishermen. I fought for every centimeter of my success! I worked my butt off at the graduate school in Oslo, and later teaching in Trondheim. What did *you* ever fight for?"

"You don't know anything about how hard it was to get my father to help me, Aresh. Don't assume! Besides— I *have* been fighting! I have been fighting for justice for my daughter! The only one who actually paid for her life, because of Tan! Also, oh, I don't know— some sort of *resolution*, I guess, between us and what we shared, once and for all…"

"Yeah, right," Lar remarked. "I think it just flatters you that I confessed holding on to that summer of the two of us. Aside from an ego boost, it seems— what we had can't be anything more to you! I'm smart enough to realize that now, *Jaan*. Especially since you'll always hold Linette's death against me. As if *you* were some ideal father for her all these years."

"Don't you dare go *there*," John wagged his forefinger into the cell phone, breathing heavily through flared nostrils.

"And don't you dare hold Tan's death against *me*, either, Aresh! Remember- your boy did this to himself! Stop trying to punish me for it as if I were responsible- though the bastard surely deserved at least life in prison for killing my innocent girl! And you know it, too! That's why you've been running, and avoiding. You

blocked my number so I can't believe I've had to resort to your office phone!"

"Why are you even calling me in the first place?" Lar questioned. "To cause anguish, and confuse me further? You could never leave that comfortable wife and life of yours and be with me!"

"Oh, come on— is this really about Helen and my marital status?" John's voice was firm and insistent. He took in a deep breath and continued in a lowered voice. "I was never *gay*, Aresh! I was never fully like you, apparently. I'd just assumed we were *both* bisexual, and exploring. Come on, now! This whole grudge you're holding against me is simply unfair! Why would you harbor a romantic future with someone who's not fully like you and with your homosexual-partnership dreams? And then hold him accountable punitively? And I didn't just get married for money, for God's sake! Helen is a sweet woman, and I met her long after you and I..."

"Alright, alright, whatever, I don't want to hear it!" Lar interrupted. "You're the one with a grudge...as if I killed your daughter."

"You harbored her murderer!" John raised his voice. "Put yourself in my place, Aresh: I'm a father! I was...Look, I appreciate that you at least tried to make things right toward the end, with you and your followers going to the police with evidence and all. But you shouldn't have protected that young man in the first place! A man capable of actual murder! It was too little, too late. That's not the young man I remember in the Emirates."

"I told you- you already killed that romantic, naïve man!" Lar replied. "We both know by now the world isn't a perfect place! I told you I'm sorry for what happened to Linette. How was I to know she was your daughter?"

"Does that matter?" John bellowed. "Why should *anyone's* child have had to die for our own issues, Aresh? Can you tell me

that!?"

"People die all the time from various causes," Lar continued. "It was her fate, perhaps? I don't know. Tan had to get over her and his obsession, I suppose. It's just how the events turned out. He had love for her, too; Tan never meant to bring her pain. I know he did it with as minimal of pain as possible. The flow of life just took us all to that point where..."

"John? Dinner's ready...." a woman's voice had broken into Aresh's words, and he knew just who it was. He sighed, welcoming her voice as the harbinger of the truth he'd finally brought himself to face.

"Go eat your dinner with your wife, *Jaan*," Lar mumbled, distancing his mouth from the receiver of the landline phone. He was resolved to face his sorrow alone. "Thanks- for trying, anyway. But just leave. Please. Leave me in my misery."

"*Aresh*...I ...I don't know what to say," John stammered with his words. "I've just been trying to make you feel better. Ever since I found out what Tan did to himself. I know you. I couldn't stand to know you were suffering. I could feel it, too."

"You've done and said enough," Lar cut in. "You're never going to be able to look at me the same anymore, I guess. You're just trying to lead me on and ensure my continued affections. You've become an egomaniac."

"I'm the one who has become an egomaniac?" John's voice was trembling. "I've been calling non-stop just to make sure you're alright! Despite having every reason in the world to shun you for good after what's been done to Linette! I..."

"Don't let what Helen has prepared for you get cold!" Lar interrupted as he slammed the phone shut. His hands were trembling like loose leaves in the wind, the weight of his grief and heavy burden pressing down on his chest.

CHAPTER 6

THE MOVING HANDS OF THE EMBELLISHED OAKWOOD CLOCK hanging by the alabaster floor lamp imitated the slow and steady rhythm of Nora's lips dancing with Stig's own. *How fortunate to have found each other*, both would often think. A union that worked regardless of her youthful, human existence, and his mature, jinn one; one where he'd be able to manifest as the same, adult male in human flesh-form of his jinn-realm appearance for over four decades now. A union of two souls satiated in the beauty of their present joy together, willfully unfocused on the human one's mortality and aging, and the other's mainly-invisible form and other logistical difficulties.

"Is it me, or has Master been praying more frequently than usual?" Stig whispered in Nora's ear, slouched on the leather sofa. Both of them shifted their gaze toward the closed door of the space Lar used as his bedroom: one of many in the luxurious suite used as a live-work unit by group members. They were all technically 'offices'- including Nora and Stig's own room together.

"Didn't he only perform the last *Isha* prayer like all of us try to fit in before midnight? With the occasional one around noon? I mean, it's later in the afternoon now…"

"I think he's just been trying to figure himself out, perhaps through doing more customary rituals," Nora said, gently disentangling herself from Stig's grip now and twirling her long blond strands around her pointed-nailed fingers. "You *do* know that pious Muslims pray five times a day, and this is actually a norm, baby. Maybe Master is simply trying to improve himself spiritually, doing all five prayers from now on rather than one or two?"

"Yeah, but aren't you finding it a bit strange, too, baby, how he's *doing* one thing while *preaching* to us another?" Stig questioned, crossing his bulky arms.

Nora shrugged. "Honestly, baby, I think he's just let us off the hook this entire time. He never forced his religion on us from the beginning, though we know the importance of his practicing his maxims in our everyday lives for the *mission*. Perhaps we've simply been spared the harder rules and restrictions all this time?"

"I wonder when he's going to give up his daily glass of wine at this rate, then," Stig retorted with a smile, referring to the taboo of drinking alcohol in Islam. His eyes traveled to the wine rack adjacent to the bar stools surrounding the shiny-lacquered kitchen island.

"*Or*, maybe he's been fooling us all along- secretly drinking grape juice instead," Nora added with a wink, giving Stig a kiss on the cheek. Her lips sizzled with his heat. She'd not only gotten used to his various jinn characteristics over the years, but actually found herself *craving* them whenever they'd be apart during his business and recruitment trips.

The rumbling sound of drawers being opened and shut caught Nora's attention. She rocked back and forth as she sat, unease creeping into her posture. "Maybe you should return to your unseen form, baby," she whispered. "Master will be coming out of his room any minute now. We don't want him to feel disrespected, thinking we've been fooling around on the couch while he was praying. He may be feeling extra sensitive."

"But…we kind of *did* do just that, didn't we, sexy?" Stig bobbed his eyes up and down. He added a little pout. "I was thinking you'd enjoy my extra shot of post-gym energy today."

"Well, yes, of course I did, baby, and I do," Nora tilted her head playfully. "But this is about *Master*…and it just feels like bad timing."

"Okay, okay, good thinking," Stig replied, standing up and stretching out his arms. "But only if you promise to make it up to me later, my clever kitten. I'll be in the room."

"I will, *meow*," Nora giggled. "Now, *shh*, go, go, go!"

Lar's door flung open right as Stig's physical form vanished out of human sight.

"Master!" Nora stood up straight on the couch, keeping her back as straight as she could. She straightened out her tight-fitting dress and smoothed out her hair.

"Is everything alright, dear Nora?" Lar asked, eyeing his surroundings. I thought I heard you talking to someone."

"I… was just on the phone with Anja, Master! She updated me on, *uh*, that Craig Stevens character."

"Oh, the moneybag entrepreneur, right, right," Lar walked over to her and took a seat. "Has he bought the bait? Will he be paying us what we asked?"

"They've apparently had dinner, Master, and Anja reports he was particularly flirty after a couple of drinks," Nora reported. It wasn't technically lying if you were reporting a phone conversation you actually *did* have that day- just a bit earlier than spending some quality time with your jinn boyfriend- was it?

"She's recorded his slurred speech discussing intimacy with her, and will send it to his wife if she has to," Nora continued. "As of this morning- our accounts show Mr. Stevens has paid the first installment already, though. So far, so good!"

"Good, good," Lar responded nonchalantly. He slumped his weight on the armchair reserved just for him in the loft. "Excellent job, ladies! You and Anja can both expect that bonus at the end of the month."

"Thank you, Master," Nora heaved a sigh of relief. She wondered which designer-label handbag it would be this time.

"All for the cause, my girl," Lar took in a deep breath and rolled his shoulders in all directions. "All for the good cause."

"Right, Master," Nora nodded. She'd long been drilled on the importance of some necessary sacrifices and secretive behavior with their clients, to be used as alibis with the legalities if the need arose. The sustainability of 'The Group' in expanding its literary following and membership- as well as their opulent lifestyle- depended on it.

"Where did Stig go?" Lar asked, his focus now on the view outside the window.

"He left while you were in prayer, Master," Nora responded, directing her gaze to the couch. "Probably returned to his current mission task. He should be back soon, though. I mean, I guess..."

"Hmm," Lar said, slumping deeper into the armchair, with eyes still looking at the overcast sky. "I hope you're not bothered he's been having to chat up that pretty student in Stavanger, are you? My dear Nora?"

Nora mumbled '*no*' as she shook her head, stammering through the lump in her throat. "I have no intention on breaking the maxim on our jealousies, Master. Besides, I know he's just doing his task for our greater mission."

He only loves me, Nora added in her mind. She wouldn't dare verbalize it to Master Lar, however. He'd not only ridicule her, but lecture her again on the dangers of romantic love.

"Good girl. Yes, we all contribute here as members do for the good of the whole. We are family." Lar's voice sounded lethargic as he spoke. He reached over to the small black cabinet by his feet shod in slippers, removing his favorite cigar gently from the wooden crate. Nora smiled with sympathy after him as Lar stood up and took a deep puff from the cigar as he walked closer to the window.

§

GAZING AT THE VEHICLES ENCIRCLING THE WATER FOUNTAIN roundabout, Lar shut his eyes to his present. Tan's weeping voice echoed in his memory. "*I'm a murderer, Master*." The painful reminder of one of their last conversations together- sitting side by side adjacent to that very fountain.

"You're hungry, Master?" Nora chimed, clearing her throat. "We're worried about you. You haven't been eating. You've lost weight and your skin is losing its color."

"Who do I have to look good for?" Lar muttered. Tan had given him the first sign of his returned affections by the same window. Lar had told him not to worry about what had occurred with Linette, and confessed that he was inside his heart. "*I think I like being there, Aresh*." Tan had responded. His voice and blushing look would never leave Lar's memory for as long as he lived; nor would the way hearing his birth-name coming from Tan's mouth had made him feel.

"Maybe you need to get away for a while and clear your head," Nora interjected into Lar's memories. "You haven't been outside of Norway for so long. There's that book conference in Paris that Bjorn and Stig are going to coming up ..."

"Yes, we're on the same frequency, my gal," Lar bit his lip as he nodded. "With regards to travel, that is. I need to renew my residency permit card first, if I want to travel anywhere without issues upon my return. I can do that from the Norwegian embassy in Dubai."

"Why the United Arab Emirates, Master?" Nora questioned. "I'm sure you can apply for a renewal here as well, from the Emirati embassy."

"Perhaps, yes," Lar took on a somber tone. "But I also want to visit my mother while there. Two birds, one stone. See how well my brother has been taking care of her. The pandemic has hit her particularly hard, with her fragile respiratory condition. We were blessed not to have lost her during the peak of the damned virus."

"I thought you'd said that your family wasn't very kind to you, Master," Nora questioned. "That we've all had to re-create our own families here. I can understand how the coronavirus could have made you think more sensitively, but…"

"Tan's death has been making me think about a lot of things, my dear," Lar interrupted, his voice trailing off as he continued to glance out the window. "About life, death, my mother, my brother, the afterlife…I've been reflecting a lot since Tan's death, you know? How I've let him down. Maybe I need to make amends where I still can, during however long I have yet to live on this earth. Before it's too late."

"With your brother, too?" Nora inquired. "Didn't you say he was actually violent with you?"

Lar smirked and closed his eyelids. He may have exaggerated some things to gain his disciples' trust. Yes, his brother, Muhiddin, had been aggressive after discovering his homosexuality. But there was nothing beyond a push here and a shove there- with which Lar himself had retaliated.

"My brother," Lar's mind traversed back in time. "Oh, yes, yes…"

One of the last conversations he'd had with his brother in person reverberated in Aresh's memory. *"You are a man, as you were born to be,"* Muhiddin had iterated. *"Allah has intended for you to be a man! A man with an organ to have intercourse with a woman in the natural way of our organs- not another man! Allah doesn't make mistakes!"*

Lar wiped away the tears tickling his face and stood up, leaving Nora behind as he walked away from the window. The cloudy sky matched his somber mood, tears rolling down his cheeks as memories flooded his mind. "I can handle my brother," he assured. "It's been years. And I'm not the same naïve, unaccomplished and unconfident man I was back then."

Despite the more recent and painful memories with his family, Lar couldn't deny the good times he had shared with them growing up in Dubai. He smiled as memories flashed by of the warm-beach summers with his *umi* and brother, drinking rose-flavored *Areej* drinks.

How nearly careless those days had been. Their father had just walked out on their mother, and yet she'd be doing fine on her own. His *umi* would go to work with her head held high, leading a relatively more progressive life compared to many other more conservative women he'd witness among their neighbors- never seen anywhere without their husbands present. Regardless, his mother could never get her mind around the thought of her eldest son- her precious first-born- not being anything other than an 'ordinary' man as expected of him.

She hadn't been as cruel with her words as his brother had, but she'd withdrawn her affection from Aresh as soon as she'd found out about his sexual orientation. And that had somehow hurt Aresh even more.

Just *'a psychological condition'*- she'd called it- for '*seeking the father he never knew'*. Aresh couldn't fully look her in the eyes up until his final departure to Europe. *Yeah, right,* Aresh would think. *If that's the case, mother- wouldn't my brother be interested in men as well?*

Only Aresh knew the full truth behind why he hadn't dared risking visiting the Emirates for all those years since leaving it behind. It had been easier to hide behind the cloak of familial heartbreak. The truth- as always- was much more complicated than what he had allowed to meet the eye. All those loyal clients he'd depended on- using his academic status as well as his convincing disciples in 'The Group'- to obtain funding to grow and secure his business.

The truth. About what had happened in Dubai- and whom he had met- that had catalyzed his arrival in Norway. The *Sharia*-law abiding authorities wouldn't let him get away for sure after discovering his homosexuality. If certain neighbors of his didn't get to him first- that was. He'd acquired so much wealth and respect through his influential book and business. And, with 'The Group', he'd even acquired a new family, of sorts. But at what cost?

It was no use fighting it any longer. He wasn't getting any younger, and neither did he have much else to lose. Aresh had to return to his homeland and face his family. It would no longer matter if they'd spit in his face or offend him; he'd just wipe it clean and go on his way. All Aresh knew for sure in his heart was that he would just have to wipe everything as clean as possible to feel any sort of relief on however long he'd had to live on this earth.

As much as they had indeed broken his heart, his mom and brother weren't the sole reason for his final departure from Dubai- as he often told his disciples. There were details of that portentous year he had never shared with anyone, not even Tan or Nora.

It all started on that fated day on his motorbike. The flames. The jinn.

His own Master.

CHAPTER 7

Dubai
1990

SHAFTS OF THE LATE AFTERNOON SUNLIGHT PENETRATED through the dark corridor, and Aresh knew he had to be swift. "I'm going out, *umi,"* he called over his shoulder to his mother in the kitchen, grabbing his shiny black helmet from the closet. "I'll be back for dinner."

"Going to meet your secret, infidel lovers?" his brother's lowered voice snuck up on him right as he reached out to open the main door to leave. Aresh gulped frozen in place.

"I like riding to clear my head, Muhiddin," Aresh's voice stood firm. *What in Jahannam is my brother saying?* "I know it's hard for you to get your thick head around, but motorbike riding has become my hobby."

"Just as sucking off men has, too, become a hobby- I'm sure," Muhiddin mumbled under his breath.

How could his brother imply him performing fellatio? The truth was: Aresh hadn't taken any sexual steps with someone yet in his life. But how did his brother even know about his sexual orientation? Even Aresh himself had been coming to terms with it in the more recent months. He certainly hadn't ever discussed it with anyone! It was enough to make his blood boil. He turned around to face him, tilting his head toward the door.

"Care to take this conversation outside?" Aresh said in a lowered tone. “Unless you’re purposely trying to give our mother a heart attack with your bullshit.”

“Can you deny it?” Muhiddin was persistent. “I saw you,” he muttered.

“What was that now?” Aresh asked in an exasperated whisper that made his throat felt sore. “There hasn’t been *anything to see,* you liar!”

Surely, Aresh had indeed *felt* what he had while looking at the young man in their neighboring apartment complex for some time now. In private, of course. Confused. Embarrassed. In pain. All of it. But he hadn’t even been able to make eye contact with the handsome neighbor boy around his age since he’d recognized his inklings, let alone anything further! He’d been too shy to do so!

Aresh had been discovering everything about himself mostly in the privacy in his bedroom. With his hand on himself underneath his bed sheets, and mind on the boy next door.

“I saw you masturbating, Aresh!” Muhiddin’s scratchy voice responded. He pointed his finger out their door and toward the direction of the apartment next door. “To *him*!”

Oh. Aresh squinted his eyes. Could it be true? Could Aresh have been caught in self-pleasure? Even if so- how could his brother know who he had been fantasizing about? That was…unless Muhiddin had caught that one particular time about a week ago. Aresh’s neck and chest begun to flush just thinking about it.

He hadn’t been in bed, but by the window. Watching the neighbor with the shiny black curls piled on his head. The one Aresh had seen around town, especially at the markets where he’d often accompany a young hijabi woman. His mother had recognized the woman and exchanged *‘salaams’*, explaining to him that she was the man’s sister- much to Aresh’s relief. They were not husband and wife, but rather orphans living together with an aging grandmother Aresh's mother knew from neighborly tea time.

Is that his bedroom, or some guest room? Aresh couldn't tell. He had begun eyeing the curly-haired young man regularly after discovering that his bedroom window had a direct view of one of their rooms. It felt good to deduce that his neighbor liked him, too, judging by a smile he'd thrown in Aresh's direction when he'd caught him watching behind the lace-sewn, white curtains his mother had placed all around their home. Aresh had gotten additional stimulation from the soft fabric, while his hand caressed his manhood to the point of climax.

Aresh could also have sworn the mysterious young man was frequenting that same room with the direct view more as of late, particularly lingering near the window that week- as if on purpose. The man would fidget through some stuff around the room that Aresh couldn't make out, though his nearly naked body was almost always pressed to the window, and his glances would dart in the direction of Aresh's room.

He's trying to communicate interest in me, Aresh soon knew almost for certain. And he couldn't help himself as his hand glided down his hips to his genitalia, comforted momentarily by the admittedly illogical- he recognized now in-retrospect- notion of a nearly transparent lace curtain hiding him. He'd paid no thought to glance at his bedroom door to check if it'd been closed or not, in case his mother or brother walked in on him. Aresh had just allowed himself to revel in the excitement of his self-discovery and the moment.

"You're telling me you don't touch yourself, brother?" Aresh fired in Muhiddin's face. "Oh, yeah right, come on."

"Not gazing at another man, I don't," his brother retorted. "No use denying your…*interests*, little brother. Look— I'm just trying to look out for you. Just give up on them, and Allah will forgive you— perhaps even reward you since it may be a particularly hard struggle for you. Give it up, and focus on procreating naturally with a woman!"

"Not everything is about having *children*, Muhiddin!" Aresh wagged his forefinger before his brother's face. He'd rehearsed the potential conversation he always knew he'd have to have with his family to defend his orientation— if it ever had to come to it— and he knew reproduction would always be something thrown at him. "What about disabled or even disfigured babies between heterosexual couples? Not to mention many of whom can't even conceive no matter how hard they try…."

"Everything in life is a part of our *test* for our placement in the afterlife, Aresh!" Muhiddin grabbed Aresh's finger, twisting it with intent. "Get that finger away from my face! You can't question Allah! He created you as a man- you're a man!"

"I'm *not* questioning our Creator," Aresh insisted, trying to ignore the anguished look on Muhiddin's face. It had appeared to be painted permanently as of late.

"But you have to admit: our world isn't exactly built on sustained perfection. Look around you at all the violence and bigotry. Besides, I'm not trying to be a woman. I'm happy being a man. I just happen to desire another man! And even if I *were* feeling like a woman and wanting to become one: so what? What *harm* would that cause anyone?"

"What *harm* does that crazy goon in the village who's been said to screw his goats cause, too, Aresh?" Muhiddin crossed his arms and laughed.

"That's not fair to compare me with him, brother," Aresh shook his head quietly, unable to meet his gaze.

"With your twisted logic- it very damn well is fair!" Muhiddin crossed his arms across his chest. "I'm sure the goon *loves* his damn goat, and the goat's still alive and well, so, no physical harm, either, I suppose. Right? But we all call him 'crazy' and tell our neighborhood kids to stay away, don't we? We're all aware how he's going against the natural way of a functional, healthy society: aren't we?"

"It's *not* the same thing!" Aresh burst.

"Yes, it is! And- oh- what *harm* can a brother and sister cause if they commit incest but are of age and feel affection for each other, right? Now *there* would be some poor, disfigured children likelier to be born, since you brought that topic up…"

"Again, with the procreation topic," Aresh finally stared his brother straight into his eyes, inching his face closer. "Maybe I don't *want* to breed children! Have you thought about that? Maybe I just want to love who I love, and die an old man in peace!"

"It's all for our community!" Muhiddin was shaking his head. "You're not getting it. You have to tame your personal desire for the greater good!"

"You're still lecturing me, as if we were still twelve and nine," Aresh retorted. "Yet I've seen the way you look at that young woman, *Fatima*. You— my big brother, and a married man! You don't exactly 'lower your gaze', as the Quran dictates, when her full-bosom-highness walks out to the market!"

"Maybe I can marry *her* too!" Muhiddin crossed his arms and lifted his chin high. "You know it's allowed!"

"Such backward thinking!" Aresh placed his arms on his waist. "You think you can care for her and Mina equally financially and emotionally, as the often-ignored fine-print of the Quran mandates? The part of the *ayah* that selfish, greedy perverts who just want more women for pleasure tend to conveniently ignore?"

"You're calling *me* the perve?" Muhiddin scoffed, shoving Aresh enough to cause him to take a couple of steps back.

Aresh was on a roll and continued regardless. "With what finances, could you even potentially have a second marriage? *Hmm?* My dear, market-owning brother? Through miraculously selling more chewing gum and nearly expired milk?"

"You watch your mouth!" his brother shoved him lightly again. "I work hard to keep my business afloat, and put food on my family's table. What do you think you are- some big shot businessman now, after that damned internship last summer? You're ashamed of me? Of me and *al-umu*? We're your 'backward' family— is that it?"

"Maybe I am!" Aresh regretted the words as soon as they escaped his mouth. But it was too late. They had.

"Oh yeah?" Muhiddin took two steps closer and leaned his face toward Aresh. "Well, we're more ashamed of you! You faggot! What good have *you* accomplished? You're lucky I discovered what you did looking at that other faggot before *umi* did!"

"*Awlad*?" their mother's voice called out. "Everything alright?"

"Yes, mother," Muhiddin called over his shoulder. His eyes were still locked on his brother's. "Aresh was just giving his opinion on my market again!"

"Don't make me leave my TV series and come there with my bad leg, *awlad*," their mother continued. "You brothers need to get along. Don't break my heart."

"Yes, *umi*," Aresh called out. "I was just leaving for some fresh air, anyway."

Inhaling deeply, Aresh added in a whisper. "Don't you dare call me that ever again, my brother!"

"Oh, yeah?" Muhiddin started laughing hysterically. "And what are you going to do if I do, *faggot*? Huh? Shoot me? So, you can go to jail to become in closer proximity to other men?"

Aresh's already-clenched fist could no longer be restrained as it lashed toward his brother's face with a punch!

Muhiddin kept silent for what felt like a good minute before caressing the cheek that had just born witness to the painful blow. "That's all you've got, little brother?"

"Don't provoke me further, Muhiddin," Aresh shook his head side to side. "I don't want to do this. We're family. I don't mean to hurt or offend you…You just got to watch your mouth, for the love of Allah!"

"Don't you dare utter Allah Almighty's name, faggot! Unless you want to lose your freedom in prison- though I'm sure you'll relish it, being accompanied by other men! I'll tell them exactly who you are, and you'll beg they do not do worse to you like the laws in Iran or Saudi Arabia."

Muhiddin ran his forefinger across his neck. "But then again- it *would* perhaps clear our family's honor…"

"Really brother?" Aresh's voice stood unyielding. "Do you think that inflicting such evil on me could give you any more of your so-called 'honor' on Judgement Day?"

As Muhiddin spit in his face, and quickly opened the door to step outside- Aresh followed suit to take in the fresh air, wiping his face with a sigh. *We both need to calm down.*

He would never forget the thunderstruck expression on his mother's face, taking him by surprise by the front yard. *She must have used the back door!*

Their mother was standing frozen, looking at her sons with one hand on her chest and the other on her knee. She was heaving against a tree, and tears were rolling down her wrinkled cheeks. Aresh knew that she'd heard. She knew.

§

THE WIND BRAZED HIS BARE ARMS HARSHER THAN USUAL, CLUING Aresh in to the fact that he must have been speeding way over the usual limit. But he didn't care. The tears that cascaded down his cheekbones were fogging up the visor, and he knew he soon had to park somewhere and take a break for safety.

At the red light, Aresh took in a deep breath. *Just relax.* The look of utter shock on his mother's face popped up in his mind. *I haven't done anything bad. She'll understand. I'll return home when everyone has calmed down, and talk to them like grown adults.*

An animal sound somewhere to the left of him returned him to the present. Aresh noted it came from a sole, black bird with piercing yellow eyes crackling loudly, as his attention was guided toward what appeared to be a park. The bird was perched atop a bench by a small, man-made waterfall area surrounded by boulders and colorful flowers. How relaxing the area looked.

I just need to take it easy.

Making a left turn at the green light, Aresh parked his motorbike at the parking lot and took off his helmet. All around him he could make out women in black abayas walking together- many with baby strollers. One or two were holding hands with bearded-men, who must have been their husbands. Premarital or extramarital dating in general, Aresh knew, was punishable by law for 'indecency', after all—let alone harsher labels and codes against his deemed 'unnatural' homosexuality.

Aresh smirked and shook his head side to side. What in the world was he going to do? He needed to get out there into the world! Somehow, someway. Just break free! Make something of himself! Explore other countries. England, perhaps?

Heck, he'd even change his religion- if he needed to. Aresh felt certain in his belief in *Allah*- but he couldn't bring himself to accept people like Muhiddin's version of *Him*. A God who wouldn't accept his creations simply for loving who they did? It was absurd to Aresh! If God had hated homosexuality as much as he did disbelievers and polytheists, surely he would have said so more directly as well, wouldn't he? An *ayah* on the prophet Lot condemning rapists who also happened to perform sodomy wasn't direct evidence of such a 'hatred' to Aresh. As far as he could make sense of it— rape and savaged sexuality was the evil underlined there rather than one's orientation. Surely there must have been some mistake in scholars' interpretations?

"*As-Salaam-Alaikum*, brother," a voice from somewhere behind him interrupted his thoughts. "Nice motorbike."

Muhiddin? Had he followed him out here? *No*. He couldn't have. He must have been comforting their mother at the moment, likely continuing to be her 'hero'- ever the suck-up that he was. Assuring her he'd 'find a way' to 'clean the family' from his brother's homosexuality 'mess'. And if not, he'd be assuring their mother that he could 'change Aresh's mind'.

Besides, this was a different voice of a slightly younger man. "*Wa Alaikum As-Salaam*," no sooner had Aresh just begun to utter in response, when he turned around to lock eyes directly with those of his curly-haired neighbor!

Ya-Illahi! How handsome he'd looked this close-up now, sporting tight-fitting blue jeans that highlighted his bulge, and a sleeveless white tank-top showcasing his sun-kissed, lean arms. *His voice is so silky.*

"Surprised to see me?" the man smiled, hands outreached to his sides. "Surely, I must look familiar…"

"Oh, yes, I think so," Aresh smiled back, blushing. "I think, *um*, you live with your sister in the building next door, don't you? We saw you at the market, my mother and I…"

The man nodded. "Yeah, the market." The man added a wink at the end of his sentence. "It's nice to see you here. Looks like you know this park, too."

"This park?" Aresh looked all around him. "Well, no, not really. It's my first time here. I just wanted a little break from traffic, you know? Maybe take a walk. It looks nice, though. Do you like it here?"

"Oh, come on, just *say* it," the man winked again. "It's okay. You can admit it. You came here on purpose." He checked his wristwatch. A rubber, black Casio. "Although it's a bit early, don't you think? Lots of us wait until after the Maghrib prayer. Before sunset there are too many guards also patrolling the area."

What in the world was this man talking about? Frequenting the park only in the evening hours? Was he a drug dealer, or something? "I'm afraid I honestly don't know what you mean," Aresh stammered. "*Jar*, my neighbor, forgive me- I don't recall your name from our market meeting."

"Oh, I bet you want to know my name…" the man smirked.

What in *Shaitan's* name was going on? All the attraction Aresh had been feeling toward this man was quickly dissipating with the eeriness the bold chatter was now causing him to have run down his spine.

"I already know yours, Aresh Jahan," the man inched closer to his face, smelling his cologne. "Ask me *my* name. I want to hear you ask directly. It's hotter that way."

A sinking pit in the core of Aresh's stomach started to rival the hardening of his penis. "I don't do drugs, or anything, just so you know." He looked around them. Luckily there was no one else in sight. *Maybe unluckily so, rather.*

"Drugs?" the man smirked. He folded his arms across his chest and leaned his body against Aresh's motorbike. "You're so cute. We're going to play this game, are we? You're going to pretend we both don't know how you've been…*watching* me? And stroking your cock through the window?"

"Oh," Aresh cast his eyes onto the pebbled ground, chuckling as he began to scratch his head. "You saw that, huh? I'm sorry about that. I live with my family, so it's hard to, *um*, find privacy sometimes, you know? As a young man…"

"Just ask me my name already," the man whispered, grabbing Aresh by his arms and lightly shoving him onto the seat of the motorcycle. He had a slick smile on his face, but his voice now sounded more threatening than inviting to Aresh.

"I think I should head back home now. My mom is expecting me. It was nice running into you here, though…"

The curly-haired man's facial expression shifted to a menacing one, matching his voice tone.

"Oh, you're going to play innocent now, huh, momma's boy? Is that it? You're going to pretend like *I'm* the only one?" He shoved Aresh off his bike and onto the ground. The stones scratched his arms and cheeks.

"Was that necessary?" Aresh managed to squeak, despite his body curling up in pain. "What are you doing? I'm really confused."

"What's the matter- too chicken to actually *fuck*?"

The man stood before Aresh now as he was laying on the ground, parallel to his vehicle. "I *finally* find one like me- close and convenient, too-as hard as that is to do in our repressed society here. And he's going to play hard to get?"

He kicked Aresh so hard, his mind went to the punch he'd landed himself on his brother's face earlier. "You're a tease- is that it, Aresh?"

Was Allah punishing him?

"No, no…" Aresh stammered, trying to block his face with his arms while also attempting to stand up. "Stop, please! You're getting everything all wrong. I did admire you- yes! You're very good-looking. And no— I'm not trying to play, or tease. I'm just really confused right now, as to…"

"Look, I don't like games, Aresh," the man stated through gritted teeth. "Or cowards."

Aresh held out his hands before his body, slowly getting back up on his motorbike. His eyes travelled to his helmet that had rolled way behind where the man was now standing before him. He had no time to grab it. "I'm not playing, man. I swear. I'm sorry you feel that way. Let's just discuss this calmly..."

"Oh, yeah?" the curly-haired man actually smiled now. His eyes travelled up and down Aresh's body now on the motorbike, inching his face closer to him in a whisper. "Where do you want to...discuss things, more *calmly*, then?"

"Um, perhaps we could...," Aresh stuttered with a feigned smile while his shaking foot attempted to locate the gear shifter. *Bismillahir Rahmanir Raheem,* he said a little prayer before shoving the man with all his might, right as he turned his torso back to facing forward.

"You'd *better* run!" Aresh heard the man bellowing behind him as he managed to take his vehicle back onto the road. "Go! Take your last ride before I conveniently run you off the road! I got people in the police force, you know! I'm going to get you fucking arrested for coming on to me...If you don't get killed first, that is!"

He glanced over his shoulder to see the man get into a white sedan and follow him out. *Oh, shit*! Aresh had to get away fast!

To his surprise, the man pulled up next to him once on the road, rolling down his window. He smirked at Aresh without a word.

Damn it. The light turned red, and they both halted their vehicles side by side! "I don't want any trouble," Aresh said in a loud voice toward the man. "Please, just let me go home."

"You forget I know where you live, fucker!" the man barked, subsequently beginning to laugh heavily. Aresh looked in his rear mirror to see that some people had their heads out their windows to observe what the commotion was about.

"Yeah, we're neighbors, my brother- come on," Aresh managed a smile despite his heart pounding so hard and stabbing his chest so much he could almost swear it was what having a heart attack must feel like.

He prayed for the damn light to turn green already! "Maybe we could even be friends, after you've calmed down."

"Just don't forget *my* little friend, wise ass," the man snickered, carefully raising a black revolver until he assured that Aresh's eyed widening in fear had seen it. He then put it away as the light turned green.

Ya Rabbi, what am I going to do? How could Aresh return home, knowing this hot but psychotic man would be near- armed and feeling some irrational form of wrath toward him? He sped through the traffic, weaving his motorcycle between cars and getting honked and cursed at.

Aresh suddenly felt something crash into the rear of his motorbike so heavily that he jettisoned from his seat. *This is it*, he thought, preparing for a painful death. *He must have caught up and crashed into me,* was his last thought as billowing flames began to spread rather quickly toward his motorcycle.

Aresh shut his eyes and said a little prayer inside his head- just as a force he could not visually make out pushed him toward the side of the road. He was thrust and rolled into a grassy area, and away from the flames. He coughed and brought his now dirt-covered hand to his mouth.

Did I make it? A plethora of thoughts were rushing through Aresh's befuddled mind. *Did I survive? But how? What pushed me out here?*

All he could see were flames engulfing the white sedan back on the road. Traffic nearly came to a halt as people slowed to stare at the horrific sight. Some were even on their cell phones, and Aresh heard a siren approaching.

The curly-haired man became visible just then, crawling out of the passenger seat with the gun still in his hand. Through coughing from the smoke and blood flowing down from a wound on his forehead, the man was able to place his hands on the trigger, and shoot several rounds from his weapon.

Aresh felt a stabbing pain on his arm. *I've been shot!* He grimaced and rolled over in anguish, screaming. With his other hand, he held what felt like a gunshot laceration. As his body completed a full roll, he dared to face what the man would do next. To his surprise- the man could now be seen with his hands around his face, struggling with some bird that appeared to be pecking his eyes!

"Everyone, stay where you are!" Aresh heard a police officer call out, just as his neighbor, with all his remaining might, stumbled up and ran off into a residential area somewhere behind him on the side of the highway. *Where did that bird go?*

All noise- except a continuous ringing in his ear- suddenly came to a halt around him, and Aresh's eyes began to shut. To his surprise, his arm wound wasn't hurting as much anymore. Perhaps the bullet hadn't hit him in a dangerous area? Or perhaps he'd lost sensation in that region by now. Was this what it felt like to die? Would the Angel Azrael be coming to take his soul?

The ambulance siren neared as what looked like the same, dark bird flew toward him, hawking in his ear. "No!" Aresh begged, still laying on the floor on his side. Maybe he should try standing up and make a run for it too? "Don't hurt me, too! Please!"

The bird simply continued hawking, and staring at him. It felt refreshing to know his hearing sense was still working, and Aresh found himself smiling at the black bird! *How curious*, he thought, suddenly recognizing the yellow eyes.

What in the world? Was this the same animal from the bench he'd glimpsed before entering the park? It looked like the same bird, alright. Was it a crow? It certainly looked like one, yet it had beautiful colors on its rather elegant and slender tail.

Aresh's eyes looked around to locate any potential source of the force pushing him off his now enflamed motorbike, and in the process rescuing him. No one. A couple of people had stepped out of their parked cars, looking concernedly at him and the approaching emergency workers getting off their vehicles in the near distance. A couple of firemen were busy working on extinguishing the fire from the sedan that had ensued the crash.

No one was there that could have helped him. *Except the bird.* Aresh smiled. Was it an angel that had saved him? The bird whose eyes hadn't left Aresh's face hawked again just then, almost smiling at him mischievously.

"What are you, little bird?" Aresh called out frantically, the blood and sweat mixing on his face. He tried to lift his arm to touch it but to no avail- his left one nearest to the bird was hurt so badly it hardly budged. "Did you save me? Oh, angel. Tell me, please."

"Are you alright?" a man dressed in a paramedic uniform approached him. Aresh turned his face to answer him, noticing the cop run off in the direction of the murderous curly-haired man. *I hope he catches the bastard.*

"Oh, wow, this arm has some first-degree burns," the paramedic spoke gently. "And there appears to be a bullet stuck inside, too. Don't worry, *habibi,* we're going to take you to the hospital, alright?"

Aresh smiled and nodded at the man, tears rolling down his cheeks as the bird fluttered its wings behind the paramedic.

"Who are you?" he called out to the bird.

"Me?" the paramedic answered him in a confused voice, glancing behind him and then back at Aresh. "I am Ahmed. What's your name, sir? We'll call your family as soon as we gather your information. Just…stop trying to speak. Save your energy. We're taking you to this hospital now. My colleagues are now after that driver. We'll get him. You're safe. It'll be okay."

Aresh drowned the man's voice as his eyes focused solely on the bird, mesmerized as the creature changed form into a well-built figure of a relatively young man, with a bearded jaw and piercing eyes. Something in those eyes looked familiar.

"I want to thank you," Aresh smiled at the figure, as the vision of the paramedic began to fade from the corner of his eye. All Aresh could now see, as clear as day, was this floating man. "For saving my life."

"I am called Amir," the being spoke, a call and all-knowing smile playing on his lips. "Remember me?"

CHAPTER 8

Sandnes

WATCHING AS MALIN CURTSIED BEFORE HER IN A WOBBLY manner, Kaitlin was delighted to see her daughter's adorable vision in a pink tutu. "I'm ready, Mommy," Malin announced proudly, flashing her front-tooth-missing grin.

"Oh, is that so, my little ballerina?" Kaitlin chuckled, crossing her arms. "And just where are your slippers, if I may so ask?"

Malin blushed and looked around. "Go get them, Mommy! Hurry! Ingrid will take my spot at the barre, again!"

Kaitlin groaned, shaking her head. "You know that looking out for your belongings is your responsibility, sweetheart." She retrieved Malin's pink duffel bag from the closet, knowing full well Paul and her mother would criticize her for 'spoiling' Malin if they could see her just then.

Whatever. They weren't the ones juggling everything on a daily basis. A mother had to do what a mother had to do. "Come on, get in and buckle your seat belt, baby. We need to beat Ingrid and her oh-so-friendly mommy there!"

Kaitlin smirked as she locked the apartment door behind them and helped her daughter buckle up inside the white Volvo sedan. Finally mastering driving was one of several aspects in which motherhood had catalyzed her attempts to improve herself. Despite Paul's opinions, Kaitlin felt she *had* also genuinely tried to connect with other local moms during school and extracurricular activities, albeit with limited success.

Most of their interactions never progressed beyond superficial-feeling, unrealized promises of coffee or playdates.

Once at the studio, Kaitlin gave Malin a kiss on the cheek and patted the small of her back to encourage her to walk toward the smiling teacher awaiting inside with only two other children. Was one of them Ingrid? The little girl Malin would feel *was* her friend during one week and *not* during the other, based on the girl's actions towards her sensitive daughter.

Oh, they've beaten us here. Kaitlin spotted Ingrid's mom, Bergdis, standing out with her acrylic nails and designer labels. She could tell from her light eyebrows the woman was a natural blonde, albeit currently carrying straight, jet black hair. Kaitlin found it amusing that while many women in the world tended to lighten their hair for a change: in this Norwegian land of mostly natural blondes, a lot of ladies were doing the opposite.

"*Hei, hei,* Katherine!" Bergdis chirped, spotting her from the direction of the reception area and walking over with a smile.

"*Hei, hei,* Berg-dis!" Kaitlin replied, emphasizing the correct pronunciation of the woman's name, in hopes it'd alert Ms. Sunshine to her mistake. Looking around the lounge area, she detected the absence of the blonde-bobbed mother with whom Bergdis usually conversed, often ignoring Kaitlin after a mere smile. *Must be why she's suddenly Ms. Sunshine to me again today.*

"Sit down, Katherine!" Bergdis chirped. "Let's watch the girls practice from the monitor. I know this will just be a small thing in preparation for their first big show before the *Jul* one in December, but it should still be adorable."

Oh, boy. Kaitlin nodded politely despite her irritation, turning her attention toward the view outside the studio. The sun's rays were peering through the window, tickling her skin. *A walk would be so good just about now.*

"Ingrid simply will not stop dancing the routine at home," Bergdis muttered, her eyes on the monitor showing that the teacher had started the girls' routine.

Not today. Kaitlin just wasn't feeling the patience to deal with idle chatter. A swaying of the trees played with shadows around the women's feet, pulling Kaitlin's attention toward the outside view again. One particular bird was fluttering about the front yard of the one-story studio that was obviously once used as a home. *I wish I could be as free as you, little creature*, Kaitlin thought. The ebony bird halted its flutter as it perched on a branch, almost staring at Kaitlin for several seconds before taking off for flight.

I need a walk. A sharp pain began to stab Kaitlin's forehead. Her chest felt heated and flustered, as if she'd suddenly broken into hives. *It's too stifling in here*.

"Hey, Bergdis? You'll be here, right? I…*uh*…just remembered I'd scheduled something during Malin's class. Silly me, still sitting here! You know how it is sometimes- barely any other time to do anything on our own with these little ones, God bless them!"

Bergdis' painted nail brushed a strand of hair off her face. "Oh? What did you schedule?"

Kaitlin hesitated before fibbing, "My… nails!" She wiggled her fingers with a sheepish smile, hoping her mom-buddy candidate would bite. "So, I'll go do that to come back before the girls are done with their class. I should go…"

Bergdis seemed to buy her unrehearsed lie, and Kaitlin felt a sense of relief. "Oh, of course. Alright, then. Well, hey- you still have my number if you need anything, right? I have yours, too."

"I do, yes," Kaitlin replied at the door before making her escape. "Thanks, Bergdis, you're so sweet. I'll be back for the end of class. It'll just be a relatively quick, natural manicure and hand massage."

A glance at the monitor showed Malin smiling through the *plié* activities the teacher had started for the class. For a moment she considered just circling around the studio to get some activity and steps into her system, while still staying nearby for Malin.

Bergdis would see, a thought popped into her head. *It's better to head toward the wooded trail*. Kaitlin let out a weary exhale. She turned her focus toward the hiking trail across the street from the small strip with a bakery, two small boutiques and the dance studio. Stepping out the door, she took in a deep breath of the crisp, fresh air. Some isolated time in nature was calling to her, and Kaitlin was hoping she could get a half-hour walk in with her thoughts and later get back to Malin without any interruptions.

Kaitlin found her legs moving toward the wooded path before she could calculate the details of her plan before returning to pick up her daughter. She trotted quickly, glancing behind her a couple of times-noticing the back of Bergdis' dark head. Kaitlin thanked her lucky stars the parking lot was jammed that day and she had parked out of sight of the dance studio; she didn't need Bergdis peeking her nosy head outside to notice she hadn't exactly hopped into her car for any supposed nail appointments. After all: there weren't any nail places within a walking distance.

"We must connect with nature on a daily basis," Meredith and some of the others in 'The Group' had tried lecturing her when she'd first met them in Stavanger. *"It allows us to connect with our own natures."*

Despite the scary events that had unfolded soon after with 'The Group', Kaitlin had to admit she had obtained some intriguing insights, and made interesting memories, through her brief time spent with them. She found herself agreeing with, for example, their lament on how modern society has caused more human ailments of the body and the mind ever since urbanization bombarded it with chemicals and manufactured materials over natural ones.

An uncanny shape in the clouds piqued her interest, and Kaitlin tilted her head toward the sky, reveling in the bit of sun rays peeking through the trees as she ventured. The present lull in the avian fluttering and wind-current-dancing felt soothing, albeit a bit unsettling as the silence highlighted Kaitlin's solitude. She stretched her arms over her head, briefly considering the thought of summoning *him* in flesh again-something she'd internally categorized as a forbidden taboo for the longest time.

With Malin fully immersed in the bilingual Nordic school system now, and her own routine established with her website- Kaitlin supposed she could certainly be able to make time and space in her life for an old friend. Would Finn still look the same? Would he still be kind and understanding with her, continuing to respect the boundaries set between them and just keeping everything as platonic and non-dramatic as possible?

Realizing she'd grown out of breath, Kaitlin allowed herself to take a seat on an oddly-shaped boulder. The gray mass with green moss around the corners appeared to be large enough to accommodate her momentarily, albeit uncomfortable for her bottom.

The terrain in Sandnes had more uphill inclines than the Stavanger woods where she'd met Finn. Kaitlin beamed as she recalled their initial meeting. He'd attempted affinity between the two of them with their mutual knowledge of French— he, claiming to being of a Belgian background, and her being Canadian— in a foreign, non-French speaking land like Norway.

Monsieur Du Feu. She laughed out loud at her thought of his name, causing some crowing sounds of nature to respond somewhere nearby. *Miss Kaitlin,* he'd insisted on calling her during those days, ignoring her marital last name.

Through a myriad of birds, from starlings to finches and larks, a bright, petite yellow goldfinch with black fuzz atop its head matching its wings caught her attention. The nestling was chirping softly and watching her inquisitively. *"Are you alright?"* the bird seemed to ask, to which she shrugged, as if the creature had actually uttered the question.

Was she alright? Why couldn't Kaitlin be like those women shopping in flocks and laughing over coffee. She'd spot them on the seldom occasion she'd run to the stores to pick up something, rather than ordering online like her as of late? They'd reminded her of her own coffee dates back in Toronto with friends and professional acquaintances.

Would she be feeling more fulfilled if she'd stayed behind at the dance studio instead to remain engaged in dance chit-chat with Bergdis? Kaitlin longed for connections and deep conversation, yet somehow never gave people a chance. *We either click with some people or don't*, she decided. *I just wasn't feeling her vibe.*

If Kaitlin didn't go easy on herself, and give herself more credit- how could she expect her mom and Paul to do so? Speeding up her steps as a natural decline in the terrain's slope approached fast, she held out her arms for balance. Kaitlin wasn't sure how— if at all— therapy with Freya may have been helping her. All she knew was- at least she was able to consciously engage in more 'positive self-talk', as advised.

How fervently Kaitlin wished Finn and the entirety of the mystifying occurrences surrounding him could have somehow cured her of her social dilemmas, rather than add more complexity to her life.

I suppose I've always attracted the marginal types, haven't I? Kaitlin scoffed, thinking back on all the 'disappointing' men she had snuck around with and dated throughout her youth in Toronto— much to her mother's dismay.

Didn't everything supposedly occur in life for a reason? When she was getting married to Paul, Kaitlin had convinced herself the purpose of all those previous, heartbreaker guys had been to make her appreciate the relatively conservative and domestic values of her now husband. *Too bad marriage has taught me other ways in which a woman's heart can be broken outside of infidelity,* Kaitlin mourned. *Like constant disapproval and lack of passion.*

What could the 'greater purpose' of Finn still being in her life have been? Why had she ever come across '*The Group, Inc.*' in the first place? Was it merely by association— because she was Paul's wife, and his implications to Tan during an office visit was blamed for Tan's toxic love toward his girlfriend turning into jealous, deadly wrath?

Allowing yourself to think you've always been a victim will not help you heal, Kaitlin. Freya's words from one of their sessions reverberated inside her mind. *We nearly always have the power to choose an alternative way in life. Acceptance of our decisions that lead to certain outcomes is key.*

"She was right," Kaitlin told the bird, unable to take her gaze away. The little fledgling cocked its head to the side, as if to ask her who the heck she was referring to. "*Freya*, little guy. *That's* who I mean. My therapist. She was right. I have to take responsibility for my own choices in the ultimate determination of my fate."

So what if Finn had sought her out? She'd found out the true nature of who he was, as well as the questionable practices of 'The Group'. And yet, *she* had *chosen* to remain in touch. Even after they'd landed the father of her child in jail. Even after Finn insisted he believed the child could be his after that night still shrouded in mystery to her— a night where Kaitlin had thought it had been Paul waking her up in the middle of the night for intercourse. She'd discovered through her religious inquiries it could not technically be so between a jinn and human.

"A potential for a jinn-human offspring goes against the natural

order of things ordained by our Creator, Kaitlin," Sibel had even assured her. "*You should have confided your concerns to me before you took that paternity test, alerting Paul to unnecessary drama. It's impossible for a jinn and human to breed naturally; just like a same-gender couple, or a bird and a dog, or...oh, you get it! Don't make me have to go on!"*

As the goldfinch fluttered away, a long breath whooshed out of Kaitlin's lips in a quiet release. Maybe this wasn't really about Finn, or even her unresolved cognitive fog and questions with regards to her childhood and her father. Paul was right in that, perhaps, she *had* been working too much from home! She drew in a lungful of air, taking in the natural aroma of pine and flora around her and allowing herself to come to terms with what she realized she'd been feeling for a long time.

Lonely.

Trembling, Kaitlin stood up, shook out bits of soil from her beige sweatpants, and continued her walk.

"Perhaps we need to explore why you fear being alone," Freya's voice echoed now in her head, rivaling the shrieking of some more birds in the near distance. *It hasn't been good to you to be as such, Kaitlin. As you've discovered from your experiences."*

"But how can I dread being alone, Freya?" Kaitlin had posed. *"Am I really that weak?"*

"Not weak, Kaitlin, no. Just fragile. But you've now become conscious of your tendencies, and can hence strengthen your vulnerability."

"Through...what?" Kaitlin had asked. *"Ensuring I'm never physically alone, somehow?"*

"Not necessarily," Freya had inched her face closer to the screen, her warm blue eyes ever accentuated by one of the lighter-colored headscarves she preferred to wear as a Norwegian woman who'd converted to Islam. A few times Kaitlin had seen her blonde locks

uncovered and tied up in a ponytail; those were apparently instances where Freya would hold their sessions from the comfort of her own home, and away from the potential gazes of men in contrast to working on her laptop in public spaces.

"But you can ensure greater awareness and mindfulness of what you're vulnerable to, and then actively fight against it. That will make you recognize your inner strength. Your self-actualized and recognized willpower."

Sudden vocal commotion from the birds startled Kaitlin, as their loud-squeal-pitch from somewhere behind her broke the silence amidst the grove. Where had they all flown off too? Kaitlin felt a rush of heated tingling across the back of her neck.

Finn.

"No, I *can't* summon you in person," Kaitlin closed her eyes and mumbled under her breath the moment his name popped in her head again. "You're right, Du Feu. I considered it. But I'm sorry. I just can't anymore! Malin needs me strong and clearheaded."

Kaitlin turned her head to try to discern the source of the squealing that had made her little bird friends take flight and disperse all of a sudden. A small, black bird with a beautiful, eggplant-purple neck that extended out to its wings was staring at her intensely atop a branch. It had a downward-curved bill, and was supporting a rather lengthy, keel-shaped tail, adding to its elegance.

"Hey, little fella! Aww, what are you- a crow? A raven?" Kaitlin smiled at the creature which now began screeching at her. He'd had something red in his mouth he was munching on. A cherry? Kaitlin felt her stomach rumble.

"What's that, little bird? *Quoth the raven nevermore*?" she smiled, quoting one of her favorite poems by Edgar Allen Poe. This particular one was smaller than the ravens she'd seen in pictures, though- and with brighter, almost-golden eyes. Was it a grackle of some sort?

Ding!

A notification alert from her phone halted her thoughts, causing Kaitlin to shiver. Looking all around her to ensure she was indeed alone, she allowed her focus to check her message. It was an e-mail. From Salim. *Oh, yeah, my other buddy lately,* Kaitlin thought, snickering. *Albeit he's mostly online and long-distance, too.*

Salim Saed was an entertainment lawyer/marketing director whom she'd paid to first design her website and later give her further professional advice. Kaitlin had mixed feelings about remote connections being necessary for her professionally while isolating her socially. But with regards to helping her website take off- Salim had proven himself to be worth every dollar she'd spent.

Hey Kaitlin,

I just wanted to send you a little update on the recent shipment. I'm afraid the stock delay from Amsterdam hasn't yet been resolved, but I'm on it! I told them to call you directly this week, as you're in the same time zone at least. I mean- heck I'm barely just waking up here in NY as I write this!

If you want, I can try to come up with a time to discuss it with them on the phone myself. So just drop me a line when you can, let me know. E-mail is all good and well but I think these guys prefer the phone.

Hope all's well,

Salim

Kaitlin smiled. She had only seen Salim via webcam, yet the positive energy she'd felt communicating with him could always be counted on. He'd let her know he was married, too; and so it had felt *safer*, somehow, for her to chit-chat with him as friends sometimes, long after they'd become collaborators.

Sandy had even vouched for Salim's legitimacy after meeting him on her behalf at a professional event in Manhattan. *"After our experiences with The Group, we can't take any chances, girl!"*

Kaitlin chuckled at the memory of Sandy's words. *"This Salim guy seems legit- but we've still got to make sure this one ain't some jinn too!"* Her friend had been burned by a jinn-friend she'd made during her visit in Norway herself. Sandy had gotten a little too nosy into Kaitlin's business and got herself entangled with one named Bjorn, also from 'The Group'!

The hairs on the back of her neck stood straight again, heated despite the chill in the wind blowing her hair around her face. Kaitlin wrapped her loosened shawl tighter around her neck, feeling static of electricity on her fingers. Her eyes searched for the peculiar black and purple bird again, but to no avail. In fact, no animal sounds could be heard in that utter, eerie quiet of the moment.

"Something isn't quite right," Kaitlin mused once more, feeling the need to return to the strip mall where the dance school was located. What time was it? She was just reaching for her cell phone when she heard a second notification sound.

Again? Kaitlin glimpsed at the screen, squinting her eyes to traverse through the glare from the daylight. It was a text message this time.

Kaitlin!

New development! The teacher just announced their decision to have the girls do a double-lesson today, for those who can stay! Something about making up for some absence Mrs. Hansen has to have apparently next week. The woman received a call during the class after you left- maybe some emergency happened last minute, who knows? Regardless, don't you worry! I'll be here through their extra session, too.

So take your time at the nail salon.

xoxo,
Bergdis

What the hell? It was odd of the woman to text her, and even odder for class to run overtime. Kaitlin began shaking her head side to side. What was up with these Europeans? Could they not have just scheduled a make-up class at another date and time? Should she call the office of the dance school herself to double-check?

Everything will be all right, a calming thought crossed her mind. A sudden chirping of the birds piqued her interest. Several male cardinals with red crests had now joined the others, standing out among the aviary crowd. Kaitlin smiled in amazement and put her cell phone into her bag. Her eyes lingered on the flying spectacle by what seemed like a body of water. It was the same group of colorful birds that she had seen earlier, before they'd run off! Where had that grackle gone off to, though?

Feeling herself drawn closer to the group of birds, Kaitlin took slow but steady steps, awing at the birds circling around what now became clearer to be a small stream. Why hadn't she noticed it before? She considered taking a photo of it with her cell phone.

No pictures necessary, a voice inside her said. *Just savor the moment, and you'll remember.*

Maybe she could walk here with her daughter after the class, instead, and share this beautiful sight with her if Malin was feeling up to it. How long would it take her to walk back to the dance school? Just as she reached her hand back into her bag to call the receptionist, Kaitlin was pleasantly-surprised to see Paul calling.

"Paul?" she asked, her voice fumbled. "Hey, I was just taking a walk. But I'm walking back to the studio now to pick up Malin. Apparently they're having a longer class today…."

"Oh, I know, babe," the voice answered. "I'm at the studio now, actually!"

"You…you are?" Kaitlin stammered.

"Yes!" the voice went on. "I wanted to surprise my girls! I left the office early. I was feeling bad for working on a Saturday, you know? But alas! Some lady here told me you were out for your nails or something?"

Kaitlin felt her cheeks redden. She let out a little laugh. "Bergdis. Yeah. And, oh- that was just something I made up to be able to take a little walk in peace. Don't tell her, babe! I just wanted to get some time walking in nature, but I was going to return in time. I mean, I…."

The voice chuckled as it interrupted her. "No sweat, darling. I'll take Malin out for ice cream or something. Some quality *daddy-daughter* time. We'll see you at home later! Go straight there."

"You sure?" Kaitlin replied. A smile formed on her face, despite her unassured surprise. "Alright. Thanks. Paul. That's sweet of you! Malin will like that."

"Yes, I hope so," he responded. "Take your time. Bye, love."

"Bye, babe," Kaitlin answered, though the other line had hung up.

What on earth was going on that day? What an odd coincidence it was to both have the dance class run overtime, *and* for Paul to decide to pick Malin up!

Well, I suppose he did go there expecting to see both of us. Kaitlin smiled. Why was she questioning her husband's surprises? Did she only like them when she was expecting them- like what he'd better have been similarly planning for their anniversary?

I'm being silly. Kaitlin's mind clouded with fogginess as all she could think of in that moment were the birds. Three or four particularly blue ones with elegant dashes of white on their wings were hovering over a rather high branch concentrated with twigs.

"You guys building a nest?" she cooed, strutting over to the small-sized birds. They chirped louder as she neared— their lack of disturbance upon the sudden proximity of a human surprising Kaitlin. Normally birds would fly away whenever she'd lay some bird food on their balcony bird feeder.

I'll just relish in nature a tad bit longer, she mused. *It'll be all right. Malin is with her father. Malin will be all right.*

§

MALIN'S EYES WERE GLUED TO THE CLOCK ON THE WALL AS SHE MADE click-clack noises with her tongue against the roof of her mouth, and fiddled with her thumbs. Where were those fidget toys that she'd made a collection of in her room when she needed them? Her mother had packed her two favorites in the pink bag, hadn't she? She couldn't find them.

"Is Mommy coming?" she asked up at her dance teacher for the third time.

"I'm afraid we still can't reach Mrs. Maverick's phone, honey, but I'm sure she just has bad reception or something," Helga Hansen responded. "Let me just get that emergency contact sheet again…."

Amer-gency? What was the word? Was it, like, *Amer-ican?* Malin wasn't *American.* And *urgency*? She remembered her mother saying the word a couple of times on the phone when she'd speak with her dad in English, aside from French as well sometimes. *"Call me back, babe,"* she'd say. *"Soon, please! It's urgent!"*

What was *American* and so *urgent* now? She watched as her teacher typed in something on her cell phone, later speaking into the receiver. Malin looked around her to see that she was the only child not yet picked up. She bit her lip. Just as distress had begun to set in her stomach- she spotted a tall man rushing through the doors, eyeing his surroundings with utter curiosity. He'd had on a blue baseball cap, and was wearing dark trousers with sneakers underneath an army-green coat.

"Daddy!" she exclaimed, smiling eyes squinting up at the tall man before her. Relief flooded through her as she ran into his arms.

"Darling!" the man hugged Malin back before turning to face her dance teacher. "Apologies, Mrs. Hansen. Kaitlin had an urgent errand to run. Asked me to come."

Helga Hansen watched as the man kneeled down and wrapped his arms around Malin. "Oh…Mr. Maverick?" she asked, sizing him up. "I just left you a message, sir!"

"Yes, I'm Paul," the man stood up, giving Malin a kiss on the head before reaching his hand out to shake her teacher's. "Nice to meet you."

"I'm Helga…and likewise," the teacher replied, before quickly retracting her hand. "Oh my, I think that was static!"

"Yes, it happens sometimes, doesn't it?" the man smiled sheepishly.

"We were beginning to get worried with our little ballerina here, Mr. Maverick, as all the parents have left."

"Oh, yes, we're so sorry about the scheduling confusion," the man spoke. "My wife couldn't return from her errand in time, but has asked me to pick Malin up. Thank you! It's all good now! Come, let's walk, *chérie*."

Chérie? Malin couldn't remember her dad ever calling her that. And he often spoke French terms of endearment mostly to her mother. *Maybe he's trying to compensate for being too busy with work lately*, Malin thought with a shrug. She'd been eavesdropping on her parents' arguments in the home, noting how her Daddy had been criticizing her mommy's business on her computer, though he hadn't been making much time for her himself! "Where are we going?"

"Let's get some fresh, forest air," her dad replied, leading her by holding her hand. He was pacing slightly a step ahead of her. "Away from the crowds. Let your mom stay cooped up by her computer. Nature will do us good, honey!"

§

THE LONGER THE PHONE RANG, THE MORE SIBEL PAK'S stomach began to bundle up. Her friend still didn't pick up after the third phone call. "Come on, Kaitlin, pick up!"

This time- the call went straight to voicemail. She was surprised when Malin's teacher called her about being unable to reach her student's mother. *Where are you, Kaitlin?*

Sibel had already had enough on her plate now with Aylin and Hakan being sick at home with the flu, and her husband's growing legal troubles with a politically unjust witch-hunt occurring in their native Turkey under an authoritarian regime. Fear of wrongful imprisonments, as had happened to some of their friends and colleagues back home following a questionable coup attempt, had been preventing them from going there for what would usually be their annual summer vacation.

What a shame it was. And on multiple grounds, too. A summer trip back home had always given their family a much-needed doping of Mediterranean warmth that lasted them throughout the colder seasons of Scandinavia.

What the hell was going on with Kaitlin this time? Sibel bit her lip and closed her eyes. She hoped her friend wasn't getting herself into any jinn trouble again.

CHAPTER 9

MALIN COULDN'T RECALL THE LAST TIME HER FATHER HAD remained so quiet, choosing to simply observe her while she skipped through the rugged terrain. Usually, he'd be more concerned about ensuring her coat had been zipped up all the way, or that her gloves were on even in slightly warmer weather if there had been even a hint of a chilly wind!

"*Ouchie*!" Malin exclaimed as the bare skin of her ankle underneath the mauve leggings she'd had on scraped against the edge of a bush.

"Are you okay, Malin?" her dad halted his stroll next to her to slightly tap her hand. A jolt of electricity traveled between them shocked her skin.

"Yes, but— double ouch, Daddy," her eyes looked up at him. She giggled. "You zapped me!"

"Zapped you?" her dad chuckled softly, his eyes holding her curious gaze. Was it just her, or were father's eyes sparkling a lighter color than usual? "Oh, the *static*. Yes, yes, it happens sometimes, doesn't it, Malin? We're almost at the lake I wanted to show you before we go home. Just bear with me for a couple more minutes…."

"You have to zap me two more times!" Malin said, blushing. "It has to be three times, remember?"

"Three times?" her father asked, looking puzzled.

"My monster thoughts, Daddy, remember?" Malin rolled her eyes. "You forgot my OCD?"

"Oh, right, right," her dad said with a chuckle, playfully inching his finger to her hand to tap it twice. "Zap! Zap!"

"Thank you," Malin smiled. Was everything all right? Why couldn't her mom pick her up, again, as usual? Where were they going, exactly? "Is Mommy meeting us here?"

"No, my dear. Not Mom. She'll meet us back home. But there *is* someone special, Malin, whom I do want you to meet by the lake."

My dear? Malin? Her father never really called her by her full name, now that she thought about it— preferring her nickname, 'Mallie', instead. Perhaps he was feeling sick, and unlike his usual self?

"You won't be scared to meet a special animal friend, will you?" her dad said, scratching his head. "Will you, Mallie?" he added.

His expression looked so desperate to make her happy somehow that Malin started laughing despite her trepidations about her dad's strange behavior, including changing up her nicknames. *Mallie.* That was more like it. It was as if he'd read her mind!

"I do like animals, Daddy. But I never thought *you* did! You and mom never let me get that puppy I wanted! You said I had to wait until I was older…"

"Well, *um*, I've been thinking…Your mother and I, that is. We have been thinking that, in the house— yes, it's a big responsibility. But I recently, *um*, made a friend who hangs out here! Freely out and about in nature! And I thought— hey, I don't see any reason why we can't all play a game of 'fetch' and hang out sometimes… when we won't be making a mess in the house!" He winked at her.

"Fetch?" Malin's eyes opened wide. "You mean— your animal friend is a *doggie*?"

"Indeed, he is," her father crossed his arms and stood up straight, tilting his head up. "Are you ready to meet him? I'll whistle to him. Look! You see the water just behind those trees over there?" He outreached his arms to point at a direction just a few steps away now, where the sparkling of a body of water could indeed be viewed from behind three particularly long trees Malin saw.

"Whoa, those trees are super tall!" she eyed them as high as she could. Her neck hurt she had to lift her face so high. Had they really walked that fast? Where had those big trees come from? Malin hadn't seen such spectacularly tall trees back when they entered the wooded area- she was sure she'd have remembered. Nothing but a couple of small ones and some bushes and dead leaves.

The sound of barking interrupted her befuddled reverie. Malin's hesitation in this unfamiliar environment became assuaged by the sight of a beautiful golden retriever puppy staring at her with big brown eyes. She gasped. "He's adorable!"

"Bo!" her dad called out to the animal eyeing them without movement, staring at them as it rested in place. "Come here, boy! Don't be shy!"

Malin took a step back and she turned her face away as the puppy barked and began running toward her. She outreached her hands in front of her, but the canine simply stopped right before making contact with her. It lifted its front paws and gave her a lick on the cheek before wagging its tail speedily.

"Aww, nice to meet you," Malin touched its paw softly, and turned to face the man. "Bo? That's its name?"

"Yes, Bo," he smiled at them both. "Bo, meet Malin."

The dog barked and lay his body on the soil before her feet. It comforted Malin, who kneeled and began stroking his soft, light brown fur. "How old is he?"

"He's still a kid in my book, so I call him a pup," Finn smiled. "Though he's a young adult in human years."

"Aww, I still think he has a puppy's face, too. And he's so clean, Daddy! For an outside dog. Not muddy at all!"

"Yeah, living amongst nature doesn't mean one is some beatnik," the man scoffed. "Your dad wouldn't get it…"

Malin's stomach suddenly felt topsy and turvy, spinning in all directions. "Whoa! What…do you mean? Are *you*…not my dad?" She took three steps backwards, her voice quivering along with her increased heartbeat.

The man threw his hands on his face and took in a long breath, trying to pull the words together. He took a step toward Malin. "Well, not exactly, but, I'll explain," he smiled at her. "There's nothing to be afraid of, Malin. Please allow me to explain. Just be calm, sit down, and hear me out. I'll take you right home afterwards to your mom. I promise."

Malin's eyes surveyed the wooded area all around her. Aside from this man's dog, there was no one else in sight to hear her crying for help. As far as her eyes could see, anyway. He wouldn't hurt her- would he?

"Who are you?" Malin asked feebly, voice stuttering. "I knew you were acting strange! But how do you *look* like my dad? And why did you kidnap me?"

"I didn't…well, I guess technically I did," the man smiled with blushed cheeks. "But, come on now Malin! *Kidnap* is a strong word! Because—you see— I'm…*family*, actually."

"Family?" Malin was shaking her head, a disgusted look now plastered on her face. She had no idea what was going on. But this man who had led her seemed like the only one who knew the way to also, then, get her back to her house. *And— family?* She supposed it could eerily be possible, seeing as how he resembled her father almost to a T. She had to cooperate. What other choice did she have?

"I'm…your dad's twin brother, Malin," the man said. "I'm your Uncle Finn!"

§

FINN WATCHED AS MALIN'S TINY BODY SHIVERED DESPITE THE relatively warmer temperature that day for a Norwegian September. His eyes darted back and forth between himself and Bo. *I'm an idiot,* he thought.

He had planned to wait longer. For Malin to play with Bo longer and get more comfortable. *I finally talk to her, and introduce Bo- but I mess up and blurt all that*! He'd been so close to keeping up his act for a little bit longer! Finn knew Kaitlin was distracted by his fellow brethren in animal form— mostly as birds, since Finn knew how Kaitlin adored them.

Master had insisted on the speeding up of Kaitlin's recruitment into 'The Group', chastising that Finn alone hadn't been able to do 'the job' for years now. Finn hadn't fought it. He'd allowed it, as long as it meant he'd soon be spending more time in her company. He'd kept up the excuse of his concern for Malin and her need to 'grow up first' before her mother could become a member and be able to live in another place.

"Hurry up, lad— that human isn't getting any younger!" Lar had pressured. *"Any later, and she won't be of use any more to our mission. And may I remind you, Finn Du Feu- neither will you."*

Finn closed his eyes and took a deep breath. His place in 'The Group' was threatened by his 'negligence', he knew. His status was already shaky with his estrangement from his parents, though they'd initially helped Lar secure several regional cabins on their property in forested lands.

His parents— who had disapproved of the jinn-human relationships they discovered their son's new alliance with 'The Group' supported. Their disappointment and distancing from their son had grown even further with Finn's declaration of his love for a human woman—Freya— for the first time. Now, Finn had gone and disappointed Lar as well with his pursuance of Kaitlin. It was unfortunate timing, too. Particularly as he and Meredith were also raising Bo— an offspring Lar merely tolerated only in his jinn form.

At least Finn had been able to secure this precious opportunity through Malin's class time, while the real Paul was taken care of as well- still at work, and unaware. Finally, he could spend time alone getting to know this little girl he'd watched from afar as she grew up.

Remembering how she could always see him and smile at him ever since she was a baby, a tear rolled down Finn's cheek. As far as he was concerned- that had to have indicated a special connection. *Damn it!* This was one of the pitfalls of manifesting in universally visible human flesh. In addition to how much energy it'd taken out on his jinn nature, too, of course.

"Okay, confession time..." Finn tried to fight back his tears with all his might. He removed the cap he'd been wearing, revealing his golden blond hair with curly ends— much lighter than Paul's brown waves.

"You're...blond!" Malin gasped. With more curiosity, this time, and less fear. "Whoa! I can't believe I didn't notice it! Though I *did* sort of think your eyes looked a bit lighter."

"Yes," Finn chuckled with relief, sensing her heartbeat slowing. Normally, his eyes were the only parts of him he could not manifest in a different form other than their natural state. But he had manifested so fast in his hasty decision to take advantage of the dance class opportunity and Paul's busy schedule that day- he'd forgotten to change his hair color! It was a detail he'd noticed only as he'd glanced his human-flesh reflection on the glass window of the dance studio before entering.

Luckily so, he supposed. He had adjusted the cap more carefully to hide his hair. Finn didn't want to imagine just how differently things could have turned out if Malin had reacted scared by his completely different hair as well in front of her teacher! She would have known something was off much sooner! He doubted she'd buy it if he'd said he'd dyed his hair that day, either. Smart girl she was, the sweetheart.

"I just want to go home!" Malin's voice trembled before Bo came to lick her, fleetingly causing her to smile.

"Bo, down boy! Sit!" Locking eyes with Bo, Finn sent him a mental message to be a little more patient to play. *Poor kid.* He'd been told about Malin for so long that he'd been looking forward to this playdate for days!

"Your mom knows me, sweety," Finn continued, facing back toward Malin. It took all the energy he could muster to fight back a downpour release of the storm cloud tears building up inside. "Kaitlin and I are friends. We keep in touch. But your father, he, *um*, doesn't think too highly of me. From our youth days. Lots of drama. Let's not tell him we've met yet. As his twin, Malin— you can call me Uncle Finn."

What had happened that day was the second time in his life he had to manifest as Kaitlin's damned husband, Finn realized, and he wasn't enjoying it one bit. But a jinn had to do what a jinn had to do.

"What's happening?" *Stranger, danger,* Malin was thinking, and Finn supposed her mother had always warned her not to talk to strangers. And she must have learned it in school, as well.

"I'm not a stranger, sweety..." Finn insisted.

It's as if he read my mind, again! Malin was now thinking, as she cocked her head to side and eyed him up and down. *Maybe we really do have that family connection.*

Finn smiled, reassured.

"Uncle Finn?" Malin asked sweetly. "If what you're saying is true: why does my dad have a problem with you? Do you kidnap people for a living, or something? Like a bad guy?"

"Bad guy?" Finn smirked, shaking his head. What violent shows had Paul and Kaitlin been allowing her to watch? "Oh, no, not at all. Our issues stemmed more from…a high school fight, let's just say."

Finn was surprising himself at how smoothly the lie was escaping his mouth. Then again, he wasn't exactly on speaking terms with his own brother. The perfect, married jinn with two children. His parents' pride and joy. No wonder he'd found himself drawn to the topic of estranged family members!

"You see, Malin- I sort of, *um*, went out with this girl that your father liked as a teenager," he continued. "Our little rivalry later spilled over to our first jobs in Canada and our family members began taking sides on who they supported more. After Paul moved to Norway- we lost contact. For good. He told me never to call him again! But I'm a single guy, and have no children of my own. When I found out I have a, *mm*, niece— that's you, Malin— I thought it only fair they should let us form a relationship as family, at least. Don't you think that's just?"

"Yes, I guess that's fair," Malin shrugged, kneeling down now to pet Bo. "But I'm still not sure..."

"Okay— let's hear it," Finn interrupted. "Why don't you ask me something? Anything! Anything at all about your parents, for example. Go ahead."

"Okay..." Malin crossed her arms, twisting her lips around in thought. How adorable she appeared to Finn. *She's going to challenge me, like her mother.*

"Got it! What is my father's job? And your birthdays? And...hmm... my mother's favorite color?"

"Let's see," Finn placed a finger on his chin, and looked up at the sky. "Well, good old Paul Maverick- he's an *IT* guy...our birthday is on March 12th... Your mother's favorite color is red...," the corner of Finn's lips in human form curved into a smirk.

Cardinal red. Try as he might, he could never get the image of his first official meeting with Kaitlin in the Stavanger woods. Her nearly crimson jacket. Hugging her curves in all the right places. Accentuating her facial features of the sweetest heavens.

"Wrong!" Malin crossed her arms and made a face, interrupting Finn's thoughts. "My dad is a computer expert! He's not ET! And my mother's favorite color? Well…to tell the truth, I don't think she even has one. She randomly wears whatever she likes that day."

"*IT* means 'informational technology', clever girl," Finn smiled. *ET. How endearing.* "It is his official field, and it pretty much means the same thing as being a 'computer expert', as you've coined it. You can ask him…just don't share how…"

"…Don't share anything about *you* as a reason for why I want to know- I understand," Malin blushed, eyeing Finn up and down before taking a look around the entirety of the field right before the forest entrance.

She's still cautious. Finn prayed to God that he wasn't doing her a disservice by making her lay down her artillery for any potential actual predators that may lurk around her in the future. Though, of course, he wouldn't let that happen for as long as he lived.

"You're lucky you look just like him…except your eyes." Malin bit her lips. "Oh, and, your hair, of course."

"They say blonds have more fun," Finn winked at her, playfully nudging her shoulder. "Come on! Ready to play a quick round of tag with Bo before going home?"

"Where do you live?" Malin pursed her lips and crossed her arms.

So she is intent on continuing the questioning game. Finn chuckled. *She's actually quite precocious for her age.* "Oh, we, *um*, live in the woods. Close to here, in Stavanger."

"Oh, I visit Stavanger sometimes with Mommy. Her friend lives there- I play with their kids. They're super fun!"

Yes, that Sibel woman, I know, Finn thought. He decided to keep it to himself. He didn't need to further scare the little girl with how he could know so many details of her life with her mother as an 'estranged family member'. "Oh, is that so?"

"I always think a dog would be a good friend, too- or even like a brother or sister!" Malin went on. "Mommy won't let me get a dog. She says it's brought bad luck before when she and Daddy first got married…but that's not fair to me!"

"You're right…" Finn clenched his fist and took in a deep breath. "It's all been very unfair, indeed. And unfortunate. To you. To me. To all of us."

Bo started circling Finn's legs, pushing some wooden sticks that had fallen from the tree branches. He got the hint. "I think Bo here is restless to finally play," he spoke to Malin. "Shall we?" He picked up one of the sticks, and handed the other one to Malin.

"Okay, we shall!" Malin smiled and nodded. "You throw first, Uncle Finn! Or…better yet- let's see who throws the farthest for Bo to fetch! Deal?"

"Deal, sweetie," Finn replied, his eyes welling up again. He took a sniff and shook his head. "On the count of three: one, two, three! Fetch!"

CHAPTER 18

THE BUZZING SOUND OF THE DOORBELL RATHER THAN THE clacking of Paul's keys to enter the house surprised Kaitlin. After all- he hadn't done that since their earlier years of marriage. He'd insisted, at the time, that it was lovelier for him to have his wife open the door. Kaitlin tensed her shoulders, then released.

"Paul?" she called out, inching closer to the door with her feet in fuzzy house-slippers. She had just come in from her hike and washed up in the bathroom.

"Special delivery," a husky voice answered.

What were they doing home already? Kaitlin peeped through the hole. Sure enough it was her husband, holding Malin's hand. She didn't see any cones or cups for her, though. *Dang it, I was really wishing they'd have surprised me with some ice cream on their way back! With my favorite maple syrup topping draped over it!*

Something on his countenance caught her attention just then. *His eyes!* They weren't light brown like Paul. They almost looked like….

No!

"It's…*ahem*…Finn, Kaitlin, yes," he spoke, leaning closer to the door. "I was in the area and I…picked up my *niece* from her class today, and we played a bit outside. My *brother* doesn't know I'm here." His one eye locked straight into her own even through the peephole.

Please play along, Finn mentally sent her way. *For Malin's sake. It'll all be okay. She's fine. It's all good.*

"No!" Kaitlin uttered out loud this time, mouth still agape. She grabbed her hair by the roots, her hands quivering with both disgust and shock. How dare he manifest himself as Paul before Malin, and apparently pretend to be her father's brother?

"I've already introduced myself to my *niece* here, and don't worry we had a good time taking a walk after her class and…"

"Oh you have, have you?" Kaitlin asked, slowly opening the door. Her eyes had popped open as wide as saucers. "To your…*niece*?"

"Yes, Mommy," Malin smiled at her, walking inside and taking off her shoes. "I've met Uncle Finn! Can you believe it?"

"No, I really can't sweetie, *heh*," Kaitlin flung open the door further and drew Malin closer. She eyed the jinn-man standing before her, from his feet to his head. Yup! Sure enough- he'd even got Paul's build right. She didn't even want to imagine how confused her daughter must have been!

"Are you okay, baby?" she pulled Malin closer and held on tight, giving her a kiss atop her head while continuing her glare into Finn's green eyes. The difference in eye color stood out in what otherwise indeed appeared to be Paul's body. "Finn! What were you thinking?"

"I'm good, Mommy," Malin reassured her. "Don't worry. I know Uncle Finn's secret now." She brought her forefinger before her lips. "Daddy is upset with his twin brother, so, *shh*, we'll both be quiet about his visit to Norway."

"Uncle Finn," Kaitlin was trying to take it all in as she nodded, heart beating fast. "Your dad is upset with him…his *twin* brother?"

Her eyes met Finn's. He was biting his lip and nodding. *See? No harm done. Come on. Play along. We'll talk.*

"Right, well, sweety?" Kaitlin grabbed Malin's bag and helped her remove her shoes. "Why don't you go wash your hands and head to your room for a bit, okay? Mommy's a bit surprised at your...*er*...uncle's visit. We need to talk alone for a little bit. As grown-ups. Okie?"

"Aww, man," Malin shrugged. "Adult time, again? Like you and Daddy?"

Finn snickered until Kaitlin's subsequent look in his direction made him mouth '*sorry*' and stop.

"Yes, adult time, sweety," Kaitlin softly nudged her daughter inside. "Come on, go wash up. Go, go!"

"Bye, Uncle Finn!" Malin waved before heading toward the bathroom.

"Au revoir, ma chérie!" Finn waved back.

Kaitlin scoffed, shaking her head. *He's certainly keeping up his character with the French.* Though he'd told her he descended from Belgians who spoke French at home also growing up- she supposed Finn could have acted like some typical Norwegian man- speaking only Norsk or English with Malin, instead.

Trotting down the hallway along with her daughter to make sure Malin closed the door behind her, Kaitlin took in a deep breath of the air tasting heavy and thick. She muttered an internal prayer for strength, strutting back toward the apartment door. Finn had now taken off a baseball cap she'd seen him have on earlier, and was now fully discernible in his usual, blond male form. "May I come in?" he asked.

Looking in all directions to make sure any neighbors weren't lingering around, Kaitlin pulled him inside and closed the door gently behind them both. Her hand sizzled touching his firm arms, and she was praying Malin didn't have to touch him or hold his hand or anything of the sort that'd make her notice the unhuman sensation. She lunged her forefinger onto Finn's chest and began with a harsh whisper.

"No '*au revoir'*," she began, pointing her forefinger centimeters away from Finn's face.

"No 'seeing' her 'again', Finn! You will not be showing yourself to Malin, again! Understood? I cannot believe you'd stoop to scaring a little girl- luring her into the woods like that!"

"Miss me?" he smirked his sly smile, eyeing her finger still on his beating chest. He even dared to bob his eyebrows up and down suggestively.

Kaitlin crossed her arms, swallowing hard before continuing. "What in the world were you thinking? Why would you do something like this? How *could* you?"

"First of all— 'scaring' her?" Finn took a step back and held his hands out in front of him defensively. "I'd never hurt my girl…relax!"

"She's not your…" Kaitlin began, but halted herself mid-sentence. It was not the time to antagonize him further. "The audacity of what you've just done, and everything else, aside—Finn, how did you even know her class had run overtime, and that we'd be picking her up later than usual? And…Paul! Where's *he*? I mean he called me to say that *he* would be picking her up. How did you get around that? How did you…?"

She watched in horror as Finn's lips twisted into a smile.

"No way…you didn't! Oh, but you did, didn't you..? You orchestrated this? *You* messaged me? As 'Bergdis'?"

Finn nodded and crossed his arms with a smile.

"And then pretended to be Paul on that call?" Kaitlin couldn't believe all this. She mostly couldn't believe how she wouldn't have been able to recognize one of his jinn games by now.

"It's easy to intercept my energy through to his phone line, Kaitlin," Finn went on in a casual tone. "Relax. Paul has no clue— he's still at work on a Saturday, the poor bugger."

"Oh my, God. No wonder! I mean, I should have known that woman would never message me. She even spelled my name *correctly* in that text message! I was just, like, in this…trance-like stance with the birds in the woods." Kaitlin paused as a thought occurred in her head. Her eyes opened wider than before.

"Wait a minute. Did you have something to do with me stalling in the woods, too?"

"Some of my friends, in bird form," Finn shrugged, still smiling. "They were helping me. We wanted to make sure you were relaxed, and assured that all was well. They let me know when you'd felt alright about the whole thing enough to head home, so I could head out to the woods with Malin myself…"

"I can't believe what I'm witnessing here," Kaitlin shook her head rapidly side to side.

"Speaking of relaxing— can I rest a bit on your couch?" Finn leaned down and held his knees. He appeared to Kaitlin to be in genuine discomfort, and she pointed invitingly toward her sofas with a sigh.

"Thank you," Finn said with a smile, taking his place on the leather couch with his legs extended over the coffee table. "I'm exhausted having had to walk with Malin over here, rather than transporting us here quicker and risk scaring her. I mean— I did make the return route feel quicker for her, through my methods…but these legs are killing me…"

"Um, Finn, you still haven't told me *why* you've done this?" Kaitlin interrupted him. "I mean—I've *really* been in a sense of brain fog lately, taking my medication, prescribed by my therapist. I was just in here, chalking my forest gaze up to this, before you guys came. Oh, I should have known you were involved! I would have otherwise certainly questioned such a message from that woman, and not entrusted her— as someone I barely know— with looking after my daughter! Even if the class really had run overtime! Why did you go through all this trouble just to see me?"

"Um, Ms. Kaitlin?" Finn interjected. "Are you done with your rambling? You know by now that I *can* be *anywhere* if I simply wanted to see you, don't you? Except in your private quarters, of course, unless I hear you call out to me and am hence welcomed..."

Ms. Kaitlin. There was that nickname he'd tended to resort to when he was peeved with her again.

"Yes, I know physically...you *can.* I just didn't think you *would.* After your promises. Which one did you break again this time? I've lost count..."

"Look— today wasn't about you, actually," Finn started. Kaitlin didn't exactly sound to him like she would welcome any invitations for her to visit Master Lar to begin the recruitment process. He'd have to leave that part for later. "The weather was pleasant, and I just wanted to hang out with Malin after her class, that's all."

He outstretched his arm toward Malin's bedroom. "It's all good now, see? She's here. She's playing. Paul's not here. All good."

"Why *now*?" Kaitlin was shaking her head.

"I just felt like," Finn was searching for the right words. "...it was a fun opportunity to introduce her to Bo, you know? I mean, I know you're probably going to become extra paranoid about this: but I can tap into her thoughts, too. It's just my nature. She's *in tune*, too, Kaitlin! Just like the rare human-jinn bond you and I share. And she's been feeling lonely. I feel it. She's been wanting a sibling...and has been praying lately for a puppy, at least, if you guys won't give her that. My heart went out to her. So, I thought that maybe..."

"Sibling, huh?" Kaitlin bit her lip in frustration, folding her arms across her chest. "You felt she wanted a sibling, so you thought—*Bo!* What a convenient solution for everybody! Is that it? A dog and a sibling, of sorts, rolled into one package? Just lovely!"

"Watch your mocking tone, please, Ms. Kaitlin," Finn raised a light brown eyebrow.

"Mommy, where's my red-haired Barbie?" Malin's voice interrupted her as her head popped out from her bedroom door. Kaitlin took in three deep breaths and counted inside her head. This, too, was recommended to her in therapy— for whenever she'd started to feel her anxiety take over.

"Mommy?" Malin tried louder this time. How much had Malin heard?

"Oh, I'll be right there, sweety!" Kaitlin called over before returning to Finn. She took in two deep breaths and went on in a near-whisper voice. "Look, thank you for bringing her home, Finn, but didn't you realize how this will be traumatizing her? Regardless of your intentions. And didn't you think I taught her not to talk to strangers? Did you think I taught her better than to allow for this! She's seven! Didn't you think she was going to be revealing what happened to her parents…eventually?"

"Kaitlin…you simply have to calm yourself," Finn smiled as he shook his head side to side. "I didn't approach her as some *stranger*- I told you! At first she and that teacher thought I was Paul, but I soon told her I was Paul's twin! I said that me and him were estranged due to some disagreement in our youth— *blah blah blah*— and that it'd be best for her to keep meeting me a secret. I told her that I simply wanted to meet my niece. And didn't reveal my real form."

"An estranged twin, to be kept a secret…" Kaitlin repeated. Shaking her head, she chuckled. "That's some imagination. And potentially a dangerous one! What if Paul *does* eventually find out? What if Malin asks about you to him, or even to her grandparents?"

"I couldn't think of anything else that wouldn't scare her, Kaitlin!" Finn exclaimed loudly—causing Kaitlin to put her hand on his flaming lips. Her hand reacted in retracting itself with the subtle burn, but she didn't care.

"I certainly didn't want to switch my form in *front* of her and *actually* traumatize our darling!" Finn continued in a lowered voice.

Our darling. Kaitlin's heart sank at the sound of those words from Finn's mouth. She opened her mouth to speak but no words came out. She couldn't believe how close her daughter had gotten to actually witnessing all the supra-human craziness things that she had. What if Malin had actually seen the dog transforming, or Finn himself? What if she actually told her classmates about seeing different forms, and people ridiculed her? Certainly, her therapist would have more to worry about.

"Whoa!" Finn reached his hands out before Kaitlin's mouth with a chuckle. "Now look at who's got the imagination! Enough with the negative thoughts, Ms. Kaitlin. It was all good. It is all good…and it'll be all good. Malin played a little with Bo, she was happy. I won't do it again if you don't want. I promise."

"She *played* with Bo?" Kaitlin's mind raced back to that day in the woods. After she'd just witnessed Tan's suicide, standing before Meredith as she and Paul had joined the police on their way to take him into custody. Kaitlin had raced behind Meredith- in her jinn form and invisible to the police. She'd joined Bo- the dog she and Paul had named while they'd temporarily had him as a younger pup. Before Meredith and Finn took him. They'd kept his name.

Meredith and Finn. Her blood began to boil. She closed her eyes and took in a deep breath.

"You introduced my daughter…" Kaitlin managed in a lowered tone. "…to your *son* in his canine form?"

To her surprise, Finn didn't speak for a good minute, looking down at the floor. Finally, he met her eyes, and spoke. "Meredith told me she's talked to you. I know that you know."

Averting his eyes and scratching the back of his head, Finn continued with a heavy sigh. "That is— at least— you know what she's convinced of, regarding Bo's paternity, anyway. As for me? I'm just not sure. She was still back and forth with Tan when we had, our, *um*, drunken moment at one of our events. But I'm helping her raise him regardless. Bo is a good kid. Children are innocents in adults' dramas."

"He must have taken after his mother," Kaitlin scoffed, pacing around with her hands on her face. "Yeah…he was a good puppy the short time he stayed with us too. Until his *dad* apparently— you— took him from us with a threat note!"

"I love Bo…" Finn placed his hands on Kaitlin's shoulders. They wobbled. "But I'm not exactly very comfortable with you assuming he's my son. Paternity can be…*tricky*, as you know, Ms. Kaitlin. But let's not digress. Please. I'm not here to reopen old wounds."

"Who else would Bo's father be, Finn? Are you trying to implicate Tan? He was human, for God's sake! But Bo is apparently of the jinn who can change form like the both of you— you and Meredith!"

"I just meant- we can't exactly give Tan a paternity test anymore, can we?"

"Finn— humans and jinn *cannot* interbreed!" Kaitlin had done her research on Islamic scriptures and gotten confirmation as such from an imam Sibel had connected her with. "I know now! I've learned. No test needed! And, unless there's some other jinn-buddy you are accusing poor Meredith of also having potentially fathered Bo with- I think you are well aware of the damned truth! You can't fool me again! Which is why I don't know how you can still imagine that Malin could possibly be of anyone else's except me and my husband!"

"Oh, stop it, Kaitlin!" Finn exclaimed. "Malin *sees* me! She's seen me since she was a baby when I wasn't manifesting as a human…."

"As do I!" Kaitlin bellowed. "So what? I'm, not biologically connected to you for being able to do so, for God's sake, Finn! Though, I've got to be honest, I've still got to figure out why *I* precisely can see you and your kind, whereas many others…"

"*Children*, Kaitlin!" Finn interrupted, throwing his hands in the air. "I walk around town and they barely notice me. Many animals do, and some humans, yes…but not the little kids. Jinn are mostly unseen to them!"

"Maybe she has a gift, or something!" Kaitlin shrugged.

"Or maybe you're in denial…" Finn whispered. "You see me. Yes. But do you think it's because you have some 'gift'? Is that it?"

"Regardless, Finn: science and the natural order of things don't lie," Kaitlin remembered Paul's tormented rage when the paternity test results had been revealed to him on the phone by an amateur lab employee. Of course, the tests had shown that he was the father. Yet the very reason why Kaitlin felt she needed to perform a secret test in the first place had driven him mad.

"Neither does my intuition…." Finn commented in nearly a whisper.

"Finn…" Kaitlin started, unsure what to say next. *Is denial limited to humans?*

"I heard that!" Finn raised a brow.

"Sorry, but it's true…" Kaitlin was still in shock as to how Finn could have kept up his supposed parental feelings for Malin for all the years. She had to give it to him— his support felt sincere. Finn had even been there for her and Malin at one of the lowest times in her life- at Malin's first birthday party she had to throw alone when Paul was thrown in jail. Sincere in his affection- despite the near impossibility of blood relations between a jinn and a human, proven further by a DNA test.

"Look," he began, exasperated. "All I know for certain is how I feel. About you, and about Malin- as a part of you…and even me somehow, in some way. And even if she *is* biologically Paul's: it wouldn't change a thing for me! I care for you, Kaitlin….and naturally for your child, as well. Regardless of whether or not it was our love and forms that particularly bred her body as a vessel for her soul to exist on this plane."

Kaitlin was at a loss for words. She settled on shaking her head with a half-smile. *How do you manage to perpetually vex, scare and move me so- all at the same time?*

"And she loved playing with Bo in the woods," Finn continued. "Whether they're half-siblings or not- just let the girl play with him in his dog form, at least!"

"Why not in his *human* form?" Kaitlin questioned, genuinely curious.

"Well, what excuse could I have as a grown man introducing her to some young kid— unless he were my son, or something? I didn't want it to be too weird, so I asked Bo to…"

"But *isn*'t he?" Kaitlin cut in, crossing her arms. "Your son?"

"He…" Finn began, but stopped himself and shook his head side to side. "As per Lar's instructions, Bo hasn't been told about me…as his, *ahem,* potential father or whatnot. Meredith just hasn't told him any facts about any father figure, and he hasn't yet asked."

"Poor Bo…"Kaitlin's maternal instincts were activated. "He must be holding so much in."

"Regardless of his paternity, I couldn't introduce him as a human boy, period!" Finn went on. "I mean, it'd have been further suspicious for Malin to meet Bo as her 'cousin'- since he'd be introduced as my son, then, wouldn't it? She'd then perhaps wonder why she couldn't even mention a 'cousin' to her dad."

"I don't know…" Kaitlin shrugged, grabbing her hair. "I just don't know what to say, or think, or do, anymore, Finn. You've dragged me into this whole thing, *again*! With kids, this time…innocent offsprings who deserve to be spared. Spared our drama, our trauma…our, whatever!"

"She feels *lonely,* Katilin!" Finn blurted out. "Bo is a strong lad- he's rather social in our circle. But I worry for Malin. She hasn't been able to make many friends yet. You won't even allow her a pet!"

Why does he care so much? Kaitlin was taken aback by how deep their conversation had apparently gotten in a short amount of time. "How do you know all this? She told you that? The pet thing?"

"She didn't have to…I feel it," Finn responded with a shrug. But she did…yes…and I do *care*, yes!" He added a wink. "I told you— I understand her! Heck, I *was* her! I had a very lonely childhood, all right?"

"Oh, *merde*," Kaitlin cursed, biting her lip. *Helpless*. That was certainly how she felt in her inability to control her thoughts, feelings or even actions around him. "My darn, overthought thoughts…especially around you. Anyway. Look, I'm sorry for your childhood. You've been so kind with my father stuff. Helpful with my…mental confusions. I'd love to listen if you ever want to…"

"I don't want to talk about it!" Finn barked. He took in a deep breath and added more calmly. "But thank you."

"Finn, forgive me for trying to protect my daughter's thoughts… her well-being overall! She's adjusting to school. I wasn't exactly *Miss Popularity*, either, when I was her age. It's a gradual process. Do you think I'm a bad mother because of the *dog* thing? Oh, come on! It's a lot of responsibility! Speaking of which— just why *is* Bo a dog, anyway?"

A clanking sound from a bag of blocks got both their attention. *Malin!* Kaitlin had completely forgotten! She shot a warning look in Finn's direction, and proceeded to smile at Malin upon her arrival.

"Baby!" Kaitlin went over and caressed her daughter's head. She knew it was unavoidable that Malin hadn't heard anything at all at this point. Kaitlin was just praying her daughter hadn't heard too much at least.

"Mommy, you know Bo?"

"Um— let me get you that doll, sweetheart," Kaitlin said with a sheepish smile after nodding. "Sorry, I got lost talking to your uncle, I forgot…You can leave the blocks alone for now."

"Oh, I found Ariel already! She's going to play blocks with me."

"Is that so, my little mermaid?" Kaitlin asked, ignoring Finn shaking his head with concern from the corner of her eye. *She's just creative,* she thought with intent this time for Finn to hear cognitively. She made sure to direct it to him, looking straight into his eyes. *And kids can have make-believe playmates.*

"Yes," Malin announced. "Although, she'll be more like my student. My archi-techie student! She'll have to watch how high I can build my building first!"

Finn chuckled, taking a step toward Malin. "You know about architecture? Well, would you look at that? My niece is going to become an *architect* when she's older, it seems."

"Thank you, Uncle Finn," Malin swayed side-to-side with her arms crossed behind her, blushing with a smile. She took several steps to make room between her and a shapely-metal figure her parents had had in the corner of the living room for décor. "Come, build with me, Uncle Finn! I like building higher than this thing!"

"Oh, alright," Finn smiled, turning to face Kaitlin. *She's inviting me. May I? Please?*

Kaitlin was just about to say 'alright' with a sigh when a loud hiss from the corner of Finn's lips took her by surprise. He'd developed a cringing look of grimace on his visage the moment he'd neared the metal object. He took a couple of steps back toward Kaitlin.

"Are you okay?" Malin asked.

"I get migraines, Malin," Finn explained. He darted a sheepish look between Kaitlin and the décor object. *Being near that thing hurt. Why do you guys have that ugly thing displayed like that, anyway?* He shook his head out and drew in a long, labored breath.

Kaitlin smiled and crossed her arms, recalling Finn's discomfort with her metal flashlight in the woods, as well. Something she'd found out was a fallacy of jinn. *It's just art*, she mentally sent his way with a repressed smile. She found herself feeling too amused to be offended.

"Your uncle was just about to leave, sweetheart. He needs his medicine. Go to your room while I see him out, and I'll come play with you."

"Feel better, Uncle Finn," Malin said with a shrug. " You're going to play with Bo? I heard Mommy knows Bo, too?"

"Yes, Malin. Mommy's met him before. I should get back to Bo. He's been waiting by the door all this time. I don't want to leave his leash tied for too long. He hates that."

"Awesome!" Malin said with a smile, waving to Finn as she turned around to walk back to her room. She suddenly stopped in her tracks and faced Kaitlin. "Isn't he adorable? Can Bo come up to play with me for a little bit, Mommy?"

Kaitlin clapped her hands and shook her side to side. "Yes- Bo is adorable. But-no can do, baby, sorry. We've all got to get going with the rest of our day. Chop chop!"

"But you'd be seeing him again, too, Mommy," Malin insisted. She folded her hands together in a pleading manner and opened a toothy grin, making sure to squeeze her eyes tightly shut as she knew her mother found to be extra adorable. "Pretty please?"

"No means no, baby," Kaitlin stood firm. "Maybe some other time. Uncle Finn was just leaving."

After darting Finn a look for one more attempt— and receiving a polite shaking of his head as a reaction—Malin finally conceded and walked inside her room.

"To answer your question— he's not a dog, by the way…" Finn whispered to her once Malin had taken a couple of the blocks and walked out of sight. "He's just taken the strongest liking to his canine form, is all. Especially as it's how Lar is most comfortable in having him around.

Master is not exactly child-friendly. As for me? I've personally found it easier to hide out among humans as a cat."

"Oh, I see," Kaitlin replied, reflecting back on Finn in his cat form. He had followed her around for a while- a distinctive black feline, albeit his green eyes shone just the same.

"Figures, I guess. I remember Sandy told me about Bjorn's- *ahem*- admiration of the snake form." Kaitlin chuckled, surprising herself that she was feeling more relaxed despite the insanity of what had just happened.

"To each their own, Ms. Kaitlin," Finn winked. "We all have our various tastes."

"Just don't do it again. Finn!" Kaitlin insisted, letting out an audible breath. "I mean it! You had your little play date arranged with Bo and Malin. Fine. Okay. But that's enough now, all right?"

"No harm done, Kaitlin," Finn rolled his eyes. "She had fun. Relax, please."

"You also promised you wouldn't do *this*- whatever you're doing- period!" Kaitlin's eyes searched the floor for any lint or pattern that could maintain her focus long enough for her to avoid looking into his mesmerizing eyes.

"*This*?" Finn questioned.

"You, or those peeps of your kind, *clouded* my mind! In the forest. That fake text message- the phone call…Now that I think about it, you didn't even *sound* quite like him! But…I couldn't question it, I couldn't put my finger on what precisely was off in that moment. It was as if my mind had been…"

The phone ringing stopped Kaitlin's rambling. "That could be Paul. *Shit!* What the heck do I say?"

"Nothing," Finn shrugged, casually pursing his lips. "He's working overtime, remember? For all he knows, you picked up Malin and returned home, like usual."

"But he could be near!" Kaitlin was shaking the phone in her hand frantically. "Paul could return home any minute! You have to leave, now! And what will happen when he finds out?"

"He won't," Finn winked. "And I don't sense him near yet. All good."

"Don't you dare do that to my mind, again!" Kaitlin kept going, ignoring the phone screen. "You could have just tried asking for a playdate. I appreciate the friendship, as I've told you. But you can't do this! Not like this! Malin needs her mom to be headstrong…and…"

"*Have* you been headstrong, though, Kaitlin?" Finn smiled. He rubbed the back of his neck, his green eyes flickering between Kaitlin and the phone.

"Think about it…you mentioned *medication*? Maybe you need something better than whatever Freya's been prescribing you, that's for sure. What does she know, anyway?"

Kaitlin took a step backward. "How did you know her name?"

"You've mentioned it…" Finn responded with a shrug.

"I have?"

"Yeah…" Finn's eyes went toward her phone again. "Um, Kaitlin? The call?"

Ding. A text message cut into Kaitlin's suspicions.

"Oh! Shit, I missed the call! One second…" she rolled her eyes as she went through her missed call. "It's Sibel! She's messaged something, too…."

Kaitlin felt a little more at ease upon seeing that it wasn't Paul who'd called, but not too much. She didn't exactly need Finn to criticize her choices, too, like she'd already become accustomed to Paul doing for so long. What problem could Finn have with a therapist trying to help her, anyway? *Sheesh.* Especially after everything he'd done to cause her current state?

"She says it's urgent," Kaitlin clicked on her friend's name and placed the phone onto her ear. "I'm calling her back!"

"Oh, your jinn-wary friend," Finn rolled his eyes. "Go ahead."

"Hello?" Kaitlin threw an angry look at Finn and placed a finger on her lips to signal him to keep quiet.

"Kaitlin!" Sibel's voice panicked on the other line. "Thank goodness everything's okay. Is Malin with you?"

"Yeah…yes, she is, honey. Why wouldn't she be?" Kaitlin knew her friend had strong instincts, but she couldn't possibly have foreseen the entirety of the eeriness that had just transpired with Malin and Finn in the woods, could she?

"*Um*, her dance teacher said you hadn't been there to pick her up from her dance class? You also haven't picked up any of my calls. I was going to call Paul, too a little earlier, but I was tending to the kids. They have been home sick all week with bronchitis. If you hadn't called me back just now…"

"Aww, I'm so sorry to hear that," Kaitlin cut in. "I hope the angels get better. Give Aylin and Hakan my regards."

She soon realized by Sibel's subsequent silence after a softly uttered *'Thanks'* that she owed her friend an explanation. "Oh, the phone call! Right! Girl, it was just a miscommunication and misunderstanding. But it's all worked out now…"

As Kaitlin spoke, Finn's eyes were palpable on her sizzling skin. She had to tread carefully.

"I had put you and Paul as the emergency contacts, and I was having some technical issues with my phone…but it's all good now. Paul has…*um*…picked Malin up, actually, and she's with me here."

"Hmm…" Sibel didn't sound convinced. "Okay. Good. Are you all right otherwise?"

"Yeah, yes, *um,* I've just been preparing food for later…left the stove on, honey. So…"

"Oh, okay. I've got you," Sibel's voice sounded more comforted.

She'd long learned by now how panicky Kaitlin would genuinely get over cooking close to the arrival time of her picky husband. "Well, call me later, then, when you can. All right?"

"Will do. Thanks so much. Love ya!"After hanging up, Kaitlin's frustration turned to anger as she saw Finn twiddling his thumbs with a smirk.

"Finn- they've contacted Sibel! That means they contacted Paul, too! The two of them were my emergency contacts!"

"Yes, yes," Finn dismissed with his hands, rolling his eyes. "But no worries. Mr. Maverick's phone went straight to voice mail, and his message got deleted."

Kaitlin raised an eyebrow.

"Whoops," Finn teased with a sly grin, snapping his fingers. "Poof! Just like that! A glitch in technology."

CHAPTER 11

Dubai
1990

COULD SILENCE HURT THE SENSES MORE THAN LOUDNESS? Watching the shadows of nurses' steps pass by his glass-windowed door, Aresh let out a weary exhale. He made sure to take in an extra loud breath, letting out a soft hum as he exhaled to soothe his troubled soul. It felt refreshing to fill the room with some noise other than ticking of the old, plastic wall clock he had for a view. The only window in his hospital room was a smaller one close to the ceiling, where all Aresh could make out were some clouds.

It must have been mere minutes since his mother and Muhiddin had left his bedside. None of what had been spoken between himself and his brother was mentioned. Their last argument was buried, like this part of his identity and being Aresh knew he had to bury as well. They asked about his wounds after being told of the 'motorcycle accident', and that had pretty much been that. They hadn't even inquired much about a potential perpetrator.

His mom had asked if he was all right, and his brother had said they'd return to pick him up when he had healed. Did they even care that Aresh had almost died? Or were they just feeling the need to keep up appearances as 'concerned family members' after the police or doctors contacted them to let them know about the crash?

Maybe it would have been easier for them if I had died, Aresh mused. *If I had just disappeared without them being responsible for it- removing my inconveniencing self out of their lives.*

A sudden orange beam appearing before him startled Aresh, spreading gradually throughout his recovery room before condensing into the now more familiar human figure. "How's your arm, Aresh?"

"Amir," Aresh whispered, smiling at the inviting light-amber eyes. How quickly this figure had become more familial with him than his own mother and brother. He attempted to sit up straighter with his back higher against the pillow propped behind him on the bed. "It's you."

"Don't try to move, it's alright," Amir floated closer. "Are you in any pain?"

"The wound still hurts a bit," Aresh explained with a shrug. "They discovered it was a .22 bullet from an older-model pistol. There was a lot of bleeding. The doctor said it's going to leave a scar. A deep one. Luckily the bullet didn't rupture any veins or muscle. *SubhanAllah*, I'm alive. Thanks to you."

"*MashAllah*," the figure spoke, elevating into the air as he completed one full circle around Aresh's bedside. He inched closer, and Aresh could feel sparks of heat radiating from his aura. "I could help your scar disappear altogether, but in due time. We do not want doctors or anyone catching on to our supra-human bond with my speeding up the healing process, do we? Where would the sacredness be in such a revelation?"

"I understand...." Aresh spoke, mesmerized. "Sacred."

"Yes, there's sanctity in having secrets," Amir spoke. He proceeded to release a soft chuckle. "You always were a most curious, yet ultimately faithful little boy, too, Aresh. I've always admired you."

"You knew me as a child?" Aresh asked, in awe. Scratching his head, he smiled. "*Ya Rabbi.* I'm still surprised we're conversing like this. I'd been taught Angels don't interact with humans!"

"I'm no angel," Amir smirked. "I'm of the jinn. I was assigned to you since birth."

"You're...a jinn?" Aresh had been told about the jinn by his mother, but it had often been in passing and in quiet voice tones. "*We cannot call attention to them out loud and risk piquing the bad ones' interest,"* she'd say. *"They can even possess us!"* She had told him about the Quranic verses and hadiths. That humans are assigned one angel and one jinn from birth on- with the former advising our 'good deeds' and the latter advising the 'bad' ones to 'thwart us off a righteous path'.

Amir's nostalgic smile as he spoke further comforted the wound inside Aresh's heart. "I've always observed you, and I think you saw me a couple of times when you were a young boy, because I remember you'd smile at me."

Aresh vaguely recalled seeing a mysterious presence in his youth, indeed, and chalked it up to seeing an 'angel', as he hadn't felt scared. Though admittedly Aresh couldn't quite make out if Amir's face in particular had been familiar.

"I've tried to remain mostly invisible unless absolutely necessary. Earlier on that road with that evil Kareem about to hurt you- it was a matter of life or death, and I stepped in."

"Kareem?" Aresh asked, a gulp lingering in his throat. "Is that his name? The neighbor who did this to me?"

"Forget him and his name!" Amir held out his palm before Aresh's face. "I don't like him one bit. He's no good. He's escaped the authorities for the moment, but he will not leave you alone once you've healed enough to return home."

"He'll...continue to bother me?" Aresh asked with a whimper. "How do you know?"

"Do you question me?" Amir fumed. "Your savior?"

"No, forgive me, Amir," Aresh shook his head and turned his eyes toward the ground. "It's just that- only Allah knows the future."

"Yes, but some of us are given special knowledge from the Almighty," Amir's voice softened. "And I am one. I know, for instance, that you need to leave Dubai! For the West! As soon as possible! It's been ordained!"

"Leave Dubai?" Aresh was befuddled. "But how? I mean, I also have my university here."

"Your voyage and safety abroad will be taken care of," Amir went on, folding his hands together before him. "I shall ensure the plight of anyone who crosses you, and guarantee they and their loved ones see destruction for doing so, as well. All as a favor to you."

A being that would protect him, and ensure that whoever hurt him would pay for it? A being that would only be looking out for Aresh's well-being? Maybe his mother had been wrong about the negativity associated with jinn assigned to humans. His own- after all- had already proven himself to be a protector, saving him from the flames and that sneaky Kareem.

"You are too kind, Amir," Aresh spoke. A tear rolled down his cheek. Perhaps God was rewarding him after all for his innocent suffering. "I'm grateful."

"It's not purely kindness, Aresh," Amir spoke with a smile. "It is my mission, and I shall ask for a favor in return later on. But the favor you will repay me with will ensure your success, as well! If you cooperate, our mutual allegiance to each other will aid us both for as long as we both live."

Success? Aresh was all ears. "How so?"

"First— you will tell your family of a natural cure for your arm abroad, and venture to Europe for it," Amir began immediately, taking Aresh by surprise. He'd sure thought a lot about all this.

"I only speak English other than Arabic," Aresh began, pouting. "And even that is of an average-level, at best."

"If we cannot get you into the UK, we will try the Scandinavian countries," Amir assured him. "Norway in particular has English as a widely-spoken language. Once you get to one of those, you'll then stay longer for your higher education. We will take care of a school transfer afterward, don't worry about that part. There, with my help- we shall create an organization of such immense beauty, and global strength, that we will leave everyone in awe…"

"We will leave everyone in awe…." Aresh's eyes twinkled as he repeated, staring blankly at the wall across his bedside.

"Your family will accept and even rejoice at the fact that you've gotten an opportunity to study in Europe," Amir continued, still elevated off the ground, with his fingers wrapped around one another. "Especially as you'll soon make enough to send them money back home."

"Europe…" Aresh had stars in his eyes.

"Yes, it is a start, at least," Amir went on with a shrug. "You need to set your feet outside of these borders. Kareem feels insulted by you, that misguided thug! I've visited him and his thoughts. He's feeling repressed and unable to live out his desires- unless he forces himself. He is a criminally-inclined lowlife."

"Criminally-inclined…" Aresh repeated with a blank stare fixated on Amir.

"Correct," Amir went on in a sympathetic tone of voice. The corner of his lip had twisted upward into a smile. "If you stay here- he will keep harassing you and hurting you. And you can never go to the police, either. If you do, he'll make sure you get in trouble with them, too!"

"But Muhiddin and my mother will never believe me!" Aresh exclaimed, shaking his head side to side rapidly. "I don't have much experience to actually make it to Europe! You either need to come from money, or get super high grades…or score a great internship experience, like the one I did in Dubai last summer with the Emirates Group. But they'll never accept me beyond that, I'm afraid."

"*Shh*, the minor details will not trump over your grander destiny," Amir reassured him. He then raised an eyebrow, pursing his lips. "Can you go into the city on an internship again this coming summer? One with a western company headquarters this time, perhaps? Try it. If you can't, I shall intervene. Regardless- do not fret. It will be done."

"Hmm," Aresh turned his eyes toward the ceiling in consideration. "I suppose I can ask my cousin, Mahmoud, about the one he completed last summer with another company. Some foreign one with a European CEO. He said it'd helped with his English, too! I think it repeats every summer."

"Perfect!" Amir exclaimed. "Along with the medical breakthrough excuse for your scar- this internship opportunity should be enough to convince your family you've earned studying in Europe. You can only advance yourself and your mission on earth away from them."

"I will try my best," Aresh whispered.

"You will *do* your best," Amir insisted.

"I will do my best," Aresh repeated.

"My poor Aresh," Amir spoke, his nearly-yellow, light amber eyes sparkling. "Humans and jinn aren't always fortunate to be born into the bodies, nor families they were meant in order to feel whole- like they *belong*. Sometimes we have to make things happen ourselves."

"Make things happen…" Aresh repeated. From the corner of his eye he spotted a nurse dart a quizzical look from the window in his direction, before walking off. *She must be thinking I'm talking to myself.*

Amir paid no mind. He kept up his explanation.

"We're free spirits— both of us, though you as a human, and I as a jinn. We should be capable of making our own choices in how to live and love. We can co-create a beautiful arrangement, you and me. An umbrella to cover all fellow brethren and sisters- lost in their misplacements and suffering needlessly. In doing so, we'll have performed an absolutely splendid mission on earth, and be rewarded by Allah for our servitude."

"Why do you suppose that's so, Amir?" Aresh asked. "Allah doesn't make mistakes. He's All-Mighty! All-Knowing. Right?"

"Oh, yes— but there's just so much to take care of in the world, young Aresh!" Amir chuckled. "And the Creator simply has too much on His hands to take care of to ensure all the spirits he creates enter the most appropriate forms and families for them."

"I can imagine," Aresh said.

"I must go now," Amir floated toward the window. It was cracked open to let in some fresh air. "I hear them. The nurses are returning to check your blood pressure."

"They can't see you, right?"

"No," Amir responded. "I assessed them- these two on this floor can't....but I still don't want them seeing you talk to me and think you insane. We can't have you taken into a mental institution! We have a big mission together ahead of us."

"I understand," Aresh nodded.

"Good." Amir smiled. "Rest home for a day or two, and don't go outside! We'll have to watch out for Kareem until you can leave the country. I'll appear to you in my animal form during the day to remind you, and then just wait for my further instructions in your room. I shall visit after your mother has fallen asleep, and Muhiddin goes in his own room with his wife. Until then- be well."

"Animal form? What do you mean, Amir? Where did you go?"

Aresh glanced frantically all around him, until he spotted the same black bird he'd been seeing since that day with the violent neighbor.

"I'm here," the bird spoke- surprising Aresh to his core with human words! "Don't be afraid. I'm most comfortable in my grackle form. Animal forms are easier for us to manifest in the human plane physically than human ones. I'll be able to accompany you easier as a bird, and in nature- away from large human concentrations."

The grackle turned its head toward Aresh one last time before flying out his hospital room window.

CHAPTER 12

Sandnes

KAITLIN COUNTED THE MINUTES UNTIL PAUL LEFT FOR WORK throughout her morning coffee routine, fiddling with her fingers on the glass table in the middle of the living room. On it, a stack of the latest fall-fashion magazines— once one of her favorite pastimes to flip through— now only served as house décor. She'd woken up feeling the utmost urgency to talk to someone about Malin's incident with 'Uncle Finn'. Merely thinking about it trembled her entire being senseless.

Sandy and Sibel were her only two friends who'd known about him, yet Sandy was in a different time zone, and Kaitlin knew Sibel would most likely freak out on her. Especially as she'd inadvertently gotten involved through Malin's teacher calling her!

Could she tell Freya? She was the only other person who knew her jinn secret. It was the reason, in fact, why Kaitlin had even agreed to remote therapy with her, with Sandy having confided in her about it, too.

She's been helping me after Bjorn, Sandy had told Kaitlin. *I think it'd be good for you, as well. To talk to someone. A professional, who also understands. After the whole Finn thing. You know?*

Despite never giving too much detail for confidentiality reasons, apparently the therapist had 'experienced jinn' herself- and that's all she'd say about that. Freya didn't chalk it up to 'insanity' for her clients- and that had been enough to convince Kaitlin to give her services a shot. She hadn't stated as such directly to Sandy, but feeling so sure she'd heard and seen her estranged father on those cliffs had had Kaitlin questioning her sanity for the longest time.

Oh, right, Paul knows too, Kaitlin remembered. She snickered. *Discovering this latest incident, as it involves our daughter and Finn, though, would drive him up the wall!*

Malin's secret outing with Finn had come close to becoming revealed during dinner. Her husband had returned home the previous night and already sensed that something was out of the norm. That was one of the perks of living with someone for so long— one partner could even physically sense things like confusion or despair in the other.

At first, Paul had bought that it'd been 'a typical day', where his wife had picked up their daughter from dance class, with nothing else occurring out of the ordinary as they chewed on their potatoes.

But Kaitlin had long learned that temporary avoidance in her family didn't necessarily mean that she could delay for too long the almost inevitable drama to ensue. Something had to give, and too often in her life— it did.

Surely enough, Paul had soon felt something was off. During their final dish of some thawed pecan pie, after all, he'd shot Kaitlin a look of concern upon hearing Malin's one-word answers about how her dance had gone.

"What's going on girls?" he'd asked. "Did anything interesting, or out-of-the-usual happen today? Anything you're not telling me?"

"Of course- the big uncle visit…." Malin had started to blurt out, just as Kaitlin laughed and tickled her with a warning look, causing her daughter to quiet down in remembrance, and flash a toothy grin to her dad.

"Uncle visit?" Paul, who only had sisters, had asked in a confused tone. "What's going on, Kaitlin? Is Aidan here or something?"

"Oh, nothing, babe," Kaitlin had shrugged, stuffing her mouth and averting her eyes from Paul's sharp gaze. "No, Aidan's still in New York. It's just…well…he called us yesterday….talked to Malin."

"Right…" Paul had spoken softly, moistening his lower lip with his tongue. "But, so what? He's done that before. Malin said 'visit'."

Merde! Kaitlin felt at a loss as to what she could possibly concoct on the spot. "Well, he suggested that he could *try* to visit us. Or that *we* could *visit him* in New York. You know- since he hasn't met his niece in person yet. And it's so hard for him to take time off of work with all his responsibilities in New York. I'm always telling him he should have stayed at the Toronto office, and be closer to mom, too, but you know he's been insisting on living out on his own as a bachelor still, and…"

"Okay, okay, I see," Paul uttered, twirling his tongue around his mouth. "Well, when were you thinking of doing this New York visit, then, Kaitlin ? You *do* know my family is visiting us in the summer. Her *Nanna* has only seen her once!"

"Right…of course, babe, of course," Kaitlin cut him off, adding a smile on her mouth, in hopes it'd distract from her trembling eyelids. How could she forget? Paul had reminded her practically every other day almost not to make 'summer vacation' plans as a family for the three of them, since two of his sisters and his parents had finally 'coordinated' the 'opportunity' to visit them.

"Which is precisely *why* I was thinking, babe, that…um.. New York could work better, perhaps, during Malin's upcoming winter break from school, then!" Kaitlin added a smile and a playful shrug after her impromptu declaration. She was feeling just as surprised as Paul appeared to be at her own sudden, yet necessitated 'plan'.

"I mean, it was just a random suggestion. We didn't really plan much. We could discuss it later. There's still time."

"Hmm…" Paul muttered, chewing on his meatball. "Is that so, my Mallie?" He leaned closer to Malin and playfully pushed her arm. "You want to visit Uncle Aidan in New York City?"

Malin had simply shrugged. A smile was plastered on her countenance as she looked back and forth between the two of them.

"And Grandma Linda, too, right, sweetie?" Kaitlin reminded, winking at her daughter as she flipped her hair back. She tried clearing her throat to catch Paul's attention. "After all— she hasn't seen you in person for quite a long time, as well."

It'd felt like a game of 'tit-for-tat', to Kaitlin. Her own mother had visited her and Malin when she was a baby, and then her mother-in-law was immediately flown in to visit as well. Though, alas, she couldn't stay too long. She had other grandchildren to take care of back in Canada.

Both ladies had made excuses like a 'fear of flying' and old age to try to get Paul, Kaitlin and Malin to fly to Canada instead, but several passport issues and Paul's busy schedule had had all of them relying more on virtual camera calls as of late. *"When Malin is a bit older, and she actually understands who and where she's visiting,"* they'd say.

Kaitlin sighed in remembrance. *That was too close last night!* Now that she thought about it calmer, she figured it wouldn't be so bad, perhaps, to actually fly back to the western hemisphere for real! It'd been a while, and the passport issues had recently been taken care of. She and Paul were blessed to be able to afford the tickets, after all. And she could keep up with her work through her laptop anywhere in the world.

Still in bed, Kaitlin thought back to how something else had been nagging her in the back of her mind the prior evening. Something Finn had said. Something she didn't really catch until it triggered something in her as she was lying in bed with her thoughts, and Paul's back had been turned to her.

"You see me," Finn had told her. *"You think it's because you have some 'gift'? Is that it?"*

Did she have a gift? Freya had contributed the episode of seeing her father on the cliffs to 'hallucinations' caused by anxiety and stress. Perhaps Kaitlin was simply developing some sort of intuitive powers, instead? Something Malin may also have had?

Kaitlin sighed. Finn had sounded like he didn't buy that, though. Was he implying that it was due to some special connection? Or perhaps he had sarcastically tried to imply something worse- something Kaitlin had secretly been fretting over since her father-seeing incident atop the Dalsnuten cliffs. *Jesus, I truly hope I haven't gone mad.*

As much as she wanted to avoid Finn for as long as possible after their confrontation following Finn's little forest rendezvous with Malin-Kaitlin knew she had to face him again, as well as her own lingering fear about the incident of seeing her father on the cliffs.

In the meantime, she would pester a professional. Freya was, after all, getting paid out-of-pocket for her help! Kaitlin's health insurance wasn't under the realm of the American-licensed therapist's coverage.

"Good morning, Freya! Can you see me?" Kaitlin waved her hands before the screen following her FaceTime dial.

Freya's sparkling blue eyes lit up the screen after half a minute or so. Her usually-covered, dirty blonde hair was long and cascading down her shoulders. "Good evening, Kaitlin!"

"How's New York going?" Kaitlin almost kicked herself as soon as the random question spilled forth from her mouth. Usually she'd just vent about something her mother or Paul had said to her that she wanted to get off her chest- getting straight to the point so as not to waste the punctual therapist who wouldn't talk to her beyond sixty-minutes exactly. She hadn't prepared herself for how she'd spill the details of Finn visiting Malin, but Kaitlin had to start somewhere.

"Pardon?" Freya's petite, angelic features— which made her appear younger than she actually was— genuinely looked puzzled.

"Oh, I mean with Covid," Kaitlin let out a short, nervous chuckle. "I heard the death tolls have finally begun to decline. I want to visit with Malin."

"Oh, yes, yes- the vaccines appear to be working, Kaitlin," Freya's visage relaxed. "People have begun returning to life as normal, little by little. Thanks to God. My husband still prefers I work from home, though, and not return to the office just yet. Safety first."

"I see..." Kaitlin said, biting the bottom of her lip. She wondered if working from home would soon become the new norm worldwide or something.

"How are you doing this week, Kaitlin?" Freya's soft voice interrupted her thoughts. "You mentioned wanting to visit New York with your daughter?"

"Yes, oh, yes...I have been thinking about it lately, yes," Kaitlin started. "You know Sandy is there, and Aidan- my big brother- too. I thought, um, it'd be a nice little experience for Malin to travel during her winter break from school. We could mask up on the plane. It'll be worth it, I figure. I was also just thinking we may go up to Canada the second week. See Grandma and her Mommy's hometown in Toronto, too, perhaps, before our return to Norway..."

"Wow," Freya responded, nodding thoughtfully. "Sounds like a big, North American trip. How does Malin feel about it?"

"I mentioned the possibility in brief to her," Kaitlin started. "It's still not even officially autumn yet! But she's adventurous. It should be good."

"And Paul? How does *he* feel?"

"He...seems to be on board," Kaitlin forced herself to chuckle. "Probably thinking it'll give his own family's long-term visit to us in the summer more validation. Heck, I wouldn't even be surprised if he insists we catch the train to visit them in Montreal, too- if we do end up visiting my mom in Ontario."

"Yes...yes...I see," Freya smiled. Her eyes squinted as she asked her follow-up question. "Above all- how do *you* feel about this decision?"

Kaitlin gulped. “Me?”

“Yes, you,” Freya smiled. “Are you sure there isn’t anything else going on for your sudden desire to travel? A subconscious desire to…*get away*, perhaps?”

“Get away?” Kaitlin stammered. “Oh, no, I don’t think so. I mean, I think I always just want to see my family. We don’t get along too well in close proximity for long, but when we’re at a distance- my family is always in my thoughts…and phone calls. Do you know what I mean? Especially with all this news of pandemic death worldwide.”

“Family—hmm, interesting,” Freya smiled.

“What do you mean?” Kaitlin asked, leaning closer to the screen.

“You *are* with your family there in Norway, though, aren’t you?” Freya smiled. “Your core, immediate one, anyway- with your husband and daughter?”

*Touch*é. Kaitlin bit her lower lip and took in a deep breath. Her therapist wasn’t one to soften her words, but somehow that had become what Kaitlin liked about her. “Yes, of course, but…oh, I don’t know. Maybe you’re right, after all, Freya! With the wanting to get away bit, you know? Finn is still headquartered here in Norway, and Paul gets to see more people at work and beyond than I….”

“You have to *write*, Kaitlin,” Freya leaned over onto the screen. “Have you been writing more creatively as well as I’ve been telling you? Personal writing in poetic or free-verse form?”

“Well the blog has been kept up with, of course, and…”

“You have to get all of this out,” Freya interrupted. “There’s simply too much you’ve gone through! Too much inside you that could absolutely explode without an outlet. Hallucinations may have only been the tip of the iceberg, I’m afraid!”

“I should write all this out…right…right,” Kaitlin nodded. She was gradually trying to bring the conversation to getting Malin’s forest incident with Finn and Bo off her chest. This bit about expressing herself through words was feeling a bit out left field, but she'd take whatever she could get.

"That's right," Freya continued. "I know you've been writing poetry. You've turned to art for healing. That's an excellent first step in recovery after trauma."

"Trauma..." Kaitlin considered. Freya had once called Paul's imprisonment and her suddenly being thrust into the role of a lone parent 'trauma'. That's what she meant, wasn't it?

"Yes," Freya said in a serious tone. "You also need to connect to a community of other survivors- survivors of....*er*, familial problems, like yourself. Or even connect, perhaps, to your mother's own stories of your family's past? Some people inherit familial trauma and language of fear and victimization. Often thinking of the worst-case scenario. I believe that your father, in this particular case, may have a story that needs to be told..."

Kaitlin considered Freya's word, biting her lip. "Perhaps my father has a story to be told, you're saying..."

"Yes," Freya said with a smile. "The mystery of him needs closure in your mind. By the way, I really do congratulate you, once again, on making this decision to seek therapy. But our sessions simply must be supplemented by side projects for you. Other outlets..."

As Kaitlin chatted on about her long-ignored childhood hobby of writing, the digital time caught her eye. She hadn't gotten to discuss the latest forest incident yet. She had to bring the topic to jinn, and quick!

"Freya, is there a community specifically for people like myself, or Sandy? With regards to being people who have faced visitations from *them*...?"

"I'm afraid that's the end of our session today..." Freya cut in, scratching her head. "Kaitlin, I wasn't particularly referring to being a survivor of jinn visits- but, sure. We can discuss that too, next time, if you wish. I'll send you links, in the meantime, if I find any information online. Don't forget to take notes separately of things to ask me about whatever's bothering you—so we can address them directly next time, and make more efficient use of our time. Okay, Kaitlin?"

Was it just her or did Freya sound upset with something? Maybe she just had somewhere to go, or another patient waiting? Either way, Kaitlin was feeling reassured by Freya's smile as they said their goodbyes. She clicked off the app screen- fighting a tear struggling to let loose from her eyes. Finn came to her mind, and Kaitlin's heart began beating faster- excited with anger, or lust, she did not dare face.

She still couldn't believe he'd not only have shown himself to Malin, but also have intervened through Paul's phone. Not to mention fogging her mind with various jinn in animal form in the woods!

Despite the danger of what Finn had done—both with Malin as well as involving others within their social circle—Kaitlin realized how badly she'd wanted it to be real. If what was described on the phone to her, with Finn in disguise as Paul trying to make time to 'surprise' her and Malin, had actually been her husband.

§

WITH MALIN FRUSTRATINGLY RUNNING OFF TO CATCH HER FAVORITE television show in the middle of it and not finishing her peas, Paul's lack of his usual chatter that evening had their dinner routine pass by in simply said *Bon Appetit*, and excused himself to the couch.sh her dinner at once'Kaitlin tried to lure Paul's eyes away from the laptop screen he had flipped open almost immediately. She peeked to see if he'd been doing work. *Nope.* Nothing but scrolling through an online retail website for designer-name shoes on *salg* as his feet stood extended on the couch in an almost laying down position. *Guess it's better than some other websites he could get addicted to instead as a man*, she mused.

Paul's eyes were still glued to the website. "You should look through these fall boots on sale, babe. Some great deals."

Kaitlin didn't even dignify his random comment with a response, instead adjusting the long sleeves of her skintight red blouse as she inched closer to him. She situated herself on the carpeted floor next to him, placing her chin on his shoulder. *Surely I'm more interesting than some bargain shopping?*

"Paulie, I was thinking…I feel Malin's been spending so much time with me, lately. When she's not in school or her activities, that is. Is there any way you could, perhaps, you could get some ice cream together? You know. Spend quality time together in person with her? I mean…you've been working a lot lately. Even on Saturdays."

"Where's this coming from, Kaitlin?" Paul shot her a baffled look from the side of his eyes. "I'm sorry I had to work on Saturday, yes, but we all went to the playground afterwards."

"That was the Sunday before that, babe," Kaitlin reminded him, ensuring her voice remained soft.

"Well, right, right," Paul pursed his lips. "But I hadn't worked that weekend. This past Sunday I was still tired from working the day before. Kaitlin… what are you getting at?"

"I don't know…" Kaitlin started, grazing the tip of her forefinger gently across his arm. "I think I'm feeling there may be a need for just you two to bond more. Perhaps, since you adore online shopping, it seems- you could go shopping with her in person, for example, or…."

Paul looked up with quizzical eyes, shutting the lid of the laptop. *Bingo.* "You're upset I'm browsing the net? It helps me distract from stuff at work, and to clear my mind."

"I could help you clear your mind..." Kaitlin fluttered her eyelashes playfully, adding a suggestive wink. "I could still do that, can't I? Like when we were dating?"

"Oh, babe," Paul started with a heavy sigh. "Is that what this is about? I can never get you if you're not direct and clear with me. I mean- is this about you wanting me to spend more time with our daughter, since I've had to work a lot lately? Or with *you*?"

"Well...maybe...*both*?" Kaitlin added a pout.

"You girls are always on my mind," Paul leaned over and kissed the tip of her nose. "My cute, woman-child wife, you."

Kaitlin's smile quickly became overshadowed by his following statement.

"It's just that...well...someone's had to pay the actual rent and bills. In addition to just Malin's extracurricular activities and toys. You know?"

Oh no he didn't. Kaitlin sulked her shoulders, leaning back and away from him. "Was that another jab at my website, again? Because you of all people know how hard I've been working for my dream. It's not just a website for me- I express myself through it, Paulie, and affect others positively doing it. It's my labor of love! I've just been home for too long..."

"Where do you want to go?" Paul asked with a sigh. "Stavanger again? If you want to see Sibel— how about we invite them over for dinner? Or maybe we could meet them somewhere there if they don't invite us? I don't want you to go there alone."

Argh— really Paul? "This is not about Stavanger!" Kaitlin steamed. He'd seen what the jinn are capable of himself- was her husband really going to still suspect she would have to make excuses to travel to Stavanger if she wanted to see Finn?

"What is this really about, then?" Paul straightened himself up on the couch and aimlessly picked up the remote control on the corner table, only to plop it back down again with a thud.

"This started as me asking if you could perhaps make more time for us!" Kaitlin exclaimed. "And just us! No family members or friends necessary. Just you, me and Malin. Heck, I'd even be happy if you two just spent some time- as father and daughter. You haven't been doing so lately. Your work has been taking up more of your time…"

"You wished you were working in person, too, is that it?" Paul folded his hands together. "You know how I'd love to switch places with you? I'd rather you work and I sit home all day and raise our daughter! But I can't."

Be careful what you wish for, Kaitlin thought. Sometimes she mourned how much more sympathetic he'd been to her when he was imprisoned for the brief time that he was- where he'd actually been 'sitting around' himself in his cell, albeit forcibly so. "I don't just *sit around*!"

Paul shook his head side to side. "I didn't mean it in a way to imply you were lazy. Why must you take everything I say as a jab?"

Kaitlin drew in her shoulders. *Perhaps it's better to emphasize the part of it having to do with our daughter.* "I'm just worried about her…."

"Malin?" Paul raised an eyebrow.

"She's been saying the other girls are talking about play dates," Kaitlin folded her arms and let her shoulders fall. "No one's offered her, yet. She's always with me. I just don't know…"

"Hmm, if you say that's so—I'm beginning to think that her uncle may have been onto something," Paul's breath hitched before slowly easing out.

"Her uncle?" Kaitlin's heartbeat began to quicken. *Finn*

pretending to be as such did say he worried about Malin's loneliness, but surely Paul couldn't have found that out?

"Maybe this spontaneous winter trip suggestion by good old Aidan just may be perfect timing, after all," Paul shrugged.

Kaitlin chuckled with relief at the sound of her brother's name. She knew that he and Paul didn't exactly like each other. Certainly not more than she liked his spoiled and greedy sisters either—as far as she was concerned—in fairness.

This trip that she'd resorted to making up on the spot actually sounded increasingly like a good idea. And like she'd told Freya-perhaps taking the return flight from Toronto after a short time there too would be good. Not only would Malin see two countries, but she'd also see her uncle and mom, as well as her mom's childhood friends and home.

Paul interrupted Kaitlin's ponderings. "And my 'overworking' paycheck can get the tickets as a New Year's surprise for my girls, all right?"

He was smiling, but Kaitlin didn't like her husband's economical implication. Regardless, she knew she just had to grin and bear it. She noticed Paul's face shifted as he asked in a whisper. "Have you…heard your father's voice again, or something, babe?"

Kaitlin's stomach did a little somersault as she shook her head 'no'.

"I'll tell you what- let's finalize this trip," Paul went on, slapping his thigh. "I think a change of scenery may be good for you."

Kaitlin smiled, but then another thought popped in her mind. Why was he so on board with this? Was he eager to have them away from the house? Was he having some affair?

"Are you sure?"

Paul shot her a curious look. "What do you mean?"

Kaitlin eyed Paul up and down whilst twirling the tips of her auburn locks. "I mean, yes— I suppose a trip out may be nice for me and Malin, sure. But I don't know how I'd feel leaving you lonely here. After the jail ordeal…."

Kaitlin closed her eyes and took in a deep breath. After his return, Paul had to take several therapy sessions to get over the nightmares that had plagued his sleep for some time. He'd never shared with her if he'd divulged his jinn experience with his own therapist he visited in person. Nor did he really talk about why he'd stopped going. *"I feel better now, babe,"* he'd simply said one day. Around the time when Malin was three years old. *"I've come to terms with it all."*

Paul ran his finger playfully across Kaitlin's cheek. "Oh, babe, we're not discussing the past, remember? That was a horrible, unjust nightmare that luckily ended. We've opened a new chapter in our lives. The three of us together. As a free man, you know I'd be bothering you girls on virtual calls every chance I get from work. If they let me, anyway."

Kaitlin noticed her husband's voice had trailed off toward the end of his declaration. "What do you mean by, if they *'let you'*, babe?"

"It's nothing," Paul waved his hand across the air, his fingers drumming nervously against one another as they met. "It's just a super busy time at work. Forget it."

"But you've always been busy," Kaitlin insisted. "Is there something you're not telling me? Something troubling you at work?"

"No, I told you," Paul went on, biting the corner of one of his fingernails. "It's nothing."

"Is…any one— seen, or widely *unseen*— still visiting you at work?" Paul was avoiding her eyes, and Kaitlin wasn't liking the secretiveness of what she was sensing from her husband. She would never be able to forget how one of Finn's fellow cult members had apparently tricked Paul at work to implicate him in Linette's murder, and later visited him in jail.

"Not every problem has to be caused by fucking jinn in this world, does it, Kaitlin?"

What the hell was going on? Kaitlin's lips and body began to quiver in shock. "Whoa…I'm a little confused here, Paul."

Paul bit his lip and eyed her up and down. "You're not the only one who's confused. Have you considered that?"

"What do you mean?"

"I have a headache," Paul sighed heavily. "I'm sorry. Work was just a little stressful today, all right? Yes. You got me. I can't talk about this now, though. Please. I'm sorry. I'm going to hit the sack a bit early. I'll tuck Malin in too. Goodnight."

CHAPTER 13

COUNTING HER BLESSINGS THEY RESIDED IN A REGION OF Scandinavia aided by the Gulf Stream—where temperatures didn't feel as freezing in comparison to the other areas— Kaitlin still felt the need to shut the living room window she was gazing out of. It was mid-September, yet the Norwegian winds were already feeling January-sharp against her bare arms in her favorite white t-shirt.

Malin was rehearsing in front of the full-body mirror by the door. Her daughter had procrastinated until the last minute to practice the dance moves she'd be performing the following day, but Kaitlin couldn't stay angry with her for longer than a few minutes.

"Turn this song up, Mommy!" Malin took Kaitlin by the hands and began to twirl her.

"You've turned on the radio, sweety?" Kaitlin's gaze flicked upward in silent exasperation. "What happened to the song on YouTube? You have to repeat those precise steps with the beat! Especially toward the end."

She managed to air out her concerns right before caving in and allowing herself to enjoy the moment with her daughter. Lowering herself closer to Malin's height to help her 'twirl', Kaitlin fell down on her bum in doing so. It caused both of them to erupt in laughter.

As she stood back up, she noticed her daughter had her eyes closed and was now singing along to the familiar tune. Kaitlin had learned by now it was no use trying to get through to Malin when she was in such particularly high-energy moments.

"Let's take this step seriously, sweetie pie. You'll mess it up if you don't do it to the beat of the actual song for tomorrow. Mrs. Hansen might put you in the back row again!"

"But this one's more fun!" Malin exclaimed. She darted over to her mother's laptop, tapping a shortcut to crank up the volume—a trick Kaitlin hadn't even realized was possible without using the mouse.

"Hey! I just met you...and this is crazy...but here's my number...call me, baby..."

Kaitlin remained transfixed in place for a good minute. *Mon Dieu!* Wasn't this the song she was humming to herself on that fated day when she met Finn in the Stavanger woods? It hadn't been a hit in years! What were the odds of the radio now playing it now so randomly?

"Mallie: you won't believe this, sweetheart, but this song has been around for years!" Kaitlin was surprised to feel her eyes well up with tears that returned to her present moment. "I can't believe I have a daughter now who's also listening to it."

There was no way around the truth, even as much as she avoided admitting it to herself. Kaitlin wasn't sure if it'd been Finn, or the naivete of those earlier days- her optimism in honestly thinking she'd somehow been lucked out by fate to run into both a new professional and social opportunity in the woods. Regardless of the reason- she felt it. *The yearning.*

"I have to cook before your dad gets home," Kaitlin sighed, sinking onto the couch. "Just five more minutes, and then you're helping me crack the eggs again. Deal?"

At least I better not be cooking on our frigging anniversary after tomorrow, she thought, snickering as she shook her head. Since their morning conversation, she had begun cutting Paul some slack—enough to stop obsessing over whether he was planning a surprise for their big day, anyway. His behavior the night before had indeed been odd, but all he'd managed to share was that his boss had been acting colder since his jail term—a relatively short and undeserved one, but enough to stir gossip among clients.

"I feel watched," Paul had admitted in the morning. "Like I'm still there only as a favor for my years of service—not because they actually want me. They're still loading me with work- but more of the administrative stuff that the interns could take care of instead."

If that was true, Kaitlin had half a mind to call Lars, his boss, and his wife to smooth things over. She'd even suggested inviting them to dinner, but Paul had thanked her and said it didn't feel right at the moment.

At least he'd agreed to use one of his sick days to take off work for Malin's dance show and even suggested a family dinner afterward. Kaitlin knew Malin got fussy eating out, but she figured some kid shows could keep her entertained if needed.

It was cringeworthy now to think of her former self before becoming a mother—so quick to judge *those parents* who allowed their kids *too much screen time* to avoid playing with them. Not anymore. She'd learned that sometimes, screen time was all her child wanted- even when she as a mother tried to suggest other games. And if it kept her little one smiling instead of kicking and screaming in public- well, God bless technology, as far as Kaitlin was concerned.

He's still not saying anything about our anniversary. Kaitlin told herself to keep calm, and have a nice outfit prepared in any case. Maybe he truly was trying to keep his plans on the low and surprise her. She'd give her husband the benefit of the doubt this time. She figured he deserved that much at least.

"Upset about Finn, Mommy?"

Kaitlin jumped on the couch and cleared her throat. "Sorry, what was that sweety?"

"Because I know I am!" Malin continued, shrugging her shoulders though still observing her feet in the living room mirror whilst they practiced the ballet-like dance routine. She'd already managed to turn off the online radio channel and revert to the YouTube music video playing the melody that would be used in the actual show. Was it her, or had children evolved to becoming more adept with technology from a younger age than she and her brother had been growing up?

"Uncle Finn!" Malin responded to her mother's questioning look. You know. Daddy's twin? I just hate having secrets, Mommy! I'm sorry it almost slipped out. I really want to ask Daddy why he and Uncle Finn are not talking, though! It's not fair he's making me keep this to myself. I mean- they're *twins*! Isn't that supposed to be special? Like in *The Parent Trap*? Maybe they can make up!"

"Oh, yes…yes sweety," Kaitlin smiled at her daughter's reference to the children's movie they'd watched together. "But, like your Uncle Finn said: it's best we keep this between us. Your daddy had a big fight with him and…we don't want to upset him. At least for a while…"

"You told me that lying is bad, Mommy," Malin made click-clack noises with her tongue.

"Yes," Kaitlin started, unsure of how to explain herself. "It is. But sometimes, we must tell something called 'white lies'. Innocent ones, to ensure peace. Only temporary ones, too. Until problems get resolved. That's all."

"Hmm, I don't know. It's strange, Mommy. They looked alike, except for the hair. I mean, his hug *did* feel different. And his eyes. His eyes were bright green, unlike Daddy…"

A small, uneasy exhale escaped Kaitlin as she looked away from her daughter's imploring eyes. *Emerald-green, to be exact.* "Yes…" she stammered. "Not all twins are exactly identical, my love."

And not all white lies are so pure, or easy to excuse.

§

THE HISTORICAL SETTING OF GAMLAVÆRKET- ONE OF SANDNES' TOP-rated restaurants housed within a beloved hotel—evoked in Kaitlin a nostalgia for simpler times she'd only glimpsed in movies and literature. The cozy charm of the antique-shaped windows and doors was rivaled only by the heartwarming father-daughter interactions she now watched with a grin from across the table.

"I'm going to print out photos of you on stage from today and send them to *Nanna* and your aunties this week, Mallie!" Paul said, rubbing Malin's cheek with affection. "My princess looked even more adorable than ever today! Your cousin, Gigi, also started ballet classes in Montreal. Had I told you that?"

There went Kaitlin's visual pleasure as her auditory displeasure at Paul's words took precedence! Her eyes did a full lap around the room before landing back on him. If her eye-roll had a sound effect, it would've been deafening. Of course Gigi had started ballet classes, too, hearing that Malin had started them- go figure! She knew that Gigi's mother, Shana—Paul's sister—always felt the need to compete with Kaitlin for her brother's attention, often using her kids as a way to keep him focused on her. As if they hadn't grown into adults with their own families formed.

"Malin's dance routine was good, too, her daddy-dear, wasn't it?" Kaitlin darted a serious look in Paul's direction while cutting her salmon with her fork and knife. She was intent on raising her child as an individual- not yet another, unremarkable member in Paul's large extended family.

"Of course, of course," Paul smiled, letting out a small laugh that didn't quite reach his eyes.

"I want chocolate cake!" Malin exclaimed! "I've *earned* it at the show. Right, Daddy?"

"Right," he winked at her.

"You're going to spill it on your tutu," Kaitlin reminded her. Malin was still practicing eating neatly on her own. "Since you insisted on not changing into your regular clothes after the show, sweety, I insist we get take-out dessert for later, then."

Kaitlin had to admit they'd had a wonderful evening—the post-show dinner and the seaside stroll downtown by the North Sea had been perfect. Watching Paul and Malin's smiling faces as they both held their daughter's hands and swung her into the air warmed her to her very core.

Tucking Malin into bed well after her bedtime—after she'd eaten her triple-layered chocolate cake with the whip cream, as promised, of course— Kaitlin went into her closet to retrieve the black-lace nightgown with the spaghetti straps she had set aside earlier. Sure, their anniversary was technically the following night. But she liked celebrating events a little early. She glanced at the clock. Besides, midnight was approaching, and it'd soon technically be the 17th anyway.

Sliding on her high-heeled slip-ones and strutting into the bedroom, Kaitlin cleared her throat to capture her husband's attention. To her delight, his jaw dropped, and he put down his phone. "You look astonishing…"

"Happy anniversary, Paulie," Kaitlin walked closer and whispered into his neck, giving it a wet kiss before blowing on it. She relished her power to tickle him in surprising ways.

"I'm a lucky man," Paul cooed, holding her lower back and turning her face toward him. He gave her a lingering kiss on the lips. "But isn't our anniversary tomorrow? Impatient lady."

"Hmm, is there anything waiting for me tomorrow?" she smiled suggestively, bringing her nail-polished hands together before her. A chip at the corner of the nail of her ring finger with the diamond ring she'd put on caught her eyes. *He used to admire my hands.*

Over the years, the specific compliments had faded, replaced by more general ones about her being "beautiful." She'd learned to accept it. Her hands, stomach, and thighs no longer looked as smooth as they had a decade ago, but fair was fair—neither did anything on Paul's body.

"I guess I'll have to adorn your beauty tonight," Paul said, opening the bottom drawer of his wooden bedside table to reveal a navy-blue box with a scrunched-up white bow taped to the corner. "I hope you like it."

When she flipped the box open, a white-gold-plated butterfly necklace—with a diamond at its center as the body of the delicate creature—gleamed back at her. Kaitlin kissed him and cooed with delight. "It's so pretty. Thank you, baby."

Later, after managing to make love—a shorter session than the foreplay of suggestive talk sparked by dinner wine—they'd both drifted off to sleep. Kaitlin had only had a few sips, being the designated driver, while Paul—as he often did—had seemed to need more of an extra nudge to get in the mood.

The following morning had Kaitlin's internal clock waking her up half an hour earlier than usual. As she stirred, Paul walked back into the room from his morning shower, wearing only a towel. "Good morning, darling," her husband greeted her. Kaitlin smirked and reached for the towel, playfully tugging at it while bobbing her eyebrows up and down with implication.

With a soft chuckle, Paul placed his hand over hers, signaling her to 'stop' with any further sexual suggestions. "I have to drop by the office again for a little, babe."

"Oh…" Kaitlin said, letting her shoulders droop. "How about later? No dinner or anything else planned for us tonight?"

Paul genuinely looked like he meant business. Much to her dismay, he didn't appear to be playing into some *"just wait and see- it'll be a surprise"* sort of surprise, teasing game either, as far as Kaitlin could tell. "No, babe. Why? But let me know if you want to do something or go somewhere."

Twirling with her fingers the butterfly on the necklace she'd still had on when she woke up, Kaitlin lowered herself back under the covers. "Okay."

Buttoning up the striped work shirt he'd put on, Paul released a breath: part annoyance, part exasperation. He leaned close to give his wife a kiss on the cheek.

"Look, anniversaries are just another day, babe," he said. "All days with my girls are special to me. We don't need to buy into capitalist inventions. I mean, I'm not an idiot. I know it's our tenth, and yeah, it's a big milestone. But we just had a beautiful dinner last night—together, as a family. Isn't that romantic? Besides, didn't you say you wanted us to focus on spending time together as a core family?"

"I understand what you're saying…" Kaitlin managed a smile, despite a gulp in her throat.

"I mean, *I* don't understand," Paul continued. "What- do you not like the necklace? The guy said it was the most special diamond they had…."

"It's beautiful, no worries." Kaitlin attempted to force a bigger smile. "Really. Thanks."

"You're beautiful…"

"Thank you", Kaitlin repeated in response, the words feeling hollow. If only compliments and gifts were enough to make her feel happy. Happiness was always as close yet ultimately elusive to her as catching the exact moment the sun set each evening.

§

WIPING AWAY AN ESCAPED TEAR FROM HER CHEEK, KAITLIN FLIPPED open her laptop screen. The radio station website where Malin had played music the other day was still visible. She smiled. *I have to actually press 'shut down' if I don't want this technology to disappoint me, too.*

"…Before you came into my life, I missed you so bad…"

Fuck! The same Carly Rae Jepsen song was wrapping up. It was playing two, three days in a row? Could she ever believe in anything being coincidence, anymore?

Finn? Inexplicably, Kaitlin wanted to talk with him. Just be in his presence and have a conversation. Joke with him about the song coincidence. About how she was singing it to herself before first meeting him.

Would seeing her special friend make her feel better? Kaitlin scoffed at the idea. He'd likely see right through her, and of course- read straight into her thoughts. Finn would chastise her for only coming to him after her anniversary disappointment.

Kaitlin's heart started pounding as another thought also subsequently occurred in her mind. Had Finn seen them last night? Making love? Had he watched? She gulped. He'd insisted he couldn't see her, unless invited. He'd also said he wouldn't. Whether out of the pain of it, or just out of some sort of jinn-human or duty or boundary- Kaitlin hadn't a clue.

Then again, he sure had gone to pick Malin up from her dance class uninvited, hadn't he? Had Finn misled her, and been watching her this entire time?

Could she ever have any real privacy in her life? Forget the occasional sex with her husband— the frequency of which was so dwindled in more recent years that she could count the number of times they even touched each other in any sexual way during the course of a year with the fingers of one hand. What about when she was in the shower? Using the restroom? Just being her casual self, going about on her laptop at home? Occasionally touching herself? Or picking at her pimples or whatnot?

Eww. Kaitlin needed to talk to him- now! Yes! She'd channel him. And she wouldn't feel a tad bit of guilt over it, either. This was not because she'd 'missed him' or anything like that. No longer even just to chit-chat to him about the song and socialize, either. *Nope*. She merely had to get to the bottom of when he'd be seeing her exactly. She deserved to know that much. That's what she would do.

Finn, she closed her eyes, focusing intently to channel him. *Can we talk?*

It took about forty seconds or so longer than an instant like before— and, yes, Kaitlin had counted—but she let out a sigh of relief as the familiar sensation of slight burns in the hair follicles of her neck occurred. "Are you here?"

"Ms. Kaitlin?" Finn's voice resonated in her room first, followed by his sturdy silhouette, materializing from thin air. He was wearing his usual denim jeans with the black blazer that Kaitlin really liked to see on him. She could also make out the unbuttoned collar of his red and white plaid shirt underneath. "To what do I owe this pleasure?"

"I'm sure you know. You always just *know* why I want to talk to you, don't you? You don't have to act like you don't listen in and watch me all the time."

"Excuse me?" Finn sounded genuinely confused.

"It took you longer than usual this time," Kaitlin went on. She crossed her arms across her chest. "Busy day?"

"Um, yes, a little," Finn squinted his eyes at her. "What is it, Kaitlin? Are you all right?"

To her dismay, Finn wasn't sounding particularly warm or flirty—something she had grown accustomed to. So, she blurted out a question that had seemed to come out of nowhere the moment it left her mouth. "Were you with Meredith and Bo?"

Finn's mouth stood agape for a good second or two before he continued. "Kaitlin—I was with 'The Group'. I *do* perform actual tasks with our business, you know, as hard as I know you find it to believe at times."

"Right—tasks, yes, I know y'all also log for pulp mills and ship paper to companies," Kaitlin nodded. She cleared her throat. "Yes, but in all seriousness—and with respect—just how *is* Meredith? I'm curious."

"She's alright, thanks for asking," Finn shrugged. His casual attitude further fumed Kaitlin.

"You know…I once thought I could consider her a friend. She used to be so nice to me. After my shocking initial experiences with you guys- she'd call me and make sure I was alright, once upon a time. After I found out she slept with you, though... I guess now she can't face me, huh?"

"That's not fair…" Finn was shaking his head. "She's still fond of you, and just doesn't want to bother you. She knows you're trying to keep away from 'The Group'. She has nothing but warm words to say for you, always."

Yeah, right, Kaitlin thought. *Maybe she was indeed fond of me at one time— until her and Finn slept together*! However they would have done so- in whichever of their jinn forms- she had no clue, but Kaitlin didn't even want to think about that.

"Okay…I'm sorry, I didn't want to offend your fellow-jinn lover and the mother of your child."

"Kaitlin," Finn flashed close to her and placed his hands on her shoulders with concern *Sizzling.* Kaitlin leaned her face into his strong arm, bare through a short-sleeve, gray shirt. She turned her back toward him, causing him to embrace her from the back.

"You're not alright," His voice was sounding softer behind her ear. "Tell me—what happened?"

Kaitlin couldn't utter anything in that moment, allowing herself, instead, to relax into his hug.

I don't know what this is, God, but thank you for allowing his touch to feel real, at least. Even if he somehow isn't. Even if I've truly gone mad. Even if that's why I can't apparently discipline my daughter well, and my husband has already grown cold with me and I haven't even turned 40 yet, and—

"Shh, your thoughts aren't healthy," Finn turned her around to face him. He placed a finger on her trembling lips. A falling tear from her eyes reached his finger before her mouth.

As Finn took his own finger to kiss the spot where the tear had landed, he smiled into Kaitlin's eyes. She finally managed to smile as well.

"I'm sorry. You're right. I'm not doing too well today. I bet you're regretting coming here with my stupid talk. As if I have any right questioning where you are or who you're with. Right?"

"I'm just happy you wanted to see me," Finn whispered softly in response.

"I'm sure you know," Kaitlin wiped her eyes, and took in a deep breath. "I'm sure you've either seen it, or have intuited it. So, just say it. Yes- I was a little disappointed lately with Paul…But this isn't fair to you. I know. I can't just call you on a whim, only when I'm in need of some attention because I'm sad!"

"It's okay," Finn's fingertips grazed her cheek. "I'll take whatever I can get just to see if you want…whenever you want. No questions asked."

"That's actually what I wanted to talk about," Kaitlin spoke softly, swallowing some spit that had piled around her throat. "The part about seeing me: you'd said that you couldn't do so…unless I called out to you, or something…"

"I'm not some creepy voyeur." Finn's voice sounded stern and defensive. "I meant what I said- I only come to you when you call on me!"

Of course he must sense that's what I've thought. Kaitlin took in a deep breath before continuing. "So if that's true— how come you were able to visit Malin? *She* didn't invite you! Or, for instance- how was your friend from 'The Group' able to visit Paul at his office and later in his jail cell?"

"That's a bit more complicated discussion, Ms. Kaitlin," Finn sighed. "Let's just say— not all jinn interactions with humans exactly have to be 'invited', of course. But those only include ones for our mission, or initial meetings. The ones where we can physically get close enough- even to embrace or kiss as we have- do, on the other hand? For personal reasons? Those require an invitation. Yes."

Kaitlin cleared her throat. "Malin says you… hugged her?"

"And?" Finn exclaimed. "Are you trying to insinuate something sinister?"

"Oh, nothing like that- I trust you," Kaitlin welcomed the look of relief in Finn's face as she spoke. And for whatever unexplainable reason, she really felt in her she truly *did* trust him with Malin. "I just meant— how could that have *physically* happened, when she didn't *invite* you, then?"

Finn drew in a long breath, stretching his arms in front of him before folding them together behind his head. "Well I *had* to give her a little hug when I picked her up. That dance teacher was watching closely! I'm grateful Malin had her thick coat on and couldn't sense my additional warmth and react."

"Okay, but see? That's precisely what I mean! She didn't *invite* you, yet….!"

"Must I spell it out for you, Kaitlin!" Finn interrupted. "By physical closeness I meant…romantically…or sexually. In such ways- we absolutely cannot do so unless the human invites us. But regular, platonic physical contact with a human- one that can see us, that is, like Malin- *can* occur."

"Hmm," Kaitlin's forehead was still wrinkled in thought. "So, her dance teacher saw you, then…"

"Yeah- I'd scoped her out before during my preparatory research. I visited the dance studio to ensure that she could see me. She's a lonely, sensitive lady. Otherwise my plan wouldn't have been able to work out, and I'd have to create some other opportunity to hang out with Malin..."

"What does her being 'lonely' or 'sensitive' have to do with seeing you?" Kaitlin was genuinely confused.

"Let's not talk about these things," Finn spoke warmly. "Come, sit down." As he gently lowered Kaitlin onto the bed, he went on with a smile on his face. "Malin is the best hugger, that angel."

Way to change the topic, Kaitlin thought. But she didn't push it. She was in need of his company, and she realized she'd take whatever she could take, as well.

"Malin did notice your different eyes though," Kaitlin smiled.

"Malin talked about my eyes?" Finn's green gazers couldn't conceal the sentimentality welling up within him, Kaitlin perceived.

"Finn," her eyes shifted toward the ceiling. "She just questioned how yours could be green while your 'twin'— her dad's— could be darker. In all seriousness: can't you change your eye color too when you—*you know*—manifest yourself?"

"Anything can deceive....but the eyes, cannot, Ms. Kaitlin," Finn's eyes gleamed as he talked. "We can manifest ourselves as someone if we must, though it's very painful to do so if we have to in a swift manner. The eyes, however...really are the *'windows into the soul'*, as you humans have put it in your literature; we can't change those."

"Hmmm..." All Kaitlin could do was nod with a blank expression.

"I must say, though, I'm surprised, Kaitlin." Finn smirked. "*You* surely must have noticed my eyes in their extremely up-close form...before."

"Finn..." Kaitlin's voice grew stern. "I don't think you want to remind me of that night. Of that...*violation* in my home back in Stavanger, do you?"

"Whoa, there!" Finn's voice grew even more serious than her own. "Are you....still trying to imply that I...raped you, or something? Kaitlin..."

"Okay, okay, you can save it," Kaitlin held out her hand in front of Finn's face, as fear began to take over her being. "I wasn't trying to start anything...."

Finn gave a heavy, almost reluctant breath. "For the *gazillionth* time— you knew it was me that night, as far as I could tell..."

"Um, come on, *Monsieur Du Feu*," Kaitlin said with a forced smirk, folding her arms. "You could have, then, transformed yourself into your regular form if you had thought that was true, right? If you were so sure I recognized you and let the intercourse take place willingly— why would you choose to remain in Paul's form?"

"I didn't want you to be taken aback and scared at first!" Finn raised his voice. "But as soon as I came face to face with you, up close... you stared into my eyes, Kaitlin. You knew it was *me* and not him....I *felt* that."

"Just, don't show yourself to her again!" Kaitlin implored, a tear falling from her eye. "Please. I don't want her to become- *messed up*- in any way."

"*Shh*, I'm never going to let anything mess up Malin, ever," Finn spoke softly. His blazing touch ran across her cheek, caressing it.

Kaitlin released the rest of her long held-back tears, burying her face into his chest. "I don't want her to have to pay for whatever mistakes I may have made, knowingly or unknowingly, what I may or may not have allowed...."

"Hey, look at me," Finn's fingers softly grazed Kaitlin's shoulders. "I just wanted her and Bo to play. I never want to see little ones sad. Just relax. And trust the flow. Please."

"Mm," Kaitlin moaned, allowing her chin to rest in his palm. She focused her gaze on his skin, waiting for the sunlight to reveal any potential pimples or scratches that would be highlighted in a regular human. *Does he have any physical flaws*? *Nope*.

There was nothing but smooth skin. Nothing that she could perceive, anyway. Even the blond stubble Finn continued to support around his jawline appeared to be glued on in perfection- the hairs were so evenly distributed and without any hint of razor cuts. She knew by now he'd had lots of years on her, yet physically — he didn't appear a day older than her. His physical manifestation appeared—if anything—younger, in fact.

Her mind thought about the dimples on her thighs and stretch marks after her natural birth with Malin. She hadn't been intimate with him in his own, jinn-form to truly look at him close-up like that. *Not in the daylight anyway*, she supposed. Her mind was travelling to that night of intimacy back in Stavanger when Finn had first pretended to be Paul.

"Am I, *er*, done with my well-visit check-up, Dr. Kaitlin?" Finn chuckled, clearing his throat.

"Sorry, was I so obvious?" Kaitlin giggled, holding her face with her hands in exaggeration. "Argh, sometimes I hate how you can read my thoughts! Especially when I'm not particularly in control of them, and am just daydreaming in a natural state, like just now..."

"That's alright," Finn smiled, his firm hands gracing both her shoulders. He continued in a whisper. As he did so, the heat of his breath tickled her skin.

"Besides— even if I couldn't read your mind, your actions gave you away. Your eyes have been studying me up-close for the past minute. I'd had no idea a human minute could feel so long in silence."

"Well...maybe I just missed kissing you...and was just leaning closer for a kiss..." As soon as the words left her lips, Kaitlin wanted to slap her forehead. What the hell had come over her? If only she had the willpower to pull any part of her body away from his encompassing touch now.

"Anniversaries are just another day...."

Paul's voice was resounding inside her head. Kaitlin closed her eyes and clenched her teeth, letting out a breath to release the tension. Opening her eyes again, she stared right into Finn's own- as if latching on to his gaze would steady her as she was falling, sturdy as a rope.

Kaitlin licked her lips and inhaled deeply. She cupped her hands around Finn's chin in haste, and planted a deep kiss, sucking in his lips for dear life.

"Whoa…" Finn softly pulled his lips back just enough to whisper in a gentle moan. "To what do I owe this additional pleasure? Your calling out to me was heavenly enough."

"I…I'm sorry," Kaitlin stammered, feeling her cheeks burn- and not from her physical encounter with this gorgeous creature made up of fire energy before her, either.

"I'm so embarrassed. I think I just needed to feel you're real or something for a minute there. And not some figure of imagination- as perhaps my father was. I just wanted to thank you once again, and say, *hi*."

"Well, *hello*," Finn smiled his slick smile. "Hi. And you're….very welcome, indeed."

I love it, Kaitlin thought. Immediately afterwards, though- she shook her head. "Though, I know, I know. It's wrong…It's a sin. This is all wrong."

"A reconnecting kiss?" Finn made a confused face. "A sin?"

"*Sin*- yes," Kaitlin nodded, gulping in the heavy air around them. "Don't you see, Finn? I've been thinking. I think *sin* is a land I like to frequent from time to time, but I could never make my home there…" Kaitlin's tears almost froze on her skin.

"Have you been drinking from your little Bailey's liquor bottles again, Ms. Kaitlin?" Finn asked. "That was quite poetic....albeit a bit dramatic."

"No!" Kaitlin scoffed. She didn't like it when he'd remind her of how he'd found her with a little bottle or two that fated day on her hike when she could have sworn she'd seen her father. It wasn't as if she was an alcoholic!

"I've been writing. But mostly— I've just been thinking. A lot, in fact."

"You're always thinking," Finn began to shake his head. "Too much so, as I always tell you. And what existential dilemma are you turning this mutual enjoyment of the present and appreciation for this rare connection into this time?"

"Sin...," Kaitlin managed to get out again. "Finn— we can't."

"Interesting," Finn rubbed his chin as his eyes stared off into the distance. "And just what is *sin* to you? According to whom? What book? I mean, Lar's mostly had us read the Quran, but nowhere in there, nor in the Bible or the Torah does it mention love being wrong. Just advisement exists on getting married if two can do so, is all."

"Well- then, I guess: *sin*, according to whatever my conscience tells me isn't right. And whatever doesn't feel... light!"

"That rhymes, *Poetess*," Finn winked at her.

"We're from two different worlds," Kaitlin sulked her shoulders, rolling her eyes in exasperation. "Human, jinn. Married, unmarried...."

"Attempting to control the *future* versus grateful for living in this beautiful *present*...," Finn added, pursing his lips playfully.

"You forgot the *past*," Kaitlin smiled.

"Look, Kaitlin," Finn began, after winking at her. "God tells us 'sin' is merely going against the self. Against our most pure, natural selves— *that's* sin. God loves us and wants us to be happy. All his creations. *He* just wants us to do so without hurting anyone— including ourselves— and respecting and loving Him. That's all."

"This is too heavy, Finn," Kaitlin waved her hands around her face. "Okay. I think I just missed you, all right? And I needed to kiss you! To lighten up."

"*Miss you...just wanted to kiss you*, huh?" Finn bobbed his eyebrows up and down. "Cute."

"Finn, I'm serious," Kaitlin chuckled nervously. "This is all just too heavy to bear. I already carry quite a bit. That's what I uncovered in therapy…I…"

"Therapy.." Finn smirked, adding under his breath: "What do therapists know?"

Kaitlin inhaled and sat down. "I also needed to ask you something, Finn. What do you think happened to me on that mountain?"

"Kaitlin…I told you. I believe it's best we leave that experience behind us…I don't feel you're quite ready to handle…."

"No, it's okay," Kaitlin cut in. "Really. It's okay. Like I said, I'm talking to a therapist now. A good one. Sandy recommended her to me. She says repressing my experiences without closure from my youth and bothersome thoughts from my past haven't helped. I need to *talk* it out, and where I can't— to *write* it out. And I'm on this anti-anxiety pill. But I saw him…I know it doesn't make sense…but it was him. I wasn't imagining it…."

"I believe that you somehow…simply…missed your father, actually," Finn explained. "That's all."

Twirling the ends of her hair strands, Kaitlin considered it for a moment. "How can I miss someone I barely even remember?"

"Perhaps your subconscious does, and is unsettled," Finn explained.

Unsettled. Kaitlin shut her eyes, allowing the way that word was resonating to sink in.

"Look- if you must know- I did some research for you, Kaitlin," Finn continued. He cleared his throat and took in a deep breath whilst gently nudging Kaitlin toward her vanity table. "Please. Have a seat."

"Finn, what's going on?" Kaitlin's heart began to race as she pulled out her chair. Finn didn't talk until ensuring she'd settled in, situating himself across from her on her bed as he took her hand in his.

"After Dalsnuten, you know I was worried for you. I visited Canada. Your father's... *still out there*."

Kaitlin blinked, once, twice, as if she hadn't heard him correctly. Her breath hitched, and a shiver ran down her spine. "What did you say?" she whispered, her voice cracking like a splintered mirror.

"He's alive, but alone and...stuck," Finn continued, rubbing her fingers as his gaze awaited a return from Kaitlin's eyes. "He was never here in Norway. And there's no way he could have visited here, either."

"No," she stammered, her lips trembling. "That's not... that can't..."

Her voice broke, and she felt a lump rise in her throat, choking off the rest. Memories she had locked away for years resurfaced unbidden—her father's face from her one or two remaining memories from long ago flashed across her mind, shadowy and blurred, like the echo of a dream she couldn't quite grasp.

"You're lying. You have to be lying. Right?"

But Finn didn't flinch. The truth in his eyes struck her harder than his words.

Her mind was racing ahead, colliding with fragments of memory—dreams of a face she was sure she'd invented, whispers she'd dismissed as wishful thinking.

She stumbled back, her legs refusing to obey. "You're saying..." She trailed off, her chest rising and falling with shallow, uneven breaths.

The question she wanted to ask hung unspoken in the air. It was too dangerous to voice. Too much to hope for.

Finn met her gaze, his expression steady, impenetrable. The truth shimmered in his eyes, a mirror of her own fragile yearning. Kaitlin felt the room close in, the edges blurring, until there was nothing but Finn, his words, and the one name she'd been afraid to utter her whole life.

"But I saw him, Finn!" Kaitlin shook her head. Was Freya right-had she truly hallucinated hearing and seeing her father on the cliffs? "I mean, it's been years. We haven't been in contact with him. Aidan's been too proud- and my mother, too, of course. They say he may even be dead, with all that drinking. No- you must be mistaken."

"Kaitlin!" Finn insisted. "Zachary Ramsay—I saw him!"

The sound of her father's name coming from Finn's mouth stopped Kaitlin mid-ramble.

"What… what are you talking about?" she whispered, her voice taut. She couldn't recall ever mentioning his name.

"Yes, Zachary Ramsay —your father—is alive. He's in Ontario," Finn said evenly. "And he's not 'happily off with some other woman,' as you've been led to believe. Maybe at one point, but for a long time now, he's been in… a darker place."

Kaitlin's fingers tangled in her wavy hair, pulling tight. "What the heck is that supposed to mean? Finn, what did you find out? Tell me!"

"It's not my place…"

"Not your place?" Her voice broke, the disbelief slicing through her words. "You tell me everything! I've answered your questions—hell, you've *read* my thoughts when I couldn't answer. You owe me this! What did you mean about him not being able to visit Norway? Is he locked up? What's going on?"

Finn hesitated, biting his lip. "No, Kaitlin… not exactly. I'm sorry. But I've already said too much. This is between you and your family. Ask your brother. I should go."

Kaitlin recoiled, her arms dropping limply to her sides. "Oh, I see," she said, her voice trembling. "So, you're only 'there' for me when it's convenient. Or halfway, like this, *eh*? You know- I've accepted this—*whatever we are*—and still, when I need something from you it's *too much*?"

"Kaitlin, I think this is coming from your very real need to feel cared for and supported, which is valid," Finn said gently. "But I'm sorry I can't always be that for you."

"How is it fair that I've sacrificed my sanity for you, but you—what have you sacrificed?" Her voice cracked.

Finn winced. "Sacrificed?"

"Yes!" Kaitlin grabbed her scalp with the tips of her fingers, raising her voice. "My sanity! Didn't you say it yourself? That only 'sensitive' people could see your kind? Are you trying to imply that my mental health is the reason I can see you?"

"I…" Finn faltered, his gaze shifting. "I didn't mean it like that, Kaitlin. I've been here for you, accepted your boundaries, respected the rare times we meet. I didn't realize you saw it this way."

"You're avoiding the question."

"You're asking too many questions!" Finn's voice rose, a rare flicker of frustration breaking through. "Your mind is spiraling in so many directions I can barely keep up! That's why… I've realized— it's time for you to find out the truth. About your family."

"My family?" Kaitlin whispered, her heart pounding.

"Yes," Finn said, his tone softening. "Uncover everything. You're a natural detective—I've seen it. With Linette's murder, with Tan, with 'The Group'… you've always searched for answers. Now it's time to ask the right questions, and get to the root of everything."

"Questions?" Kaitlin whimpered.

"Yes," Finn replied with a sigh. "About your father."

Kaitlin's lips parted, but no words came. Finn leaned closer, his voice firm. "Ask your brother, Kaitlin. That's all I can say. Start with Aidan. It'll be quicker."

Kaitlin exhaled sharply. "Fine. I'll ask Aidan."

"Good," Finn said with a small smile. "And in the meantime, please try to relax. Think of something that makes you happy when your mind runs wild."

Kaitlin took in a deep breath, allowing his words to sink in. Maybe she was overreacting? Finn had just admitted to traveling at his jinn, warp-speed to Canada to look up her father for her after the incident.

"I'm sorry, Finn. I'm just still in shock. I know you were trying to help. I appreciate it."

"I'm used to your harshness," Finn teased, throwing his hands in the air.

"Malin's crazy dance moves," Kaitlin said after a pause, a small laugh escaping her.

Finn looked puzzled. "Sorry?"

"You said to think of something that makes me happy when I get a rush of anxiety like this," Kaitlin explained with a smile. Her face turned solemn as another thought occurred in her head. "I just hope my craziness isn't rubbing off on her—or maybe it's already in her genetics."

Finn chuckled softly. "Kids should be allowed to be kids. Malin will find her way, too."

How different his advice is from Paul's parenting style, Kaitlin thought.

"And for the record," Finn added, "I don't think you're crazy. Your society's judgments are shallow at best. The line between 'normal' and 'not' is far too arbitrary. Stop putting words in my mouth."

"Alright," Kaitlin sighed, a trace of resolve settling over her. "Time to call her uncle. He's apparently got a lot to explain."

"Yes, he does," Finn said with a grin.

Kaitlin chuckled again. "You know, it's funny. Malin's got the strangest uncles—one real one in New York, and one fictional one here in Norway."

"I'm not that strange, am I?" Finn blushed, stepping closer. "Just a tad… magical, perhaps."

"See you," Kaitlin said, swaying slightly as she clasped her hands behind her back.

"Au revoir," Finn winked, and before her eyes, his human form dissolved into the air.

CHAPTER 14

New York

TWO SPOTLIGHTS SHONE ON THE WOODEN STAGE PLATFORM, and Sandy was staying out of them as much as possible. Bjorn smiled at the self-effacing energy radiating from his human lover, watching her from his red velvet seat in the front row. He noted the leather flats on her feet with plastic bottoms—a wise choice to avoid making additional noise to the lines being rehearsed. Attracting attention from any potentially lingering staff or acting students, Bjorn knew, was risky. After all, Sandy didn't need to be viewed as talking to a seemingly empty chair in the audience.

Jimmy, Sandy's friend as well as resident stagehand at the downtown theater space with all the access codes, had allowed her to use the stage for an hour before her upcoming audition for *The Pretentious Young Ladies*. Sandy had suggested running lines with Bjorn in the privacy of her apartment again, but he had insisted it'd help her the most if she could practice now in the same exact spot where she would soon be facing the director. This was a make-it-or-break-it audition for her career, she'd divulged to him, and Bjorn knew she'd go into a prolonged period of despair if she didn't land this part. Desperate times called for desperate measures.

The beat in which she had taken a pause ended, and Sandy inhaled deeply before delivering her subsequent line. "*...To come out point-blank with a proposal of marriage- to make no love but with a marriage-contract, and begin a novel at the wrong end!*"

Sandy slowed her haphazard stroll, positioning herself to a halt centerstage, delivering her dramatic final line as 'Madelon'. Bjorn's smile met her glance. To his dismay, she smiled back— causing him to shake his head with disapproval.

"Once more, father, nothing can be more tradesman like, and the mere thought of it makes me sick...."

"Uh, Sandy?" Bjorn called out to stop her before she could complete her sentence. Standing up from the creaking audience chair, he pointed out a finger for Sandy to halt for a moment, looking around the small auditorium. *It's a good thing no one's here to see.* The poor woman wasn't getting any younger, and neither would she realistically be able to sustain a living on bartending and table-waiting alongside small gigs here and there; the entertainment industry was cruel, Bjorn knew.

Beaming next to her in a quick flash, Bjorn softly placed his hands on her quivering, sparkling chocolate-brown shoulders. "You cannot break character and make eye contact with any particular audience member at any time, Lady Liberty," he whispered into her ear. "Remember?"

"Oh, right, right," Sandy replied softly, chuckling excessively as she tucked her curly locks behind her ears. She closed her eyes and inhaled deeply. Twisting her torso to meet Bjorn's gaze again, he nudged her instead to face the empty seats. He'd promised to help her land this well-paying part, and he was intent on keeping it. Any intimacy could come after her practice time. Right now—Sandy had to stay focused.

"Relax, bae..." Sandy teased, whispering toward his heat, though keeping her face toward the audience as he'd instructed.

"I take your craft and my task seriously, bae," Bjorn kissed her subtly on the cheek. Their nicknames for each still had the power to turn him on—Sandy was different from all the predictable, small-town girls he was used to back in Europe. "This is not about us. Maintain focus on your character's goal in this scene."

"Okay, Coach," Sandy feigned a pout toward him and cleared her throat. "But wait—I'm saying these lines to my father in the play. So, shouldn't it be okay to say them looking at you? I mean— I can say them *to you*, pretending you're the actor who'll end up playing my father. Would that help?"

"No, love," Bjorn assured her. "Not these last two lines. They're major! The audience knows you've been talking to your father all this time as you've been pacing around. But you have to end this genius soliloquy by the great Molière directly to the *audience*!"

"Molière the Great, huh?" Sandy teased. "Did you know him in real life, too—my handsome but *older* jinn-lovah?"

Master Lar's crazy for thinking she can lead 'The Group' here, Bjorn thought as he dragged a hand down his face, settling on his mouth which he cupped with his hand. *A child-woman fledgling*, he thought. Possibly an aide: that's all Sandy could be for the NYC-based American branch Lar had had on his mind on for some time now. She wasn't mature enough in spirit to be a recruiter, in his opinion.

"I'm not *that* old, baby," Bjorn winked at her, before gesturing for her to take it from the top. There was no need to make her feel chastised now. He beamed back into his chair. "Action!"

Sandy rolled her shoulders and shook her arms about, taking several leaps in the air to get back into the play. Taking a deep breath in, Bjorn could see her countenance reflect the despair of the character in an instant. It was almost as if a switch were turned on inside of her.

She wasn't a bad actress by any means— he had to give her that. Bjorn had observed as much through the time he'd been traveling to the States to casually continue seeing this curious woman he'd first met back in Stavanger. Yet she'd had her self-esteem issues plague her once the theatrical spotlights— or a camera lens, as he noticed from her headshot photoshoots—focused on her.

Bjorn had also come to know the economic troubles Sandy had been facing as of late—troubles she wasn't even sharing with her best friend, Kaitlin Maverick. He was subtly keeping an eye on Sandy and Kaitlin's friendship, as she was his buddy Finn's recruit candidate for their brethren.

He'd come to feel sad for this beautiful young woman, orphaned at a relatively young age, and oblivious to her sweet charms. He wouldn't go so far as to say he'd developed romantic feelings for Sandy, per say. *Nah.* Bjorn wasn't like Finn. He knew damn well the strict lines that had to exist between their jinn realm and the human one—particularly outside 'The Group'. But he had surely come to sympathize with her struggles, and sincerely wanted her to make a living off of her talents and aspirations rather than 9-to-5 jobs that would only stifle a free spirit like Sandy Burns.

As much as he'd ridiculed Stig for years for caring deeply for his assigned human girlfriend, Nora, Bjorn could never feel as such for his own— Anja. It was why he'd lingered longer, instead, on his 'overseas task' of acclimating Sandy into being initiated into 'The Group' as a New York representative.

"Good heavens! If everybody was like you a love-story would soon be over..."

"Keep going— yes— but you have to be firmer, Sandy!" Bjorn called out. "You're upset with your father here, but also making an assured statement. Remember."

To his pleasure—Sandy listened but didn't break character this time to place her focus on him.

"Matrimony ought never to happen till after other adventures. A lover, to be agreeable, must understand...."

Bjorn let out a sigh of relief, relaxing in his seat as she wrapped up her audition monologue again. *Not bad.* Sandy was taking his directions in, but he knew the director of this particular play. A man named Steve Bernstein who had used the services of one of the girls from 'The Group' before—including Anja.

Bjorn chuckled. It was all work to both of them. But there were also no coincidences, he knew. Life was funny sometimes. Bjorn was simply meant to help Sandy speed up in performing at her maximum potential to impress a former client. He could extort Steve if he needed to. But Bjorn wanted Sandy to do this herself. And if Sandy's nerves got the best of her last minute, and Bjorn had to enter her being and possess her performance – he'd do it in a heartbeat.

§

AIDAN RAMSAY WAS AN IMPATIENT MAN, BUT HE FOUND HIMSELF waiting patiently in traffic as a mother and her twin-baby stroller passed his car at a turtle's pace— despite the light having turned green. He returned the woman's apologetic smile toward him, and cursed the car behind him for honking loudly. Didn't anyone have any common decency anymore? What was he supposed to do—run the woman and her children over?

Taken aback to see that the car passed him illegally anyway—with the driver flashing him his middle finger in doing so—Aidan actually found himself chuckling despite his rage.

"Alright, asshole," he spoke, alone in the driver's seat. "You win. Go to it—wherever you're hurrying off to— you lowlife excuse for a man."

Damn. Was it just him or was he growing softer lately? Aidan smiled. Ever since what happened with the young woman at work— his life had changed, that was for sure.

All of a sudden, Aidan was no longer a bachelor living alone in the city. And yet, no one could know about it, due to his company's policy regarding his supervisorial role over the woman in his life. How he was supposed to hide it from his sister and niece when they'd be visiting soon was still a mystery to him. Even more worrisome— how was he going to hide it all from his mother? The woman's sixth sense had been so keen that sometimes she could even perceive if a decorative item in a room had been moved around!

Aidan gulped. He mostly wanted to avoid having to explain himself. Autumn in New York was proving to have a warm wave of weather lately, but it was going to be a long, dark winter ahead for him with family stuff to deal with, for sure.

A ringing of his phone interrupted his ponderings as he stopped at another red light on his way to Wall Street. *Oh, it's Kaitlin*, he thought with a heavy breath. *She'd better not tell me they're coming sooner than in December, as planned.* He hadn't yet prepared.

Then Aidan had another thought. Malin, his little niece, had school— didn't she? He'd been looking forward to seeing her the most. Kaitlin wouldn't be as crazy as to actually take her out of school for some overseas trip, right? Besides, the holiday season in December was the best time to visit the city. *I think I may have grown paranoid.*

Aidan accepted his sister's call with hesitation, putting her on speakerphone. It was better to get this conversation over with now before he had to return to more pressing matters at the office.

"Baby Sis! What's up?"

CHAPTER 15

KAITLIN TAPPED HER LONG, UNTRIMMED FINGERNAILS ON THE phone screen, sitting on the bench by the Sandnes pier. Her gaze wandered, taking in the breathtaking Norwegian scenery, including the stylish, smiling passersby. She had just strolled along the harbor, and called her mother regarding the idea of the winter visit.

Linda had been thrilled— ecstatic even—about her daughter and granddaughter flying out. She insisted, in fact, on flying down to meet them in New York—relieving Kaitlin of the need to throw in an extra place to visit on the short break— and couldn't wait to reunite. But as always, Linda also couldn't resist letting her *concerns* slip into the conversation: *What did Paul do this time? Is Malin all right? Is Paul back in jail? Did he hit you? Is he cheating? Are you?*

The familiar interrogation lingered in Kaitlin's mind, leaving her feeling unexpectedly sympathetic toward her brother. The poor guy now had to accommodate three ladies in his apartment for the holidays—no easy feat for someone as undomesticated as Aidan. How would he juggle family time while sneaking in his endless flings? Kaitlin smirked, picturing the chaos.

She glanced at her watch. Two hours until Malin's bus would drop her off at their apartment door. This time, Kaitlin vowed not to get distracted or led astray by any of Finn's jinn or cult acquaintances in animal form—not after last time. *Focus,* she reminded herself. She *could not* be late to meet her daughter.

Her thoughts wandered back to last night. What had she been thinking? Calling Finn over and kissing him like that! Maybe it had been bravery, but it felt more like foolishness now.

Paul's words replayed in her head, just as they had before she'd kissed Finn. His voice, sharp and wounded, had cut through her thoughts like a knife. *"You're not the only one who's confused..."*

What was up with him? Was it his boss's apparently dismissive attitude since his jail release? His colleagues' icy stares? Silent pressure to resign? Kaitlin had so many questions Paul refused to elaborate on with his short answers. She inhaled the strong, salty scent of the North Sea, letting the waves soothe her fraying nerves.

Oh, well— someone else has some questions to answer. Kaitlin picked up her phone and dialed her brother. "Tell me the truth for once in your life, Aidan," she demanded after their initial pleasantries wrapped up. "About our family."

The silence that ensued stretched long enough to make Kaitlin doubt herself. Finally, her brother spoke. "Did you wake up today determined to bombard me with drama, Kaity?"

"Don't dodge the question," Kaitlin pressed. "What are you not telling me about our father?"

"First, you ambush me with this visit—now this?"

"Oh, so your sister and your niece visiting is something that'd burden you, is that it?" Kaitlin inquired. "Fine! I'll ask Sandy for a place to stay, no sweat. Or, better yet, I'll look in to some hotels. Don't worry your busy head, *big businessman*!"

"Oh, stop, drama queen," Aidan giggled playfully, to Kaitlin's pleasant surprise. "You know I've missed your crazy ass. Love you, and Malin already. I'm happy about the visit! Truly! But you're asking me about our family history on the phone— it's making me think you have ulterior motives for coming out here! What are you— leading some investigation? What's brought this on?"

"My *sanity*, Aidan," Kaitlin snapped, lowering her voice. "That's what brought it on. You, Mom—both of you. You treat me like either a delicate princess or a useless idiot. I'm done. I'm asking *you* first. Tell me about Dad!"

"What *about* Dad?" Aidan's voice quivered.

"Is he alive or not?" Kaitlin pressed. "I could have sworn I saw him out here several years ago, and I never thought to mention it to you until now. If he is alive—do you know if he ever visited Norway? Are you in contact with him?"

The pause this time was shorter, but Aidan's tone carried a hint of panic. "Someone's told you something? I don't know what's brought this on now, but you couldn't have seen him over there, Kaity."

"Oh, so you *do* know where he is!" Kaitlin exclaimed with a squeal. "*Merde*! He's alive and well? Spill! Where is he?"

"Kaity…" Aidan began with a heavy breath. "I'm driving to work over here! Why don't we discuss this when you come here, eh?"

"Please, Aidan!" Kaitlin begged.

"Alright— yes, I do, Kaitlin!" Aidan proclaimed. "Happy? I know where he is. Yes—our father is alive, though unwell…"

"Not well…how?" Kaitlin's mind raced even faster, recalling Finn using the same terminology to describe Zachary.

"Wait…give me moment," Aidan exclaimed. "Let me park in my spot. I just arrived at the office."

"I'll wait," Kaitlin spoke as her heart sank.

What could possibly be so 'unwell' about their father? Was Zachary trying to reach out to her? Did he need her now, as she'd needed him all those years? Being torn between her empathy and anger was paining Kaitlin to her very core.

"Alright, so, are you seated?"

"Yes!" Kaitlin couldn't wait any longer.

"He's…in an institution," Aidan went on, audibly taking in a gulp of air. "Just north of Toronto, at the Waypoint Centre."

"What?" Kaitlin's voice cracked as the word escaped her lips, barely audible. Her mind struggled to process the statement, the world tilting as if the ground beneath her had been yanked away. "Isn't that the mental institution by the Georgian Bay?"

"Yes," Aidan spoke softly.

Kaitlin shook her head, her breath quickening. "Why's he there? Mom knows, too, doesn't she? Oh, *mon Dieu!* Why have you guys been keeping something like this from me?"

"Of course, she knows," Aidan said. "But we agreed to spare you, and you never asked. You also had enough on your plate. Between Mom's meltdowns and you dealing with your 'amazing' husband…"

"Aidan!" Kaitlin bristled. Paul was hers to criticize—not anyone else. Yet, as usual, she found herself defending him. Regardless of all their issues.

"We didn't lie," Aidan continued. "We just… omitted the details. Dad wanted it that way, too. He was ashamed. He told us that it was too late with regards to us, as we'd already discovered him. But he didn't want you to see him like that— as a failure. 'Loser' was the exact word he used."

"But you could've told me!" Kaitlin's voice trembled. Tears spilled down her cheeks, her pulse roaring in her ears. "He's my father, too! I deserved to know! I would have liked to know!"

"I thought I could restore him back to health first, at the clinic where he is," Aidan's voice sounded calmer now. "Just so you know—I haven't been able to visit as much as I used to before moving here to the States. For a while, it had seemed like he was improving. We were going to tell you once he had fully recovered. But the nurses have been telling me he's regressing again. He, *um*, has his cycles."

"He didn't have to be in perfect condition for me to get reacquainted with *my father*, Aidan!" Kaitlin exclaimed. "It would have been nice just to see him..."

After a moment, Aidan continued. "*He* has asked us not to tell you, too, Kaity. Didn't you hear me?"

"Oh, please!" Kaitlin exclaimed, her chest tightening. She couldn't believe what she was hearing.

"I'm serious! He insisted, in fact. He didn't want you to be impacted negatively. That is— on the seldom occasions he was improving and cognitively himself and rational enough to even discuss such things."

"How *did* you discover him, by the way?" Kaitlin removed her face from her phone just enough to check. She still had time to talk. *Good.* This would all indeed be better discussed in person. She knew that. But too much had already been revealed, and she needed to know more. Maybe this impromptu New York trip she'd gotten herself into truly would be for the best.

"That's a whole other bag of worms, and an even longer story," Aidan continued with a sigh.

"I'm all ears." Kaitlin tapped her fingers nervously on the empty beach seat next to her, as her feet followed suit on the concrete ground. What in the world was her life lately, with so many mysteries unraveling themselves ever since she met Finn in the woods nearly a decade ago?

"I ended up having as a client a half-uncle of ours, Zachary's half-brother," Aidan continued a minute or so later. "Turns out— the two of them grew up estranged from each other."

"Estranged...," Kaitlin repeated, frozen in place.

"So, get this," Aidan continued. "I'm driving him one day, and I tell him I'm originally from Canada, as well, since he reveals to me he misses 'back home' already and then answers when I inquire as to where that is. He tells me he recognizes my last name—and asks if I know a *Linda* Ramsay! Our mom! What are the odds, right?"

"You still *chauffeur*?" Kaitlin asked with a raised brow. She knew that's how her brother had started out, but as far as she knew Aidan now had other employees for that. Just how much had her brother been keeping from her?

"I was stepping in for one of my men, Kaity," Aidan said with frustration. "Let's not steer from the matter at hand, here. So, anyway, this guy, John, tells me that he'd met mom once as a young man when she and our dad had come knocking on their door one day as newlyweds."

"Knocking on whose door?" Kaitlin asked, squinting her eyes. "This John guy and his family?"

Aidan's voice had a small tremor as he agreed. "Well, yes—John and his mother. Zachary apparently wanted to show solidarity with his mother after discovering the affair going on behind her back, and Mom went along for support."

"Solidarity with…Grandma Mabel?" Kaitlin asked. Her paternal grandmother had passed away when he and Kaitlin were just teenagers, and they'd been told their grandfather had died way earlier when they were little.

"That's right, Grandma Mabel," Aidan continued with a heavy sigh. "Apparently Grandpa Robert was a bit of a *playah* with the ladies—and was seeing John's mother on the side, though he was married to our grandmother! Mabel discovered he had opened up a whole other house for them after his mistress gave birth to John!"

"Oh, damn," Kaitlin yelped, subsequently chuckling to herself-more to relieve the shock and stress. She added in a giggle. "Now we see where you get your womanizing ways from—Grandpa Robert."

"*Haha*, very funny," Aidan mocked.

Kaitlin couldn't believe her ears. She needed to draw a family tree or something if she was ever going to get anywhere with all the information being thrown in her direction! Regardless, she had Finn to thank, she supposed, for catalyzing this at least.

"What else do you know about this half-uncle of ours—this *John*?" Kaitlin asked, adding with a lump in her throat. "And I'm confused—how does *he* connect to your discovery of Dad and his condition?"

"John runs a successful software company and visits New York and Chicago often," Aidan continued. "When we discovered our little 'small world' moment, we went out for drinks. He told me about how his mother defended herself to Zachary. Saying she didn't know Robert was still married when she began their relationship, and so on and so forth. But our dad kept harassing John's mother, apparently. Blaming her, as Robert's mistress, of causing all the stress of his now broken family that led to his… double life, causing his conditions and becoming institutionalized and stuff."

"Oh my God…Aidan….wait, wait, wait…" Kaitlin shook her head. *What the hell? Forget the cheating!* Was *this* something in her bloodline she had to worry about? "Grandpa Robert was *also* institutionalized?"

"I know, Sis," Aidan said mournfully. "It's crazy to even think about, isn't it? I asked John when he last heard from his father, Grandpa Robert. And even from Dad, for that matter…"

"Go on…," Kaitlin pressed him to continue after his voice trailed off.

"That's when he told me," Aidan's dolorous voice was almost a whisper. "John apparently didn't receive much support from Grandpa Robert any more than Zachary did when he was growing up, as he was diagnosed with *schizoaffective disorder* soon after Mabel left him."

"Schizoaffective disorder…," Kaitlin managed, shaking her head. The ground beneath her feet felt as if it could crumble at any minute, and swallow her whole.

"He was kept at the psychiatric center for years," Aidan went on. "It's apparently a rare combination of both schizophrenia and bipolar disorder. And when John went to visit his father, Robert, during his final days, he was surprised to discover yet another family member that was also later admitted as a patient there."

"Our father," Kaitlin understood in a feeble voice.

§

"YOU STILL THERE, SIS?" AIDAN FELT A PULL ON HIS HEARTSTRINGS with the silence coming from his sister on the other line. This couldn't have been easy for her to uncover all at once. Lord knew it'd taken him a good while to come to grips with everything himself!

"Do you think Dad inherited his—*err*—ailments, from his father before him, then?" Kaitlin finally asked.

"We think so," Aidan nodded, wishing now his sister could have seen their father as he had. How long had it been that he'd buried this family secret inside him? How freeing it was now for him to finally get it off his chest. Sobriety after AA meetings for years had also helped him get his act together— but nothing worked as fast as responsibility had.

He was beginning to be grateful Kaitlin had come up with this planned visit to see him after all! *My own secret can wait*, he thought. *All in due time.*

"Grandpa Robert died at the hospital," Aidan continued. "That part we'd all known about growing up, as you know."

"Well, yeah," Kaitlin said, pursing her lips. "We just assumed it was 'old age' stuff that had had him in some typical hospital. Not a *mental institution*! And Dad— what's his diagnosis? Has his treatment helped? How long has he been there?"

"It hasn't helped..." Aidan chose his words carefully. He didn't want to upset his sister any further with all the details. Their father's scary switches between two different personalities. His paranoid and sometimes even violent accusations of everyone around him— including even Aidan during one visit— claiming they're trying to trap and hurt him. He shut his eyes and held the tears in.

"Maybe you should visit him if you end up going to Canada too on your visit out here across the Atlantic?" Aidan couldn't believe the suggestion was coming out of his mouth, but he was now realizing that perhaps seeing their father again would help Kaitlin, too, as it had helped him— especially as she had found out the truth, anyway. And through her own vision or whatnot, according to what his sister had just relayed! How crazy life was!

"You think you can maybe do a quick solo visit to Mom's soon? Like in October maybe? You know Thanksgiving is coming up there."

"Aidan, I can't leave Malin and she has school…" Kaitlin reminded him. "I wish you'd had settled down with kids already so you could finally get me. I'm unable to be so mobile."

Settled down, Aidan scoffed. *If only she knew*. How ironic life was. And how his sister could manage to sound like their mother sometimes. He cleared his throat. "Right, right. Well—you'll visit whenever you can, I guess. If you want to, that is."

"How's his behavior….exactly?" Kaitlin pressed on.

"Dad? He gets extreme manic episodes, on top of paranoia. But the nurses are usually able to have us wait in the waiting room until it's a suitable and relatively safe time."

"Wow," Kaitlin managed to whimper. How Aidan wished he could hug her across the telephone.

"Yeah, little sis. You have to read the full report. I'll send it to you, now that you know. I was surprised. Explains some things, actually. How we both, I suppose, inherited his thrill-seeking obsessions in life…though you more than me. Do you remember Mom telling us about his random, scary motorcycling adventures?"

"Yes, but speak for yourself!" Kaitlin answered him in a feisty voice. "I've settled into a boring marital life. Look who's talking! It's surprising *you* still haven't been on that TV show you guys watch over there. Sandy watches it all the time. *The Bachelor*? *The Bachelorette*?"

That's the spirit, Sis. Aidan liked to hear Kaitlin sounding like her usual, defensive self again—despite her judgmental assumption about his life shifting his mood. His eyes shot downcast on the floor. "Right, right."

"I'm just teasing, Aidan," Kaitlin stated. "Hey—are you okay? Did one of the ladies break your heart or something? Talk to me…"

"*Or…something*," He stammered. "Enough about me. If you come, you'll see in person."

"See *what* in person?" Kaitlin sounded genuinely confused. "Dad?"

"Well, everything," Aidan said with a sigh. He always knew his mother and sister would discover the truth about his current life eventually. It'd been a miracle he'd been able to keep his mother away from his home in New York lately, in fact. *I guess it was always going to be Kaitlin to find out first.*

"I meant that…we can talk. I can get you up-to-date with Dad, my love life, all of it…."

"*Ooh*, okay…" Kaitlin muttered, her voice taking on a slightly playful tone. "Are you dating someone seriously for once? Holy cow-Aidan, how much have I missed out on over here?"

"Patience is an underrated virtue, Kaitlin," Aidan teased. "You'll see when you come here."

"So, you're *sure* Malin and I can stay a bit with you in December?"

"Of course, Kaity," Aidan went on. *She doesn't trust me.* He supposed he only had himself to blame for his lack of communication sometimes. Had he been able to be there for his mom and sister as much as he could have? How could he—though—when he'd had so many of his own demons to deal with? One thing he knew for sure was this: he could not afford to turn out like their father had.

"Mom suggested visiting you for *Noel*, too," Kaitlin continued. "I just spoke with her before calling you, actually. We can all be together in the city with you for a while. We have to talk about all this in person!"

"Oh, did she?" Aidan scoffed. *Oh, boy*. "What's Paul got to say about all this, by the way, Kaity?"

"Aidan, didn't you hear me?" Kaitlin asked. "Mom also wants to stop by. What do you think? Would that be…?"

"If I can handle you, I can handle Mom, Kaity," Aidan smirked, silently praying that could be true. "So…Paul?"

"Oh," Kaitlin began. "Paul is…preoccupied with work, as always. He won't mind. You know— I was even thinking Malin could improve her English over the winter-break, and possibly even French. Her Norsk has gotten native-like here, as you can imagine. Heck, perhaps even an entire semester in Toronto or New York won't hurt either, down the line."

"Whoa— you're considering staying beyond a winter break?" Aidan couldn't believe what he was hearing as he interrupted his sister. "An entire school semester? I thought it was just two weeks or so!"

"Don't worry— we'd find another place to stay for a longer-term, if need be, somehow," Kaitlin said with sorrow in her voice. "Anyway— it's just a possibility. You know. We have to go with the flow in life. I have to think about Malin's education and well-being. If anything, I just meant for when she's older, that's all."

"Why do you think such a 'need' may even be a possibility?" Aidan asked with concern. Was his sister contemplating divorce or something? What the heck was going on?

"Kaity—Are you guys okay? Tell me the truth. The Paul I know wouldn't be 'cool' for you to visit for a prolonged time like that. How long have you guys been together now? Nine…ten years? Though, I've got to be honest— it always seemed more like a platonic arrangement than some big romance, but regardless…"

"It's just a consideration, big brother," Kaitlin cut in. "And Paul and I are cool—I was just thinking it may be good for Malin, that's all. Socially. But just what did you *mean* there, with what you said about my marriage?"

Aidan groaned, his eyes performing a dramatic sweep skyward. "I still remember your wedding, Kaity. The guy didn't look into your eyes once— even during the dance his kiss was theatrical…rehearsed."

"Um, Aidan?" Kaitlin asked in an exasperated tone. "It *was* rehearsed. Nothing unusual about that. Come on-- lots of couples rehearse their wedding dance..."

"Well, yes. But during the actual day wouldn't they be more emotional about it? Even his vows were robotic—despite the deep words about you *rescuing his wrecked ship*, or something like that. Did he even write those vows himself?"

§

CLOSING HER EYES, KAITLIN TRAVELED BACK TO THE MEMORY OF HER first glance at herself in the mirror as a bride. It was a beautiful, breezy, warm evening on September 17 in 2011. Right before she'd stepped out of her bridal room and joined Paul at the altar where they had said their vows.

"You are my mermaid, Kaitlin," Paul had spoken, holding her hands and staring lovingly into her eyes, while everyone else's eyes were on them. *"I'd been batting the stormy waters, about to sink in my secluded ship and go overboard when you saved me. Rescuing me from a lavish but dull existence in a Scandinavian paradise..."*

Kaitlin took in a deep breath, and shouted into the phone. "Of course Paul wrote them, Aidan! It was ten years ago almost exactly, actually. I remember distinctly. And since when did *you* become Mr. Romantic? How come you didn't tell me all this back then if you were so concerned?"

"I don't know, doll," Aidan continued. "I've wanted to believe my sister was finally happy. You'd been through so much and I really wanted to believe marriage would be the best decision for your life. I just remember the dude had been more preoccupied with attending to the guests while you twirled in your beautiful dress mostly by yourself or with your friends...."

"You remember my wedding dress?" Kaitlin snickered. Something was definitely up with her brother. Had he fallen in love with someone, and envisioned marrying her, or something?

"Wait; you mean you just had your tenth-year anniversary?" Aidan cut her thoughts. "Wow! A congratulations is in order, I suppose. It's been ten years, eh? How did you guys celebrate?"

Kaitlin found herself releasing the tears she'd been holding in. *My father. My marriage.* Everything she thought she knew for sure was suddenly a source of confusion for her.

"Kaity?" Aidan asked softly. "Oh, shoot. Something happened, didn't it, Sis?"

"It was *terrible*, okay! There. You happy...?"

"What did he *do*?"

Aidan's voice was almost as angry as that time Kaitlin could still recall when she'd been nineteen. Her brother had found out how the star quarterback of her university team had forced himself on her and almost raped her—until she screamed and pushed him hard enough to get herself away. She hadn't told anyone and hadn't intended to—until she caught mono, 'the kissing disease', from the bastard.

"*You could fool Mom with the 'allergic reaction' excuse, but you can't fool me, Sis,*" her brother had told her during her weekend visit home. "*Who the hell gave you this yucky thing on your face? I'll punch the living daylights out of the asshole.*"

"No, no nothing violent or anything like that, Aidan," Kaitlin went on with a smile. She was hoping her sustained gratitude to her brother for that—despite years of various moments of being disappointed by him as well—could be discernible through her tone of voice. "I know you're always looking out for me in your own way. Thank you."

"Of course," Aidan responded assuredly. "So what did you mean, then?"

Kaitlin took in a big gulp of air. "I just meant it was horrible in that, well; I spent the entire day of our anniversary crying to myself…hugging my daughter—grateful for her, of course. But I felt alone…so alone…"

"He *forgot*?" Aidan guessed.

"Not technically…I mean he did give me a lovely necklace the night before. After the dinner we had as a family..."

"Oh," Aidan said, befuddled. "Alright. Cool. So— what was the problem?"

"Aidan—the entire day, he ignored it, and didn't even plan a night out for just us two! He used to wake me up with little notes by the coffee machine when he went to work."

"*Um*, Kaity? "Aidan interrupted her. "Okay, I don't want to sound like a macho, but I'm afraid I'm going to have to give this point where it's due to my man Paul over there. You ladies sometimes exaggerate these things. If he remembered and got his present, then, okay—I'll give the guy some slack. What were you expecting, little Sis? Fireworks? Besides, you guys are parents now. Who was going to watch over Malin if you two had gone out alone? Didn't you tell me you haven't found any babysitters you like over there?"

Good point, Kaitlin had to admit. But then again—Paul could have at least considered it, and asked if she could arrange some babysitting, as far as she was concerned. It would have shown added effort—and interest. That would have helped to make her feel better. Wouldn't it?

"It's not about a present or big event, Aidan! He's supposed to know me by now! He knows I'm impatient and will become like a little girl around my birthday or our anniversary. We'd even celebrate our kissing anniversary and such, for Goodness' sake! And he knows I always like to make an entire day of it…."

"Sis, I've got to go!" Aidan spoke quietly into the receiver. "Sorry, I have to take this other business call. Do you want me to call you back?"

"Oh," Kaitlin sulked. "No, that's okay. I'll talk to you later. Thanks for listening…and sharing. But you still owe me!"

"Okay, you let me know if you need me, alright? Can't wait to see you girls soon!"

Kaitlin sighed and hugged her body closer for warmth after their conversation ended. What the heck had her life come to? First, she'd seen what had appeared to be like some ghost of her father on the Dalsnuten cliffs. An incident even Finn had felt sorry for her for—enough to research her father to help. A jinn 'friend' who then decided to also visit her daughter! And now— Kaitlin just found out her father was apparently alive and in some mental institution rather than living happily ever after with another family. Let alone all that craziness with her late grandfather, too! Not to mention some mysterious half-uncle!

She didn't want to face whatever could possibly happen next. Whether it was aging or just a lack of enthusiasm: she wasn't feeling the energy, nor the strength. Was Finn right to imply that her medications may not have been helping her? Kaitlin considered for a second whether she'd forgotten them that morning. *Nope.* Her mind recalled the trouble she'd had, in fact, with opening the cap that morning. She'd taken them, alright!

Should she start exercising again? Like she used to do with Sibel? Maybe another friendly coffee date would do just fine to help her feel better. She checked the time. Stavanger was close enough to Sandnes for a quick snack or drink. Was her friend available to hang out for a bit? Although she was sure Sibel would be lecturing with some spiritual stuff again, Kaitlin couldn't help but smile as she typed her text message, inviting her for a quick catch-up session.

For a moment, she hesitated— unsure if she should call Sandy instead, or Freya.

No, she finally decided. *I need some company, in person!*

Kaitlin had just found out too much. She needed warmth from a friend she could trust— a human. She supposed she had to prepare herself for religious lecturing from Sibel, but it was still worth a shot.

Licking her lips and inhaling the crisp sea air once more, she pressed 'send'. Whatever she could get to feel better again, and replace the sunken feeling in her stomach and soul with—she'd take it.

CHAPTER 16

SIBEL'S VOICE WAS MELODICAL AS SHE TOOK IN THE AUTUMN AIR next to Kaitlin, eyeing her surroundings. "Sandnes is just as pretty as Stavanger, girl, though perhaps a bit quieter?" Her thick, dark brown hair was pulled back in an unruly ponytail, accentuating the Burberry scarf wrapped around her neck. An exotic Turkish-accent in her English was faint but still detectable.

This is nice, she thought. Even an hour spent outside of the house felt good. After Kaitlin had invited her out, Sibel had agreed to drive over to meet her as soon as she could. Kaitlin had visited her much more often already— and she wanted to return the favor. Their kids were in school, and Sibel knew Kaitlin couldn't really afford ruffling any further feathers with Paul by letting him know she'd be visiting Stavanger again. And here she'd thought Turkish men tended to be more controlling!

Sibel's eyes met Kaitlin's in a forced smile. There had been enough stress at home with her husband, Engin— and his brewing political troubles in their home country of Türkiye. But she didn't want to think about all that now. Instead, she allowed herself—as she usually did—to keep her private life hidden, and immerse herself completely in Kaitlin's drama, instead. It helped somehow to ease her own.

"Yeah, Stavanger has a bigger-city feel, particularly during cruise season and all the tourists," Kaitlin retorted, biting into one of the delicious homemade pastries with dill and cheese Sibel had brought over for them. "Thanks again for coming on such short notice. I truly appreciate it."

"You bet," Sibel said, placing a hand gently on Kaitlin's lap for comfort. Her friend had quickly filled her in on the family drama that had just been revealed to her. Sibel wasn't certain she had understood all the details correctly— it all sounded like a Turkish soap opera to her! But she also knew that life tended to be stranger than fiction— just as her own drama she was facing with her husband that had left them both unable to return to their homeland in fear.

"I still can't believe your father is alive after all, but in a mental institution," she continued.

"I suppose I always knew of the possibility he was still out there somewhere," Kaitlin's eyes were focused on the ground, shoulders depleted. "His death wouldn't necessarily have become public record easily uncoverable by Google or anything, but somehow we would have heard of it from someone who knew someone and so and so forth, you know? I'd just been assuming he'd completely forgotten about us and was focusing on some new family."

"Does he?" Sibel asked, raising an eyebrow. Upon seeing Kaitlin's confused face, she went on. "Have another family as you guys suspected, I mean?"

"Hmm, that's a good question," Kaitlin answered, wrapping her arms closer around her wool coat. "Aidan didn't say anything, and I didn't ask. What I heard was shocking enough. But I don't think so. My mom swears to have seen him around with some floozy after he left us— but who knows if that particular woman remained in his life long enough? I mean— where would he have had the opportunity to get a serious love interest and father another child from *the institution*? You know?"

Sibel nodded, hoping her smile came off as reassuring to Kaitlin as she'd intended. "Do you think it'll make you feel better when you visit him?"

"*When*?" Kaitlin inquired. "I haven't even decided yet *if* I'll see him. Mom doesn't even know that I know yet….as far as I know, anyway. Besides—Aidan told me Dad explicitly instructed them not to tell me about his condition. He was alive, and in communication with everyone but me, it seems! That makes me double angry somehow!"

"I understand, but you *have* to see him, Kaitlin, or you'll always regret it," Sibel reminded. "Our parents aren't getting any younger. A father you'd long assumed to be out-of-touch, or even potentially dead…here he is! Imperfect, and with questionable choices— maybe. Yet *traceable*, apparently— no wonder you hallucinated him on those cliffs!"

Kaitlin's ears perked up. "Do you suppose that was a mini-psychic moment for me, Sibel—like a vision? Or did you mean 'hallucinated', as in, a psychological breakdown? Maybe psychological issues are in my genes, eh?"

Sibel's heart melted as she saw a tear fall from Kaitlin's eyes onto her fingers, where she was staring. "Hey, it's okay. I told you! It happens. Whatever the reason—a lot of the human brain remains a mystery to this day. I'm surprised you didn't hallucinate or intuit him *again* after that, actually!"

Kaitlin darted her eyes toward the clouds, as if trying to remember. "I mean, I *did* have a couple of dreams with him in them, where he didn't speak a word. Mom used to say that seeing the deceased silent in one's dream usually means direct communication or a visitation by the actual spirit. She used to tell me that about her seeing my grandmother often as such. But there goes that theory, I suppose, since Zachary is apparently still alive!"

"Zachary— was that your father's name?" Sibel asked, to which Kaitlin nodded. It'd been a long time since she'd been living in Norway, yet she still couldn't quite get her mind around how comfortably westerners referred to their family members by name rather than other more respectful terms for elders as she was accustomed to.

"I once could have sworn I'd seen Johnny Depp at the mall!" she went on. "The guy had the same style of hat and the facial hair and everything. But at second glance— the guy had disappeared! And we both know I gratefully haven't seen any jinn or anything, girl! So far, so good, anyway!"

Kaitlin smiled as Sibel pulled the bottom of her ear lobes and knocked on the bench three times—a Turkish superstition for protection, she'd long been introduced.

"Don't even get me started about the jinn, Sibel," she rolled her eyes, biting into another chunk of the pastry. "A part of me is thinking maybe I've even encountered them somehow for *this* purpose, girl. To somehow be catalyzed to find out about my dad…"

"Catalyzed," Sibel considered, pursing her lips. "Perhaps. Whatever it was: I think you need to see your father while you can. It could be good for his health, but mostly do so for *yourself.* I think life is giving you guys this second chance, and you need to use it."

"Finn," Kaitlin went on with smiling eyes in a daze. "You'll never believe this, but he's the one who actually encouraged me to question Aidan about all this! He had looked into my father for me. Out of concern for me on the cliffs."

"Kaitlin!" Sibel snapped, her voice sharp with anger. "You promised me you wouldn't be keeping in contact with him anymore! Have you not seen how dangerous the whole thing is?"

"Oh, I haven't meant to!" Kaitlin's words fumbled out in desperation. "Sibel— please believe me! He quite literally brought himself back, hanging out with Malin after her class!"

"*What*?" Sibel froze, shaking her head in disbelief.

Kaitlin slumped her shoulders. "I guess I couldn't hold it from you forever. I mean, I knew you were going to judge me for it, and I can't blame you…"

"*That* was why Malin's teacher called me, wasn't it?" Sibel stood up abruptly from the bench as she put the pieces together. "I knew the whole thing was too strange to be true! When you told me that all was 'fine' —even though I'd just been called as an 'emergency contact!"

"Malin's okay, girl," Kaitlin attempted to assuage her friend's frustration. "Please, sit down. And trust me—I gave Finn quite a piece of my mind and warned him never to hang out with her again!"

"Wasn't the poor thing scared?" Sibel asked softer now, slowly sitting back on the bench. Children were innocents, and the idea of a jinn being visible to them under normal circumstances befuddled her beliefs. "How could she *see* him in the first place?"

"He— *um*—manifested in human form as her father, and then went on to convince her he was… get this: Paul's long-lost twin."

Sibel burst out laughing. "Excuse me, I'm laughing out of anger. What the …?"

"Fuck?" Kaitlin finished the intended curse. "You can say it!"

"Yes, what the *fuck*?" Sibel asked, blushing. "The audacity of him…"

"Tell me about it," Kaitlin shook her head. "Malin bought it, though, and it's under control. For the moment at least…"

Sibel nodded and turned her attention back to the savory, *börek* pastries. W*hen will I actually be able to feel like I have everything under control, as everyone thinks I already do?*

Kaitlin turned her whole torso toward Sibel in the quiet that followed. "Sibel, I've been so caught up in my father and all the Finn drama, I don't think I've asked how Engin's case is going. I'm sorry. Any improvements in the situation back home?"

"The case is… going, I suppose," Sibel replied with a heavy shrug. Her eyes met the concrete ground. "It's incredibly unfair. They're prolonging everything in the courts on purpose. They know there isn't any real evidence of any crime or wrongdoing, but that doesn't matter—it's all political."

"I'm so sorry," Kaitlin said softly, biting her lip. "I don't even know what to say. At least you're here, together, without the risk of them locking him up for nothing."

"Yeah," Sibel looked up, attempting a smile. "I miss the way things were back home, though. Before everything changed with all the injustice. I guess it's easier sometimes to hold on to the past."

"I get it…" Kaitlin nodded. "Sometimes I think I've been holding on to the entire Finn thing all these years because it's been flattering. I mean, we're not in our twenties anymore, girl. And we're mothers now."

"Being mothers doesn't take away from our womanhood, Kaitlin," Sibel said, her shoulders rising and falling in a weary motion. "We're still young, if you look at the larger picture of life. But the excitement of Finn made you feel even younger, perhaps. I get that."

As Kaitlin's eyes drifted off into the distance again, the wind that had picked up was beginning to graze Sibel's cheeks and she was beginning to wonder whether they should find some indoor seating somewhere. *They won't let us in with our outside food, though,* Sibel sulked.

"He was the last one who felt like—I don't know—like he had developed this crush on me and was pursuing me relentlessly, or something," Kaitlin was continuing. "Like a boy in high school."

"Uh oh," Sibel sneered. "Don't remind me of high school. I can't imagine our kiddos as teenagers. I don't even *want* to think about which little classmates may have crushes on our children now, let alone anyone potentially creepy down the line!"

Kaitlin chuckled, playfully nudging Sibel's arms. She took a big gulp from her takeaway coffee cup. "Sibel…can I ask you something? You believe in God, right?"

The cup with tea in Sibel's hand quivered, her arched brow shooting up higher on her dewy skin as she turned to face Kaitlin. "Sorry?"

"I mean, I know you do," Kaitlin mumbled, hands moving erratically around her torso as her head shook to follow suit. "*Duh*, to me! Of course. We've talked about these things before. Sorry. And you know I do, too. It's just that— you've shared a lot about your faith with me…about the jinn kind, and our own humanity. And now, getting into some things with Freya…"

"Freya?" Sibel asked.

"My therapist," Kaitlin reminded her. "But…oh, I'm not even sure what to quite ask or what exactly it is I'm trying to uncover…"

"It's okay, Kaitlin," Sibel's voice eased as she went and sat herself closer to Kaitlin. She wrapped the paper towels back around the Tupperware she'd used to bring the snacks she'd prepared. She hoped they would still be warm enough to serve after she'd comforted one of her friend's anxieties again.

"What's on your mind, specifically? It's okay to have questions— it doesn't make you 'bad', or even a non-believer, or anything like that. It just makes you a thinking human."

"Okay," Kaitlin said matter-of-factly, clearing her throat. "How can God allow for *evil* to exist in this world?"

"Hmm," Sibel murmured, her gaze shifting to a few passersby. The question caught her off guard. Where was this coming from? Had her friend finally started seeing things clearly? After years of trying to convince Kaitlin that Finn wasn't good for her—evil or not—was *this* the breakthrough?

"It's a complicated question for sure, Kaitlin. Why? What's particularly on your mind?"

"Well," Kaitlin began hesitantly, her fingers fidgeting with the butterfly pendant on her necklace. "Your comment implying child predators too earlier got me thinking. I mean, with everything going on in the world—I just feel like I'm worrying more and more every day. I don't want Malin to ever get hurt. Yet I also know that's not possible.

How much can we really protect our children, you know? Ultimately we can't extend ourselves to everywhere at once."

Sibel nodded, though she wasn't entirely sure how the connection tracked. "I get that," she said cautiously. "Anyone can do anything at any time in the world we live in— some have a higher proclivity toward evil but the possibility is inherent in us all. The way I see it, though, is this: life on Earth is full of opposites, right? Day and night... pleasure and pain..."

"Paul and me...." Kaitlin muttered, causing both women to smirk with a smile. "I think I see what you're getting at, in terms of nature requiring a *balance* and all?"

"Well, yes," Sibel pursed her lips as she inhaled. Her eyes fixed on a spot across the walkway. "But it's more than that, Kaitlin. It's about *the test."*

"The test?" Kaitlin asked, folding her arms across her chest.

"The test of *faith,* with which, I believe Allah—God, our Creator—wants to assess us at the end of our lives on earth."

Observing Kaitlin's puzzled countenance, Sibel snapped her fingers and continued before her friend could get in another question.

"For instance: consider something we all know as fact, Kaitlin. Something like, I don't know—a math equation. Two plus two. We know it equals the number four. Right? We know it mostly because we memorized it as such during childhood, but we can also *physically* place two sets of objects in pairs, and then count them all to see that two and two make four. And with that *visible* proof before us— we don't need *faith* to *know* that sum to be true."

"Right," Kaitlin was nodding, leaning back against the bench.

"But we *don't see* God, and we don't have all the proofs in the world. And I don't believe we were ever meant to know the meaning of it all. Not on this realm, anyway. Precisely for our faith to be tested."

"Interesting," Kaitlin considered.

"God loves us," Sibel continued. "We are like His children —although not in the human, procreative sense of the world, for we don't believe He has 'begotten a child' like many Christians do. That's even in the Quran, in *Surah Al-Ikhlas.* Surahs are like..."

"Chapters, sections—right?" Kaitlin nodded.

"That's right," Sibel's face lit up. She wasn't some ideal Muslim woman, or anything, and hated risking being seen as some expert on the subject, or even as some morality police! So whenever Kaitlin seemed to connect with her and showed interest in what she shared—whether or not she agreed with Sibel's unique world schema and perspective or not—it warmed her heart.

"Very good, Kaitlin! Anyway— we're His children but just symbolically so."

"I grew up with these ideas as well, Sibel," Kaitlin assured her. "I know we have differences in Islam and Christianity about this matter of paternity—where you guys don't believe Jesus was God's son but rather an important prophet—but, once again, how can our Creator allow for such suffering? Rape, torture, child abuse? I can't even speak some of these things that come to mind...just looking at the news..."

"Yes, Kaitlin," Sibel said, concern in her voice. Her friend was sounding more and more pessimistic by the minute. "I know that part is terrible. We believe that innocents die sometimes as martyrs, whose souls are promised a better place. But it's precisely where I think I've been trying to get at. It must also be a part of *the test*. I believe we're meant to see the concept of 'hell' as some sort of preview on earth—like a trailer of an upcoming movie, in a way."

"A movie trailer," Kaitlin crossed her arms. "Wow— that's an interesting way to look at it."

Sibel beamed. Maybe it was reading one too many books while being a homemaker all these years in Norway, but she sure had thought about this, and was glad to have made a friend she could delve into such topics with rather than merely maintain quotidian chit-chat about the weather or gossip.

"I believe we are shown both extremes on earth—both heaven and hell. We are shown destruction, in order to truly be able to value peace. We see *hate*, to value *love*. If everything on earth were idyllic—we would be in Heaven, and we wouldn't be humans; humans with free will to choose…to have their faiths tested. Sometimes a preview of hell is self-inflicted, through the painful consequences of our choices."

"Jinn also have the freedom to choose... don't they?" Kaitlin's question lingered in the air, drawing a faint, knowing smile from Sibel. It was clear who was still on her mind, much to Sibel's quiet frustration.

"They have the freedom to choose between right and wrong? Between whom they…love…or, I mean, you know, between whom they express affinity towards and…"

Sibel sighed, part in empathy and part in exasperation. She placed a hand gently on Kaitlin's shoulder, the smile on her lips tinged with sadness. "Yes, they do. In the grand test of life— *in choosing from the choices destiny has bestowed upon us, we're all essentially as free as birds.* And yes, Kaitlin... I believe Finn chooses as well. And I believe he does love you in his way. As…inappropriate as it ultimately is."

"You must think I'm truly insane," Kaitlin murmured, her gaze dropping to her lap. "You don't see them the way I do... and Paul? He only saw that one jinn when he was in jail…as far as I know, anyway."

"My faith teaches me they exist, Kaitlin," Sibel replied gently. "So who am I to question what's been revealed to you, just because it hasn't been revealed to me? And honestly? I wouldn't want it to." *Allah korusun*, she recited in her mind. *God forbid.*

"Oh," Kaitlin sulked. "It's a bad sign if a human has been shown one, then, huh? A jinn?"

"Well…" Sibel knew she had to tread carefully. Particularly as it'd just been revealed to her that a little girl, too, had seen Finn, for goodness' sake!

"Not necessarily. I mean— perhaps there is something the human needs to recognize through his or her acquaintance with one? It doesn't necessarily have to mean something negative regarding the seer. I'm not too sure, to be honest."

A falling tear from Kaitlin's face signaled to Sibel to switch the topic to more calming aspects.

"Now— Paul may have seen one in jail, if what he says is true- for he was, I can imagine, feeling lower than low there. This tells me you may have been seeing and experiencing much further, perhaps, for the purpose of your *soul* in need of more healing still…."

"Healing…" Kaitlin agreed, her stare blank. "Yes, I may subconsciously need more healing."

Sibel smiled and patted her friend's back softly. "I hate to talk about the topic of religion more, I mean— I'm not some expert. But maybe praying could help?"

"Maybe," Kaitlin pursed her lips in consideration. Her thoughts went to Freya's suggestion. "Or, perhaps meditation could? Or writing..."

"Perhaps," Sibel smiled.

"Don't worry, girl," Kaitlin reached out and patted Sibel's arms. "Malin and I will be alright. Besides— I've almost gotten that *Ayat-al-Kursi* from the Quran you shared with me entirely memorized, if things ever get to that point."

"I'm glad," Sibel winked. She'd done all she could do to help her friend. Introduced her to religious clerks to talk to if she needed to on top of the prayers to ward of the jinn for good. It was all she could do— as it wasn't as if they could go to the police and complain of being followed by some invisible jinn!

Merve. The thought of the jinn-troubled former coworker in

Istanbul she'd lost touch with years ago would always plague her, Sibel knew. But perhaps life had given her a second chance as well. Unlike Merve, Kaitlin swore she wasn't having a romantic relationship, and that it was mostly a 'mutually-beneficial friendship' between her and Finn over the years. That's how she'd coined it, and there was no further warning or insistence Sibel could sustain after a certain point. She'd given her new friend the tools she needed, but ultimately— it was only Kaitlin who could help herself.

Sibel took in a deep breath and tried to shake her head to rid her of all the negativity of the entire topic. Kaitlin had suggested they head back home, and was accompanying her back to her car now. As they strolled, her gaze latched onto the sparkling jewel adorning Kaitlin's neck.

"Now— tell me about his gorgeous necklace? *Oh, la la!* A present?"

"Yes," Kaitlin smiled playfully, caressing the butterfly. "My anniversary gift. We've been married for ten years, can you believe it?"

"Congratulations!" Sibel smiled. Her expression shifted. "What did Paul say about your father situation when you told him?"

Kaitlin's cheeks reddened further than her nearly porcelain skin had already been with the chill in the air. "I haven't."

"You haven't told him what you discovered about your father?" Sibel started getting a queasy feeling at the pit of her stomach. She didn't like the idea of a secret being shared between Kaitlin and a jinn before her own partner.

"He would ask too many questions," Kaitlin shrugged. "I was thinking of telling him after our trip. I still want time to process all this on my own first, you know? Even Freya doesn't know yet, Sibel."

"What can I say?" Sibel attempted a smile as she got in her car. "I feel special, I guess."

§

THE FOLLOWING MORNING, KAITLIN FOUND HERSELF WAKING UP IN bed with one singular thought: she needed to write. Her website had gone neglected for weeks, sidelined by the chaos of Finn's visit, the tangled mess of her anniversary with Paul, and—most recently—the seismic revelation that her father was alive and locked away in a mental institution!

"Oh boy," she muttered, brushing her hair back. "Freya's going to have a field day with this during our next session."

Sibel's words were reverberating around the hallways of her mind. *"In choosing from the choices destiny has bestowed upon us, we're all essentially as free as birds...."*

As they did so, verses began to form in her conscious, almost unbidden, weaving themselves into a pattern of rhyme. The phrase stirred something deep within her, and words began forming, like a melody struggling to escape.

Her laptop awaited, its screen still glowing from a half-finished Word file left open the night before. She stared at the blinking cursor for a moment before her fingers began to type.

you long to choose, and be chosen
freedom is not a gift that can be given

the cage opens,
and you're asked to fly with clipped wings
expected to be the one that sings

Kaitlin drew in a deep breath, sipping on her hazelnut coffee as her nostrils savored the aroma. For a brief moment, she shut her eyes, wondering where Finn could be at that precise moment. Opening her eyelids, her fingers traveled back to her keyboard—typing out the melody of her heart like a pianist playing a musical one.

my bird…
I knew the day would come

the day you'd want to finally be free
for I could not promise you a nest

not out of choice
but out of responsibility

"Writing poetry again?" Paul's voice startled Kaitlin, sending her fingers jolting away from the keyboard.

"What's that? Oh, yes—it's, um, for the blog," she stammered, trying to shake Finn from her thoughts. Lately, poetry had become a way to manage the emotions she couldn't say out loud. Butterflies churned in her stomach as Paul hovered behind her, his breath warm against the nape of her neck.

"Romantic," he spoke after skimming over her shoulder. "Who is this one about?"

Kaitlin sighed, her irritation simmering "Paul, please don't start. It's *art.* Neutral, and to-nobody-in-particular. Just art. Freya says art is therapeutic."

"Oh, *Freya says*- does she now?" Paul retorted. His tone carried a slight edge.

"She does," Kaitlin replied, a bit sharper than she intended. "And, actually, Sibel thought Anine might pick up some of these poems for her music as song lyrics. Imagine that—my words on the radio!"

Paul snorted, crossing his arms. "Right. And what's next? Maybe you'll become a singer too? A duet with Anine, perhaps?"

Kaitlin turned to face him, biting back her irritation. She tilted her head. "I know you're joking, but...what if that happened? Would it bother you?"

"You?" Paul smirked. "A singer? Kaitlin, you're an educated woman with years of marketing experience, a successful entrepreneur, blogging whiz and a mother. And you want to *sing*?"

"No, I don't *want* to," she shot back. Then, softening, she smiled faintly. "But if I did, would that be so crazy? I mean, you just called me a successful entrepreneur. That's something nice to hear, by the way. Thanks for that."

"Baby, don't I always compliment you, and mean it?" Paul raised an eyebrow, his warm brown eyes traveling down her figure.

"Yes," Kaitlin cooed, twirling her hair exaggeratedly. "But calling me 'beautiful' isn't the same as acknowledging something I've achieved."

Paul bit his lip, his tone subdued. "Noted, I guess."

Kaitlin, sensing an olive branch, decided to share another poem. "I'm seriously inspired by random things throughout my day, babe. Look at this one—it's about birds again. And trees. Tell me what you think."

She opened another Word file, her fingers hovering before she cleared her throat and read aloud.

how little you make of the cut…
annihilating the proud, rooted tree with your machine
before which it remains humble and powerless

seen as a nuisance
for the garden's landscaping
removed for convenience…
its extinction excused with
'brittle twigs, sparse flora'
'ours' for the taking

until you miss, one day
the shade it provided

and the songs it once brought forth
from the birds now left homeless

how you only now call it 'beautiful'
after you've ruined it

significance of 'insignificance'
no such thing in life…
as permanence

"Ta da," Kaitlin turned to face Paul, beaming.

"Nice," he muttered. "I like the environmental message."

"Thank you," Kaitlin said with a shrug.

Paul leaned back against the counter, crossing his arms. "Sounds like this one's influenced by real life, at least. You always get worked up when people cut down trees in their yards."

Kaitlin raised a brow but decided to let his curious comment pass. "Right."

"So, about that first bird, though," Paul continued, pouring himself a glass of water. "Who's it supposed to be? You? Someone else?"

"Paul," Kaitlin groaned. "Art includes universal metaphors. Haven't you been listening to me?"

"There's a bit of truth in every fiction," Paul quipped. "You feel trapped here in Norway sometimes. Admit it."

"Maybe," Kaitlin sighed. The admission hung in the air like a storm cloud, heavy and charged. His directness had struck a nerve. Maybe this was her chance to get things off her chest.

"Sometimes, yes. But it's not that simple."

"It's never simple with you, is it?" Paul retorted.

"Look, I thought I deserved this lovely, settled life—for agreeing to it, for choosing it. And don't misunderstand— I'm very grateful!"

"But…" Paul rolled his eyes and twirled his hand in the air, encouraging her to go on.

Kaitlin softened her tone. "But…I don't know: sometimes I feel like I'm paying, *penance*, somehow."

"Penance?" Paul's jaw dropped. "As in—punishment? I thought we were past all that… jinn nonsense! After my jail experience—I've tried to move beyond the bloody creeping feeling of some hunky jinn-man possessing my wife's body! It has not exactly been a walk in the park for me to have to deal with the fact that…"

"Paul," Kaitlin interrupted, heart racing. "This is not about *that*. That's beyond us. Please. It's about…*choices*. And paying the price for my *haste.* Maybe I should've stayed in Canada, kept my job, and saved up. We were friends for a while but dated ever so briefly. Maybe we shouldn't have rushed into marriage so quickly—"

Paul's voice broke, trembling. "Are you saying you regret marrying me?"

"No—not exactly, no—"

"Wow," Paul mouthed the word with his mouth nearly as wide as his shocked eyes.

"Paul—please listen, for once!" Kaitlin pleaded. "I'm talking from my heart. I do not have any agenda! No rehearsed speech for you—please stop trying to trip me up!

Paul plopped down on the sofa and released a loud breath, slapping his thighs with the palms of his hands. He shifted uncomfortably. "I'm not trying to make you feel boxed in. I just don't want you to forget what we've built together. Our family. It's solid."

"Solid," Kaitlin echoed, turning the word over in her mind. Was it? Their foundation had felt more like quicksand lately, each step sinking her deeper into questions she didn't want to ask. "You're right. We've built something. But sometimes I wonder if I've let too much of myself get lost in the process."

Paul frowned. "Lost? You have everything, Kaitlin. A beautiful home and environment, a thriving business, a family that loves you—"

"And yet I feel incomplete," she interrupted, her voice firmer now. "I can't explain it, Paul. Maybe it's just a phase. Maybe it's nothing. But writing...it's helping me figure things out."

He studied her, his brow furrowed as if searching for the right words. "Do you...feel incomplete with me? Or is it something else?"

She opened her mouth to answer but hesitated. How could she explain that it wasn't about him—or at least, not entirely? The weight of her father's secret, the strain of holding everyone else together, and the questions Finn's reappearance had stirred all churned inside her.

"It's… complicated," she finally said, dodging his gaze. "And I don't know the answer yet. I think it may be stemming from my family roots."

Paul sighed, pushing off the counter. "Well, let me know when you figure it out. I'm heading down to the garage. The car needs…"

"Wait!" Kaitlin shouted. "*Kismet*…."

"Kiss?" Paul asked. "Kaitlin, I don't exactly feel like kissing you right now—"

"No, silly," Kaitlin said, walking slowly but assuredly toward him. "*Kismet.* It's derived from *destiny* in Turkish."

Paul inhaled deeply, placing his hands in his jean pockets. "Destiny? Great. So now Sibel's teaching you philosophy too?"

"Paul, stop. She's my *good* friend. And for once, I'm trying to say something meaningful here."

Paul exhaled loudly, clearly uninterested but gestured for her to continue.

"Maybe… maybe we weren't ready *when* we got married," Kaitlin said, her voice trembling slightly. "I'm not saying it was a mistake, but—"

Paul cut her off, his tone sharper. "But what? That you regret it now? That I'm some sort of… detour on your way to *finding yourself*?"

Kaitlin clenched her fists, the tension rising like a wave crashing against her resolve. "That's not what I'm saying! I'm saying... maybe we didn't know ourselves fully back then. Maybe we still don't."

"We're not children, Kaitlin," Paul fumed. "Speak for yourself! I know my damn self and what I want— and have always wanted. Thank you very much!"

Kaitlin took a couple of steps toward him as he walked off toward the opposite side of the living room. "Think about it, Paulie. Maybe we were destined to marry after a *longer* dating period of getting to know each other, and maybe even ourselves, more. And yet we both rushed it, perhaps? Just to ease the long-distance issue?"

"Is this what you and Sibel talked about?" Paul stopped his pacing abruptly and turned around to face Kaitlin head-on.

"What?" Kaitlin raised an eyebrow. "No, we didn't talk about you. It was good for me to catch up with my friend. Something wrong with that?"

"No," Paul pursed his lips. "I'm just beginning to think maybe I've been in the wrong for encouraging your friendship with her. She may be nice and married and relatively more stable then, let's say, someone like Sandy, for example. But she's filling your head too much, don't you think? And that husband of hers is no picnic either…"

"Oh, what did *Engin* do now?" Kaitlin inquired as she threw her head back with a huff, her eyes following suit. She'd long grown accustomed to her husband's tirades of her choices— in professional endeavors, clothes, in friends…

Friendship on fire.

Kaitlin shook her head as his voice echoed in her mind, reverberating despite it being nearly whispered into her before their scorching embrace on the cliffs of Dalsnuten. *Damn it, Finn!* Why did he always have the craziest timing? *Get out of my mind! Stop!*

"He's always running his mouth about his crazy dreams and aspirations for retirement in their native country at every game we attend!" Paul plopped down on the sofa, picking up the daily paper. "Filling me with his negative energy about how backstabbers have stolen his dreams and stuff like that."

Kaitlin couldn't believe the words coming from her husband's mouth. Why was Paul picking on Sibel's husband all of a sudden? Was it a way to deflect criticism? Freya had suggested from what she'd relayed to him about their relationship that her husband's personality tended to be 'avoidant' in its attachment style and resorted to such things at times.

"You know he's just nostalgic for his homeland, Paul. Come on now…there's a warrant out for his arrest, for crying out loud! And he hasn't done anything!"

"Exactly!" Paul intervened. "Lord knows what he did to deserve it, Kaitlin. I mean, how well do we even really know these people? Maybe he really did commit some crime there, who knows?"

"Whoa, now hold on, there!" Kaitlin dismissed his baseless accusation, waving her hands before his face. "We've been through this. It's some politicized witch-hunt for dissidents in the country, with that authoritarian president the country's got cracking down on…."

"Cracking down on opponents for some coup attempt against him several years back, yeah, yeah," Paul scoffed. "That was—when—like, back in 2016? It's been… how many years now? If he was clean, he should have been free to visit their country during their summer vacations by now."

"Their president is still in power, Paul. *You* of all people should have sympathy for the guy! Come on, now! Did *you* deserve it when *you* were thrown in jail? When people thought you were an actual murderer?"

"Touché… " Paul lowered his voice after some consideration. "Okay—so why can't Sibel return with the kids, then? If her *husband* is the one with the political issues…"

"Maybe because she's *his* wife? Apparently, they presume

people to be guilty before any evidence, even just by association over there…"

To her surprise, Paul smiled. "You know— you should have studied *Law*, instead of *Marketing*. Lots of collegiate majors are growing obsolete these days, actually. I was reading about this in the paper the other day. Malin definitely needs to pick a worthwhile major…"

"Why did you say that?" Kaitlin folded her arms. "About studying Law?"

"You're defending Sibel and Engin so well, that's all," Paul shrugged.

Kaitlin clenched her fists, fuming. "Paul—what do you suddenly have against them?"

"Nothing!" Paul exclaimed. "It's just—well, who knew that Sibel, seemingly a nice married lady, could be filling my wife's head with religious stuff or cultural mumbo jumbo that could actually take her farther from me…?"

"Paul!" Kaitlin interjected, grabbing the paper from his hand as gently as she could. "The woman said nothing against *you* personally! She drove out here yesterday just to meet me for an hour- and she even made me take home some of her pastries for you and Malin. They're in the fridge."

"Lovely," Paul deadpanned. He added a wink. "Well, she's a good baker. I'll give the lady that. I do like how she's getting you to appreciate the kitchen a little bit more at least."

"Oh, stop," Kaitlin's eyes slid upward, and she let out a small groan. "By the way….as *kismet* means 'destiny'—let me give you an example. And by example, I mean a total random one—so don't get ideas in your head."

"Ideas in my head," Paul repeated with a smirk. "You're warning me in advance, aren't you?"

"If you and I were 'meant to be'…destined to be," Kaitlin went on, ignoring his comment. "Perhaps our paths still could have crossed at any other time in our lives, too!"

"What the heck are you talking about?" Paul was shaking his head.

"Take our age difference, for instance," Kaitlin went on, unstirred. "And your expectations from me when I was barely in my mid-twenties. I was never into cooking and cleaning like you'd always expected from me—but now I'm naturally doing those things on my own. Right? And I'm actually enjoying them. Motherhood has likely matured me as well. So…maybe…I married you before I was fully ready to be married— period? Just to be married? With it not having anything to do with you, personally!"

"You've really thought about this," Paul walked over to the window, gazing out whilst he bit his lip.

"Babe…" Kaitlin began, walking over to him. She noted that his anger had transformed itself into something else entirely.

Paul was clenching his fists and releasing them. "All because I didn't schedule some separate romantic dinner with some stupid candles or special music or whatnot for just the two of us without our daughter?"

"*Shh*, the therapist just says to express everything out, Paulie, that's all" Kaitlin rubbed the back of his shoulder. She knew his sweet spots. "I'm sorry."

"My wife's telling me she regrets having married me…" Paul's eyes were still fixated blankly outside the window, with his back turned to Kaitlin.

"I was just trying to refer to the *timing*, Paul. Not marrying you in general. Without you there would be no Malin. No Norway. Nothing that makes us…us…and me…me! Everything, with the good and the bad, about this place catalyzed me….catalyzed us…in ways we perhaps never would have been ignited to make changes in our lives…"

Paul glanced at Kaitlin over his shoulder. "I hope you haven't been sharing our personal challenges in that blog. I haven't checked it out in a while...."

Oh, I'm sure you continue to Google it every morning, Kaitlin thought as she flipped her hair, taking a gulp from her water bottle on the glass table before them. *Right after checking your e-mails for pictures your sisters send you of their kids.*

"No, not publicly. I've just been keeping to my private journal."

"Where's that?" he asked, throwing Kaitlin a wink— much to her relief. He couldn't have gotten *that* possessive as to be reading her journal, too, could he?

"I could tell you but then I'd have to kill you," she leaned over to brush a soft tap kiss over his lips. "Paulie— look, in sum, I just meant that maybe even *you* may have married *me* before *you* were actually ready, as well. You know? Just because you felt pressured to from your circle— being older and paid well enough in Norway to start a family..."

"Save it, babe," Paul sighed, walking over toward the restroom. "I don't want to talk about this anymore."

Kaitlin felt herself on a roll. "Maybe it was to spite your ex who hurt you? I mean...maybe you should have dated around more— to figure out if it had really been someone like *me* you'd actually wanted more as a girlfriend rather than a wife? Whereas you could actually imagine yourself growing old with...I don't know...someone like...like....?"

"Someone like, *Jeanette*, you mean?" Paul stopped in his tracks, scowling at Kaitlin. "Really? Don't tell me we're back *there* again."

What the hell? Kaitlin couldn't ignore the sinking sensation she felt at the pit of her stomach. Had they still been keeping in touch? She knew her husband's little childhood American buddy was a married woman now, and no longer working at the same office as Paul. *Being married didn't stop me from communicating with Finn.*

"I was going to say— someone maybe more *traditional and*

domestic in general, like your *mother*, Paul," Kaitlin stammered. "Where the hell did *Jeanette* come into this conversation? But how *is* she and Tim, by the way? Haven't heard from them in a while, have we?"

"Everyone's fine," Paul's jaw tensed in exasperation. "This is ridiculous. *You* start this senseless argument— essentially telling me in your indirect, clever little ways you regret ever having married me. And now, all of a sudden, *I'm* the bad guy? One who's *fantasizing* about his friend or whatever else, according to you…."

"You're overreacting, Paulie," Kaitlin followed him as he stormed toward the door. "Why can't we have open, calm discussions without your dramatics all the time?"

"*My* dramatics?" Paul scoffed, putting on his loafers. "Look who's talking!"

"Anyway—I'm going out!" He added over the shoulder in a calmer voice, "…to pick up Malin!"

"She doesn't get out for another half hour," Kaitlin tried plastering on a smile, hoping it'd make her voice sound softer. "This week is my turn, babe—I told you I'm heading down to her class right after the market."

Kaitlin shut her eyes, trying to hold back tears, She never wanted to have a household where her child would be coming into a home with negative pent-up energy, intense residuals from her parents' arguments. Just as she vaguely remembered to have happened in her own house growing up in Toronto, right before her dad had left.

"No, *I'll* do it today," Paul insisted, zipping up his sports jacket. "I need some fresh air. You can get more of your writing done. Focus on clever campaigns for those drug-cookies. Get more of your independence and 'space', babe."

Tears rolled down Kaitlin's cheek freely after he shut the door behind him. She sped toward the living room and screamed into one of the cushions, hoping the neighbors wouldn't hear. As if they didn't hear

Paul at the door already! Kaitlin hated how he always seemed oblivious to chastising or raising his voice at her even in places and moments where people could easily overhear.

She looked at the clock on her phone. There was still time, but if Paul wanted to—he could just park in front of Malin's class and get his 'air' from the windows of the car, as far as she knew…or frankly cared.

Plopping her exhausted body onto the living room sofa, Kaitlin shut her eyes and drew in a deep breath. Opening them back up- she realized she felt glad he'd left. She turned the sound off and tossed her phone onto their unmade bed. She'd make it later. Now she had to urgently improve her mood.

Thief.

Paul may not have been a murderer as once wrongly suspected of him. *But he is a thief indeed,* Kaitlin mourned. *He always steals my energy…my last remaining joy for life.*

She opened the Microsoft Word document on her laptop and continued. Her fingers banged on the keyboard in release.

taken, but alone …

Kaitlin allowed more tears to fall and took a gulp of water from her adjacent water bottle, gazing outside at the beautiful view from the window. All her possessions. Her life looked beautiful, and for that she was grateful. But whether it felt that way on the day-to-day— she couldn't be so sure.

She peered back at the screen, yawning as sleep overtook her attention away from the words being typed. Luckily she'd saved the last poem she'd typed:

taken, but alone…
ruling emptiness, though on a throne

mental torture
always having to look over your shoulder….

as you grow older
only thoughts grow warmer,
while reality grows colder

CHAPTER 17

Oslo

THE DAYLIGHT FILTERING IN THROUGH THE FOGGY WINDOW could not disguise what the night had robbed. Finn couldn't sleep a wink knowing he had to face the inevitable vitriol from Lar Iktar. "You've summoned me, Master?" Finn's hands were folded stiffly before his body as he walked up to him, eyes glued to the carpeted floor.

"You're late again," Lar bellowed, his hands clasped behind his back as he stared out the unkept window.

"I was in my natural form in the back room, Master," Finn explained carefully. "Stig and I were discussing details about the shipment to—"

"You thought I wouldn't find out, lad?" Lar interrupted sharply, his voice cutting through Finn's excuse.

Finn hesitated, reading Lar's mind and playing dumb to stall for time. "Master, I'm not sure what you're referring to…"

"Don't try to *fool me*, you fool!" Lar spun around, his face twisted with anger. His silk pajamas clung to his frame, a jarring contrast to his commanding tone.

Finn noted Master hadn't even bothered to dress. What time was it? Lar had been unraveling more and more lately.

"I know you've been sneaking off to *that woman*, Du Feu! Not as part of your task, either— for personal companionship! And now you've shown yourself to her daughter? Have you completely lost your mind?"

"Master, I've explained this before," Finn started. "I had to ensure Malin was mature enough to be able to adjust. It's part of the process. Once we persuade Kaitlin to join us…"

"Don't bull-crap me, Du Feu!" Lar injected, bellowing.

Finn's jaw tightened, but he forced himself to remain composed. "Master, I really feel *connected* to Malin. It's as if I'm *meant* to protect her, somehow. It's given my life a…newfound sense of *purpose*. Besides, you told me—"

"Enough!" Lar snapped, cutting him off again. "Your *purpose* is to expand the mission of 'The Group', Finn! Or have you forgotten, and need a reminder? Shall I decrease your monthly benefits to remind you where your *priorities* should lie?"

Finn clenched his fists, fighting to suppress the rage boiling inside him. Lar's threats were nothing new, but the blackmail—always the blackmail—struck a nerve. He hated how both the realm of the jinn and humans were dependent on economical hierarchies and exchanges.

"Master, just give me a little more time. I can convince Kaitlin to join us. If I move her and Malin into the Sandnes cabin, it'll be closer to Malin's school. It won't disrupt their routine…"

"Look, lad," Lar hissed, stepping closer. "I've been tolerant with your…*distractions*, over the years. You're lucky your parents generously donated that cabin to us, and haven't pestered us about it since. But my patience is running thin."

"Do not worry, Master," Finn's teeth ground together, but he managed to keep his face neutral. The mention of his parents stung more than it should have. "I'll get back on track. I promise."

"How do you think your poor parents would feel if they found out? Would they be proud to know you've been using your place with our mission for your unholy, *romantic* human-jinn union?"

They haven't given a shit in the longest, Finn thought with a smirk, but decided not to say anything.

"We cannot bring *emotions* to the forefront of our actions," Lar continued coldly. "They are the devil's tricks. *Survival* is all that matters."

Flashbacks of his last meeting with Kaitlin ran through his mind, their interaction exciting him in the melancholiest of ways, as per usual. How welcomed her surprise kiss after all that time had been. And how he'd missed it already.

"I'll focus only on her place here for the overall mission," Finn lied.

"Good!" Lar bellowed. "Because your stubbornness has shortened your timeline. Kaitlin Maverick *must* join 'The Group' as soon as possible! That Malin girl is old enough to be raised by other family members, if need be. Have I made myself clear?"

Finn nodded, but Lar's words hit him like a blow. He'd been buying time, inching toward a solution that wouldn't destroy everything and everyone he cared about. Now, Lar was demanding results.

"For the last time, I'll remind you of what I told you about Freya too—the human women will age as you remain in your form for many years longer than them! What will you want of them then?"

Finn closed his eyes, nodding to feign agreement. *I don't care*, he thought as always. *If it's true love, I can just enjoy someone's company for as long as I can have them alive.*

"Tan didn't die for nothing," Lar pressed, his voice lowering ominously. "Through Kaitlin, we *will* expand into Canada. Do you want her husband, Paul, to become part of 'The Group' instead? I mean, he's been exposed to us as well. I *could* shift my strategy…"

The thought of Kaitlin's husband joining them made Finn's stomach churn. The man's presence would be insufferable at best, a constant reminder of what could have been in its place. "No, Master. Paul won't be necessary."

"Tan lived in Canada, and I want to feel closer to him," Lar's gaze softened briefly, his expression turning wistful. He cleared his throat. "To honor his memory. After all, he died as part of his mission with us. Stig has already gotten close to a student there. Poor Nora is doing her best to hide her jealousy."

Finn forced a laugh, masking his irritation. Lar's hypocrisy was suffocating. He condemned Finn's emotions for a human, but turned a blind eye to Stig and Nora's relationship- just because they were both his followers. *Never mind his own lingering romantic delusions*! The double standard was maddening.

"What's so funny, Du Feu?" Lar demanded, his brows knitting together.

"Oh, I just remembered something Stig had said about that Canadian hottie," Finn replied quickly. "I apologize, Master. Please continue."

Lar narrowed his eyes but let it slide. "We will shift to the United States next, where Sandy Burns and Aidan Ramsay will be made into our American agents, as decided. But first— Canada. As for ensuring the male human counterpart for that student Stig is chatting up, I'm sending Meredith to Quebec this week. Nora has already found a reputable young candidate."

Finn's stomach sank. "Master, with all due respect, does Meredith really need to go there to…"

"I don't want to hear excuses about raising Bo!" Lar snapped. "You jinn need to rise above these human emotions of bonding with children. They weaken you!"

Finn shut his eyes, suppressing his frustration. "Yes, Master. I'll speak with her."

Lar's voice softened, but his words carried a sharp edge. "No more delays. You *will* keep working on alienating Kaitlin from her husband, so she can eventually settle back in Toronto. She shall start by securing a suite for us there."

"Yes, Master," Finn said with a heavy sigh.

"If need be, we'll offer her wealth beyond her wildest dreams. She won't need Paul. She'll have everything she needs to live comfortably."

What about her daughter? Finn worried, but proceeded to nod numbly- his mind racing. "I understand."

Lar leaned in, his voice a low growl. "A human and a jinn cannot breed a child. It's one of the founding principles of how I've paired my disciples, and it's gotten us success thus far. Get that through your head, Du Feu, for once and for all."

Inching closer to look up at Finn, Lar patted him on the cheek. A cruel smile curled his lips. "Stop with the foolish fantasies, and you'll rise once again…as my star."

"Master," Stig's voice interrupted them, tentative but firm as his human form materialized beside them in a matter of seconds. "May I have a word with you—in private?"

"Not now!" Lar barked. "And no privacy is necessary among the brethren, as you know."

"With all due respect, then, sir," Stig pressed, "…allow me to address something I've been looking into. With how strongly Finn feels about their bond: I believe the Malin girl may perhaps be a *mugharriboon.* Half-jinn, half-human. It *has* been documented in our history as technically being possible, despite its seldomness."

"Are you questioning my knowledge?" Lar's voice was ice.

"No, Master," Stig replied, bowing. "I just wanted to help. I'll head back now. If you'll excuse me..." He allowed his form to shimmer and fade, with eyes locking briefly with Finn's before disappearing entirely.

Bro— this union is ill-advised, particularly because there are children involved, Stig's voice echoed faintly in Finn's mind. *But not necessarily ill-fated. Look at me and Nora. Follow your heart.*

Finn mentally thanked his friend. *I'll look into it.*

Lar snapped Finn's attention back with a sharp laugh. "Chop chop, Du Feu! Get to it! If you won't bring Kaitlin to us willingly, we'll have to use force."

"You wouldn't hurt her…" Finn shook his head.

"Everyone I loved is gone," Lar reminded him, shrugging. "Tan—who was supposed to be my *future*—is already dead! Directly or indirectly—he sacrificed himself because of me! And John Walker, my *past*, has betrayed me once again! Don't you see? In my current *present*, I have nothing to lose!"

Asshole. Finn clenched and unclenched his fists through gritted teeth. *You'll be nothing if you lose all of us*. He took in a deep breath as he plastered on a smile. "I'll move as swiftly as I can."

"My Finn," Lar spoke, his lips twisting into a smile. "This isn't some romance novel. There is no grandiose sacrifice for love necessary, especially when Kaitlin wouldn't do that for you! You can't denounce who you are and permanently manifest as human. You need me, as a father figure, to guide you. You need 'The Group'. You've worked so hard to rise in our community ranks. In our created family. Think of all you've accumulated. Think with your spirit – because the mind and emotions can roller coaster."

"I've accumulated many goods, yes, but also cracks in my heart, Master," Finn mourned.

"I'm giving you until I return from my trip to the Emirates," Lar sighed, pointing his forefinger near Finn's blazing pupils. "You have two options, Du Feu. If it's easier, you can convince Kaitlin to stay in one of the cabins near her home for a while to get acclimated, rather than— as ideal— directly help us assure residence for the brethren to start off in

Canada during that upcoming trip of hers. Whichever option you pursue- she *must* have at least begun the initiation process by the time I come back!"

§

NORA RELEASED HER LONG-HELD BREATH THROUGH GRITTED TEETH as Stig returned to their room, shaking his head with disappointment. "I think Finn has finally left?"

Stig plopped his human form onto their king-sized bed, flipping open his laptop. "Yeah, he was just on his way out. Poor jinn."

Nora inched closer to Stig on the bed. "Stig?"

"Yes, baby?" Stig turned to face Nora, caressing a strand of her hair off her face.

Nora's eyes were downcast. "Do you think it's strange, too, what Master said…about his family in the Emirates?"

"Baby, I'm afraid you've been running your mind overtime lately over Master." Stig shook his head side to side with a smile. "*You're* the one who told me not to question his increased attention to his daily prayers, remember? So what's up with all *this* now coming from you?"

"I…I miss my mom, alright?" Nora whispered, eyeing their surroundings to make sure Lar wasn't around.

"Why's it okay for *Master* to be interested in 'making amends', as he's put it, with his family, but when I even mention my parents- God forbid- he has to give me *that* speech? About being a cat and forgetting our 'past lives' before 'The Group'! Why's it okay for *him* to make plans to go see them after all this time, but not for me? Or you, for that matter? Or Finn, or any of us…"

Stig reached out to caress her hair. "Well Finn and I— let's just say, our families aren't exactly interested in seeing us any longer. They're very conservative in the jinn realm, and don't approve of this life we've chosen, living as liberally as we do and cooperating with humans. But I do see your point, baby…although…"

"Yes?" Nora asked, raising her brow.

"Are you sure *your* family would be open to seeing you, if you could do so somehow?" Stig continued, biting his lip. "It has been a while."

"I don't know," Nora shrugged. "Maybe I'm hoping a lot of water has run under that bridge since. You know I've been looking them up—they're alive, and living in the same place. I guess a part of me just wants to try, at least. I don't want to live with regrets after someone has passed, or something—you know? You see how Lar has become after Tan!"

"I get you, baby," Stig pulled her in closer to his heated torso. "But what did you have in mind? What can we do? You know you're bound to the house unless Lar knows exactly where you are at all times."

"I have been thinking," Nora began, twisting the blonde layers that grazed her blue eyes as she gazed poutingly at Stig, "…that maybe *you* can help me?"

Stig smirked coyly. "Of course you have. Okay, baby, I'll try. But—*how*?"

"He barely leaves the house anymore here, Stig," Nora's voice turned serious. "But in Dubai- you can follow Master. Stay disguised but surrounding him at all times once he flies over there."

"Okay," Stig looked confused. "And I'm guessing that's when you'll be leaving the premises here to visit your mom— right? But the cameras…."

"You can tap into his phone and ensure that the alerts are off."

"Brilliant, as well as sexy," Stig chuckled, interlocking his heated breath in a passionate kiss with Nora. "I always knew you were special."

CHAPTER 18

RESTLESSNESS SPREADING FROM HER CORE THROUGHOUT HER jittery legs, Kaitlin muttered into the receiver with utmost impatience. "Come on, Sandy, pick up the phone!"

As triggered as she still was at her husband for his elevation of the prior day's argument—not to mention the sour face he continued after returning home with Malin and throughout dinner and a cold *'goodnight'*— she needed to maintain a sense of excitement in her voice talking to Sandy. *I don't want her thinking I want to visit New York just to escape my marital reality here.*

"Hey, girl, hey," Sandy's chipper voice answered on about the tenth ring. "Sorry, I was entering the apartment! I'm so glad you called! I was going to call you myself!"

Kaitlin smiled. Her friend's energy somehow always managed to bring positivity to her day. "Oh yeah? Why? What's going on?"

"You first!" Sandy replied.

What if she's traveling somewhere herself for the holidays? Kaitlin thought, worry beginning to creep in. *Or perhaps she's found someone to move in with?* They hadn't talked in a while, she realized. One of those longer periods of non-communication she'd grown accustomed to with some friendships, where it wouldn't be intentional and you could just pick up where you'd left off at the next time.

Sandy wouldn't exactly be alright with her and Malin crashing over her place, if that were the case, would she? Kaitlin decided to let her friend go first. "It's nothing, girl. I insist. *You* go first! What's up?"

"Remember that major play I mentioned about a month ago? The one that I had told you would finally jumpstart my career?"

Kaitlin thought for a moment, unable to remember the exact name but recalling the amusing conversation they'd had about it. "*The Fake Bitches?* Or something or other?"

"Oh, you're good," Sandy began to laugh on the other line. "It's called *The Pretentious Young Ladies,* and I got the part!"

"Oh my God, that's great, Sandy!" Kaitlin yelped with joy. "Congratulations!"

"Thank you," Sandy's voice trailed off. "What was your news, Kaitlin?"

"Oh, *er*…nothing as major. Well, firstly— when do rehearsals start? Are you going to be busy for the holidays?"

Sandy cleared her throat. "Oh, the show is in the spring, girl! We don't do the big rehearsals until February or so. I just received the calendar. I'll mostly be memorizing lines and running them once a week or so in the beginning. Why?"

"Well, Paul and I, *um*, were thinking it would be good for Malin to have a little holiday trip. To see her North American culture. And before returning to Toronto with Mom, from which we'd fly back to Norway— I was thinking we could first see my brother in New York… and see you too?

"You guys want to visit?" Kaitlin was glad to hear genuine excitement in Sandy's voice again. "Oh my God, Kaitlin— that's great news!"

"Yeah?" Kaitlin let out a long-held breath. "Awesome! How can we make this work, then, girl? I mean— it would make more sense for Malin and me to first go over to Aidan's, I'm aware. I don't want us to burden you. But Aidan's been….acting a bit strange on the phone."

"Strange?" Sandy asked curiously.

"He's told me all this drama concerning our family," Kaitlin explained. "And I don't know what's going on with his private life—but he's definitely keeping something from me. I'm not sure how I'd feel taking Malin directly there before I go check out what's up in his place first."

"You mean you don't want your daughter to discover potential S&M bondage toys and such in her uncle's drawers by mistake, eh?" Sandy teased, chuckling. "I'm flattered you'd trust that my place would be more Disney-innocent in comparison to your brother's!"

Kaitlin remained silent, triggering her friend to add, "I'm kidding!"

"By the way," Sandy continued. "You mentioned you and Malin…*Paul* isn't coming?"

Kaitlin drew in an exasperated breath. "Oh, don't get me started on him."

"Let me guess," Sandy sighed with sympathy. "Another fight? Look. It happens. That's marriage for you—or so I've heard, anyway. Believe me, Kaitlin— even your family pressures and issues are worth more than absolute, apathetic loneliness like mine," Sandy's eyes welled.

Kaitlin didn't press any further. She knew that growing up without parents, as well as still being single and without a child of her own—was a sensitive topic for her friend.

"Sweetie….we can talk about everything like the old days when I come. Just us girls."

"I think I'd like that," Sandy said softly in response.

"Are you sure you can handle us if we fly straight to stay with you for a few days?" Kaitlin asked after a beat of silence over the call. "At least until I figure out the deal with Aidan's bachelor pad? And see if it's good to hold Malin and I, and even Mom when she visits?"

"Of course, girl! I can't imagine Momma Linda there with both you and your brother! She's going to give you both an earful, that's for sure!"

Kaitlin smiled for a moment, recalling how her mother had apparently warned Sandy on her Norway trip to visit her when Malin was a baby as well. It was how Sandy had first met Bjorn the jinn, in fact. *Speaking of whom,* she thought with wonder. "Hey, Sandy? How's Bjorn, by the way? You're still not hooking up with him, are you?"

It felt awkward to warn her friend from getting physical with a jinn-lover whereas she herself hadn't exactly been avoiding little touches here and there from Finn, albeit abstaining from sex.

"We'll….talk, as you said," Sandy sounded eager to change the subject. "Where's Mallie? Let me speak to her. I can't wait for the visit!"

"Oh, she's in her art class. Her dad's been trying to hang out with her more. He should be picking her up any minute now. I'll tell her you said 'hello'."

A worrying feeling presented itself somewhere in Kaitlin's stomach pit, but she pushed it from her thoughts as she hung up the phone call with Sandy.

Finn wouldn't dare 'visit' her again—would he? Not after they'd been openly communicating and transparent with each other. He couldn't. Besides— Paul had just picked her up from her music class yesterday. Kaitlin had ensured he wouldn't do so from her dance class — as she couldn't trust that the teacher, Mrs. Hansen, wouldn't mention anything about him supposedly having picked her up before, as well.

Luckily, today was art class. Kaitlin sighed. *My poor baby.* Maybe Paul was right. Maybe they were overdoing it with three extracurriculars in addition to school to get Malin to become more social. And with this overseas trip coming up, the girl had to rest before the break!

I'm not sending her to any classes— at least not until we get back, she decided. I'll just spend more time with her myself. Mommy-Daughter time. Just reading and playing together after she does her homework. And maybe shopping, too.

§

IF THERE WAS ONE THING FINN HATED MORE THAN LYING, IT WAS breaking a promise. Watching Malin and Bo circumnavigate a tree in all directions during a game of 'Tag', Finn sighed. How bittersweet it was: to watch these two dear children enjoy each other's company so innocently, yet do so at the expense of having to break his word to Malin's mother. Not to mention having had to resort to his human transformation into Paul's 'twin' again as he picked her up from her art class!

Lucky for him, Malin had recognized him and went up to him in a hug— not alerting yet another teacher that anything may be off. Finn snickered to himself: of course both Paul and Kaitlin also received text messages from each other agreeing that the other would be picking up Malin.

"Stay close, boy!" Finn called out.

"Aww, he's got the most adorable big brown eyes! "Malin cooed. Finn was amused to see that Bo had taken the word 'close' a bit too literally, and buried his nose into Malin's face while she was petting him.

"Yeah, I think he takes after his grandmother," Finn quipped, with his expression shifting as soon as he uttered the words. He missed the woman, his mother. Whether she or Finn's dad missed him, he hadn't a clue. *I doubt it*, he mourned.

"You knew the dog's grandmother, Uncle Finn?" Malin raised her eyebrow, caressing Bo's tawny mane.

"Yeah," he went on. *Oh, shoot.* Him and his big mouth in human form! Again!

He *had* indeed been comparing the boy's darker eyes with his mother, contrasting Bo's brown hue with his and Meredith's green ones. Yet how exactly could he explain as such to Malin? What human dog-owner thought about his or her pet's parents, let alone their grandparents-right? *I have to be smarter. Malin's too bright.*

"Yeah, can you believe it?" Finn asked. *I hope so, because I sure can't.*

"Bo— *um*—was a pup from my late dog," he continued. "A fellow retriever my, *um*, own momma had given to me as a birthday present, actually!"

As Bo's ears perked up and looked at Finn questioningly, he was met with a polite, mental warning to 'please play along'.

"My mother's own dog had given birth, so I remember that grandmother one as well; I knew both the Mom and Grandma."

"Wow— that is so crazy, but also cool, Uncle Finn!" Malin nodded. Finn agreed that it was crazy— as only something true, or something close to it, anyway, could be.

He recalled the female dog that had eventually made a home with a man named Stephan whom Paul Maverick worked with, and Meredith—a jinn family friend of Finn's since his childhood— had stayed with them during the late stages of her pregnancy in hiding. It was mostly to give birth in her dog form much quicker due to the gestation period, and to avoid arousing Lar's suspicions that she was pregnant!

Besides, though she had gotten back together with Tan at the time, he had encouraged her to get an abortion—further breaking her heart. Bo had been one of two other puppies, who Finn knew Meredith still sometimes shed tears over— yet they had formally been adopted into their new family with Stephan.

Dearest Bo. Finn smiled as he remembered the boy as a little puppy. How happy Kaitlin was to receive him as a gift. And how devastated she was when Finn had to take their son back. It had all been a part of the little game he had to play to ensure her compliance and keep quiet for 'The Group'.

His 'son'. *Shit.* Smiling at the sight of Bo playing now with Malin, it had actually felt good to at least finally admit it to himself. Finn supposed there would always be some chance Bo or Malin could both be half-breeds. He remembered the term Stig used for them with Master. *Mughariboon.* Finn didn't ask, but not because he didn't dare challenge

Lar Iktar. No. It was because he'd inquired into the possibility himself.

He'd conducted his Islamic research and had even visited several Head- Jinn scholars since Malin had been born. Some outliers mentioned the possibility of the half-breeds— much to his initial excitement, of course. But many were saying how, from a scriptural point of view about the two different makeups of their kind— *unfortunately, no*— that it was highly unlikely. The chances that Malin could technically be his offspring were quite slim, indeed.

He'd never admit as much to Lar, of course. Mostly to keep Kaitlin safe— as his protective feelings over Malin were the only thing allowing him time before Lar pressured him into finally initiating Kaitlin into 'The Group'. "*Or else*," he would always say. And whatever Lar meant by that— whether it was actual murder, like with Tan's ex-girlfriend, Linette Peterson, or some other sort of blackmail that Finn knew would ruin Kaitlin's life, he couldn't risk it.

Finn had come to realize that despite her seeing him since she was a baby—his love for Malin was ultimately from a place of genuine affection. Perhaps he cared simply because she was the daughter of the woman he loved—he now supposed—rather than being genetically linked to her.

This is how some good stepparents must feel like, he thought with a smile.

Moreover, Finn was also feeling the sorrowful truth in his heart as of late. A truth he had to come to terms with and accept— especially now that he had come so close in contact with Malin Maverick. She had indeed grown to be a spitting image of Paul— that lucky bastard! It had also allowed Finn to accept Bo's own similarities with himself and his family lineage. *Albeit Tan had brown eyes, too,* Finn shook the thought from his mind as soon as it arose.

"What was her name?" Malin's sweet voice interrupted his self-questioning.

"Whose?" Finn shook his head and cleared his throat.

"Bo's mommy? And her mom-dog before her? And what about his daddy?"

"Oh, well— I don't, *uhh,* remember his dad, but Bo's mom was named, *uhh*—Freya!"

Merde. Where the heck did the name of his human ex-lover reveal itself in Finn's mind again? Was *she* thinking about him as she used to? Because that was when he knew it usually happened. Had *she* broken up with that man she'd left him for, finally?

Finn rolled his eyes. He supposed he could have just said 'Meredith', as the truth. What was the name, after all, to Malin? *No*. Finn had to have blurted Freya's name for a reason. His old lover was overthinking about him lately. He could sense it!

"Freya...cool," Malin said with a shrug. "And the Grandma doggie?"

"Oh ...Anja!" This time Finn grinned, mentally apologizing to his friend from 'The Group' for aging her as a 'grandmother' in his fictional tale to Malin. Why he couldn't just share his own mother's name, Stefanie, was beyond him. He just wasn't feeling comfortable in uttering her name—especially as he knew his folks could always be around the woods they tended to frequent. Eyeing him from afar. Judging him.

"Wow...cool beans!" Malin went on excitedly, caressing Bo's mane. "They all sound so European. My own name is European, Daddy says."

"Oh, is it now?" Finn asked, raising an eyebrow. *Her 'daddy', she says.* Paul Maverick, with his frequently-dumbstruck expression on his face flickered across his mind. *Fuck him*.

How Finn had wished that Paul dude had truly been guilty of murder and locked up forever. Finn would not go as far as to actually mess with her husband beyond the jail stint he had helped 'The Group' devise, though. That wouldn't be right. As much as he was sure Lar would find some way to excuse it—as he had for Tan's murder of Linette…Finn couldn't.

Besides, he thought— *Kaitlin had freewill.* Finn wouldn't want Kaitlin to live with him and accept him and his world out of *necessity* if Paul mysteriously disappeared. If he wasn't *chosen*— it couldn't be real love, as far as Finn was concerned. And he didn't want to chase after anyone if he truly felt they didn't choose him or love him. He had his pride, despite how it may have appeared to the women at times.

The freedom of choice. The concept lingered like a spider web in the inner workings of Finn's sub-conscious. *The mission.* Lar's rude reminder, and threat, recurred in his mind. Finn took in a deep breath. "Hey, Malin?"

"Yes, Uncle Finn?" Malin asked with curiosity in her sweet gaze, as Bo continued to circle her.

Finn bit his lips. "You like these woods out here, right? You've been having a good time?"

"Of course, Uncle Finn!" Malin responded, smiling as Bo nuzzled her leg.

Finn's eyes fixated the soiled ground, unable to look at her directly. "How would you like it if you and your mom stayed with me and Bo for a while? In our cabin out in the woods!"

Malin's facial expression shifted, Finn noticed, as he glanced up to gauge her reactions. "Like a holiday? Or camping trip?"

Finn attempted a reassuring smile. "Sure, yes, we can say that!"

"But Daddy will miss us! Besides, Mommy and I are already going to visit overseas soon."

"Right, right," Finn managed a soft chuckle. "Well, it's just a thought. Think about it."

What the hell was he doing? This entire thing was going to be harder than he thought. *If even necessary.* Stig had confided in him about

Nora's plan to visit her family behind Master's back, while he kept an eye on him in the Emirates.

Maybe it was time they all had their voices heard against their once savior who had increasingly begun to feel more like their captor.

CHAPTER 19

New York

RAISING HER CHAMPAGNE FLUTE INTO THE AIR, SANDY WAS pouting as she toasted, sitting up in her bed. "I wish you could drink with me, Bjorn. It's no fun celebrating alone."

Bjorn smiled with sympathy, with his thick arms embracing Sandy's body covered only in a red slip without undergarments. "You know my diet is minimal and different from yours, home girl. Besides, I never got why humans felt the need for alcohol to celebrate anything when all it does is ultimately bad to your bodies."

Sandy rolled her eyes as she took a sip of the bubbly. "It's just to toast with! Would you like me to put juice or something in your glass? I could get some from…"

"Shh," Bjorn began, the sound slowly turning into a hiss as his form transformed into a snake.

"Bjorn, what are you doing?" Sandy giggled.

"Congratulations, bae," Bjorn hissed, his serpentine form now moving lower on Sandy's torso, wrapping around her upper legs. "I knew you had it in you."

"Thank you, bae," she said as she caressed his scaly skin, giggling. "I couldn't have done it without our practice together. Oh, come on! Turn human again. I want to kiss your lips."

"Okay, Ma'am," Bjorn hissed, his eyes remaining icy blue even in his animal form. They fixated on Sandy's warm brown peepers, mesmerizing her beyond all logic. "But first— your favorite…"

Sandy moaned with joyful pleasure as Bjorn untwisted himself in a whirlwind, causing her body to elevate several centimeters off the bed. He turned back into his human form just as quickly, catching her in the air with his arms before she could fall down.

"That's how *I* say cheers," Bjorn winked, pulling her closer on the mattress.

"I'm not complaining," Sandy whispered, kissing his torching lips. "Ow!"

"Sorry— too hot, again?" Bjorn raised a hand to his own lips. "It gets like this immediately after my transformation. I think it's the excess energy."

Sandy tried to smile through her grimacing expression. "It's alright," she placed her lips on the cold champagne glass to cool them down a bit. "By the way—thanks for believing in me, and telling me I had it in me."

"You also had *me* in you," he winked at her as Sandy ran her fingers through his long blond hair. She suddenly stopped, as a quizzical thought occurred in her mind.

"What's that supposed to mean, slick?" she snickered, forefinger playfully grazing Bjorn's cheek. "You mean to say that you doubt I would have landed this part if I wasn't sleeping with you, or something?"

"No, not at all…" Bjorn started, his tone of voice serious. "Your talent has gotten increasingly amazing over the years, baby."

"Right…." Sandy's voice was uneasy.

Bjorn continued. "I just meant—you know…since I always tell you about the softness of your voice on stage…I just sort of… spiritually took hold of your body during the audition. Just a tad bit, but mostly—"

"What?" Sandy whispered in shock, cutting him off. Her heart palpated as tears began to form in her eyes. She pushed Bjorn backwards through his chest. "Are you saying you…you *possessed* me? And that's how I got this part?"

Bjorn shook his head rapidly. "Don't think of it like that—it was just a quick jolt to make you sound louder and more confident to the judges. But I quickly exited—I promise!"

"Bjorn," Sandy murmured, a single tear sliding down her brown cheek. "How could you? I didn't feel anything different…if I had known…Oh, how stupid am I?"

"Home girl, what's the big deal?" Bjorn shrugged. "It was still mostly all you, baby! And it was unseen, don't worry. I just helped you with your stage presence and voice tone. Isn't the result more important here? You got the part, and did your best."

"I wanted to *earn* it, Bjorn!" Sandy shot back.

"You did! It was all you— I just amplified your sound and presence is all," Bjorn's light blue eyes were wide open. "You're acting like I paid the Director off, or suggested you've been *whoring yourself* by sleeping with the guy or something, sheesh! Now *that* would have been 'not earning it'."

Sandy placed the champagne flute so hard on the counter it nearly broke. "I thought you believed in me! I thought you sincerely believed I could become a successful actress! Where I didn't need to be frigging possessed by a jinn during my performances! Or 'whore myself'! I can't believe how long I've been with such a…such a…*chauvinistic pig…snake*!"

Bjorn floated close behind as Sandy thrust herself off the bed and began to pace through the corridor of her apartment. "You can make it! I know you can! I'm just trying to help you! I have no reason to be in the States right now if not to help you."

"You pity me…and feel guilty," Sandy crossed her arms. "It's okay. I don't want my feelings for you to burden you anymore. Thanks. You can return to Norway. Go ask Lar Iktar to task you with another woman!"

Bjorn opened his mouth to speak, but quickly shut it momentarily, hesitant. “What are you talking about?”

“Oh, spare me—haven’t I been a *task*, Bjorn?” Sandy took a step closer to Bjorn, sticking her head out toward him.

“I know I’m not the sharpest tool in the shed with men— but I’ve read his works. I know how y’all work. I know you wouldn’t have been allowed so much time with me and still remain under the organization’s auspices had I not been part of some plan your damn leader has got going on. But I chose to ignore all that! I told myself it was worth it because we’re not exactly some conventional couple anyway….”

“Whoa…baby…your imagination’s been running wild,” Bjorn began to chuckle nervously. “Come on— you’re going to have guests soon. You won’t be able to welcome me here as easily. We were just getting started with the party, baby. What are you doing right now? The timing of this conversation is a bit dramatic, don’t you think? We’re celebrating you today! Maybe I can pour you another glass of—"

“Whatever,” Sandy stood firm, avoiding eye contact. “The timing is never going to be perfect. And yes—we have been celebrating, but apparently not my natural success at my audition as I’d thought… I think…I think we need a break.”

Bjorn took in a deep breath. He bit his lip. “I think you’re using this as an excuse. I’m so sorry you’re feeling this way.”

Sandy nodded rapidly along with the irritated tapping of her foot. “I’m the one who’s sorry, Bjorn. I’m sincerely sorry I was stupidly under the impression that this may have been more than a hook-up for you. But apparently you view me as some loser and an easy lay— if anything beyond some task to initiate yet another woman into your little *group*. Now, if you’ll excuse me, I need to get some rest. I just want to be alone. Or maybe I’ll *whore myself* out of the pain and heartache as you implied…”

"You are so sweet," Bjorn chuckled, transporting himself instantly next to her sulking body, lifting her face to meet his, grabbing her by one of the curls in her hair.

"You're overreacting, baby. None of that is true. Save the dramatics for the stage! However you got it— you *got* this role you were meant to play!"

"I'm not even sure I want to go through with the damn play anymore," Sandy wriggled herself out of his touch.

"Don't be absurd— you can't give up your professional future out of some false sense of pride!" Bjorn reached out for her hands again. They were trembling. He placed a soft kiss on them, ensuring she wouldn't let go this time. Yes—she needed to earn more money to become a stronger member for 'The Group'. But he also genuinely wanted her to accomplish her dreams.

"Why do you underestimate yourself? I never got that about some women. If I'm not mistaken, a 'whore' by definition uses her body for money— whether by choice or destitution. Or uses her sexuality in exchange for favors. I've given you nothing in return for your beautiful body, except my own. If you're a whore, then I must be one, too."

"You act like you joke, Bjorn, but I'm no fool," Sandy bellowed. "I've dated too many 'red flags' to not see through this one. As if your being a jinn wasn't enough, your words use humor to disguise your cold judgements about me!"

"I know what I said," Bjorn stood firm. "I referred to our exchange, yes—but we have also genuinely had a connection, Sandy. I just wanted to help you with your dream."

"Your words go from sounding deep and sincere one minute, and light and silly—almost insulting to me—the next. I know we have this chemistry…but half the time I can barely even understand you, Bjorn!"

"Just *experience* me," he smiled. "Understanding is…overrated," he added a wink. "I love you, Sandy. I think I really do."

"No, you don't," Sandy retorted, in a calmer voice. She found herself chuckling at the subsequent thought. The laughter felt freeing during the heated exchange. "Maybe just your…*snake* does."

"You're going to miss my snake," Bjorn winked at her. "And it's going to miss you, Lady Liberty. Come on. You don't have to do this!"

"Oh, but I do. This has been fun, and sweet. I'll admit. But it's more than just about you, Bjorn. It's beyond you. I have to do this for myself."

She turned around to face him once more. "Thank you, actually."

"For helping you land the part?" Bjorn asked, befuddled. "You've already thanked me for that. Painfully so, but…"

Sandy gave him an incredulous stare. "For helping me realize I actually have to *be* 'Lady Liberty' now. And not because I somehow represent New York City for you, like the statue. I actually have to embody what she stands for. For independence, and for strength."

Bjorn smiled softly, inching his face lower and so close to Sandy she could feel his heartbeat. "I've always thought you were already those things, baby girl."

The heat coming from his breathing made the hairs on her skin erect. Sandy smiled. "Goodbye, my Thor."

"Say goodnight, not goodbye, baby," Bjorn teased her. "Summon me when you've come to your senses. This new play you've gotten into is going to have an intense schedule. You'll be overworked. Stressed. You'll need…*release*."

Sandy grinned through a teasing eye roll as he dissipated from sight. She really hadn't decided whether she'd actually ever see Bjorn again. Or whether or not she even wanted to. But for the first time— it no longer mattered.

She had to prioritize her own well-being, and not summon him because she felt it necessary to maintain his interest and attention. Whether this was a break or a break-up; Sandy was going to give herself a break.

§

FREYA OLSDOTTER BRUSHED HER FAIR HAIR IN THREE LONG STROKES before looping it in a bun and tucking it all beneath her beige, bonnet-style under cap. Smiling at her reflection, she threw on her favorite lavender, silk headscarf, meticulously pinning it together under her chin and tossing the ends over her shoulders.

Where are you, Merve? She had to meet her husband for some furniture shopping soon, but throughout the morning she inexplicably wasn't able to get her untraceable former patient out of her mind!

This wasn't the first time, of course. Merve would occasionally cross her mind ever since her patient, Sandy Burns, had mentioned *them* years ago in connection to her and her friend's experiences in Norway. Freya had noticed improvements in Sandy—her focusing more on work than dating and no longer mentioning jinn— and so had decreased the frequency of their phone calls to once every two weeks. She was just about to suggest the same to Kaitlin Maverick, as well, until—alas— she'd brought *them* up again! And there went the accumulation of an entire month of willpower she'd had to regularly work for all these years of having escaped them!

Freya had to be fair. Yes, Sandy had mentioned having a friend with jinn experiences and that's how Freya had taken Kaitlin on as a patient, as well. Yet that didn't mean she wanted to discuss them in every session! She knew that being plagued by the jinn in the human realm usually meant mental suffering—usually stemming from familial trauma. And that's what she wanted to discuss with her patients—to actually be able to ameliorate the root causes of why they'd be plagued by them in the first place.

Just even someone alluding to them hit too close to home. The jinn. The Group. *Finn.* "Argh!" Freya cursed herself for thinking of his name again, flinging one of her puffy bed pillows across the bedroom.

Inhaling deeply, she closed her eyes and recited one of her daily salah prayer openers to ward off negative energies. *"Auzubillah Minashaitan Nirajeem."*

Freya opened her eyes, fighting back tears. *I can't risk madness,* she thought, the name of her first failure as a therapist returning hauntingly to her mind again. *Merve.* She glanced towards her ceiling by instinct, though she knew God was all around humans, closer than one's 'jugular vein'— as the Quran dictated.

Allah—I think you're trying to tell me something. I think there needs to be some closure, right? Or the past will never let go, will it?

She'd left that old part of her— and Finn—behind a long time ago. Freya had come to New York to advance her studies in Psychotherapy, while actively doing all she could to improve her own mental state. In her initial loneliness in a new city, she'd taken to social media— anonymously posting about her jinn experiences and attempting to find someone to commiserate with. She'd only had one person respond to her with a sad story of her own—a woman by the name of Merve. They'd chatted enough for her to reveal her identity and meet offline— initially as acquaintances and later eventually in her office once she'd obtained her license to practice psychotherapy.

She had also found new love, clinging on to him like a lifeline to push Finn away. A practicing Muslim man, Salim, who'd introduced her to his faith. He hadn't pressured her to convert, but in Islam she'd found acceptance— as well as the ever chance of repentance and forgiveness by Allah. Her new faith had given her the strength and self-value she needed to actually believe all those motivating pearls of advice she'd been giving to her clients about self- love.

It hadn't been easy, but alas— she'd done it! Freed herself from 'The Group', and made a thriving new life for herself in New York. She'd obtained several other clients through word of mouth— enough to accommodate her bills, though Salim had been paying most of the rent and everything else in more recent years, as her husband.

Most of her patients ended up being domestic abuse survivors or drug addicts, who'd thank her for getting them out of the most delicate of situations. Freya liked to be pragmatic, outlining concrete steps in getting over their addictions to substances and mistreatments. Dealing with just one person—Merve—who had reminded her of her own past demons had been doable for Freya. Until one day, it wasn't, and she simply couldn't.

What had started as cathartic commiseration and relief to know that she wasn't alone in the world with her experiences had soon brought back darkness into her life. She'd tried to encourage her patient in reconnecting with her family back in her native Türkiye, and landing better jobs to support herself in the United States; the young woman had mentioned some wealthy aunt sending her money to help her out but that wouldn't be sustainable. Yet Merve just wouldn't let go of her main focus being the jinn! And Freya had had it! In her new life, she didn't want anything, or anyone, disturbing her newly adapted peace of mind.

She needed to be away from jinn hauntings as much as possible. Reciting the prayers in her head to keep Finn and the rest of them away could only work for so long. Merve's frantic rambling of her fears with some jinn of hers kept reminding her of the past— and maintaining that energy and presence in her life in the process. And she wouldn't have it any longer.

The memory of their last session would plague her for as long as she lived, Freya was certain. Particularly the latter part of what Merve had divulged right before storming out of her office and changing all her information. A crucial part to which Freya hadn't even really paid attention until later in regretful retrospect.

"I've gotten myself into a whole new intense relationship as soon as the other one ended,

Freya," Merve said in an exasperated tone, flopping down on the chair. " I know I need to be alone for a while, but I just don't know how."

"We've discussed your patterns of co-dependency, Merve," Freya said calmly as she nodded, thinking *God, help me.* "And how it's ultimately up to you if you want to break the cycle..."

"The cycle," Merve repeated. "Yes, I know- but I've been feeling so lonely here in the United States, you know? I wanted to believe I've at least left all that...otherworldly stuff I talked to you about behind me..."

Freya gulped as she nodded. How could she forget? What were the odds that the jinn stalking she herself had experienced and attempted to escape from back in Norway had also happened to one of her first new clients in this new country? Right as she'd finally been freed of Finn's memory lingering over her psyche. Possessing her thoughts, fantasies...her soul.

"I said my prayers and I thought the drama in general was finally removed from my life," Merve went on. "I mean, silly me. I thought I'd be alright, finally dating a man I thought I could freely hold hands with in public. Someone visible, accepted, you know? How was I to know that my heart would continue to become completely shattered? How was I to know he'd...*hurt* me?"

Freya smiled politely, recalling the man from Merve's office whom she had started mentioning during their last couple of sessions. "Why do you think you ignored the red flags, dear Merve? That guy exuded womanizing energy since the beginning, from what you've told me. Have you discussed your concerns with him?"

"It's not just that," Merve spoke softly, eyeing the floor. "He swears there's no other woman and that we simply have to keep our relationship on the low due to office policy against us being together, especially as he's technically my manager..."

"Have you tried contacting your family yet, Merve?" Freya interrupted. "Your father in particular?"

"I know I promised you I would," Merve began, biting her lower lip. "But I'm still angry at him for practically paying off my boyfriend from Istanbul—like he probably saw from those old Turkish movies! I

don't want him to trace me here— at least not until I make something of myself and can face both my parents with pride."

"I want you to face the roots of why you may have a habit of being attracted to unavailable men, Merve," Freya spoke softly with a smile she hoped appeared more comforting than she was feeling in the moment. She leaned in closer toward Merve on her swivel chair.

"Your ex— Emir—right? He was the one with whom you first came here to study in New Jersey?"

"Don't say his name too much—" Merve's voice trembled as she almost whispered, eyeing her surroundings. "Yes, we both started off at a language school here."

"He wouldn't have taken that money had he loved you," Freya continued. "We've discussed this— how you can't solely blame your father. Regardless of their imperfections, I'm sure your parents must be missing you terribly, and you don't want to carry that burden on your shoulders."

"He has still been following me, actually," Merve cut in. "It's what I also wanted to talk about today. He'd been away for a while, but I felt him. I saw him, in fact. We had a holiday party at the office, you see, and afterwards…"

"Merve, before you go on about the jinn— I'd like to tell you a little about another thesis," Freya intercepted with a sigh.

"Maybe this could help you since you're not listening, it seems, to a lot of my other advice. In our profession, we have something called the 'Charles Bonnet syndrome', where studies have been done of nearly blind patients reporting seeing strangers dressed in historical or geographically-different clothes. At times these strangers would ignore them but at others, interact with them—either kindly or sometimes even unkindly."

"No, no," Merve shook her head frantically. "Freya— I'm not blind or anywhere near it. This jinn— using a similar human form as my ex, Emir— is not a figment of my imagination! You said you believe me!"

"Yes, I've experienced that the jinn are real, as well, but I just want you to consider other, more *scientific* possibilities sometimes,," Freya insisted. "It's for your own good. Look— there have also been instances

of similar hallucinations by non-blind patients who nonetheless – during brain PET scans – showed reduced blood flow in their occipital and parietal lobes, as the cause. If your visions become more severe I may have to prescribe *quetiapine*. Quetiapine is ….”

“I don’t need some *prescription*, Freya!” Merve burst out. “I’m not crazy! I need comfort and understanding from someone who believes me!”

Freya closed her eyes, inhaling deeply and then exhaling as she counted to four. “Prescribed medication isn’t something to be ashamed of, dear Merve. It’s natural, after some experiences in particular, for our brains to become deficient with some chemicals such as serotonin and others.”

“Freya, please…” Merve begged, but Freya was adamant.

“There are also some victims of sleep apnea that have reported hallucinations accompanying their paralysis—being unable to speak or move—as they wake or fall asleep, Merve. It’s more common than you’d think, albeit more amongst people with social anxieties. Sometimes experiences like yours can be attributed to these reasons as well, beyond the supernatural—just an inability of the individual to properly pass through stages of sleep, for instance.”

Freya had offered Merve all the scientific explanations she could think of. Whether she was trying to convince her patient more, or herself, at the time— she still wasn’t too sure.

“I know jinn are real, Merve. And that’s how we’ve bonded. But as your therapist I just need to remind you that there are other reasons why we may experience things similar to jinn surrounding us. That’s all. As much as I care for your well-being, I am not your friend. I have to help you through a place of logic and practicality—not personal empathy.”

“I don’t suffer from any of those scientific claims, Freya,” Merve’s voice was hard.

Freya took in a deep breath. “Merve- it’s been a pleasure. But I’m afraid I have an announcement to make- something I’ll be discussing with

my other clients as well. I...have decided to take a break for a while."

"What do you mean?" Merve responded, eyes welling with tears and her mouth twisting into a childlike pout. "I don't have anyone else here I can talk to about this! You can't!"

"It's not you!" She'd blurted, further adding puzzlement onto Merve's face. *You idiot!* She'd cursed herself. *Why would you even imply as such to a patient?*

"It's just that I need to supplement my License to practice Therapy with additional training," Freya said, blushing. As an alibi with some of her other clients as well- she truly had signed up for the additional license- for which she could have waited but had decided to sincerely go through with in order to recuperate from all the negativity with Merve.

"I've also been ignoring my home. My husband has been needing me more lately. I'm afraid it's for the best, at least for a little while I recuperate and, *um,* study."

"You don't truly believe me about the jinn!" Merve shook her head side to side. "That's what this is ultimately about, isn't it? You think I'm not only mildly troubled like some typical patient, but irreversibly crazy? That I'm just imagining things?"

Freya attempted a reassuring grin. "No, no, no! My dear, no! Of course, not! I am not judging you at all! I am far from perfect myself, believe me. I'm just seriously at the beginning of my profession still, as I've told you. Don't worry- I'll be referring you to some numbers of other therapists you can contact in the meantime to continue your treatment that work with your insurance. Maybe they can help you better than I ever could."

"Freya- how can I share my experiences with other therapists?" Merve pleaded. "I thought you and I had a connection- as patient and mentor, I mean- because you've told me you've been there, too! How can I tell any of others about this, without them thinking me bonkers?"

"Now, don't you worry," Freya had offered her a tissue, which Merve picked up reluctantly as she wiped a fallen tear. "You've already come a long way in recognizing your patterns since your childhood, and I'm very proud of you. I want you to know you can always reach out to me

only in case of any emergencies. In the meantime, not to worry. Like I've said- I will send you an entire listing of other local resources that can work with your insurance...or maybe you won't even need therapy for a while...."

"What?" Merve blurted out.

Freya had lied, knowing full well from her studies this woman would naturally have the inherent need to continue talking out her experiences for long-term therapeutic healing. "You said it yourself – you've been able to remain distant from the drama through prayer and focus on your work. Perhaps dating this manager guy has just triggered you and thrown you off your kilter, and maybe staying away from dating him could work out better for you. In the meantime, just remain in the present and focus on your well-being."

"Freya...." Merve burst into full-blown tears this time. "I'm desperate. Please. I don't know who else I can turn to! You don't understand. Aidan—my manager; he didn't just hurt my pride or my heart, Freya! He—well, I think that the jinn, through him—*violated* me....and my body!"

All Freya could think in that moment was, *No more jinn talk...No more anyone reminding me of the past....No more.*

"I'm afraid we've also logistically come to the end of our session, Merve, my dear— looks like our time is up! As I've said; you can get through anything on your own. You're stronger than you think. You've already been excelling at finding jobs and living on your own here in a new country. You have to give yourself more credit. And in the meantime, as promised, I will certainly send you that list of other therapeutic resources. One of them was a classmate of mine and I'm sure she'll be non-judgmental about the jinn, not to fret."

"I get it....." Merve stood up and uttered with a clenched jaw. "Thanks anyway."

She stood frozen in place for the longest minute of Freya's life. Even her sobs had turned quiet. Merve had turned to stare at Freya's face

one last time with the most tormented expression, accompanied by a disappointed shaking of her head.

"You're a terrible person for doing this to me," were her last words as Merve had stormed out of her office and out of her life. Untraceable from thereon forth.

That was the last Freya or anyone had apparently heard of Merve Turan— according to Google, anyway. What if something terrible had happened to her because the one person she'd had in the world she could entrust with her issues had stranded her?

Merve had also revealed that she'd been 'violated'—had she been raped? What if her rapist later murdered her? How the heck could Freya ever know which manager named 'Aidan' that could have been?

She could never forgive herself. *I was so selfish!* What in heaven, hell or both on earth had she catalyzed?

Life had given her another chance. These two women— Sandy and Kaitlin—could not have become her clients through some coincidence. Merve may have been her first failure, but Freya had to be brave— and more ethical, this time— to ensure that she'd also at least be her final one.

§

AIDAN HAD TO RING THE DOORBELL TWO MORE TIMES BEFORE SHE finally answered. The woman who had changed his life forever. The one he had never expected to fall in love with, but had.

How was he going to ask her to temporarily stay somewhere else over the holidays because of his mom and sister visiting him—he hadn't yet prepared. But he'd do whatever he had to do in order to avoid conflict for as long as he could. He'd have to tell the truth eventually, of course. To her. To his mom and sister.

But first things first— he wanted everyone to get over the drama with his father before he could throw his own stuff into the mix.

"I'm coming, I'm coming," Merve's voice was teasing as she opened the door in only a towel wrapped around her body. Her blonde-highlighted brown hair was wrapped up in a towel turban-style.

"To what do I owe the pleasure of this trip, Mr. Ramsay?" she teased.

"Mmm," Aidan cooed. Was that vanilla bean, again, he smelled? It was subtle, yet he loved it. And his wife knew it.

"May I come in, Mrs. Ramsay? Your husband's missed you."

CHAPTER 28

FINN CLEARED HIS THROAT EXTRA LOUDLY FOR ATTENTION, IN addition to the ignored thought he had already sent her way. "Mer? You up there? We're back." It took several seconds but Meredith's soft voice responded from the second floor of the upscale wooden cabin.

"Welcome back, guys," her voice called out in response finally. "Sorry—I'm just cleaning up here!"

Bo, in his human boy form with shaggy brown hair and matching eyes, plopped himself on the rocking chair by the living room fireplace, causing Finn to fleetingly smile. His grin soon turned into a giggle as he watched Bo rock himself harder and harder. "Be careful you don't break it, boy. This isn't a playground swing. It's an antique!"

"Can Malin and I go to the playground next time?" Bo asked. He looked down at his slender body. "And why can't I hang out with her like *this*? Why do I have to be in dog form all the time?"

"Bo, we've talked about this," Finn pointed out. "For the time being, Malin needs to believe I'm her 'long-lost uncle', and we can't have you accompany me as anything other than my 'pet' at this time. Because otherwise, that would make you her supposed 'cousin' and that may risk complicating things with regards to our secrecy."

"A pet," Bo snickered, sulking as his rocking slowed.

"Hey," Finn flashed next to him, placing his forehead against his. "Bo, look at me."

Bo managed to look up, gazing into Finn's eyes with need. It warmed his heart.

"I know this isn't easy. You're a kid, and you just want to have fun. Especially as you've made a new friend, but..."

"Why can't I just lead a normal life like the other kids?" Bo jolted up from the chair. "I don't care if I must attend jinn school, and not human ones like Malin does. I just want to be normal."

"Things are...different in our brethren, you know that," Finn replied with a heavy sigh. He heard Meredith moving through some furniture upstairs. "One second. I have to talk to your mom for a bit. I'll be right down. Hey, why don't we do a drawing contest again, what do you say? Take out your sketchbook and start without me."

As Finn heard Bo mutter 'okay', he flashed up the stairs and peeked through the open crack in the bedroom he shared with Meredith. Their jinn forms didn't require much sleep, but when they did— it was reassuring for both of them to cuddle in doing so. Though they hadn't been intimate for the longest time, it all felt more and more like *home* to him over the years.

He smiled as Meredith's long straight her running down the back of her petite frame came into view. "Looking at Tan's pictures again?"

Startled, Meredith wiped her tears and shut the drawers. "Oh, no, no, no, I was just cleaning."

Finn gave her an all-knowing smile. They both knew she was still in love with her ex-human lover. And in his own crazy way, Finn always felt Tan had loved Meredith as well. Tragically, the man was just too obsessed with his murder of Linette and its repercussions to ever focus on the two of them.

Oh yeah, Finn thought, rolling his eyes. *And focused on impressing Lar, too.* Meredith shot him a look, causing Finn's hands to go up defensively.

"Alright, alright, let's focus now on your trip," Finn went on. "You sure you can go through with this, Mer?"

"I am," Meredith said, sulking her shoulders. "I need to get on Master's good side just as much as you do. Show my continuing worth to maintain my standing in our community. It's just business."

Yeah, Finn chuckled. *A business trip named Jack.* Or was it Jackson? He couldn't quite recall the name of the Canadian man Meredith was tasked to 'coincidentally' meet, only to then lure into 'The Group'.

"It's just that…" Meredith started.

"What is it?" Finn asked, noticing her distracted sadness.

"Bo," Meredith replied with a shrug. "I'm worried about leaving him behind."

"Don't worry," Finn placed his hands gently on her shoulders. "I've got Bo. He's safe with me. No one can hurt him. Not Master, not anyone!"

"Thank you," Meredith's blazing lips neared Finn's own. "It means a lot to me that you've been taking him out to play. Even if it is probably more for Malin than for him."

He softly placed his fingers on her lips. "Don't. You know we shouldn't."

"Why not?" Meredith asked. "Is this still about Kaitlin? I thought you'd gotten over her already. Time heals all wounds."

Not lasting ones, Finn thought. "Have they truly healed yours? Over Tan?"

"That's not fair, Finn," Meredith said, taking a step back. "He's gone! He's dead, do you understand that? I can mourn the dead— but you cannot be a father to Bo and mourn your living little human girlfriend who won't make the same sacrifices as I have!"

"Meredith!" Finn bellowed, caught between his anger and sympathy upon seeing her fragile, emotional face. Her childlike features expressed immense sorrow.

Something he hadn't recognized had been brewing in him lately—particularly after he'd discovered that Lar would be sending Meredith off to Canada soon. Alone.

His voice shifted. "Hey, Mer?"

"What?" she whimpered.

He worried about her. Meredith. This was the actual mother of his child—children, in fact, counting the other two they'd given up for adoption. Finn was more convinced of it now. Sure, he wasn't in love with her. But they understood each other, and could actually make a living together. He knew he had to do the right thing.

Something he had been considering more and more lately, in order to benefit everyone. Something that could even appease Lar; as much as he preferred jinn and human unions in the brethren to avoid children, he and Meredith had already gotten through that and could promise to be more careful to avoid another jinn offspring.

Something that also wouldn't necessarily be betraying his love for Kaitlin, either. If she ever cared enough, that was, to finally be with him. To finally choose him. For it didn't have to be a marriage in the traditional sense, but rather more of a platonic, respectable one.

Maybe it would turn into love in the long run. Maybe then his parents would even be proud of him. He'd had a fleeting run-in with his brother not long ago, and he'd relayed that their mom and dad had found out about how Finn and Meredith had been living with Bo 'in sin'.

Bo. Part of him told him to help him escape. Lead a better life than the addictive hellhole that the mission of 'The Group' had turned into— despite starting off as somewhere 'exciting' for him to live and feel accepted in. *Bo deserves just as pure and wholesome a life as Malin*, Finn decided. How that could be achieved— he wasn't yet sure.

Lord knew Meredith had been begging to run away and lead a new life together, away from Lar and the cult— just the three of them. *"Lar would be even angrier with me than he's already been lately, Mer,"* he told the only woman who'd always been there for him. Someone he truly loved as a friend- aside from a couple of nights of conciliatory passion. *We were both trying to get over broken hearts each time*, Finn told himself for the millionth time. It was just sex. Wasn't it? Yet how had they gotten to this point?

He sighed. He knew his parents had always wanted him to marry one of his own. Like his brother had done. Their kind didn't do such things in the same manner of humans, but he knew Meredith to be a romantic. Finn also didn't have a ring on him, but he got down on one knee.

"I know we're more coparenting as friends than anything else. But I also know that we both want the best for Bo, and for each other, too, for that matter. Meredith Olsen…will you marry me?"

§

KAITLIN GASPED AS SHE JOLTED UPRIGHT IN HER BED, FLIPPING OFF her sleeping mask. She had been awakened with the now familiar tingle on the back of her neck and the nearly-whispering voice in her ear again—one she'd come to recognize as actually being a thought inside her head, only through his voice. *Can we meet and talk…?*

Kaitlin rubbed her aching temples, focusing on her own mental response. *No, Finn. Just say what you want to say like this.*

Finn was persistent. *Please? In person. I'll meet you by our pier.*

Hugging her pillow and rocking her body back forth, Kaitlin shut her eyes to concentrate on her telepathic message to Finn again. She glanced at the bedroom door to ensure her husband wasn't coming in to take her by surprise. *Paul's home today. I can't, even if I wanted to. Which I don't. Sorry.*

Finn's voice resonated louder this time. *We need to talk— it's about Malin.*

§

THE SEAGULLS PAINTED A NEAR-WHITE PICTURE RIVALING THE SEA'S foams before Kaitlin's eyes. Her favorite bench—the one she'd been hanging out on with Sibel the other day—was occupied, and so she had to settle for sitting on one closer to the water this time. Luckily, it was also away from the pedestrians on the sidewalk, many of whom would be seeing her as 'talking to herself'. She wanted to avoid feeling stranger than she had already been feeling as of late at all costs.

I'm here. The familiar tingling sensation traveled from her back and throughout her body, and Kaitlin turned her head toward the direction she was being pulled toward— almost magnetically. Finn was leaning backward on one of the larger boulders. For the longest time, the two of them stood looking at each other without verbal utterances. Sorrow lingered in the air. It was heavy, and didn't leave room for words.

"You promised not to see her again!" Kaitlin finally managed to mutter after Finn initiated taking a couple of steps toward her. She had insisted on not meeting, until Finn had convinced her to do so following yet another shocking confession: that he'd just arranged a second play-date between her daughter and Bo! It hadn't been easy to get by Paul this time, but Kaitlin had fibbed something about surprise-shopping for Malin and needing to be by herself.

"How could you risk it like this— again? What if Malin told her dad her 'uncle' picked her up from art class, instead of her mother?"

"She wouldn't, and didn't," Finn rolled his eyes, sighing as he flopped down next to her. "She's a clever girl, and she's bought this entire *'it's a secret since Daddy isn't talking to his twin'* charade. I'm proud of her—she apparently didn't even tell you. She keeps her promises. She's a good girl."

"Finn, this is becoming ridiculous," Kaitlin retorted, still in disbelief. "Frankly, I'm feeling disrespected and even a little afraid."

"Afraid?" Finn asked, sounding hurt. "I thought you would trust me by now…"

"There are bouts of time when you keep *your* promises- until you don't," Kaitlin observed. "I can never trust when and if you're going to randomly show yourself! It's constantly making me on the edge in daily life, and…"

"I promised to stay away *if* you didn't want me to," Finn cut in. "As a jinn, remember, I'm guided through your *specific instructions*. Specific beckoning. Specific sensations I'm in tune with as well. You were feeling concern for Malin again, and I felt it. And I showed her and Bo a good time again, that's all. You and Paul try to almost get her out of your noses, buried in your work while keeping her occupied with extracurricular activities when all she wants is more quality time!"

"Well, good. I hope you had your last *hoorah* for a while as some babysitter, then, 'Uncle Finn', because—and maybe you've heard me think this as well— I'm seriously planning on cutting back Malin's after-school activities! What excuse are you going to have then, I wonder, to orchestrate your playdate schemes?"

Finn took in a deep breath and shut his eyes before opening them slowly. "You're already traveling overseas in December; I will miss you girls. Bo will miss Malin, too. There won't be any playdates for a while. So cut us some slack, will you?"

"Stop using Bo as an excuse," Kaitlin steamed. "And—here goes, Finn—my *explicit, specific* instruction for you to not visit us on our trip to the United States or Canada, at least! Alright?"

"I won't, but, *ahem,*" Finn cleared his throat. He hadn't a clue how to open Lar's demand to Kaitlin. "I wanted to talk to you about the trip, actually. I will do more than promise- I will *swear* on my very own life not to present myself to you or Malin in your United States and Canada trip, *if* you promise to do one little thing for me."

"I'm listening," Kaitlin crossed her arms after a moment's hesitation.

"Lar is watching me like a hawk. He knows we're still, *err*, friends. And he's pressuring me to ask for *your* help— as a human with citizenship over there— in securing a suite in the city in Toronto for us."

"What?" Kaitlin remarked, spit nearly coming out of her mouth.

"For legitimacy purposes," Finn explained. "We're required for tax information and such to present ourselves to our paper clients as reputable as possible. We need actual humans with their names and information on the papers to take care of the overheads and utilities."

"You want me to like, what—rent out some suite for you guys? And with what money, Finn, may I ask?"

"I'll take care of all that," Finn said dismissively, his hands waving in the air. "You can even stay there yourself…whenever you need, or feel overwhelmed and don't want to stay with Sandy or your brother, anymore. You can think of it as a hotel room, of sorts."

"Finn, if I wanted to stay in a hotel room— Paul would have arranged that for us," Kaitlin raised her chin. "He just didn't want us to feel alone in New York while he's stuck working here for the time-being, that's all. He's used up his vacation days already, and so…"

Finn smirked and shook his head. "I didn't ask you why Paul isn't coming with you girls, Kaitlin." He leaned close to her face, his fiery breath tickling her face.

"You don't have to make excuses for his absence on the trip— or why his inherent stinginess hasn't considered hotel accommodation for merely ten days or so in both places."

Kaitlin opened her mouth in defense, but quickly shut it. It was no use with Finn. She raised a brow. "You asked to meet me here to request my help for your organization?"

Finn glanced at the North Sea waves surrounding the *Gandsfjorden*, and then back at Kaitlin. He drew in a deep breath. "I also wanted you to hear it from me: Meredith and I are, *um*…you know, as fellow kinds, thinking of making things official in raising Bo…and…"

"You two are…getting *married*?" Kaitlin's voice trembled in spite of her resolve to keep as cool as she could. "You could just cut to the case."

"Technically, yes: I suppose we'll be doing just that," Finn cleared his throat, averting his gaze away from Kaitlin's own fixed blankly on his visage.

"Why, though?" Kaitlin demanded.

"Pardon?" Finn asked, genuinely befuddled.

"You already live together," Kaitlin continued, folding her arms across her chest. "I didn't realize a legal marriage was of importance in your, *err*, circle."

"Well, it is, Ms. Kaitlin," Finn stood firm. "Mostly so for my parents. They've found out about Bo, and, well they're traditional. And for their continued support of allowing our use of the local cabin—it's just logistics."

"That cabin belongs to your family?" Kaitlin shook her head, recalling her visits there in Stavanger. *How the heck can jinn own property?*

"I heard that," Finn teased. "Lar constructed it, and it's under his name. But it's on my parents' property. A lot of natural land belongs to my kind, Kaitlin. We preside in our most natural states in locales freer from human residue. In our own realm, of course. Anyway—they've allowed it, at a price."

"A*ha*…right," Kaitlin nodded, as confused as ever.

"I had to get Lar's blessing first for the marriage," Finn chewed on the inside of his mouth. "He was initially upset, but came around rather quickly when he considered its professional benefits."

"Hmm," Kaitlin uttered, still avoiding eye contact. "You'll still be living with the other members?"

"Yes," Finn relayed. "Anya has been the head of the main cabin for a while now—remember her?"

After Kaitlin nodded with a smile, Finn went on. "It's exciting for her and Bjorn, though on paper she's technically married with Serdar and…"

"I know Bjorn, but *Serdar*?" Kaitlin asked quizzically. Why did that name sound familiar to her?

"Yes, Ms. Kaitlin," Finn grinned at her thought's questioning. "You've heard of that name before. We met brother Serdar through the late Tan—he was his old roommate."

Kaitlin could swear she was losing her mind. "Oh, wow, okay, so, let me try to get this straight—I suppose anyone who is or has been a friend to any of you is somehow fair game to be recruited, eh?"

Finn tilted his head and furrowed his brows. "Not really, Ms. Kaitlin. We wouldn't 'befriend'— as you're terming— just *anyone*."

"Oh, right—only 'special souls' like me, was it?" Kaitlin inched closer to his face. The heat radiating from his skin added a rosy flush across her cheeks, his breath a most warm and subtle breath tickling her skin.

"You know you've been the most special of all for me," Finn caressed her chin, his expression stern as he lowered his face to stare deep into her eyes. "I really wish *you* would stay with us."

Kaitlin placed a palm on her face and slowly stepped back from the kiss for which she realized her entire body had been quivering in anticipation. "Trust me, Finn: I'm not some ideal wife or partner or whatever you imagine you'd have in me, even if I were to throw it all away to run off with you. Besides— I would not want to intrude on your marriage with Meredith."

"Meredith's my friend, and we'll mainly be coparenting, " Finn shrugged. "You should be aware that it's a technicality."

Kaitlin scoffed. "Just as your consummation of Bo as an offspring, too, was a 'technicality'?"

"And yours of Malin with your husband, too, I suppose…." Finn pressed in a sarcastic tone. "Yeah, something like that I guess."

"Wow," Kaitlin clicked her tongue to the roof of her mouth. "Well, I guess I'm glad you're finally admitting Paul is definitely Malin's father, at least."

"It was one drunken night…" Finn went on, ignoring Kaitlin's last comment. "You were keeping away from me, and she'd just had a big fight with Tan. As she's told you— we just comforted each other. We're not perfect either, just like humans, Kaitlin. But let's not digress from what this is really about."

Kaitlin let out a sharp sigh. "You're right- *I* came here because you said you wanted to discuss Malin. I really don't want to talk about *us* right now."

"And I *did* talk about Malin," Finn continued. "I wanted to tell you about our latest play date before you heard about it. As well as these…other updates."

"The *last* play date, Finn," Kaitlin begged. "Please."

"Okay," Finn nodded. He took a couple of steps back, arms resting his own trembling body against the bench he was leaning on for support of his manifested human form.

God I wish I kissed those lips when he was closer to me, Kaitlin mused, observing Finn biting his lips.

Oh, merde! She thought, catching Finn smiling at her. Of course he had heard her.

"I'm still right here, you know…." Finn said with a smile. "And please don't force yourself to explain the 'impossibility' of 'us', again, Ms. Kaitlin."

Kaitlin raised her chin, tilting her head backwards almost as if the act could throw the tears back into her body through her eye sockets.

"No—I'm genuinely amazed of your acceptance that Malin was indeed consummated by my husband and I."

"Why do you feel the need to bring that up again?" Finn asked. "I love Malin—simply because she is yours, and is a sweet child, Kaitlin. Regardless of which male she carries the blood of..."

"Thank you," Kaitlin smiled, blushing. "I mean it. It's nice to hear that from you, I suppose, so I think I wanted to celebrate with a kiss out of joy. Let's forget it."

Finn cleared his throat. "I can try, but I don't *want* to forget it. Couldn't you at least *try* to give *us* a chance? You haven't all these years— are you happy?"

You must not forget your mission, Finn- or else. Lar's voice echoed at the back of his mind. Seizing upon Kaitlin's quiet contemplation, Finn went on.

"Let me just introduce you to the only person whom I've still got remaining in my life as family…Professor Iktar."

"No way! "Kaitlin yelped.

"Kaitlin…don't judge him based purely on hearsay, without having met him. Why don't you and Malin come to stay with us? You know—when Paul thinks you'll be in New York. You girls should return a week earlier. Just a week is all I'm asking you for. A trial, if you will."

"Finn, we're not talking about some gym membership," Kaitlin scoffed, crossing her arms.

Finn continued, sidestepping her comment. "I'll meet you girls when you're at the airport, after he's waved goodbye and left. You can stay with us for a few days before you and Malin actually fly out. You can do your work from your laptop from anywhere!"

Kaitlin released laughter despite herself. "Are you frigging serious?"

"We'll get to see each other," Finn shrugged with a smile. "I want you to test it, at least. Give it a chance. You'll see Malin can grow up happier with another child her age around— Bo. And she'll be in nature—it can help transform her into becoming a more confident version of herself. Malin likes nature!"

He added with a wink. "She's a bit like her mother in that way, but more observant—and less high-maintenance in the woods."

"You're insane," Kaitlin shook her head side to side, smiling. "Besides—isn't the high and mighty Lar Iktar against any more children? You said it yourself…."

"As you will be contributing to our brethren, Lar will manage—not to worry," Finn insisted. "You've visited our cabin before, Kaitlin. Was there anything to be afraid of? No. So, come on. Lar's not so bad once you get to know him. He helps us all. To be ourselves. You can be yourself, without judgements. You can stay for as long or as short as you like…Just—*stay*."

"Finn…" Kaitlin began more firmly this time. "Thank you. But I am not interested in joining 'The Group'! And to even think you would try to convince me to do so with my *daughter* this time? That's nuts!"

"You did translations for us before!" Finn claimed with a casual shrug. "Why not?"

"Don't get me started with those translations you lured me with, Finn," Kaitlin said matter-of-factly.

Finn's face turned more serious. "You got paid, Kaitlin. We'll pay you again. You have my word."

"I get paid from my website now, thank you," Kaitlin said, hugging her arms closer around her torso. She took in a deep breath, running her palms across imagined creases on her jacket.

"It'd be like an adventure," Finn inched closer, placing his hands gently on her shoulders.

Kaitlin stepped back, doing a couple of little jumps in place for heat. "Not under our circumstances, Finn. We can't. I'm sorry. You know this cannot be. Not like that. Why are you so insistent?"

"Circumstances may be bad, but connections aren't," Finn wrapped his arms around her torso, passionate desire flowing like hot lava from his manifested skin onto hers.

"I will not go through with this marriage with Meredith if you come live with us! Alright? Happy? That's why I'm *insistent*, as you say. All of this isn't my first choice. *You* are."

"Finn," Kaitlin whispered feebly, looking up at him as his green eyes planted themselves into her soul. "This is all…*chaos*."

"I find lust in your chaos, Kaitlin, and heaven in your fire," Finn began, whispering softly on her titillated skin. "I've put trust in your rust."

Kaitlin pulled her face back, smiling as her hands lingered on his arms. "What was *that*?"

"A poem I wrote," Finn said with a wink. "I know you've been writing too. I'm trying to impress you. Are you impressed?"

"Finn," Kaitlin rolled her eyes despite being unable to resist a chuckle. "It's beautiful. As all of this is. Thank you. But I cannot join your damned cult! Please understand—put yourself into my shoes!"

Finn took in a deep breath and raised his palms to the air, stepping back. "Okay, tough cookie. You're still insulting us. I give up. I figured you'd be stubborn, again. But I wanted to try, at least. I don't want to think back and regret not having taken a chance with any possibility, at least, when it comes to you."

"Finn…" Kaitlin was once again feeling at a loss for words.

"Why don't you at least help me by allowing Lar to think you've accepted?" Finn's eyes implored. "Help me with the Toronto leasing of a suite for us. As my friend at least. For everything. Please?"

Kaitlin sighed. "Very well. I'll see what I can do. Will Lar insist on seeing me afterwards, though? I really don't think I can handle such a thing."

"He'll be convinced you've accepted being a member if you just later meet him at the cabin with the keys to the place you'll be securing in Toronto," Finn assured. "I'll aid with placating him, just as I will with the actual economics. Can Paul find out you've leased a place in Canada?"

Kaitlin's eyes shot up in thought. "I don't think so. It's funny— my legal status is technically 'single' back home, as we legally got married here. Over there I'm still 'Kaitlin Ramsay', and we don't have a joint account in Canada."

"I think I'll like you better in Canada, then," Finn said with a slick smile.

"Don't get any ideas," Kaitlin warned him with a smile. "No visiting us over there— remember?"

Finn's hands shot up in a surrendering motion. "A promise is a promise. You need to have this family time, and heal the wounds with your mom and brother over your dad. I'm giving you your space, as long as you give me your word, as well. You just mentally let me know the amount you need for the space, and it'll be in your bank account."

"You have my word," Kaitlin spoke softly. She watched as Finn placed his hands into his trouser pockets, his dark coat highlighting his blond mane glistening in the sun.

"And, hey, Finn? Congratulations." Kaitlin hated awkward silences. "If you feel that marrying Meredith is the right thing to do— who am I to stop you? Please— by all means. Please do what is best— especially for Bo. And thank you for everything."

"Thanks for your well wishes," Finn shrugged. With a sudden thought, he placed his forefinger in the air close to Kaitlin's face, as the sea breeze blew more strands across her face. "I know you think our union can't be lasting because it can't build toward some purpose or future in your human realm. But haven't you and Paul solely worked toward a purpose – that of being married ? Think about it: how did those times work out for you?"

Kaitlin shook her head rampantly, fighting back tears. "I don't know, Finn. All I know at this moment is that I need to actually go to New York. I have my family drama to deal with, as you know. Figuring out what's going on with my dad and showing Malin a good time— those are my priorities right now. I need to do the right thing. One step at a time. Baby steps are all I can handle even contemplating right now."

"Alright," Finn pulled himself back, inhaling the chill in the air. "Go—deal with family drama. Maybe it's time I recognize my true place in your life. Maybe it's time I focused on a little family of my own."

As the nearby seagulls croaked and cried out, Kaitlin glanced at them with a melancholy smile. "I am like these seagulls, Finn."

"The seagulls?" Finn asked.

Kaitlin allowed herself to experience the weighing sensation of disappointment penetrating through every cell in her body. "Remember feeding them when we saw each other again by this harbor? Back when Malin was still a baby? They were fighting for a mere chunk of those cardamom buns from your fiery hand. The buns weren't enough to fully satiate them…and yet they were good enough for the seagulls. I'm like that, too, Finn. I'm still drawn to whatever is offered to me, even when I know it can never be enough…for I also know in life there isn't any guarantee of something more filling ever coming my way if I let the opportunity go. "

"Hmm," Finn simply uttered, his hands grazing her hair. "I remember even then watching the breeze blow through your hair. I had kept my promise to stay away, but then I saw you, and fell in love with you all over again. You're still wearing it long."

"Oh!" Kaitlin exclaimed as if in remembrance of something, pulling her head away from him. "I almost forgot! This time, I've come prepared."

Finn's eyes dimmed as his focus grew stronger on Kaitlin, watching her fumble through her slouchy hobo bag before finally taking out a circular pastry from a bag.

"Don't tell me you've packed something metal against me," he teased, right as Kaitlin unwrapped the food item.

"*Voila*! The quintessential Canadian bagel- let's see your *hveteboller* compete with this!"

"Alright, Miss Kaitlin," Finn chuckled, placing his fingers on his chin with one hand as the other grabbed his elbow. He added with a wink. "Glad to hear my buns made a lasting impression on you! Now let's see what you've got! Let's feed these babies!"

Kaitlin placed her arm straight and behind her, preparing to throw half of the bagel she'd ripped in the direction of the croaking seagulls, when the bread dropped into the sea. "Oh, no!"

As the water splashed into Finn's eye, he wiped it immediately, cursing under his breath. "*Putain*! Water isn't good for my kind."

"Oh, that must have hurt," Kaitlin said with a sympathetic smile. "I'm sorry." *Doesn't he take showers, though?*

"Our natural forms don't need water for cleansing, and the human flesh we manifest in stay pure as long as we don't remain in them for too long," Finn explained, answering her unuttered question with a wink.

"I see," Kaitlin nodded with a grin, holding out the other half of the bagel.

"Fire and water may not make good companions, but *we* just might…for life."

"Okay, poet," Kaitlin rolled her eyes but with a smile. "Oh, look! One of them grabbed the bagel from the water! Smart fella! I feel bad for the other ones, though. Here goes. One…two…."

"Wait!" Finn called out, holding her arm. "Your placement is all wrong. How are you going to teach Malin to throw stones and pebbles far into the sea with a stiff arm like that?"

"Not all of us have supra-human powers, Mr. Super Jinn…" Kaitlin winked.

To her enticement, Finn's eyes opened as wide as saucers as he let out a small chuckle. "You've got nicknames, too, now, eh?"

"*Eh*?" It was Kaitlin's turn to laugh, albeit her burst sounded more like a snort. She took a small bite off the corner of the plain bagel she'd bagged from the local bakery before meeting Finn. *"Es-tu un canadien aussi maintenant?"*

"Canadian…Hungarian…Bavarian…Planetarian," Finn's face expression turned serious. He placed his hands into the front pockets of his tattered jeans. "I'll do my best to be wherever and whatever you need me to be. You must be aware of this by now."

"Finn…." Kaitlin began. *Why can't things ever just be lighthearted between us?*

"I like depth," he winked at her thought, clearing his throat. "You can't desire *passion* in life and then be upset at its source for having too much of it."

Kaitlin rolled her eyes at him playfully as a particularly eager seagull began to hover near them.

"Oh, look at this guy!" Finn exclaimed. "Give him his share!"

Kaitlin looked at him with panic. "Won't it hurt my hand? I've never hand-fed a large bird before!"

Finn rolled his eyes at her. "Stop struggling so hard to chase it…just be still, and wait for it to come to you to retrieve the nourishment!"

"How?" Kaitlin stammered, placing the bagel piece in the middle of her palm. "Will it just pick it up from my…"

Her question froze mid-air as a particularly grayish seagull snatched it from her hand and flew off. "*That*…was surprisingly easy….and exhilarating! And I didn't even have to throw anything like some American batter."

He inched closer behind her, his flaming breath tickling the back of her neck. His scent— an ever-curious mix of sulfur and the evergreen woods—was creating goosebumps all over Kaitlin's body.

"If you want to try to be more athletic, though, you can raise your arm with your elbow loosely bent, like this," Finn motioned, moving Kaitlin's arm backwards. "Reach all the way back, and….throw!"

Two seagulls fought for the piece of bread now in the air, one of them acting more competitive and eager to catch it. Kaitlin squirmed as she actually saw the creature turn his head behind his body to grab the piece of food before his seagull friend could.

Was that a snapping sound she'd heard? Kaitlin closed her eyes, dreading perceiving any potential struggle for life in the poor animal. "Oh— *no*! Finn! Is it okay?"

Watching as Finn transformed into his invisible form of energy to quickly grab the falling bird in the air, Kaitlin followed behind as he walked back to the shore line and gently placed its body onto the concrete. The animal's screeching sounded more and more faint by the second as it flapped its wing to no avail.

Kaitlin's eyes began to well with tears. "Finn— do something! We have to save him!"

"I think it's simply its time, Kaitlin," Finn said softly back in his human form once again, caressing the animal's face. "There is nothing I can do."

The animal gazed into Finn's eyes and let out a feeble screech. "*Shh*," Finn spoke softly to it. "You'll soon be at peace, my friend. Not to worry."

"You're just going to let it *die*?" Kaitlin yelped with trembling hands on her face. "You're a jinn! Can't you….I don't know…"

"What?" Finn demanded. "Bring it back to life or something? We are inferior before God, just as your kind. I'm afraid there's nothing I can do."

The animal lacked movement now, allowing itself to repose fully in Finn's hands. "I'll bury it in the sand."

"I killed the seagull!" Kaitlin wept, trying to catch her breath between sobs. She rocked her body back and forth gently across the boulder she'd sat on. "It was flying along just fine on its daily flight. Until I had to tease it. With my stupid throwing game. I had to lure it out of its routine."

"Hey…hey there," Finn shot back over her shoulder, tilting his head forward to imply she should follow him as he walked. The seagull was still in his hands, and Kaitlin couldn't take her eyes off it. "No need to get so hysterical, now. Your intention was good, Kaitlin. God knows. It's okay. It's all right. You were just trying to feed it."

"What good are intentions if the results are horrendous?" Kaitlin uttered through her tears. "I killed it, Finn! I killed it! I'm just as messed up as my father is— apparently still alive, and unwell, out there."

Finn didn't say anything further, sitting next to her. Instead, he stroked her hair and placed his free arm around her shoulders, allowing for her to cry into his arms.

Circling above their heads, a black and purple grackle was staring intently at the both of them. Its gaze remained fixed on Kaitlin, until Finn hissed at it and willed it mentally to leave.

CHAPTER 21

WATCHING AS HIS DAUGHTER HUMMED A FAMILIAR POP TUNE while sprawled on the couch, Paul peeked through the corner of his newspaper with a smile. He was going to miss Malin in the two weeks or so she'd be away, much more than arguing with her mother— that was for sure.

"You sound good, Mallie," he called out to her, holding his gaze on her until she returned his smile. "That's my princess."

"Thanks Daddy," she replied with a casual shrug, returning to the coloring book she'd been occupied with on the couch, blue color pencil in hand. Kaitlin had gone out to get some coffee that had run out—doubling also as a walking exercise for her, Paul knew. Getting movement out and about was essential in her mental well-being. Besides, it was a Sunday and he didn't mind the only chance he had to relax a bit.

Was it just him, or had Malin been talking less and less with him lately? Had Kaitlin voiced needless concerns with their daughter, as well? Filling the little girl's head with more emotional stress than she was equipped to handle? She hadn't been snuggling on the couch with him lately as much as she used to.

"Mallie—sweety?" he called out to her, placing the newspaper atop the glass table in front of him. He leaned forward in his daughter's direction. "Can we talk for a little bit, before Mommy comes back?"

"We are talking, Daddy," she said with a smile and a shrug.

"Is there anything you'd like to tell me in particular?" Paul insisted, reaching out to caress the top of her soft head. "Come on. You'll be away from me in New York soon. I'm going to miss my angel so much! Let's hang out today. Would you like to go to the mall? Someone has a birthday coming up— we can get some early shopping done!"

"My birthday is next month, Daddy," Malin said, her tone growing increasingly excited. She jolted up. "Although you *could* get me a Halloween present since it's October! I want a costume and Mommy said I should recycle the fairy one from last year since no one in my class has seen that yet!"

"She has, has she?" Paul said with an exaggerated look of shock on his face. He walked over to sit down next to her, caressing her silky brown mane. *And yet Kaitlin can splurge on designer clothes with the gift card I just bought for her own 33rd birthday,* he thought with a snicker. "Malin Maverick cannot repeat a costume two years in a row!"

He couldn't believe he'd just said what he had— particularly as he didn't get what the fuss about this satanic-seeming holiday for children was about. But if it got his daughter excited, he'd pretend to get excited with her – at least until she was a bit older and he'd have to warn her about all the dark stuff.

"This year I want to be an animal of some kind, *hmm*," Malin tapped a finger on her mouth playfully. "Maybe a dog! Ooh— I want to play in the woods again!"

The sudden sinking feeling at the pit of Paul's stomach rivaled its growl from hunger. "*Again*? What do you mean, Mallie?"

"Oopsies!" Malin's eyes widened. She placed her hands over her mouth.

"The woods?" Paul got down on one knee and placed his arms gently on Malin's shoulders. "Mallie? Sweetie, look at me. What are you not telling Daddy? There's something you and Mommy have been keeping from me, isn't there? I feel it. Tell me! When were you last in the woods?"

§

KAITLIN JAMMED THE KEY TWO MORE TIMES INTO THE HOLE TO GET IT to turn— it had been hard to do so with one hand, as the other was still holding on to the heavy plastic bag. "Paul?"

She finally rang the doorbell. *Something's not right.* Her husband would have usually heard her fidgeting about, offering to help her with her load. Kaitlin watched as the door opened slowly and Paul gave her a slight nod to welcome her— rather than a kiss or even his usual gesture of picking up the groceries.

"*Um*— hi, Paulie, what's going on? Where's Mallie?" Kaitlin began feeling worse as her husband shot her a head-to-toe look-over, walking back to the living room.

"All good— she's getting dressed, we're going to the mall soon to get her a Halloween costume."

"Oh, yeah?" Kaitlin asked, removing her shoes and closing the door behind her. "Thanks for offering but I think I can manage the one bag into the kitchen."

Taking the bag toward the kitchen area and looking into Paul's eyes for a response—Kaitlin's stomach sank even further to witness his nonchalance at her sarcasm. "So, she convinced you of a need for something other than the fairy costume, *eh*?"

Paul still wasn't looking at her, instead focusing on the closed television. "She's grown fonder of…dogs…it seems than ever before, wife dear."

Kaitlin placed the items she'd just bought into the refrigerator and closed its door. She stood still in place as Paul continued.

"Have a seat, Kaitlin. We need to talk."

Kaitlin took in a deep breath and walked over to sit next to him. *What the heck is this about?* For her life, she had no clue what it could be this time to have gotten Paul to act this way with her.

"Our daughter asked me something while you were out— about walking in the woods."

And there it is. Kaitlin thought, her chest feeling flustered. "The woods?" she itched the skin around her chest through her sweater.

Paul continued. "She inquired about my 'brother Finn'…with whom I have apparently not been talking to for a while, and who was told to be kept a secret from me while they have been hanging out in the woods."

Oh, shoot. Kaitlin cleared her throat. "What? Brother? Our girl's got a vivid imagination. I…"

Paul's sudden turning of his body to face Kaitlin head-on jolted her in surprise. "*Don't* try playing me for a fool, Kaitlin! Not this time. You told me you weren't meeting with them, or him, anymore!"

"I'm *not*!" Kaitlin whispered loudly, straining her neck to ensure that Malin was still in her room. "Please—keep your voice down. Paulie don't assume anything before you know the details. This all happened behind my back, too, believe me—but our daughter is safe. I'm assuring it!"

"She said you *knew* they played fetch with some dog in the damn forest!" Paul's forefinger was merely centimeters from her eyes.

"I swear I didn't at first," Kaitlin stammered. "As you know, she's been wanting a dog. And…and I was promised it was a safe opportunity. I think that the jinn genuinely wanted a …a friend for his son…"

"A friend…for his son…" Paul's voice had eerily become softer now. "Gee. How sweet. Finn Du Feu, was his name, wasn't it?"

"Paul— I'm serious!" Kaitlin nodded frantically. "He's with that woman, Meredith, from 'The Group'! They're a couple! And they have a child together— they're all of the jinn kind and I think the kid transforms into a dog form. There's nothing to suspect— they're even getting married! It's just been a play date. Their son is a kid who likes to take on the dog form, apparently. You've met him, too, Paulie. It's…*Bo*."

"Bo?" Paul asked, his brow raised until a look of remembrance clouded over him. "That puppy I'd brought home to you, from Stephan at the office? The one that was taken from us—that was some *jinn*-dog?"

"Can you believe it?" Kaitlin chuckled nervously. "It turned out that our daughter played with our once-pet. One that we first named. What a small world."

"Yeah…some play date," Paul nodded. The eerie smile continued to be plastered on his face, creeping Kaitlin out. "A play date where the both of you had to concoct some lie about my 'long-lost twin brother' in order to plan out! I can't believe you have been hanging out with damn *jinn* again— and now our daughter's involved too!"

Paul crossed his arms, waiting for a response from Kaitlin.

"And you think telling me he's with some jinn woman is supposed to make me feel better?" he continued upon her silence. "Trust you more, somehow? Why the fuck is a jinn luring our daughter to the woods and you're not telling me? How long has this been kept from me?"

"Mommy!" Malin called out from her room. "I can't put on my pink sweater!"

"I'm coming, sweetie pie!" Kaitlin called out, taking in a deep breath and heading toward her daughter's room. She stopped to turn back and glance at Paul. "It's…complicated…but please let's not confuse Malin, please! Go do your shopping— I'll come too, if you'd like. But please don't say anything to her regarding this. What did you tell her, by the way? Please tell me you obliged the lie!"

"I ignored it," Paul scoffed. "She apologized for seeing my 'twin' behind my back, claiming curiosity about her 'uncle' and the company of some dog of his. I had just told her it was 'alright' and accompanied her to her room before you came in."

He inhaled deeply, shutting and reopening his eyes before continuing. "How could you put our daughter at risk by involving her with a supernatural being, Kaitlin? Why are you even seeing him still in the first place? After everything we've gone through, nonetheless!"

"I'm not, Paulie," Kaitlin reached out to brush her hand across his scruffy cheek. "You have to believe me! He just met with me to confess he'd carried out this play-date for our children behind my back. I got so upset—believe me! And I met him again to ensure an oath from him that it would not happen again! Apparently he needed to look like you in order to pick Malin up from dance class, and that's how the 'twin' excuse started, and…"

"Is *this* why you gave me that whole thing about regretting marrying me too soon or some shit like that the other day?" Paul cut in, burrowing his eyebrows with hurt hazel eyes gazing into Kaitlin's own peepers of the same hue.

"Wh-what?" she stammered.

"Because *that* conversation only came up recently, seemingly after you've met up with your jinn-buddy," Paul scoffed as he began to pace around.

"The two things have nothing to do with each other," Kaitlin dismissed.

"It's okay— you won't have to pretend to love me anymore, I guess," Paul chuckled to himself. He did a turn in place before opening his arms right before Kaitlin's face like a performer. "I just lost my job today! Ta da! Now you can have an additional excuse to leave me, if you wish. Hang out as much as you want in whatever damned hell you please— though you can bet I won't be allowing Malin to do that with you!"

"You…got fired?" Kaitlin stammered. The shock took precedence over the harshness of his words regarding her and her daughter. "You got fired from your job?"

"Not exactly," Paul explained after inhaling deeply and chewing his lips. "But they want to transfer me to a less significant department….something about being 'uncomfortable' with my time in jail after some clients found out. They want me even further behind the scenes, to 'protect the company image'. They finally admitted it, at least. At least no one has to pretend like the elephant in the room isn't there anymore."

"Oh," was all Kaitlin could utter. A text message arrived on Paul's phone before she could interrogate any further.

"I'm leaving!" Paul's eyes remained glued to his phone. "Tim's reminding me of his drink invitation. We'd discussed hanging out in Stavanger, before I agreed to shopping with Malin—*merde*! I totally forgot! I thought I could use a drink to mourn my job situation…But it looks now like I've got more reasons!"

"Wait— what?" Kaitlin asked. "Paul we have to talk about this! Don't just run away! Tim can wait, and….!"

"Oh, we'll talk," Paul scoffed at her. "When I come back. In the meantime, I hope you think about what you're doing to our daughter, let alone *us*!"

"What *I'm* doing?" Kaitlin asked, but Paul wasn't listening as he headed to their daughter's room. She paced to get to her before he could. "Malin! Sweetie, can Daddy take a raincheck on the costume shopping? His friend needs him. I'll take you there if you want!"

Malin stepped out slowly from her room with a pout, looking back and forth between her parents. "We're not going today, Daddy?"

Paul wiped a tear from his eye, shooting Kaitlin an angry look as he kneeled before his daughter. "I'm sorry, my princess. I need to go hang out with my friend Tim. Daddy's a little upset—about the brother thing."

"It's all my fault," Malin began to cry.

"Paul— please just go, if you must!" Kaitlin stepped closer to them. "Don't do this to her!"

"Mommy—I'm sorry I couldn't keep the secret," Malin looked up at her with sad eyes. "I just want you and Daddy to be happy. I'm sorry I messed things up."

Paul held out his hand toward Kaitlin, implicating with his facial expression for her to stop and let him handle this. He drew Malin closer onto his chest, allowing her to cry in his embrace. "You've done nothing wrong, my angel. It's just….grown-up stuff. Hey, look at me!"

As Malin's doleful eyes looked up at Paul, tears fell from his own face. "We're going shopping tomorrow. Play at home with Mommy for a bit. Tomorrow—it's you and me for shopping. No ifs or buts. Okay?"

As Malin nodded and Paul kissed her forehead, he stood up with a sigh, eyes focusing on Kaitlin.

"Baby, wait inside as I see Daddy out, alright?" Kaitlin plastered a smile on her face. "We'll do that puzzle together, okie?"

"Okie dokie!" Malin smiled, hopping back into her room.

Kaitlin inched toward the door, crossing her arms across her chest. "You're seriously heading out. *Tim* has invited you, has he?" she asked softly, helping him put on his jacket. "Are you sure it wasn't his wife— your buddy, Jeanette?"

Zipping up his jacket, Paul drew in a deep breath and shut his eyes. "God, give me patience!"

He inched closer to Kaitlin with his finger pointed in front of her face, causing her to pull her head back. "You have got to learn to stop projecting your own mistakes onto me!"

Kaitlin's jaw dropped, and she had to take a few seconds to breathe and recollect herself before continuing. "Look who's talking like maybe he's still attending therapy sessions since his release himself, *eh*? Good for you, Paul! I'm glad you know what *projecting* means!"

Paul ignored her as he put on his shoes and checked his pockets for his keys and phone.

"When will you be back, and…?" Kaitlin started to ask. But the door had already shut behind Paul before she could finish her question.

§

RUNNING HIS HANDS OVER HIS BURGUNDY SWEATER AND TROUSERS, Paul rang the doorbell. As he heard his friend's voice letting him know she was 'coming', he smoothed his short brown mane as well.

When the hell are these beings going to leave me and my family alone? Paul couldn't believe it was still continuing. After everything they'd already gone through. Wasn't it enough? If this Finn asshole were a human being, he'd arrange to have a man-to-man talk with him by now, alright. But how in the world did one confront a supernatural being who apparently wouldn't be leaving his wife—or his child— alone easily?

"May I come in?" he smiled as Jeanette opened the door. She was dressed in a casual black dress hugging her bulging curves. Paul smiled. Somehow, he'd always thought her extra kilos flattered his friend.

"Oh my, Paulie! Are you all right? Tim's just told me he's dropping off Brian before returning?"

"Yeah— they both kept me company in my misery. He's told you about my demotion, huh?" Paul paced back and forth speedily around the familiar beige kitchen counter. His breathing was as heavy as an animal in heat or fury, snorting.

"Paulie, come sit down," Jeanette motioned toward a chair she'd pulled out. "He'll be back soon—Tim's told me you weren't ready to go home just yet. We've gotta take care of ya! What's going on? I'll get you a cup of green tea…It's…"

"She took me *there*!" Paul cut in before she could finish. "She threw me straight into the past, Jeannie! Literally! She said that maybe we had married 'too soon', and that we should perhaps have 'dated around some more', and so on and so forth! And if that wasn't enough…if that wasn't enough, he…."

Jeanette sat next to him, looking into his eyes with concern as he threw his face into his hands. "Who? Your wife? Oh, boy. I should have known this much drinkin' was about more than your position change—I had a position change recently, as well, Paulie. You don't need to take it personally. Lars is in over his head lately…"

"You didn't go to jail, Jeanette! Thank you for trying to help, but—he actually told me the clients have gossiped."

Jeanette was shaking her head. "But the real murderer killed himself! I don't understand the fuss…."

"Sadly that part doesn't show first when someone searches up my name on Google," Paul said with a smirk. "Only the damn brief news about 'local man arrested in connection' with Linette's murder, since that made the headlines. Apparently the last two clients didn't dig deeper to read about the actual murderer's suicide."

"Lars will calm down, and return you to your rightful place in no time," Jeanette assured him, running her hand over his shoulders. "You need to calm yourself, too— so if you don't want tea you could also just drink warm water. I also have some chicken noodle soup I'd made fresh for Tim when he returns home. My poor hubby has been coughin' all week…"

Paul nodded politely. His mind was still on Kaitlin and Finn. Meeting to supposedly discuss some play date for the 'kids'. *This is going to plague me,* he thought. *I need to match what she did.*

"Too bad you're no jinn", Paul muttered under his breath glancing at Jeanette's hands before returning her smile with a gaze into her blue eyes.

"Whattu say, Paulie? Jeanette asked softly, fidgeting with her hair.

"Oh…I asked, uh, if you had any *gin*, inside?" Paul cleared his throat. "Gin and tonic?"

"I don't think more alcohol is the answer," Jeanette responded with a soft chuckle.

"Maybe a good old alcoholic-burn down my throat and into my system can calm this racing heartbeat, eh?" Paul asked more to himself. "You did say I needed something warm, didn't you?"

"Alright— I suppose there'll be no harm since you're safe and indoors, now," Jeanette replied. "Tim should be back soon. And as the designated driver of the evening, he'll take you back. Gin and tonic—comin' right up!"

Paul smiled. Jeanette had always been there for him, hadn't she? Going to the police to help him out. Always making sure he had warm lunch at work. What had Kaitlin done except complain about her life, sitting home all day on her computer? Running a business with bakeries and some colleague she never met but chatted with all the time!

"Maybe this isn't even about that ghost-like dude who apparently wants his son to play with my daughter," he said to himself, scoffing. "Maybe I've been focusing on the wrong foe… maybe it was always that guy she's been doing work with all along…*Salim*, or whatever his name is…"

"Here you go…" Paul was surprised to see Jeanette had gotten a glass for herself too as he gulped down half the gin immediately before clinking his glass with hers for the rest. "Cheers!"

"You're the only one who's ever really cared, Jeannie" he murmured. "Your alibi helped get me out of that place…and now…"

"Oh, Paulie," Jeanette took a sip of her gin, blushing as she pulled back a strand of curly blonde hair off her face. "Thank you—but I think it's the drinks talking. You were saying something about Kaitlin earlier. I'm listening, if you care to explain…."

"I wish it was you playing with me and the dog in the woods, Daddy, and not your twin," Malin's voice resonated inside his head. The sentence she had told him right before Kaitlin returned. The part he didn't relay to Kaitlin. The part that broke his heart the most.

As a tear fell from his face, his blurry vision turned to focus on Jeanette. "Maybe…it should have been you, Jeannie. All along."

Paul inched closer to Jeanette's heaving bosom protruding from her low-cut dress. "Maybe we've both made wrong decisions."

"Paul…" Jeanette stuttered, breathing heavily and maintaining her lips lingering close to Paul's own. "We can't."

"I think we need to," Paul said, his hands running over Jeanette's legs as her own fingers began scratching his back with long fingernails. Both of them allowing for a lasting kissing session that didn't sit right, but somehow felt satiating nonetheless.

CHAPTER 22

THE CHIRPING OF THE BIRDS SOUNDED NEARLY AS LOUD AS THE sunrays brushing her face felt warm. Kaitlin growled as she opened an eye, and later her mouth for a big yawn. She stretched her arms up and later to Paul's side of the bed, feeling nothing but emptiness across the Egyptian cotton sheets.

She peeked at the clock. 8:30. Where had Paul gone? It was unusual of him to be awake already on a weekend. Had Malin awoken earlier than usual? Was he playing with her?

Kaitlin smiled, mentally preparing the ingredients for the omelet she'd decided to make for them. Malin was pickier than her father, so a simple boiled egg with her peanut sandwich would have to do. Heck—she'd throw in pancakes, too.

Glancing at the subtly swaying trees outside, Kaitlin cracked open their window before heading to Malin's room. It was warmer than usual for their southern Nordic region, and the weather promised to further ameliorate the Sunday plan for them as a family Kaitlin was planning in her head.

Maybe Aidan was right. Maybe she really had inherited some things: overdramatic behavior from her mother, and adrenaline-seeking tendencies from their dad. *Hopefully nothing scarier,* she silently prayed.

Perhaps she had to make more of an attempt to grow closer to her husband, rather than Paul being expected to make the grander efforts. He had returned home the previous night, and had gone straight to sleep next to her; she'd pretended to be asleep already. He reeked of alcohol, but that was to be expected. Kaitlin was hoping he'd got enough rest to take Malin out shopping as he promised— where she'd later join them as she played out in her head, first allowing for them to have some father-daughter time.

"I don't know what came over me," she heard Paul speaking softly in the bathroom, as Kaitlin passed it on the way to see her daughter.

What the heck? Who was Paul whispering to in the bathroom? Was he on a business call again, trying to keep it secret from her? He knew she'd hated his mixing business with family time—especially on weekends. Trotting slowly to the bathroom door, Kaitlin tilted her head for a closer listen.

"I'm sorry if I've put you in a rough position, Jeannie," Kaitlin heard Paul lower his voice even further into a whisper. "Did Tim say anything?"

Her heart sank even deeper upon the next words uttered from his pursed lips.

"I never would have kissed you like that and compromised our friendship if it hadn't been for all those drinks. Luckily, I don't think Tim noticed a thing when he came, either. We can put this behind us."

Mon Dieu! Kaitlin felt her entire body begin to shake as she clenched her fists. She closed her eyes and took in a deep breath, counting to four before releasing it outwards at an even slower rate later.

"Mommy?"

Wiping a fallen tear that had escaped her eye, Kaitlin moved swiftly to comfort her waking daughter as soon as she heard her.

"Good morning, sweetie pie," She kissed the top of Malin's forehead. "Why don't you come wash your face in the kitchen while I go set up the table? Daddy is still in the bathroom."

"What's he doing in there?" Malin snickered. "Something smelly?"

"Oh, Daddy's smelling fishy, alright," Kaitlin teased with a scoff.

I cannot frigging believe you, Paul. Kissing Jeanette. Of all people.

Greeting them 'good morning' and uttering little else, Paul walked over to help with the coffee, later pouring Malin's chocolate milk for her. Kaitlin sensed his eyes on her while she set the table with pancakes, meeting them only with fleeting smiles.

"Mommy, I don't feel like honey today!" Malin decided, picking up some blueberries from her plate.

"Mallie, baby, you always have honey with your peanut spread," Kaitlin raised her voice. She'd prided herself on having gotten her daughter accustomed to honey for sweetness in the morning rather than the less healthy substitute of jelly or jam.

"Yes, but I just don't *feel* like it today!" Malin rolled her eyes, throwing in a smile at her mom.

Kaitlin smirked. She couldn't recall using those words around her daughter for her life! She shuddered at the thought of what else Malin was going to increasingly pick up from hearing around school now that she was growing up.

"Are you excited to see Grandma soon, Mallie?" Paul asked, cutting her pancakes into four smaller pieces.

"Hmm," Kaitlin just uttered, averting the gaze she felt focused on her like a hawk. "We're both excited to travel out of Norway for a bit, that's for sure."

"I am!" Malin answered the question first directed at her, looking back and forth curiously between the two of them.

"What's going on with you this morning?" Paul whispered to Kaitlin across the table, once he'd assured Malin's attention was back on the cartoon she was viewing on the television from the corner of her eye.

"Nothing," Kaitlin dismissed with a quick smile.

Washing the dishes after breakfast, Kaitlin's hands were still trembling. *Jeanette*, she thought, smirking to herself. With her back turned, she could hear the TV on but for her life could not focus on the words coming from it. Paul had kissed Jeanette. He said Tim had come in, implying that it stopped afterward. Would they go further the next time if they had the opportunity? As one of the dishes slipped out of her hand, it landed loudly in the sink.

"You okay?" Paul called out over his newspaper.

"All good," Kaitlin responded over her shoulder, wiping the plate with the towel. Taking in a deep breath again, Kaitlin walked into the living room and sat on one of the armchairs closer to the window to gaze outside.

"What's Malin watching?" she asked, hearing that Paul's footsteps had inched closer to her.

"The news," he said in a deadpanned voice. "She's suddenly developed a fascination with Macroeconomics."

"Paul…" Kaitlin rolled her eyes, finally looking up into his eyes.

"I turned on Netflix Kids for her," Paul explained with crossed arms. "Kaitlin—can you please tell me why in the world you are…"

"You guys finally did it, huh?" Kaitlin cut in with a whisper, adding a soft applause. "Congratulations, Paul. You and Jeanette have finally kissed, it seems. After all these years. So romantic! I'm happy for you guys. Really."

"Oh…you listened to me in the bathroom," Paul chuckled, red-faced and scratching the back of his head. "Well I hope you listened to all of it, Kaitlin. Because we addressed how it was a moment of drunken despair. It was not some romantic liaison; I wouldn't know what those are like, unlike you..."

"Oh, that's slick," Kaitlin stood up, glancing behind her to make sure Malin wasn't paying attention to them. "You're a really funny one. I just found out my husband made out with his childhood buddy— a fellow human with much more danger, therefore, being posed to our marriage. One who's also married, mind you. And he's going to *dare* try to turn this around on me, is he, now?"

"And I got demoted at work and came home to find out that my wife and daughter were hanging out with jinn folk, Kaitlin!" Paul exclaimed, lowering his voice toward the end.

"Malin cannot hear the 'jinn' part, Paul— please watch your tone!" Kaitlin insisted. "We cannot scare her."

"You should have thought about that when you agreed to meet your little buddy without coming to me first, as you promised!"

Kaitlin placed her hands on her hips, taking in a deep breath. "I think this space will be good for both of us, Paul. This United States and Canada trip cannot come soon enough!"

"You cannot make this about me!" Paul steamed. "It was one stupid kiss. I was drunk!"

"It's not just about some…kiss! Although, frankly, I'm still in shock..."

"What is about, then?" Paul demanded. "Do you want me to risk losing this demoted position as well by coming with you girls? Do I need to check in with you through whatever means over there to ensure the safety of my daughter away from jinn even across the damn ocean? Because if I have to, I will…"

"He swore he would not see us again, don't worry," Kaitlin explained, eyeing the ground.

"And you believe him?" Paul chuckled, shaking his head. "How can you guarantee something like that from some inhuman being, Kaitlin?"

"Because it's all *business* to him," Kaitlin said, looking her husband straight in his eye. "I guaranteed it because I said I would help secure a location for 'The Group', with their resources. They need a Canadian citizen and a human for that."

Paul took several seconds to take the information in, chortling. "You agreed to be some liaison for them?"

"Finn is not interested in me as anything other than a Canadian contact for his organization, Paul, don't worry," Kaitlin said, keeping her head raised while swallowing the lump in her throat. "And the play date was something for his son, as I've said. None of it will happen again. As for your kiss with Jeanette…."

"…It will not happen again, either," Paul finished her sentence, placing his hand across her torso. "I don't know what's going on with us lately, babe, but I'm not about some affair. You know me."

"Neither am I," Kaitlin responded, her eyes filling with tears. *I just want to feel a sense of purpose, Paul. I want to feel loved, and not alone.* How fervently she wished her husband could read her mind sometimes like Finn could—words she couldn't bring herself to mutter aloud.

"I'm mostly disappointed you would allow for that unhuman bastard to endanger our child, Kaitlin," Paul chose his words carefully and in a lowered tone of voice despite steam nearly coming from his nostrils. "How can I trust you ever again?"

"You think I would allow anything to endanger Malin?" Kaitlin demanded. "And don't get me started on trust! Of all the people to cheat on me with, you chose *Jeanette*— the one person you knew to be bugging me since the beginning of our marriage! You did it out of spite, didn't you?"

"What part of *drunk* do you refuse to understand, Kaitlin?" Paul said in a casual tone. Kaitlin could tell it was forced. "I don't know how it happened. It just did. But with this Finn—we've both seen what the jinn are capable of! It's naïve of you to trust his word!"

"People say being together with someone for a long time tends to bring out negative tendencies in every relationship, babe," she inhaled deeply, placing her head gently on her husband's chest. Freya's advice resonated in her head. *Whenever you're having a hurtful argument, make sure to establish physical warmth with your spouse before things escalate.*

"Are *we* naïve, Paulie? What made us think we could be immune to the wraths of the passage of time?"

"My poetess," Paul kissed the top of her head, as Kaitlin smiled into his eyes. As soon as she did, the image of Paul with someone else returned to her mind, and she quickly wriggled out of his embrace, getting up to head toward their bedroom.

"What is it?" Paul sighed, walking behind her.

"I don't know how I can rid the image of you and Jeanette kissing from my mind," Kaitlin stopped in her tracks to whisper, looking to ensure that Malin was still wrapped up in the show about fairies.

"The same way I've been trying to overcome all the even crazier images of my wife with some jinn-man, I suppose," Paul smirked with a shrug.

"This is bigger than *us*, now," Kaitlin said, taking a deep breath and placing her hands on her hips. The sound of Malin's off-key singing alone with one of the tunes from the show filled her with delight. "Moving forward, we have to prioritize their daughter's well-being."

"I'm not sure how we can get past this, babe," Paul started, licking his lips. "All I know is we have to. For our growing daughter above anything else—you're right. Hey, maybe…."

"What?" Kaitlin posed with hunched shoulders.

"Perhaps we could try couple counseling after your return?" Paul suggested, twisting his lips. "Preferably with a neutral third-party other than your current therapist or my former one?"

Kaitlin smiled at him and nodded. This was one of the better ideas she'd heard from Paul as of late.

§

"HI, STARGAZERS! YOU'VE REACHED SANDY BURNS, HERE. I'm afraid I can't come to the phone right now. But please leave your name, number, and message and I'll get back to you as soon as I can. Thank you!"

Upon hearing Sandy's chirpy voice, Kaitlin smiled for the first time since crying through the previous night. Paul had kissed her 'goodnight' and seemed like he had wanted the kiss to linger, but Kaitlin couldn't bring herself to it.

She had called Sandy to inquire about some trip details, but hated leaving voice messages. While hanging up, she had a thought. Okay, so she had technically kissed Finn, as well, she supposed—if not more—but somehow she never thought a jinn would count.

Maybe I was out of my mind to hold this double standard, and what goes around comes back around—eventually.

CHAPTER 23

MALIN'S LAUGHTER COULD NOT BE CONTAINED AS SHE jumped on the trampoline, joined by Sibel's two children as well as two grandkids their elderly neighbors brought for company. "Bouncy! Bouncy! Bouncy!" Three boys and a little girl from Malin's class had also agreed to come—much to Kaitlin's delight, as she'd invited the entire class since her daughter wasn't particularly close with any of the kids.

Roving her eyes to spot her husband across the indoor playground, Kaitlin found herself amused to witness Paul's grimacing smile as he conversed with Engin. *Bear with it for just another hour,* she mentally tried to relay with him—hoping it would somehow work just as it did with Finn.

Her eyes met Sibel's across the ball pit, the two of them silently knowing the birthday party for Malin doubled as a farewell party before their North American trip .

"Aylin!" Sibel called out to her older daughter who was closer in age to Malin than her younger son, Hakan. "Be careful! And don't exclude your brother!"

"*Tamam, anne!*" Aylin agreed in Turkish. With an eyeroll, she took Malin by the hand as they proceeded to jump higher in unison.

"They've started ignoring our warnings, already," Sibel whined, sipping on the Sprite in her Styrofoam cup, to which Kaitlin nodded with sympathy.

"Does Malin's teacher know she'll be missing a couple of days of school?" her friend continued.

"Yeah, yeah," Kaitlin nodded with a heavy sigh. "I assured her she'd be caught up on the work she'll miss. It's just addition and subtraction, anyway. How hard could an eight-year-old's mathematics be?"

"You'd be surprised," Sibel chuckled. "I pride myself on being a stay-at-home mom but Aylin's homework has been more difficult than I remember when I was her age!"

As the two women shared a subtle chuckle, the sudden feeling of familiar tingles on the back of her neck took over Kaitlin's focus. She looked around the premises with panic.

"What is it?" Sibel asked with concern.

Not seeing any signs of *him*, Kaitlin took in a deep breath and attempted a smile at her friend. "Nothing, nothing. I just remembered her first birthday party, girl. Do you remember? When he…."

As her voice trailed off, Sibel understood her friend in the silence. "I remember. Do you sense that he is here now? Finn?"

Kaitlin shrugged. "I'm not too sure. That's the part that unsettles me more than anything. I swear I can almost feel his presence sometimes, but unless he wants to make himself known—I can never know for sure. He has that power, and I have no choice but to trust his word that he won't show himself where and when not welcomed."

"You're sure your time abroad isn't tied to *him*, right?" Sibel asked with raised brows. "You're not trying to hang out with him and Malin easier over there or anything like that?"

"No, girl—he's promised to leave us alone there, as I've told you," Kaitlin reassured her, silently praying that would indeed hold true. She'd been too embarrassed to relay that Paul had made out with another woman—somehow, things like that felt easier to share with her best friend, Sandy, only.

Maybe, just maybe, these three weeks would be good for her to take a break from both Paul and Finn. *I need to find myself*, Kaitlin thought with a sigh. *And what I really want out of the remainder of my life.*

§

LOWERING THE ZIPPER ON HER WINTER JACKET, MALIN TOOK IN THE fresh forest air. Her uncle had zipped it up all the way, and it was hurting her neck! She smiled. Finn had surprised her by picking her up early from the last day of school she would be attending before the trip.

"I'll take you back home at the same time the bus usually drops you off," he'd told her. "Not to fret."

"Uncle Finn—where did you go?" she called out upon arriving at the lake past the two tall trees. He had led her on their usual path toward the lake, walking from behind, promising that's where Bo would be waiting for her to play with. She felt she would truly miss both of them when she'd be away from Norway.

"*Hei*!" a boy around her age, but slightly taller, appeared behind the bushes, causing Malin to scream.

"*Det er OK*," the boy assured her in Norsk.

"*Beklager, jeg ble bare overrasket,*" Malin expressed, relaying how she was simply startled. She looked up and down at the boy before her. He was wearing baggy jeans with Converse sneakers. A thick Nordic-pattern sweater was visible under his felt coat. "*Snakker du Engelsk?"*

"Yes, I do," the boy answered, smiling into her eyes.

"I'm looking for my uncle," Malin went on, looking at the floor. "He was just walking behind me. Did you see a blond man around here? He has a dog I wanted to say 'bye' to before leaving for New York!"

"You mean *Finn*?" The boy nodded with a grin, reaching out his hand. "I'm… B..Bob, by the way."

"Ooh, you sparked!" Malin smiled, recoiling her hand.

"It happens sometimes," Bob blushed, slicking his hair back with his hand.

Funny how Uncle Finn zaps me too, Malin thought curiously. "I'm Malin, nice to meet you."

To her surprise, the boy didn't respond that it was nice for him to meet her, either. Something touched the tip of her nose just then, causing Malin to jump back. "What was that?"

"What—another spark?" Bob asked eagerly.

"Oh, no, no....something fell on my nose!" Malin exclaimed, looking up at the sky.

"A snowflake!" Bob looked up at the sky with awe. "I feel it, too, now. It's on my lip!"

"Be careful— my mom says we shouldn't eat snow." Malin giggled.

"I just licked it and it disappeared...no harm no foul, " Bob took a step closer toward her.

Malin felt her heart beating faster by the second. Who was this kid? Was he leaning in to kiss her or something? She was too young! Wasn't she? They were both just kids! She had seen those classic postcards with children kissing but her mom had told her those were not real— just for show to be 'cute', weren't they?

"How do you know Uncle Finn?" she asked, taking a step back.

"I've been waiting here for him, as well," Bob spoke. "He's...a friend of my mother's, and he's been teaching me how to log. Maybe we can wait together."

"Oh, yeah?" Malin asked, hesitant but relaxed, somehow. She wasn't sensing any danger. "Alright, I suppose....I think the snow stopped!"

"I think it was just a passing cloud," Bob hypothesized. "Look! Do you see those bushes? They still have the white covering!"

"Where?" Malin asked, looking all around her. As something whizzed by her eyes in a flash, her jaw dropped to see that Bob was now almost on the other side of the lake! *How did he get there so fast?*

"I'm a fast runner!" Bob called out to her, motioning with his hand for her to walk over. "Such beautiful flowers here still."

A voice inside her told Malin she shouldn't let her guard down completely with this kid. Sure, he appeared to know Finn. But no one could run that fast, could they? It was almost magical! What the heck was going on?

"Oh, come on!" he insisted to her, motioning still with a smile.

Malin pulled her hair off her face and walked over to him slowly. "Wow, they're green though it isn't spring."

"Some blooms last," Bob said with a smile. He cleared his throat. "So you said you're leaving for New York soon?"

"Yeah, I'm so excited!" Malin beamed. "I've never been on a plane before! Well—not since I was old enough to remember anyway."

"I'm excited for you…and hey, I've got something for you," Bob called out. "Before you go."

It shocked Malin to see him reach out to his backpack and unroll a thick sheet of paper. The sheet had a drawing of a little girl on it. Her! Bob had drawn her!

"Oh, wow, is this…. *me*?" Malin's jaw dropped.

"Yes," Bob scratched his head. "Do you like it?"

"Wow, I do," Malin smiled. "You've got real talent. But—I don't remember you. Where did you see me before to draw this?"

"Finn's shown me your picture," Bob said with a smile, blushing as he scratched his head, mirroring Malin's own gesture. "As his niece, you know? Besides, I know you just had your birthday…so, happy birthday!"

"This is a present for me?" Malin asked, taking the drawing from his hand. "It's so cool! *Tusen takk*!"

"*Du er velkommen*," Bob winked at her, responding to her gratitude.

§

KNOWING IT WAS THE LAST TIME HE COULD PLAY WITH HER FOR A WHILE, Bo couldn't wait to have at least one more playdate with Malin before she and her mom left for the States.

"Mer? Are you done with your meditation?" Finn called out, entering the red doors to the cabin in his black, feline form, and Bo met him with several licks in his canine one.

He knew deep inside this jinn was most likely his actual father, but Bo played along with their game of ignorance about his paternity. It was either that—or denial, he'd often think.

"Where's Mommy, my boy...B.. Bo?" Finn blushed, transforming into his human-body form as Bo followed suit.

"Mommy's with the trees again," Bo walked over to their fireplace, hurling another log into the pit. "She said her business trip wore her out. Hey, um, Finn? Can I log more wood with you? Please?"

"If the weather cooperates, sure," Finn cleared his throat, ruffling the boy's fine, brown hair. He kneeled down next to him.

"I know it's become a fine workout for you, Bo. But remember not to chop off any more wood than we need. You know how we must be prudent and moderate with our spending. There are still more gifts to be bought for the loyalty of our clients. We've worked hard to make our company number one in the region, and we can't lower our reputation."

"Ultimately, humility bears more fruit than frugality," Bo said with a smile, quoting one of Lar Iktar's maxims.

"Whoa, look at that," Finn chuckled. "You've been getting some studying done while your mom is busy. I'm happy to see."

"Don't worry," Bo blushed. "I've heard Mom on the phone. She says there's an in-fox of customers this month."

"You mean—'influx'," Finn playfully punched his shoulder. "It means 'abundant....large in quantity'."

The chill in the air as they went to log hung like the lull of nature's uncharacteristic quiet.

"Hey, can I ask you something da...I mean, Finn?" Bo asked, blushing.

Finn took in a deep breath and bit his lip, turning to face Bo. He placed a hand on his shoulder and gave a warm smile to reassure him. "Anything."

"Can I see Malin? I've missed her."

Finn sighed. "I know you've been having just as much trouble as me with this strange dynamic and unconventional little family we've created in this place, Bo."

"What do you mean?" Bo asked quizzically. He just wanted to play with his friend.

"Forget it," Finn chuckled, ruffling his hair.

§

WATCHING MALIN LISTENING INTENTLY AS FINN, WHO HAD NOW joined them by the lake, told her about different kinds plants, Bo waited for his cue to revert into his canine form. He hated having to do so, but figured he owed it to Finn.

Bo was just glad Finn had allowed for this—meeting Malin in his human form, albeit he was to create another identity for himself. He knew they were sworn to stay away from them while they were abroad—Malin and her mother. But he couldn't have let the object of his affection travel without seeing her one more time. Besides, he'd heard about the arguments. Malin's mother wouldn't be making it as easy on Finn to allow for playdates, anymore.

He vaguely remembered Kaitlin from when he was basically a newborn—she played catch with him in her Stavanger apartment, until Finn came to take him back to his Mama.

Why couldn't things have progressed so that he could have been closer to Malin, and they could have played with each other as they both grew up? Why did deep, all-encompassing love always have to present itself in the most complicated of situations?

Why could she mostly get to know him as a puppy? He'd been told that humans call young love 'puppy love'. Bo chuckled to himself. Soon they'd both be old enough— he and Malin. Bo swore he'd find a way to reach her without needing the adults around— and in his human form, too.

And if it was meant to be— she'd remember him, and they could finally be able to see each other whenever they wanted.

CHAPTER 24

New York

THE HONKING HORNS AND EMERGENCY SIRENS WERE AUDIBLE even from the twelfth floor, Kaitlin observed, staring at the small-scale passersby rushing through the busy city street. It was certainly a contrast to her views of more animals than people in her smaller apartment in Sandnes. Sandy had told her the one-bedroom apartment was actually a large studio before she added dividers around a small corner next to the kitchen for a makeshift room. "I can feel I'm going to like it here. New York is going to be good for me and Malin."

Sandy bit her lip, smiling at Malin. "I hope so girl, no doubt."

Kaitlin sighed. The last conversation her and Paul had at the airport two snowy mornings ago before they went through the security check at Sola Airport brought a lump to her throat.

"I think this trip will be good, Paulie. It's a good thing there's no return ticket with this updated package last-minute...."

He had tried his best to sound reassuring. *"Baby, you know I'm not going to see Jeanette—or anyone else, for that matter— while you're away. We have to trust each other. And you girls are returning as soon as your mom and you figure out if you're heading up to Canada after all with this trip, or just staying in New York since you'll see her there. Once you've decided, let me know and I'm getting those tickets."*

Kaitlin had made sure to pack a metal flashlight in her luggage-since it wouldn't be allowed in a carry-on bag, along with an *Ayat-al-Kursi* prayer scroll Sibel gifted her with. After learning that Finn was apparently trying to get her into the damn group of his— she couldn't take any more chances. Regardless of his latest promise to 'stay away'.

She knew she could just buy a flashlight in the States, but who knew when he would potentially show up- and she wanted to be prepared in case that happened before she had a chance to go shopping. Her neediness for his company had just gotten her too close into some real trouble— and not only herself this time. Her daughter, too.

Kaitlin had met up with her friend one last time before her trip- and was pressed to spill the truth. As expected, Sibel had told her a lot afterwards. Kaitlin had absorbed all the new bits and pieces of information coming at her from every which way. Took them in, until they resonated within her bones. She spoke the words that subsequently flowed through her—pouring out in a rush.

"Maybe I just needed some light in my life, Sibel....And maybe his flames emitted that for me."

"So do angels, Kaitlin...I know you're being poetic, but in all senses of the word— you could have chosen to breathe new life and light into your life through less shadier sources."

Strangely enough, Paul and Jeanette making out had suddenly become the lesser of her worries.

"Look, it's clear that we've both made mistakes," Paul had told her before she and Malin had gotten on the Passport line. *"We're both imperfect humans. But for Malin's sake we need to get as close to perfection as possible as parents. She shouldn't pay for our issues....Please just focus on her enjoyment there. I'll send you guys whatever you need. Let's video-call every day and send me lots of pictures, okay?"*

She'd promised, and meant it. They weren't perfect as husband and wife. That was for sure. But Kaitlin knew both she and Paul had better be the best parents they could be for their fragile daughter's sake. Especially in her vulnerability, having been exposed to what she'd already had.

Glancing back toward the living room with a sigh, Kaitlin smiled at the sight of Sandy playing with Malin. "I love what you did with your hair, girl!"

"My hair?" Sandy asked. "You like it? Thanks, it's called a *money piece*. The stylist said the blonde highlights my face and that's enough, since I told her I didn't want too much chemical process in my hair. I like the simultaneously dark and light hair on me— feels at home."

"You're *sure* you are okay with us crashing with you for a couple of days before heading over to Aidan's, right, girl?" Kaitlin asked, raising an eyebrow at her friend. She'd known her long enough to recognize her rather sweet inability to say 'no' sometimes. And looking around the small living space in person now—where Sandy had to sleep on the couch—Kaitlin realized she had to head to Aidan's sooner than planned, and give her generous friend privacy and comfort back.

"Of course," Sandy chuckled, blushing. "You don't have to keep asking, girl! It's all good! I'm just worried I won't have as much time to take you girls around as I used to, now that I've gotten this big part! I mean, those brief weekly rehearsals start tomorrow, and…"

"Aunty Sandy is a theater actress!" Malin waved her hands right and left on the sides of her body.

"*Jazz hands,*" her and Sandy said in unison, right before tickling each other. Kaitlin smiled at the sight—her friend had taught her a couple of cutesy things over Face Time.

"We'll only be a day or two then, girl, no sweat," Kaitlin said. "I'm going to press Aidan to stay over with him earlier than next week, don't you worry."

"Are you sure?" Sandy asked in a low voice. "I mean, stay as long as you want, really! Otherwise— what kind of a friend would I be…or aunty, for that matter? It's just that…oh, well, never mind."

"Go on, please" Kaitlin encouraged.

"Well, I remembered how I've had an— *um*— acting coach who's helped me practice my lines lately," Sandy began, fidgeting with the sleeves of her ivory blouse. "But I don't think they'll be coming around anymore, so it should be all good."

The pleading look in Sandy's eyes looking at Kaitlin let her know all she needed to know. *There's a chance Bjorn could come over randomly at any time.*

"Oh, okay, yeah I got you…ahem…didn't realize that the, *um*, acting class with him was still a thing," Kaitlin winked. "Especially as you've already gotten this amazing part!"

"Right, right, it took me by surprise too, heh," Sandy twirled a curly lock of her hair behind her ear. "But, yeah. The coach and I had a fight anyway. I don't think I'll be seeing him anytime *too* soon."

"Oh, I'm sorry, girl," Kaitlin said. She looked at Malin, and motioned to Sandy with her fingers pointing to the bedroom. "Would you like to talk about it…inside?"

"Oh, no, it's okay," Sandy shook her head. "We can talk later. I'm good. Really. I'm sorry, girl. I know you're here to relax. I don't want to dump my drama as a cherry on top of your own!"

Kaitlin smiled, caressing her friend's shoulder. "I get it—I mean, look at me…practically forcing my brother to be able to crash at his place with his niece. Aidan doesn't seem…right lately. I thought it was just romantic troubles at first, but it feels like he's keeping something from me. Maybe this is my *karma* for not wanting Paul's sisters at our place for too long! I've been thinking about karma a lot lately, actually…"

"What's *karma,* Mommy?" Malin asked, flipping through the children's magazine Sandy had given her.

"It's when the universe, *um*, makes you pay a price for doing something not so nice," Kaitlin shrugged through gritted teeth, causing Sandy to giggle.

"Hmm," Malin didn't sound convinced. "*If you're not nice you pay the price*—that rhymes!"

"I suppose it does," Kaitlin chuckled.

"Give your brother a break," Sandy told Kaitlin. "It could also be virtual miscommunication. Long-distance makes things open to misunderstandings. I would know!"

"Bjorn, right?" Kaitlin smiled. She added with a mischievous whisper. "*The coach.*"

"Who's Born?" Malin mispronounced, causing both her mom and Sandy to laugh.

"*Bjorn* is a friend of mine whom I've been trying to keep in touch with under distant conditions, sweety, and it hasn't been easy," Sandy tried to explain. "Yet I'm sure the Aidan I remember— your protective brother— will be much more accommodating in person. Just give him a chance, girl. He knows you're here, right?"

"Oh, yeah, he called me when we were still at the airport," Kaitlin responded, turning her gaze back out the window. The whizzing traffic below somehow jolted her out of her own overthought thoughts. "You can never get bored living here, can you? So many people, so many stories. You can never feel alone."

Sandy took a step closer to Kaitlin and joined her gaze outside. "That's another reason why I feel proud to live in New York. It's beyond just the vibrancy of this island of Manhattan here. There's also Long Island! Maybe I can rent a car and drive you girls out there sometime."

"Long Island?" Kaitlin inquired.

"Yeah, I visited some friends in Ronkonkoma there recently, and learned about this country's indigenous history. Lots of interesting stories I'm writing sketches about, actually. Did you know that there's a story about this tribal princess named *Ronkonkoma*, who died in Long Island's deepest and biggest lake in the 1600's? She died of a love her father forbade, and legend has it that every year..."

As Sandy went on about a tragic story, Kaitlin's mind wandered off to her own. *Shoot!* Suddenly remembering she missed her virtual session with Freya as she was traveling, Kaitlin took out her phone and fumbled with the 'Settings'.

"Sandy, sorry to cut you off, girl, but do you know if I can make local calls from my cell here?" Kaitlin asked, showing her the I-Phone.

"Let me see," Sandy said quietly, looking through Kaitlin's phone. "Yeah— 'roaming' is on. It should be alright. Though you want to make sure you don't talk for too long, because that bill is going to…."

"Thanks a lot!" Kaitlin cut in, blowing her daughter a kiss as she passed her on the way to the bedroom Sandy had prepared for them. "I just have to call Freya for a second, girls. Give me a minute!"

Sandy smirked, turning her disappointed look into a smile as Malin's eyes met hers. "Want to play a game while Mommy ignores us, princess?"

Stepping out of the room with a look of relief plastered on her face a few moments later, Kaitlin was pleasantly taken aback to see Sandy teaching Malin the card game 'Uno'. She hadn't exactly had the most productive of talks with Freya, but felt accomplished nonetheless to have at least gotten through one of the tasks she'd mentally listed for herself. *Argh,* she sighed, remembering she should also schedule a meeting with Salim and discuss her orders. *Oh well. First things first.*

"Can I join you girls?" she walked over to join Sandy and Malin sitting down on the carpeted floor.

"No, Mommy—you wait for the next round!" Malin pointed an exaggeratedly angry finger in her face, pouting through a smile. "You're punished for ignoring Aunty Sandy and me!"

"Oh, am I, now?" Kaitlin crossed her arms and twisted her lips into an amused smile, meeting Sandy's eyes.

"You came here to visit *her*, didn't you?" Sandy smirked. "And I thought you'd missed your dear old friend Sandy, hon."

"Like you'd come to Norway supposedly *just* to visit Malin and I- eh?" Kaitlin winked. "Besides, this is medical, in a way—not personal."

"Touché," Sandy blushed. "What time is your appointment with Freya?"

"Tomorrow—2 pm," Kaitlin said, biting her lip. "She didn't exactly sound too enthusiastic to see me in person. You still have in-person sessions with her, sometimes, right, Sandy?"

"Yeah, one in-person session followed by a virtual one two weeks later," Sandy said with a casual shrug, holding her cards above Malin's head to tease her.

"Is 2 pm alright with you?" Kaitlin asked.

"Yeah—I have to leave for the rehearsal around 4 pm, but you should be back by then."

"Pay attention, please!" Malin crossed her arms, darting a look at the two of them. "Mommy, you're interrupting us!"

Kaitlin chuckled, looking at the couch behind them. "Alright, missy—sorry! Hey, aren't you jetlagged? We should rest while Aunty Sandy here gets through her routine."

"Jetlagged?" Malin asked.

"It's extra sleepiness that happens after long flights, sweety," Sandy explained.

"You're sure you're comfortable on that couch?" Kaitlin asked Sandy with a grimace. "Because I'll see Aidan tomorrow after my appointment, and I can ask him to…."

"Oh, hush!" Sandy rolled her eyes, getting up to head to the kitchen. "I told you—it pulls out into quite a comfortable little bed. Why don't I serve you ladies some snacks and you can rest in the room. Sound good?"

"Uno?" Malin asked, looking sadly at her playing cards.

"*Uno* can wait until you get your rest," Sandy winked at her.

"Besides—we can beat Mommy better after some snacks and rest."

§

PLACING A LIGHT BLANKET OVER MALIN IN HER FAVORITE fairy pajamas, Kaitlin's heart was as full as the tears welling in her eyes. "I think she's still in deep sleep," she whispered over her shoulder, tiptoeing her way out of the room where Malin was sprawled out across the entirety of the bed. "Let's head into the kitchen."

"Were you able to get some sleep at least?" Sandy asked, sipping on some instant coffee. "Let me mix you some of this *Nescafé* stuff—it's European!"

Kaitlin chuckled softly. "I want to be as un-European as possible during these three weeks, girl. But, sure—I can never say 'no' to coffee! I probably just got in a couple of hours in slumberland."

"Coming right up," Sandy quipped, preparing the mix for her friend. "Still little milk, no sugar?"

"Sounds good," Kaitlin said softly.

"What's up, girl?" Sandy eyed her curiously. "You're holding back. Anything specific you want to get off your chest to our common denominator, Lady Freya? By the way, you're meeting Salim, too, finally—since you're here, right?"

"Oh, yes, yes, I've e-mailed him I'm here," Kaitlin said, mouthing 'thank you' as she took the large coffee mug Sandy handed her.

"I think meeting Freya in particular will also be good for another reason. You said she's from Stavanger—correct?"

"Yeah," Sandy said nonchalantly. "You two didn't talk of such things?"

Kaitlin pursed her lips. "Not really. She changes the subject when I ask her anything."

“I’m sure it’ll be easier for her to talk comfortably with you in person.” Sandy said with a shrug, sipping on the remainder of her own java.

“I wonder if she ever knew about ‘The Group’, since you said she’d had people tell her about the jinn before,” Kaitlin spoke more to the microwave than at Sandy.

“Beats me!” Sandy shrugged. “Anything about ‘The Group’ in particular bothering you, still? Is *Finn*?”

Kaitlin took in a deep breath and placed her mug on the counter. “Can you believe Lar wants me in ‘The Group’, Sandy? Finn insisted, and when I naturally refused—he asked me for the favor of at least renting a place out for them in Toronto, and pretending to Lar that I’m on board!”

“They’re relentless!” Sandy scoffed, shaking her head. “I can’t believe it’s *that* conversation again. Must everyone encountering the jinn join their cult somehow? You know what—maybe you should ask Freya if she knew of them, now that I think about it!”

Kaitlin stuck her head out the kitchen to ensure Malin hadn’t awoken. “He’s also shown himself to Malin! He had to manifest as ‘Paul’, and later created a story about being his estranged twin, instead—all seemingly to arrange a play date for her and his jinn-son in his canine form in the woods! ”

“He….*what*?” Sandy asked in disbelief. “And…*jinn-son*? You mean that dog with Meredith?”

“Yes, Bo,” Kaitlin said mournfully. “I think that was the final draw for me. I had to get away.”

“*Um*, sorry to burst your bubble, hon, but we’ve kind of seen how we can’t exactly outrun the jinn anywhere in the world—haven’t we?” Sandy asked. “He can come here, too, Kaitlin. Like how he visited me in Starbucks way back when—remember? I don’t think you can keep him away from you here on the other side of the world.”

"I know," Kaitlin started. "I think maybe I'm trying to keep *myself* from him— and from all the reminders of him and the things we lived through, technically in Norway. Besides, he swore to me, and I can feel if he's around so he can't lie; he swore to staying away here in exchange for me renting out that suite for them."

"So I'm guessing this will necessitate a couple of days at least in Toronto for sure, then, right?" Sandy asked.

"Right," Kaitlin sighed, gazing down at her hands. It'd been due time she got herself a manicure. She mentally noted the cute nail salon she'd glimpsed on the street corner of Sandy's apartment.

"It's also Paul. He's become unbearable. I convinced him this trip would also do Malin good, in addition to giving us some much-needed time apart. Of course Paul reasoned his family could visit Malin here, or in Toronto with my mom if we end up going. I think that was the real selling point for him, honestly…"

"Oh, goodie," Sandy's voice was tinged with sarcasm. "Two Grandmas. What was your mother-in-law's name….Mila?"

"Yes, Momma Mila is always planning a visit. But she's not nearly as cumbersome as his sisters with their kids, who I'm sure will tag along with her…"

"Those are Malin's aunts and cousins, girl," Sandy said with a shrug. "Think about it that way—she doesn't have siblings, and it'll likely make her happy to feel part of a bigger family when she's older."

"You do have a point there," Kaitlin bit her lip. "Paul…"

"Is there anything else regarding him you're not telling me?" Sandy raised an eyebrow as Kaitlin's voice trailed off.

Catching her friend up on the Jeanette kiss after the tenth anniversary coldness, Kaitlin considered telling Sandy about her father, too, but stopped herself. *Sandy doesn't need to think I'm crazier than she probably already thinks I am.*

Besides, she still had unanswered questions—and further details about her lineage could wait until after a talk with Aidan….or even maybe with her father himself.

"Oh, fuck!" Sandy exclaimed, then quickly closed her mouth with her hands, mouthing 'sorry', as she didn't want Malin to wake up and hear. "I can't believe he'd kiss her! What was the name of that Marilyn Monroe movie—*The Seven Year Itch*? With you guys, what is this—the ten-year itch?"

"Please don't compare Jeanette to Marilyn," Kaitlin was relieved to find herself chuckling along. *Good old Sandy.* "Marriage is…overcoming obstacles and mistakes. Regardless of how many years."

"Marriage isn't easy, I suppose," Sandy said with a smile. "But neither is the 'single' life believe me. Girl, do you suppose I have dated so much because I can't make friends as easily as lovers? That my personality is so messed up and unappealing—I have to get by through offering my affections in order to keep people…."

"You're being too hard on yourself, again, girl," Kaitlin reassured her, playfully punching her on the upper arms. "You're still young. You can figure this all out."

"We're heading toward 40!" Sandy exclaimed, causing Kaitlin to snicker.

"We still have time for that," Kaitlin rolled her eyes playfully. "Besides—they say 'forty' is the new 'thirty'."

Sandy took out some Oreos from the cupboard, offering one to Kaitlin before munching on two of them back-to-back. "Girl, I'm seriously afraid of my patterns. It's like I can only get over someone by allowing myself to fall in love with someone else immediately…a circumstance that starts out as what I believe will be a quick band-aid solution, only to have it develop into a serious bond in need of yet another rebound connection as well …and the cycle repeats."

"Yeah, well, speaking of *cycles*," Kaitlin said blankly, breaking the cookie in two and only licking the creamy center. "I also want to ask Aidan if my hallucination of our father in Norway is something to worry about in the family."

As soon as she divulged as such, Kaitlin stopped herself. She hadn't intended to say anything—and hadn't technically, she supposed. But she could only keep it all inside for so long.

"What do you mean by 'in the family'?" Sandy asked with a raised brow.

"Oh, nothing, forget it," Kaitlin tried to dismiss. "Aidan had said he may know of something maybe about our grandfather, but anyway—I'll spill when I know more details myself."

Sandy's brow remained raised, but she shrugged nonetheless. "Oh, well, I'm sure it's nothing like that, Kaitlin….nothing like some history of mental illness or something if that's what you mean. At least—I don't think so. I've known you for—how long? If you're troubled, then what must I be?"

Kaitlin giggled. "Love you, girl."

"Remember," Sandy went on with a smile. "Interesting things don't happen to uninteresting people."

"I like that," Kaitlin winked at her, washing her coffee mug. She watched as her friend walked over to the small window from the kitchen, staring blankly outside with a stare that left no impression. "You okay?"

"You've at least advanced further ahead in life than I have, Kaitlin," Sandy sounded more solemn now. "You have your daughter if nothing else…"

"On top of all the intriguing events, you're saying," Kaitlin teased. "Yes, I'm grateful for Malin, at least. But, hey, you can't ignore how interesting you yourself are, Ms. Actress, to have tickled a jinn's fancy yourself."

"He calls me *Lady Liberty,"* Sandy rolled her eyes. "Argh—

and I'm a sucker for it! Can you believe it? So random! But, then again, what man of just the tiniest bit of mystery and strangeness hasn't intrigued me over the years?"

"Didn't you tell me he.... *levitated* you?" Kaitlin snickered, blushing at the remembrance of Sandy relaying their unconventional intimacy with her.

"*That's* definitely a once-in-a-lifetime experience. Forget all the losers before! Whoever you meet after him now—who better be a human, by the way—has only got to be better!"

"Our souls connected....until our technology disconnected," Sandy nodded, smiling. "We sort of had a little fight ourselves. And stopped texting each other."

Kaitlin raised an eyebrow. "What was the fight about?"

"Let's just say he apparently had a little more to do with my getting the part than I thought," Sandy said angrily.

"What?" Kaitlin asked in shock. "How?"

"I'll fill you in," Sandy started, taking out her phone. "I just remembered I have to message the Assistant Director with something. Wait a minute....I know they're good with tapping into our thoughts but...can they do so when they're not present with us as well? Because...speak of the...snake— Bjorn's typing a text..."

"Oh, that's a good sign," Kaitlin nudged her friend. "He's thinking of you, too." She couldn't believe she, of all people, was encouraging her friend to feel happy about a jinn. *Oh, well*, Kaitlin thought. *Anything to cheer her up.*

"Look at the three dots," Sandy continued, sharing her iPhone screen with Kaitlin. "Here's the part where I receive countless compliments in the process of my rejection...."

Lady Liberty

You're one of the sweetest, fiercest, most attractive girls I've ever met….You don't have to keep yourself away from me. You don't have to punish our souls and forms like this.

"I can't believe he texts you," Kaitlin smiled, reading the newly-arrived messaged over her friend's shoulder. "Finn never writes. Just whispers into my mind."

"Really? Wow. I'm curious how that'd be like. Bjorn can't tap into me mentally like that."

"No? I thought that's how all the jinn and human duos communicated," Kaitlin snickered. She lowered her voice. "Can Malin hear us in here?"

Sandy stuck her head out the door. "No, I think she's still sleeping. But, hey…you should do the same, girl. You have a big day, tomorrow! Go lie down next to your daughter."

"Let me help you with the dishes," Kaitlin started, picking up the plates in the sink from their lunch earlier.

"Nonsense—you go rest, I've got these," Sandy said. She added with a smile. "You'll make it up to me tomorrow."

"Deal," Kaitlin winked. "Later, girl."

As Kaitlin tiptoed back into the room, she took out the laptop from her carry-on bag. She had to write something for the blog and then advertise it on social media. "My adoring followers—and the damn algorithm—await," she whispered to herself with an eyeroll.

What could she write about. ***GREETINGS FROM NEW YORK?***

Should she let her followers and clients know she was abroad just yet? Maybe she should write a recap of her visit later on, instead.

She decided on the latter, erasing the title. ***MARRIAGE—WITHOUT THE WHITE HORSE AND CARRIAGE***

She chuckled to herself. That was more like it. Besides—she found that she'd gotten more support from the online community when relaying her troubled ponderings than by anything else. People loved, it seemed, to commiserate with total strangers online sometimes.

"What is marriage if not lifelong company, guaranteed as much as logistically possible?" Kaitlin began to type. She yawned after several paragraphs, as sleep took over her attention from the words being typed.

"Maybe we just all want to avoid dying alone at all costs…."

CHAPTER 25

Dubai

1990

WATCHING THE GROWINGLY CHILDLIKE YOUNG MAN BEFORE him intensely, Amir was amused. *He's proven to be such a loyal student.* "Are you packed, Aresh?"

"Yes, Amir," Aresh said with a sigh. "My mom has bought my medical excuse for my visit. You're sure once in Oslo I can actually stay there, right?"

"Of course," Amir replied with a smirk. "Do you still doubt me?"

"Not at all," Aresh shook his head. "I'm just nervous. I'm still trying to figure everything out. But I've been taking good notes."

"Good, lad." Amir floated to pat Aresh on his back. "You can turn everything we've discussed into a book one day."

"If I *have* any readers," Aresh scoffed, eyes downcast.

"Before readers, you need followers, Aresh!" Amir steamed, floating higher into the air. "You can only obtain that by displaying the absolutely *confident* attributes of a leader—I don't want to hear any more of this self-sabotaging language!"

"Yes, Amir!" Aresh nodded.

"We will have the members first prove *loyalty*. They shall spend a week living in nature and mostly off the nature, removed from possessions. We'll test their reactions as they meet both your kind and mine alike, coinhabiting. And if they pass? They'll have earned the lifestyle we'll be awarding them with."

"Loyalty," Aresh mourned, shaking his head as he bit his lip. "It's hard to come by. As you witnessed— I just met someone I thought I could be with myself on this last internship. *Jaan.* We became lovers. I thought we had something special. But he is in Canada, now, and hasn't returned my letter."

"Forget that boy," Amir said with a smirk. "I'll make sure he and his clan will regret it for the rest of his life, trust me. Think of it as a summer tryst and a life lesson. You're meant for bigger and better things. You've already taken the first step by sending that application to Oslo University. We can expand into North America later on. Greater things than some fling await you in Europe, now!"

"Yes," Aresh said with a heavy sigh. "I must say, though, Master. I don't know how I can focus on graduate studies if they accept me. This is all too exciting!"

"*When* they accept you," Amir began with a wink, "You'll see what it was all for. All your suffering. You will become the leader of a transnational movement for everyone who's suffered needlessly. Only the evolved souls, that is. We cannot accept just anyone into our movement."

"What about my grades?" Aresh asked.

"They…will suffice," Amir chuckled, extending his hand out toward Aresh. "Don't worry about them. Just rest assured that, together—you and I will make history. Your purpose on earth is this mission."

I've been chosen, Aresh thought as he shook Amir's hand. The burning sensation sizzling in his human palm without injuring his skin had already become familiar to him.

"How can I get people to take me seriously, Amir?" Aresh asked.

"You can start by taking me more seriously now that we're officially working together, Aresh," Amir lifted his chin proudly.

"Sorry—*Master*," Aresh said, looking down at his feet.

"That's more like it," Amir smiled. "Now—as for your followers… do not fret. We shall attract people in *dha'iyfah* states of mind. I shall whisper to you to let you know which human with such a weakened mental state you will target, and I will bring in the jinn counterpart. Later on—they shall do this recruitment process for us. We will be saving them from their disturbing lives, and provide them with everything they ever wanted but couldn't find. Money? Sex? Acceptance? Whatever it is—everyone has a weakness, Aresh, and we will find it."

"We will find it, Master," Aresh agreed, his head still facing downward in a bowing position.

"With the *brethren* we form, which will include sisters, too, of course, but I just enjoy that term— they will not only be completing their servitude to Allah, as demanded for both humans and jinn, but also be able to lead happy lives on Earth. For that—we shall create Heaven on Earth."

"Heaven on Earth," Aresh repeated.

"That's right," Amir said with a twisted smile. "We shall focus on only having highly educated, attractive members for it to truly feel like the Heaven described to us in the scriptures. We will create most of our offices amidst the beauty of nature, surrounded by flowing rivers and beautifully smelling flowers, as the Quran describes."

"The flowing rivers, Master," Aresh repeated. He was going to avoid Hell on Earth---and the heartache Jaan had caused him— once and for all. Aresh wasn't going to be some loser, burning after some love who couldn't face the depth of the love they'd experienced. He was a handsome young man, and not just because his mother would tell him so. He wasn't going to waste any opportunity that presented itself before him—especially as it was already so difficult to come across fellow men like himself, where they had to keep their attractions underground.

This jinn and his plan would be his only viable option for a way out of his misunderstood and repressed existence in Dubai— not to mention now dangerous one, as he'd already gotten further threats by the neighbor boy to 'keep quiet, or else'. Aresh swallowed the lump in his throat, turning his attention back to Amir.

"The highly-elevated brothers and sisters.... whom we'll know when we meet them.....will belong to our mission, Aresh! We will earn their trust by giving them little tasks with regards to the business model we have come up with— the paper stuff, since it includes logging out in nature—as a cover. We will pay them generously, and later introduce them to our philosophy and literature, asking them and their families to donate for their education and lodging— promising them a life, in return, worth double or even triple of whatever they've paid us!"

"Yes, Master," Aresh said.

"Say your goodbyes to your mother and brother in the morning, and I shall see you next in Oslo, where I will wait for you," Amir said.

"Where will I go?" Aresh asked.

"You will ask the taxi to take you to the address I will provide you," Amir explained. "Once there, just look out for me in my grackle form."

"I wish I could be a bird, sometimes, Master," Aresh said, smiling as he stared off in to the distance. "Just fly away from everyone and everything sometimes. You're sure neither Kareem nor the police will be on my back, right?"

"Leave them to me—I've told you," Amir said with a smirk, twiddling his fingers together.

"By the way—why do you favor your bird form, Amir? I mean—Master?"

"Wisdom," he replied in a still and even voice. "The birds always know, my Aresh. They chirp at the crack of dawn, along with the first prayer of the day way before the sun rises or even before the *Adhan* calls the community to prayer from the mosque minarets. The birds always know before any other creature about the commands of the Almighty."

CHAPTER 26

WITH HIS SISTER'S NAME FLASHING ACROSS HIS PHONE screen, Aidan quickened his steps toward Merve. "Baby, make haste. My sister can be a bit… spontaneous. Heck—I wouldn't be surprised if she just randomly shows up here now that she's in New York!"

"She wouldn't…" Merve said, her jaw dropping in disbelief.

"She *would*," Aidan replied, giving her a quick kiss.

"Well, I should be good to go in a few. We've already got my stuff at the hotel. Let me just check the bathroom one more time. Somehow, us ladies can always tell when another woman has been there first!"

"I have to take this call," Aidan whispered, bringing a finger to his lips. "Baby Sis!"

"Big Bro-ham! What's the dilly-o?"

Aidan snickered at his sister's greeting. "What kind of strange slang is that?"

"I don't know," Kaitlin chuckled. "I'm getting old, too. How's it going? All good at work?"

"Y-yeah," Aidan stammered, glancing nervously at Merve, who was moving back and forth between their bedroom and the bathroom, making more noise than necessary.

"How's my niece? You girls were able to rest? Everything good at Sandy's?"

He tried to mouth for Merve to be quiet, but it only irritated her. She dropped her entire makeup set onto the floor, exclaiming, "Shit!"

"What was that?" Kaitlin asked.

"Oh, *um*, the cleaning lady is still working on the bathroom," Aidan improvised, bringing on a disapproving look from his wife. He giggled, imagining her thoughts: *"Me? The cleaning lady?"*

"Oh, well, you didn't have to go through all that trouble, really," Kaitlin went on, seemingly buying the excuse. Aidan suppressed a groan. He could have just told her the truth— "Surprise! I'm secretly married to my colleague!"— but things were a bit more complicated than that.

Agreeing to drop by Sandy's later to welcome them and bring back most of their stuff to his place—as Kaitlin was now heading to some therapist of hers—Aidan hung up the phone and walked over to Merve. Hugging her from behind, he gazed at their reflection in the bathroom mirror.

"Thanks for being a good support about all this, my lovely wife."

"You're lucky I like the Turkish hammam services at *The Marmara Park Hotel,"* Merve teased, turning to kiss him.

"Do you remember the last time we were glancing at our reflection like this?" her voice softened, tinged with sadness.

"Don't remind me," Aidan said, his body tensing with anger at the memory. "That bastard!"

"I'm happy your niece will soon be playing here," Merve said, wiping a tear from her cheek. "Do you ever imagine how it could have been if I hadn't lost our baby—because of *them*?"

Aidan's clenched and unclenched his fists. "They messed with us, but we're beating them at their own game. The jinn won't prevail. Love will. In due time, my sweet, everything will be alright."

§

WITH THE BUZZER FROM SANDY'S DOORMAN ALERTING THEM TO her brother's arrival, Kaitlin smiled at her daughter. "Who could that be?" She had decided to let his quick visit to say 'hello' be a surprise.

"Aunty Sandy, of course!" Malin said confidently, pulling out Uno cards from a basket Sandy had placed them in. "She owes me more rounds before we leave tomorrow!"

"Now, Malin, just because we're staying over at Uncle Aidan's starting tomorrow evening, it doesn't mean Aunty Sandy won't be hanging out with us. She's already got us tickets to see the Rockettes at Radio City Hall!"

"The Rockettes?" Malin asked, but the doorbell rang before Kaitlin could respond. She peeked through the peephole and quickly opened the door.

"Aidan!" she exclaimed, leaping into her brother's arms. To her surprise, tears sprang to both their eyes as Malin joined them.

"Uncle Aidannnnnn…."

"Surprise, girls!" Aidan hugged them tightly, later kneeling to embrace Malin separately. "Welcome to New York, sweetie pie! Let me look at you—you're even lovelier than your photos!"

"Thank you, Uncle Aidan," Malin said, hugging his leg and craning her head up with smiling eyes. "I am eight now! And you look younger than your photos!"

As Kaitlin and Aidan laughed, Malin continued. "Your hug isn't as firm as Daddy's, and a lot comfier than Uncle Finn's!"

"Uncle Finn?" Aidan asked, puzzled. He turned to look at Kaitlin.

Kaitlin waved her hand dismissively. "Oh, *um*, we'll talk later. He's a family friend."

For a moment, a lump formed in her throat, making it hard to speak. Her eyes averted Aidan's imploring gaze, and fixated on her daughter's as she forced a smile. "Malin, show your uncle the luggage he's taking today. Let's go, big girl!"

Aidan held out his hand. "Wait, Kaity, wait! First—Malin deserves her 'welcoming gift'."

"Oh, I love presents!" Malin cooed, clasping her hands together and swaying.

Aidan smiled as he handed her a sizeable red carton bag. "It's…. an American Girl doll! You are an American girl now!"

"Aww, thank you," Kaitlin smiled, coming closer to him and adding in a whisper. "We're not exactly sure how long we're actually going to stay here, remember? She's still a Canadian-Norwegian at the moment."

But Malin had already ripped through the long, rectangular box and taken out the doll with highlighted hair. "I love her! Thank you, Uncle Aidan!"

"You're very welcome, sweety," Aidan cooed. "Enjoy."

"Come, sit down for a sec, Big Bro," Kaitlin motioned him to the nearby chair.

"I'll, *uh*, have a seat for a little but I feel bad staying at your friend's place without her present…where is Sandy, by the way? I've missed her!"

"She had rehearsals today for this really cool play Off Broadway!" Kaitlin beamed.

"That's good for her," Aidan nodded. "I remember it used to be off, off Broadway. She's inching closer!"

As Kaitlin playfully nudged her brother, Aidan continued. "How was your therapy session—was it weird meeting her in person after all that time online?"

"It's so nice to meet you finally in person, Kaitlin," Freya had smiled at her, giving her a warm hug as she finally met her at the office that looked familiar from the video calls. As it was their initial meeting—and Kaitlin had planned another in-person one before flying out to

Toronto—she decided to focus mostly on her marriage and father rather than the *jinn* questions she wanted to ask.

"It was okay—it went well, thanks," Kaitlin said, a smile soon crossing her face. "I wouldn't really know, Aidan. I've never met other strangers online in person before, as I'm sure you have through your Dating apps."

"*Haha*, funny," Aidan forced a chuckle.

"I miss Bo, Mommy," Malin said with a sorrowful disposition. "This doll has puppies on her T-Shirt!"

Kaitlin inhaled deeply. "Malin….not now, baby."

Malin sulked, her eyes then lighting up as soon as a thought crossed her mind. "Did you know that Bo was Uncle Finn's gift from his mother, Anja?"

"Okay, who *are* these people?" Aidan inquired. "First this 'Finn', and now 'Anja'? Can someone please explain?"

"Aidan—I'll explain when we come over tomorrow!" Kaitlin insisted through gritted teeth, trying to open the television to distract her daughter.

"And the grandma doggie's name was Freya?" Malin continued, her focus still on the doll she was now twirling in the air. "Or was it the other way around? I don't quite remember."

"Freya?" Kaitlin dropped the remote from her hand. Was it just her overthinking, or was Finn providing names of his friends to Malin back in their little forest outings? If that was the case— had he had another friend named Freya? He couldn't have possibly meant *the* Freya she knew, as in her therapist, could he?

"Yeah," Malin went on. "He said Bo got his eyes from his grandmother."

Kaitlin exchanged glances with her brother.

"Alright, I'm off," Aidan announced, straightening up. He looked at Kaitlin. "Something tells me you're in over your head again. And I can't wait to hear about all this back at my place tomorrow. For now—I'm letting you girls to it. Let me just get the luggage. Where are they again?"

"Right…right," Kaitlin said blankly, motioning her brother to the bedroom while her eyes and mind remained fixated on the words that had come out of her daughter's mouth.

§

"YOU JUST MISSED HIM" KAITLIN GREETED SANDY AT THE DOOR with a smile.

"Aww, no!" Sandy groaned. "I was going to order Chinese food for all of us!"

"Eww," Malin made a face, earning a laugh from both women.

"Yeah—something tells me that wouldn't have gone over very well, anyway, girl, thanks," Kaitlin said. "But we do need to expand Malin's culinary horizons while she's in New York!"

"Hey—I like pizza!" Malin said with a pout, placing her hands on her hips. "That's Italian, right?"

"Okay, *Signorina*," Sandy said with a grin. "How about I order a nice big pie of cheese pizza for all of us, then, on your last night of sleeping over?"

"Deal!" Malin exclaimed. "It'll be like a slumber party!"

She danced over to Sandy, chanting, "Oh, yeah! Oh, yeah!"

Kaitlin forced herself to smile along and followed Sandy into the kitchen, waiting patiently until she made an order from her phone.

"*Um,* Sandy, can I ask you something?"

"Anything," Sandy said in a chipper voice, bringing down some ceramic plates from one of the higher shelves. "Argh—I haven't used these in a while!"

"We can just eat from the box, girl!" Kaitlin said, but Sandy shook her head 'no.'

"No, we're doing this properly," Sandy said with a wink.

"Look at you, " Kaitlin started, teasing her friend. "A great actress *and* a domestic diva. Me? I can't even master one thing."

"Oh, please," Sandy giggled, setting the plates down on the counter and pulling out matching forks and knives from the wooden drawer. "You are *so* meant to be a great writer…and if not, you just may have been meant to be the 'grand story' yourself, Kaitlin."

"Oh, my crazy life shall definitely be a story someday," Kaitlin replied with a snicker. "Probably written by someone else, though. Some actual 'grand' writer."

"I'm so tired, girl," Sandy sighed, her tone softening. "Tired of rebounding from one red-flag guy to the next, just to distract myself from the drama and hurt caused by the previous one. Honestly, I don't even think I would have gotten myself involved myself with Bjorn—especially knowing from the start his entire jinn deal— if it weren't for that momma's boy ex of mine. I can't keep doing this."

Kaitlin nodded thoughtfully. "I think the hardest lesson for people like us is learning to be okay with being along for a while."

"I've always been told I was 'too much'," Sandy muttered, shaking her head.

"You're not 'too much'!" Kaitlin assured her. "Think about it—what kind of cold, miserable and cruel partners must your exes have had up to that point to think your kindness and affection were 'too much'?"

Sandy sighed again. "It's like…I thought having someone—*anyone*—was better than being alone, you know? But now I feel like such a loser for allowing for all this drama because I couldn't set boundaries or say *no*."

"Freya's helped you figure all this out, hasn't she?" Kaitlin asked with a grin.

Sandy shrugged. "She's been great. You know—she's told me

that feeling at peace with ourselves often begins with feeling at peace with our parents. But I barely remember mine."

Placing her hand gently on Sandy's shoulder, Kaitlin gave her a knowing smile. Her friend's parents had both died in a fire when she was just a teenager. "Do you think you're subconsciously angry at them, for going on that ultimately deadly trip and leaving you alone?"

"It's actually one of the things Freya's been helping me deal with," Sandy nodded, fidgeting with her fingers. "I've begun shifting my perspective. They were just going on a job interview for my father—trying to make a better living to raise me. Besides, they actually spared my life by not taking me with them. I've been writing letters to them as if they're going to read it. About how I've forgiven them, and am grateful for the life they've given me. It's helped."

"That's beautiful, sweety," Kaitlin squeezed her friend's hand. "That actually reminds me of something called 'negativity bias' that Freya has suggested I may have been holding on to with regards to my parents. I also have trouble with boundaries in my adult life, apparently, because growing up I've had to take on a nurturing role over my mother, with all her stress she shared with me after feeling abandoned by my father."

"You were so young girl," Sandy shook her head. "And I remember Aidan would often keep his emotions in, just focusing on his athletics and own life, wouldn't he?"

Kaitlin nodded, and the ensuing silence allowed Sandy to go on.

"I'm glad Freya's been helping us. Hey—you met her in person finally today, right? She's nice, isn't she?"

"Yeah," Kaitlin hesitated. Her stomach twisted. "Remind me—how did Freya say she came to believe in the jinn, again?"

"Oh, I think she said she had some former patient she lost touch with who told her about some experience with them or something like that," Sandy shrugged.

"Do you remember any names?" Kaitlin implored.

"Not really. I mentioned Finn and Bjorn, and she seemed like she recognized the names but then dismissed them…Wait a minute. No, can't be…"

"What?" Kaitlin pressed. "Don't ask how I know—but remember how I told you Finn hung out with Malin, pretending to be her dad's estranged brother?"

"Yeah," Sandy's eyebrow shot up.

Kaitlin took in a deep breath. "Well he randomly mentioned names to her with regards to the dogs...and one of them was—Freya."

"That's odd— I mean I guess it *is* a relatively common name in that region," Sandy considered. "Then again—you're right. With these beings we can never be too sure. I mean, come to think of it—I had thought she looked familiar to this photograph of a woman I saw with Finn in one of the albums I was skimming through at the Stavanger cabin of theirs, but…the woman had open hair and just couldn't be Freya. I didn't quite connect the dots…But I guess she did start wearing the hijab later on, so…."

"I wish we could take a look at that photograph now," Kaitlin said, the nerves in her stomach twisting in every way possible.

"Yeah….wait, I may still have it!" Sandy exclaimed. "I snapped a photo of Finn with some blonde before Bjorn came in and she closed the photo album. When I was at their Stavanger cabin. I think I saved a photo of the photograph on my old phone….hold on!"

Kaitlin smirked. "You keep your old phones?"

Sandy shrugged. "I am a bit of a hoarder. But—hey, you never know when something can come in handy! Give me a sec."

As Sandy went to rummage through something in her closet, Kaitlin felt more butterflies churn in her stomach. Could it be Freya in that picture Sandy had mentioned of some 'familiar' blonde woman with Finn? All she knew in that moment was—she was about to find out, and it wasn't easing any of the stress in her life. Where would all this lead? And when could she finally break free?

§

MOUTHING 'THANK YOU' TO THE WAIF, BLONDE RECEPTIONIST FOR what felt like the twentieth time, Kaitlin took in a deep breath before knocking on the door. "Freya? May I come in?"

"Kaitlin!" Freya waved 'hello' with her back turned to her, still on her computer. "I wasn't expecting you again until next week!"

"Yes, I know, I'm sorry to come in like this, unannounced on your lunch break. Thank you for allowing it."

"I was told it'd be quick," Freya's chair swiveled to face Kaitlin finally. "Everything alright? Did you forget something?"

Kaitlin swayed back and forth in place, placing her hands inside the pockets of her red coat. "There's something I have to ask you. It might not be considered professional—per patient and therapist standards—but it's urgent, and I couldn't wait, I'm sorry."

"*Um*, sure, go ahead," Freya eyed her quizzically. "Are you okay? Have a seat!"

Kaitlin smiled politely, taking a seat on the two-person sofa. "I just wanted to know—how you came to believe in the jinn yourself? What was your experience?"

"I cannot answer anything about my personal life, as you must realize, Kaitlin." Freya said, clearing her throat.

"It's harder than people realize, isn't it? To move on after the presence of such possessive power?" Kaitlin licked her lips as she inhaled. "After a jinn! For God's sake, I don't think I can ever…"

"Oh my God, completely," Freya started, rolling her eyes toward the ceiling fan nonchalantly. "It's sure been a journey for me to uproot my lifestyle and move here afterward, just to…."

"Freya?" Kaitlin pushed further as her voice trailed off. "You can tell me. In fact—*please, do*! You moved here…after a jinn? I'm just going to get straight to it— did you know….*Finn Du Feu*?"

As shocked as Freya looked, Kaitlin had a hunch it was more at Kaitlin's knowledge of it than at the suggestion.

"How would you assume that?" she finally asked, clearing her throat. "Because I'm from Stavanger?"

Kaitlin walked closer to her, taking out her phone. "No—because I saw this photo of you two together in an embrace, from a gathering with 'The Group'."

"Kaitlin…." Freya stammered, seemingly searching for her words as she glanced at the photo. "I'm afraid my ethical code of anonymity requires that..."

"Freya—I don't mind if we *never* have a session again, if that's what you must do," Kaitlin explained, banging her fist on the table. "But please help me—just woman to woman—as I can see you've obviously been close to *him*, too."

As Freya shut her eyes and inhaled deeply, Kaitlin was taken aback by the tears she saw in her eyes. "Yes—I was involved with them. In my old life—before I found the righteous path. But, Kaitlin, I want you, also, to understand—I have worked so hard to put all that behind me! I am now a married woman!"

"So have I!" Kaitlin placed her hand on her bosom, crying as well. "And I am, too! A mother, as well. I have to free myself—mostly my daughter. As you obviously have. I mean—Finn hasn't scared me, or anything. But I'm afraid of this…Lar Iktar. He's demanding from Finn to make me a member!"

To her surprise, Freya smirked. "Oh, please—between you and me, Lar Iktar is a joke. It's the 'big boss' you've got to watch out for. Lar calls him 'Master'. He is a jinn, and his name is 'Amir'."

Big boss? Amir? "H..how would I know who that is? How can I get him off my back?"

"You had said you know about the Islamic prayers, right?" Freya said with a shrug.

"Yes," Kaitlin started, when Freya cut her abruptly.

"Yeah, well, those work on minor-jinn, like Finn, but Amir…he is the mastermind. He could be around you and you would never know—you'd probably think it's Finn, or one of the others. You get shivers down your spine and such sensations when Finn is near, right?"

"Yeah," Kaitlin said, blushing. It felt awkward talking to an ex-lover of Finn's in this way, somehow.

"Yeah, well—like I said. It could not always be him. It could be Amir, and he's not a good one or even neutral one. Sometimes I heard him referred to as 'the Emperor'…he is obsessed with power and vengeance. He's *bad*."

"What?" Kaitlin scoffed.

"Lar is his puppet, and he controls the others through him," Freya continued. "I'm not sure how anyone could defeat him, really. Maybe only Lar can—as he's mainly connected with him."

"Finn…never said anything," Kaitlin shut her eyes, hoping it'd shut off the pain as well.

"I'm not surprised," Freya scoffed. "You know, I'm surprised he's still remained under Iktar's spell all this time. I remember him to be smarter, and more headstrong than that."

"What do I do, Freya?" Kaitlin whispered, leaning closer to her.

"You have to fight…with all your might," she whispered back. "I wasn't able to get much help when I discovered Amir, and later escaped him—but I did, nonetheless, one day as Lar was talking to him, in his bird form. He likes to be in dark bird forms, from what I recall. And Lar saw that I saw—and I ran! I ran, Kaitlin, like no one has ever run before! I left Norway and never looked back. I don't know what else I can tell you."

"I understand," Kaitlin bit her lip, eyeing the floor.

"Finn...." Freya started. "He can be charming, I know. He's one of the better ones, believe it or not. But many in his circle are too dangerous. You have to do what's best for you and your daughter. Now if you'll excuse me....I'll be writing out the final report on you, dear Kaitlin. I'm sure you understand, as you've alluded to earlier, that we cannot have any further sessions."

"I see..." Kaitlin clicked her tongue against the roof of her mouth. She was just about to leave when Freya called out to her.

"But wait! This doesn't mean you can't talk to me as a friend. I'm always here for you—you know my FaceTime connection. Heck—here, write down my personal number, too."

"I'm sure you say that to all clients to be polite," Kaitlin forced a smile, glancing at the notepad where Freya was jotting down some numbers.

"Believe me," Freya shook her head sadly. "I wish I could have said it to the one patient I lost track of, due to my cowardice. I'll regret it for the rest of my life. I don't want you to think I'm abandoning you. I'm not."

"Thank you," Kaitlin smiled, as Freya came to take her hand in hers.

"I mean it." Freya insisted. "You can call me anytime. Just because I'm obliged to end our professional contract, doesn't mean I can't remain in your life if I'm meant to. And I think this is too big of a coincidence binding us."

§

EXITING THE ELEVATOR AFTER LEAVING FREYA'S OFFICE IN TEARS,

Kaitlin checked her reflection in the mirror. "Have a great day, Miss!" a doorman said politely, holding the door open for her.

"Thank you, you too," she answered him. He had called her 'Miss', unlike the coffee shop boy earlier who called her 'Ma'am'—*who said New Yorkers were rude?* Kaitlin tried to smile as she took in the crisp cold air, wrapping her checkered scarf tighter around her neck. Who knew New York City winters could give Norway—heck even Ontario—a run for their money when it came to coldness?

She checked her phone to see two missed calls—one from her mother, and the other from Sandy. Paul had sent a teddy bear hug meme to Malin through WhatsApp, writing for them to video-call him whenever they could. Kaitlin smiled. *Poor Paul.* So much was going on even here across the world that she'd forgotten temporarily about their drama—and perhaps it was better that way, she figured.

Kaitlin noted the avenue and the street crossing. 47th Street and Broadway. Wasn't her brother's place two blocks away? She supposed she could just walk over, as he had given her an extra key to get inside later even if he wasn't home yet— but what would be the point? He was probably still at work. She checked the time. Besides—Sandy would be walking over with Malin soon to walk around a bit before going over to Radio City. She was in no mood for some show, but she had to do this to make her daughter happy.

Returning her friend's call to coordinate their location, Kaitlin jumped up and down in place for warmth—right in front of the clothing store Sandy had told her to wait for them.

"There you are!" Sandy exclaimed, walking over to her in the crowd as the two of them exchanged a hug and Kaitlin leaned down to kiss her daughter 'hello'.

"Did Freya upset you?" Sandy placed her hand on Kaitlin's shoulder.

"You met your Doctor Friend, Mommy?" Malin asked

innocently, warming Kaitlin's heart. That's how she had termed her therapist to her daughter.

"Yes, sweety, Mommy met up with her Doctor Friend," Kaitlin shook her head, wiping a fallen tear from her cheek. She turned to Sandy. "And—no, girl. Freya was cool. Let's just say—our suspicions were correct. And she's revealed some other information—I'll fill you in later. But I won't be seeing her as a therapist anymore."

"Oh, boy," Sandy gritted her teeth. "Maybe I shouldn't either."

"That's up to you, girl," Kaitlin placed her palms in the air. She looked around her as she took Malin by the hand and squeezed in through the crowd.

"And here I am, Sandy. Forlorn, lost…In a big city once again, bigger even than Toronto…And yet it no longer energizes me…makes me feel smaller, in fact…."

"In the meantime—let's try to enjoy the sights, eh, girls?" Sandy said, smiling between Malin and Kaitlin.

"Where's that crowd going? "Kaitlin asked.

"To the *Rockefeller Center* Christmas tree," Sandy explained. "Follow my lead!"

Leaving her mother a quick audio message assuring her she'd call later, Kaitlin smiled at Malin as they all walked in front of the touristic attraction. She giggled as Malin showed all her teeth, including a gap between two of them, and held up a peace sign in front of the tall tree as she posed for a picture.

Dingggg. Paul was calling her.

"What do you say, baby?" she asked Malin. "Shall we show the tree to Daddy?"

As Malin nodded eagerly, Kaitlin found herself comforted by Paul's smiling face on the video call. He asked if they were 'okay', and she had said 'yes'—not knowing if it was quite true.

All she knew in that moment was—at least she had gotten one

step closer to unraveling the mystery of the jinn in her life. What would happen with her business after meeting with Salim, the mystery of her father she hadn't yet been able to discuss fully with Aidan, her mother....she hadn't a clue. She had no idea how much detectives made in real life, but she sure had become one lately for free!

She had Freya to thank for more than the information she'd just revealed to her. Somehow—whether it was because she was simply good at her job, or due to this apparent Finn-connection they both had—the woman *got* her.

Whenever you're down, Kaitlin, always step outside yourself in your mind, and look at your situation from outside the box," Freya would say. *Think like a magician, or healer, or even a detective. What would you do, if you could? How could you help yourself? And then—take concrete, realistic steps to achieving it....baby steps can lead to bountiful leaps.*

CHAPTER 27

HOW IN THE WORLD COULD LAR IKTAR HIMSELF HAVE HAD SOME mysterious 'master', and one apparently in bird form at that? With Freya's words still haunting her throughout the relocation to Aidan's place, Kaitlin ran her fingernails through her scalp, applying pressure to ease the stress.

"He could be around you, and you would never know," she had said, *"You'd probably think it was Finn."*

Could this 'Amir'— the 'mastermind' of 'The Group', according to Freya— have indeed followed her? She remembered the birds in the forest distracting her the day Malin was first led by Finn outside her dance class. Finn had called them his 'friends' in bird form— could one of them have been Amir? Kaitlin shivered at the thought, mentally making a note to gaze around for any dark birds lingering around her in particular!

With Finn— she had come to understand his affections, but what the heck could this 'mastermind' jinn possibly want with her? It didn't make any sense to Kaitlin. Was it all about membership in their damned cult? She was receiving some answers yet so many questions were simultaneously speeding toward her in every direction she turned. Freya had appeared sincere, at least, in saying that Kaitlin could call her even though she could no longer 'treat' her.

Watching as Malin jumped up and down in the separate queen-sized bed they would be sharing, Kaitlin smiled with a sigh. Maybe she would ask Freya later—right now, she had to focus on enjoying the trip with her daughter.

"Where are we going today, Mommy?" Malin was out of breath already.

"Times Square, sweetie pie!" Kaitlin exclaimed. "Your uncle says the sights and lights are more magical when it gets dark, so he'll be taking us on a drive through the streets when he returns."

"Why does he have to be at work all the time, too—like Daddy?" Malin pouted.

"I'm afraid it's the way the world works, my love," Kaitlin replied with a soft grin, flopping herself on the corner of the bed. "Adults have to work and earn a living to be able to provide for themselves and their loved ones."

"Being an adult is no fun sometimes either, then," Malin said with a sulk, picking up the American Girl doll to twirl her hair.

"No, it sure isn't, baby," Kaitlin smirked, kissing the top of her daughter's head.

"I'm glad you have more time to spend with me, at least," Malin hugged her mother's leg, and it was the world to Kaitlin.

Ding.

The text-message sound alerted her to Salim asking if 4pm the following day at Bryant Park would 'work' for her. Kaitlin had suggested the location from the little she knew of the touristic area, particularly as Sandy had suggested she could take Malin ice skating there. Kaitlin figured she could meet him and still be close to her friend and daughter while having the professional coffee date— if they could find a seat amidst the typical crowds!

"Let me check the oven to see if those chicken nuggets are ready yet," Kaitlin told her daughter, heading toward the spacious kitchen which her brother also used as a dining room. Ever since she and Malin had set foot at his place the previous night, she found herself in awe; not only was it a contemporary-decorated, two-bedroom apartment that was clean for a bachelor, the decorations also all matched the modern art on the walls perfectly!

Kaitlin always knew her brother to have good taste in fashion and had already glimpsed the perfectly-arranged designer suits in his bedroom closet. Yet she somehow thought he would have gotten by all these years with simple furniture akin to IKEA! Her brother made good money, of course, but she'd never thought his spending would extend to his living décor this much as well.

Pulling out one of the bar stools with leather cushions to wait for the remaining five minutes on the oven for their quick snack, Kaitlin smiled at Elizabeth Taylor staring at her. She walked over to the Andy Warhol painting hanging atop a sleek cabinet between the kitchen and the living room corridor. Kaitlin wondered if it was a replica, later deciding—after closer inspection—that it probably wasn't. *I'm impressed, big brother*.

Mentally noting to snap some photos of the house arrangement to share with Paul for perhaps a mini furniture makeover of their own back in Norway, Kaitlin ran her fingers over the quality finish of the wooden drawers. Opening the top one to see how smoothly it glided, Kaitlin was surprised to see how quickly it did so—as it was completely empty!

She chuckled. *Leave it to Aidan to buy furniture he'd never use, just to make his pad look good.* Instinctively pulling out the second and third drawers as well, Kaitlin noticed a colorful shawl in the third one. A scarf? Picking it up to check its brand, a large rectangular pink chocolate box took her by surprise.

"Hmm," Kaitlin's mouth twisted into a smile. *I'm tickled pink,* she muttered underneath her breath. She shook the tin box only to hear what sounded like papers inside rather than chocolate. What was this—some romantic notes left to him by a lover?

A white cardboard with blue writing was on top of several photocopies of paperwork. Was it a certificate of some kind? Glancing at the top—and then all over its surface—Kaitlin's mouth fell agape.

THE CITY OF NEW YORK
OFFICE OF THE CITY CLERK
MARRIAGE LICENSE BUREAU

§

MENTALLY COUNTING TO FOUR, KAITLIN RELEASED HER long-held breath as Aidan arrived at the dimly lit apartment. She'd thought for a moment to allow her discovery to go unaddressed, yet ultimately mustered the courage to confront her brother about what he had done. Her feelings were a mélange of anger, betrayal as well as concern for his well-being, all in one soup.

Aidan was looking worn out. *I bet it must be exhausting to harbor so many secrets,* Kaitlin thought with a scoff.

"Kaity! It is so lovely to have my sister welcome me! Where's Malin?"

"Uncle Aidan!" Malin came running into his arms. "I finished all those nuggets you got us! None left for you! I'm sorry! I was so hungry!"

"I swear I'm going to cook something healthier for us tomorrow," Kaitlin shook her head with a smile.

"All good, girls," Aidan dismissed with his hand, winking at Malin. "I'm taking us to a revolving restaurant at the Marriot Marquis Hotel—it's called *The View*."

"Oh, you didn't have to," Kaitlin said softly. "You said it'd just be a mini-tour of Times Square."

"No trouble—and it is right by there," Aidan said, hanging up his coat. "Let me go put on some more comfortable clothes."

"Can I first talk to you about something?" Kaitlin bit her lip. She considered waiting for after dinner, but couldn't hide it. The excited part in her was competing with the infuriated part, and she had to satiate at least one of them soon!

"Sure," Aidan's expression turned serious, glancing at Malin, who was now distracted with watching something on television.

"Let's head to your room," Kaitlin suggested as she led the way, "I don't want Malin to hear. I'll get to the chase… I saw *the papers*."

"Papers?" Aidan questioned, closing the room door a bit to hide the sound from their conversation.

"Yeah, I guess that 'cleaning lady' forgot to clean those out of the drawers, *eh*?" Kaitlin flapped her arms and slapped her jeaned thighs for effect. "It appears that a *'Congratulations'* is overdue, big brother! You've apparently been *married* for some time now!"

"Married?" Aidan stammered, scratching his head and looking all around him. "To whom? Where are they, Kaity?"

"You don't need to keep up the act, it's okay," Kaitlin crossed her arms and bit the side of her lower lip. "I saw the certificate. You and someone named *Merve*. I think it's a Turkish name? The residence address shows this apartment. Was there a ceremony, too, we weren't invited to, I wonder…?"

As she tapped her fingers on her cheek, Aidan shut his eyes and sighed. "Kaity, it hasn't been a typical marriage; ours has been more one of convenience, mostly for me to help out a friend. Sit down, please. I'll explain…"

"A friend?" Kaitlin asked on, crossing her arms. She walked over and pushed the pink, tin box toward him as it slid across the table.

"Are these chocolates for me— as a peace offering for snooping?" Aidan smirked.

"I thought so," Kaitlin shrugged confidently, finally taking a seat. "I mean, I thought they were chocolates. That's the only reason I opened them. But— alas—your lady, Merve, here, apparently likes to use this fancy box as storage."

"Right," Aidan chewed his lips.

"Aidan—it's not like it's a *shameful* thing to get married," Kaitlin shook her head softly side to side. "I don't understand this secrecy. What's going on?"

"I want to protect her," Aidan said, eyes downcast. "She wants to keep working, and though I'm a founder of my company, I'm no longer the only executive, Kaitlin. I've had to sell nearly half of my shares. I didn't want to alarm you or Mom…"

"I knew something was up!" Kaitlin folded her arms across her chest. "You should have stayed with that diplomatic job! The car service business is tricky! But… what do your economic woes have to do with…."

"I also need to adhere strictly to our policies—of which non-romantic relations in the office is one," Aidan interrupted. "The CEO watches all of us like a hawk because of investor and board interest in compliance."

Kaitlin's eyes circled the entire room before landing back on her brother. "Once again—Aidan, this doesn't explain why you couldn't tell me or Mom that you got married, as if we were going to blab about it to your professional circle…."

"Are you going to let me get through this story or not?" Aidan steamed.

Kaitlin motioned with her hands for him to continue. *Geez Louise, someone's touchy.*

"Merve was my assistant…." Aidan began, sitting next to his sister and putting his head between his hands before looking up. "She came to the office in response to an employment ad, saying she needed work with the expiration of her student visa approaching. Despite her less than stellar English— for which she was taking night classes somewhere— I gave her a chance. She had a good CV, with higher education completed. As far as I could tell, anyway. I mean—most of her experiences were from Turkey and I never exactly called her old employers for referrals, but I didn't care."

"You offered her the job…just like that," Kaitlin continued, befuddled.

Aidan smiled. "Sort of. She is a looker, I have to admit. She'd given me 'the eye', but also had this conservative air about her. Graceful young woman. She didn't throw herself at me like some others. We became friends in addition to being colleagues, and I grew to really like her— though I couldn't admit it for the longest time."

"Some *friend*," Kaitlin darted her eyes toward the ceiling. *Finn*. His name popping up in her head again awakened her to her own hypocrisy with the platonic word. *Argh!*

"*Anyway*," Aidan emphasized, rolling his eyes at her before continuing. "At first I started her out as a paid intern instead, hiring a native speaker for the initial position. But she was getting paid legally in this country and she wasn't complaining."

"Right," Kaitlin nodded, squinting her eyes. She wished her brother would just get to the point already.

Aidan cleared his throat. "So one drunken night after our annual office party I, *um*, went too far, apparently. I mean, I guess….and….she told me later she was…. *pregnant,* and so…."

"Aidan!" Kaitlin interrupted, her voice trembling with emotion. She could not believe what she was hearing. "What do you mean *you guess,* and *apparently*? What's "*too far*"? I can't believe you! Did you …. *rape* the woman, or something?"

"Kaity, I don't *remember* violating her in any way— I swear!" Aidan pounded the side of a cabinet with his knuckles, tears filling his eyes. "I mean, for a long time I even denied it— to her and to myself. I honestly don't remember having ever been that drunk to the point of zero recollection, but I swear it's true!"

Kaitlin was appalled at the possibility, but she didn't know what to believe.

"I remember the party here and there, and leaning closer to her after everyone had left, " Aidan went on. "Merve was helping to clean up, and she looked so hot. But I just wanted to kiss her, Kaitlin! That's all! I remember I leaned in…and her big eyes were staring at me, smiling. She was not scared or unwelcoming or anything like that. And after that…it's all just a blank!"

"Aidan, you said she got pregnant!" Kaitlin shook her head, torn between sympathy and anger. "I don't understand. What could have happened, then? What exactly did you drink?"

"A whole bunch of things— I mixed too much. Rum, Gin, Vodka- three beers…"

"Wasn't that Dad's problem, too?" Kaitlin's voice became lower. "Mixing drinks? And why would you drink so much? At the office, too! Don't those people look up to you?"

"I wasn't feeling too good. Funny you mentioned him, Kait. The party coincided with the day of one of my visits to good old Zachary. I'd just returned to New York the night before…"

"Aidan," Kaitlin cut in. "I know you're insisting you, like, *zoned-out drunk* before….whatever happened. Regardless— it's no excuse! Would you want a rapist using an 'I don't remember' excuse with someone you care about? With a daughter? A niece? Me? Anyone?"

Aidan pressed his face into his hands. "Except in my case, Kaity- it's absolutely true! I would have taken a damned lie detector test, if it ever came to that! I'm not some fucking rapist!"

With tears now streaming across her cheeks, Kaitlin desperately wanted that to be true.

"I hated myself for doing that to her, though, regardless of the strange circumstances," Aidan continued after replenishing his long-held breath. "I mean, technically still… I suppose my body entered hers, because of the baby…"

"Well…as I was saying," Kaitlin threw her hands out toward her sides and took a deep breath in. "You may have apparently inherited this high inclination toward alcoholism from Dad! I mean *I've* drank before, Aidan. Obviously. But I never became addicted. I've never been too much into liquor—just enough to get tipsy. But you…I don't know what's going on, with all this I'm hearing. I mean, perhaps you've been affected by our Dad environmentally, too? Seeing him as you have. Whereas me? I was only five when I last…"

"Oh, for God's sake, Kaity!" Aidan said in a raised, firm voice, standing up. "Everything always has to be somehow turned around and be about you—you— you! *You* were five? Yeah. Well, *I* was only seven when he left! I was an innocent child, too!"

"All I meant was— you've been *seeing* him, whereas I thought he was untraceable all this time…."

"Kaity!" Aidan bellowed. "I didn't know about him for nearly two decades, either! Just like you! If I hadn't met John, our half -uncle, I may never have known…."

Kaitlin shut her eyes, and drew in a deep breath as she held her hands out before him. "I'm just trying to help us figure all this stuff out, okay? I'm so confused. I don't want to think my brother is some….rapist."

Finn. The vision of that night when he'd got into bed with her as 'Paul' crossed her mind. How scared she'd been when she had discovered the truth. What her brother was telling her now was somehow reminding her of that chapter from her own life. Could this have been something similar—a jinn thing? A way for them to have sex with a human through possessing another one's body, if not downright manifesting as one like Finn had done?

"M…maybe it wasn't the alcohol, then?" Kaitlin asked, her voice stuttering. "If you insist this hadn't ever happened to you before. A fleeting violent inclination, perhaps? Did you feel like some…*er*…force….came over you, or something, Aidan?"

Aidan's eyes began to well up. "Kaitlin, I never got shitfaced or even punched a guy— let alone a woman! How the heck can my own sister accuse me of purposely raping someone?"

Kaity shrugged with a soft voice. "I'm not accusing, I'm just trying to understand…"

"Kaity!" Aidan interrupted her in disbelief. "Can I finish? There's more—just be patient."

"Okay, okay," Kaitlin held out her hands and plopped herself further back on the couch. "Keep going."

Aidan sat back down next to her. "Anyway…. I promised to make an honest woman out of her and marry her. And I knew it would all be hard to explain to you guys—why I seemingly have had to marry her secretively yet also so fast."

"An *honest woman*?" Kaitlin asked with a smirk. "Oh God, Aidan, that makes what you've done even worse, somehow. Come on! You sound more closeminded and machoistic than Paul now, are you kidding me?"

Aidan crossed his arms and wiped his tears. The up-and-down look of contempt he shot at her made Kaitlin shiver. "Do you *always* do this, Sis?"

"Do what?" Kaitlin demanded.

"Just throw the people who love you into the fire? When something you hear isn't to your liking—by just assuming the worst about them? Dad…Paul…and now, me?"

Kaitlin gasped. "I can't believe you've found a way to bring this onto me…"

"Kait—you don't even know Merve!" Aidan exclaimed. "How are you so quick to just jump the gun on *me*?"

"What the hell are you talking about, I mean,….?"

"What if the woman was a liar, eh?" Aidan cut in before Kaitlin could finish her question. "What if she just wanted to get me in trouble, for whatever reason? What if the baby was from someone else?"

"*Was* it?" Kaitlin raised her brow and smirked. "And *did* she?"

"Oh, *now* you're asking if she was telling the truth, Sis?" It was Aidan's turn to scoff. "Gee, thanks. I love how I'm automatically assumed to be guilty based on my gender."

"You told me you married her, for God's sake!" Kaitlin went on with confidence, flipping her hair back. "Obviously you wouldn't have done so if you'd thought she was lying!"

"Touché," Aidan remarked, after briefly considering Kaitlin's words. He bit his lower lip. "The point is—she *could* have been."

"Why *did* you marry her, Aidan? And don't give me the 'honest woman' crap again, please. Spill. If you didn't remember exactly what happened and weren't sure she was being entirely honest later accusing you, then…"

"Because I *did* believe her, afterward," Aidan's eyes were glued to the floor. He took a deep breath. "And I fell in love with her."

Kaitlin smiled for the first time during the entirety of their conversation. "Whoa. My playboy brother. Fell in love? Oh, what further shocking extremes from one end of a spectrum to another will my ears be hearing today?"

"Very funny," Aidan said, rolling his eyes— but blushing before her like a little boy.

"How did you come to believe her, though?" Kaitlin asked, rubbing her chin. "First, you're saying you don't remember anything warranting her accusation. Then you're telling me she was telling the truth and that you fell in love with her, for heaven's sake! I'm very confused. She didn't, like, report you to the *police* or anything?"

"Merve quickly realized what had happened, and came to me, believing me," Aidan whispered, looking all around him. "Kaitlin—we believe that who actually violated her, using my body as a vessel…. was *Emir*."

"*Emir*?" Why in the world was that ethnic-sounding name familiar to Kaitlin? *Amir,* the name popped into Kaitlin's head. It sounded like Amir— the name of the 'Mastermind' jinn Freya mentioned. Were they one and the same?

"Shh, don't verbalize his name, too much," Aidan said with a nod, bringing his forefinger in front of his lips. "It's a long story. A remarkable and crazy one. You may not believe me, but I ask you to listen with an open mind. Because it just so happens to be the truth."

"I'm curious, now," Kaitlin said without taking her eyes away from her brother. "I promise I'll hear you out. Shoot."

"The identity of Emir…well, the *force* behind the namesake human form he tends to take on with Merve, anyway …" Aidan took in a deep breath and heaved his shoulders before continuing, "….involves something unseen to most people. Beings…called *jinn*. The jinn are…"

"Oh!" Kaitlin fidgeted, then raised her hands slightly before letting them fall. "That makes more sense now, yeah. *Easy, peezy, lemon squeezy*, as Malin says. I know who the *jinn* are, Aidan."

Aidan's jaw almost dropped to the floor. "You're fucking kidding me, right? You know about the jinn?"

"Yes—I know them!" Kaitlin went on with an eyeroll. "They're called 'the third ones'. The third beings— in addition to humans and angels— whom God describes in the Islamic holy book as being his special creations inhabiting this world, living in a separate realm from us, though sometimes crossing over. And so on and so forth. I had an inkling it may have been the jinn when you insisted you didn't rape her but I didn't want to say anything first. Go on…."

Aidan's jaw remained agape. "*You* have heard about *jinn*, before? What the hell? They're not exactly popular knowledge in Canada or the States. Have they got a whole discussion on them goin' on in Norway or somethin'?"

"*No*— but, as a matter of fact, I've *known* some, too," Kaitlin smiled, shaking her head. "I hate how jaded life has made me. I hate how nothing really shocks me anymore. But yes— dear brother. Looks like I've got a rather long story to tell you, too, myself!"

"Oh, I'll bet you do," he said with a scoff, albeit with a smile forming on his lips. "Nothing really surprises me anymore, either."

"What's going on here?" Kaitlin asked with a forced chuckle. Brooding with concern, she had to admit it felt good to see her brother relaxed, at least, despite the severity of the things they'd just discussed.

Aidan shrugged. "Beats me! Our father was in *Alcoholics Anonymous* when we were little, and you and I apparently need to join some *Jinn-Survivors Club* or something!"

All Kaitlin could do was rock back and forth in silence, eyes fixated on Aidan— the weight of their shared trauma lingered heavily in the air.

"Hey—what are you two gossiping about behind my back?" Malin demanded, her eyebrows crossed as she stormed into the room. "I'm bored! Let's go to Times Square already!"

CHAPTER 28

THE SMILE BEAMING FROM SALIM WALKING BESIDE HER AMIDST the holiday stalls radiated warmth despite the chilly winds. Kaitlin was taken aback how much taller her remote colleague was in person! “Thanks for agreeing to meet me on such short notice.”

"Are you kidding?" Salim inched his face closer to her, his breath visible in the cold air. "I wouldn’t have missed finally meeting the beautiful Kaitlin in the flesh!"

Kaitlin pulled back slightly, offering a soft smile. Salim didn’t seem to have the typically reserved, personal-space-conscious mannerisms she’d noticed in most Americans.

"Thanks," she said, adjusting her red winter hat. "Things have been a little hectic, and my daughter and I will be flying out to Toronto soon. So I really wanted to finalize that next marketing strategy you mentioned."

“You’re leaving already?” Salim stopped his speedy walking abruptly, the coffee in his hand spilling a bit onto his gloves.

"Well, we’re here for another week!" Kaitlin chuckled. "But I need to spend time with my daughter and brother, so I wasn’t sure when else we’d get a chance to discuss the cookies."

"We’re getting dinner before you leave, then—you have to promise me!" Salim grinned. "Not today, since your daughter’s waiting after her ice-skating trial, but next time, I’m not taking ‘no’ for an answer."

"Maybe your wife can come, too?" Kaitlin suggested, sipping her cappuccino. "Paul couldn't make this trip, as you know, but I'd love to meet her."

Salim waved a hand dismissively, his gaze shifting to a nearby jewelry stall. "She's out of town. I have my place all to myself this entire week."

As his eyes met hers with a suggestive grin, Kaitlin's stomach tensed. Was he implying something? She forced a light chuckle. "A week isn't that long—you'll survive."

"Do you like bracelets?" Salim asked, greeting the eager sales associate. Most shoppers, Kaitlin noticed, were browsing more than buying.

"I do." She smiled, admiring a silver bracelet adorned with delicate butterfly beads. It would match the anniversary necklace Paul had given her. "How much is this?"

"That one is $150," the young lady said with a Slavic accent.

"Nice," Kaitlin said, setting it back down.

"You like it?" Salim picked up the bracelet. "Try it on—let's see how it looks on your delicate wrist."

Kaitlin hesitated as the salesgirl winked at her. *Let it go, lady,* she thought. *He ain't my man, and the bracelet isn't that big a deal.*

"It's nice, but I don't need it. Let's go."

Salim ignored her protest and gently pushed back the sleeve of her red coat, sliding the bracelet onto her wrist.

"Beautiful!" he said, extending her arm for a better look. He winked back at the salesgirl. "You have a lot of beautiful things here."

"Thank you," the woman blushed, tucking her red hair behind her ear.

What the hell, dude? Kaitlin thought. She'd had no idea what a flirt Salim was!

"Is this the only one?" he asked the salesgirl.

"Yes, I'm afraid so," she pouted, her glossy red lips protruding.

"That's a shame," Salim said, glancing between the girl and Kaitlin. "I would've liked to buy two. Tell you what—I'll buy this one now and leave my info so you can contact me when another one comes in."

"Oh, no need, Salim, really!" Kaitlin interjected. "You can just get this one for your wife. I really don't—"

"Here it is." He cut her off, handing his business card to the sales associate with a charming smile. "I'm Salim. What's your name?"

"Luba," she smiled.

"Luba, wrap this up nicely for my dear friend Kaitlin, will you?"

Oh, merde. Kaitlin's pulse quickened. Before she could protest, a dark bird swooped low, startling them. Salim fumbled with his credit card, knocking over more coffee onto his jacket.

Kaitlin reached into her shoulder bag, pulling out napkins to help him.

"Sorry, ladies," Salim laughed. "I get a little nervous surrounded by so much beauty. I'm usually not this clumsy."

"That stupid bird!" Luba giggled, tucking her hair behind her ear again.

Kaitlin forced another smile, but inside, she couldn't shake the discomfort settling in her chest.

§

ENSURING MALIN'S TEARS HAD SUBSIDED, KAITLIN RETURNED HER daughter's hot cocoa and took her by the hand, leading her toward the seating area next to Sandy. They settled into the small, shaky metal chairs surrounding the ice rink. Apparently, Malin hadn't had much luck with ice skating and her self-confidence level had dipped.

"We'll start with roller-skating, baby. It's okay," Kaitlin

reassured her, kissing her cheek. "That's how I first learned to balance before trying the ice."

Malin dropped her shoulders, still pouting as she licked the remaining whipped cream hanging on to the side of the carton.

"How did it go?" Sandy asked, tugging her violet beanie down over her ears. "Salim was cool?"

"Yeah," Kaitlin scoffed, sipping her own hot chocolate. "Maybe *too* cool."

"What do you mean?" Sandy raised an eyebrow. "You guys discuss some wild marketing ideas?"

"Oh, we discussed some ideas, alright," Kaitlin sighed. "But actual useful ones? That only happened in the last fifteen minutes. The rest of the time, he was flirting—with me and this salesgirl! And he's supposed to be married—sheesh!"

"You're kidding!" Sandy rolled her eyes.

"Salim insisted on buying me this bracelet I was checking out!" Kaitlin was shaking her head.

"And *did* he?" Sandy asked, her lips twisting into a smile.

"Sandy—no!" Kaitlin protested. "I don't need any more drama. I turned it down, changed the topic, but he still gave his number to the salesgirl. I wouldn't be surprised if he visits her later—if she doesn't call him first!"

Sandy clicked her tongue. "Geeky married men chase flirty encounters, while handsome, notorious womanizers like Aidan Maverick secretly settle down. What's the world coming to?"

Kaitlin laughed. It amused her that Sandy had called her brother 'handsome.' She knew her friend had always had a little crush on him growing up. It was a relief to have gotten her friend filled in with what she had discovered about her brother secretly being married, albeit not the disturbing portion of the story.

That reminded her—Sibel had messaged. Kaitlin made a mental

note to share Aidan's secret marriage with her, especially since the mystery bride was also Turkish. Sibel would have a field day!

Kaitlin chuckled to herself—maybe she should have accepted the bracelet and gifted it to her mystery sister-in-law for fun. Whoever the woman was—and whatever craziness had apparently gone down between her and Aidan—she deserved to be celebrated for having gotten her brother to tie the knot!

"Luckily, a bird flew by and made him spill his coffee," Kaitlin continued. "The embarrassment got us out of there faster."

"A bird, huh?" Sandy's tone shifted.

"Yeah—why?" Kaitlin asked, then understood.

"I just remembered what Freya told you—about that jinn in bird form controlling Lar or whatever. Now I'll be paranoid every time I see a bird!"

§

HOLDING THE NOTEBOOK A BIT FARTHER THAN HER USUAL EYE LEVEL to ensure the legibility of her handwriting, Freya smiled. Despite the less-than-stellar professional implications of ending therapist-patient relationships, she often enjoyed the 'Case Summary' writing process.

"The patient, 33, seems to be dealing with her fear of abandonment through anxious coping mechanisms. Her default mode appears to be searching for her authentic self through a misconstrued sense shaped throughout her childhood and adolescence vis-a-vis her relationships with others..."

Chewing on the end of her favorite pen bearing her name, Freya jotted down another observation drawn from her studies at New York University's *School of Psychology*. Writing this final report on Kaitlin Maverick was proving to be more complex than she expected.

"Loving beyond measure what they'll soon hate without reason." **The Thomas Sydenham quote has exemplified the Borderline Personality Disorder since the 17th century. Also called *hysteria*....symptoms of which have also been displayed by the patient to some extent. The patient can speak affectionately about individuals in her life one moment, only to blame them for random things with vicious language the next. Furthermore, the patient has possibly found the narcissistic traits in her husband familiar due to early experiences shaped by her overbearing mother— where the patient was blamed for the mother's loneliness, acting as a stand-in for the absent father who had vanished without a trace.**

Freya closed her eyes and breathed in the memory of one particular 'individual' from her own past, someone she had sworn to remove from her life at the roots. Finn Du Feu's green eyes burned into her mind, clouding her vision.

It had been strange to finally meet this new object of her old jinn-lover's affection. Kaitlin was even lovelier in person, with an energy that radiated from within—something technology could never quite capture. No wonder Finn was smitten.

That reminds me! Freya flipped through the pages of her journal, searching for the section she had dedicated to her research on jinn after her discussions with Merve. She had sworn not to talk about the past—but that didn't mean she couldn't *write* about it. What kind of therapist would she be if she didn't follow her own advice about expressing one's issues? She was, after all, only human—flawed like the very people she counseled.

She had long been intrigued by the idea that God had created jinn with powers greater than those of humans, yet they struggled with their own internal battles. *"We're both flawed compared to the angels, my Freya,"* Finn had once told her in Stavanger, sitting beside her on their favorite bench. Her blonde hair had whipped in the wind, and she had been certain that passersby had seen her whispering to him, no matter how hard she had tried to disguise it. She hadn't cared—she had been so in love.

I'd been so full of unintentional sin, she thought now, a single tear rolling down her cheek onto the journal. She quickly wiped it away before it could smudge the ink.

"You humans have advantages, too, my dearest," Finn had told her. *"For one thing, you're gifted with aging and death. Your fleeting youth and experiences make life more beautiful and intense."*

"You're not immortal, though, are you?" she had asked him, tilting her head in curiosity. *"Lar's told me otherwise..."*

"No, my dear..." Finn had explained with a smile. "*We are to die and be judged in the hereafter, just like your kind. We're just less affected by physical injuries and illness, so our forms last longer. It takes—shall we say—a more elemental death for us to truly perish. But no need to cloud our beautiful day with such morbid thoughts..."*

The memory of his kiss made Freya snap out of her reverie with a small squeal. She needed a shower. Just recalling their encounters made her body throb, and she cursed herself.

"*Tawbah...*" she whispered, the Arabic word for repentance in Islam falling from her lips. She glanced at the clock above her bedpost. Less than an hour until Maghrib prayer. She needed to take her wudu ablution.

She couldn't risk being possessed again. She couldn't risk losing Salim—her fiancé in American legal terms, but her husband before Allah's eyes. Salim, who had stood by her for years, guiding her toward light and stability. The man who had supported her throughout her journey as a therapist. He would catch on if she let herself fall again.

After drying her hair, Freya tiptoed back to her journal.

"Ow!" she yelped, rubbing her toe after stubbing it on the bedpost. She noticed her pink nail polish was still intact.

"Ugh!" She would have to remove it and re-do her ablution

properly.

"Are you alright, *Habibti*?" Salim called from outside her door.

"I'm okay, my love! Just taking a quick shower."

Her mother—who had struggled to accept her conversion to Islam—hadn't approved of her living situation with him. "*Doesn't that go against your faith?*" she had sneered.

"*He married me through nikah, Mama. You know this!*" Freya had defended herself. "*We just haven't had the formal ceremony yet.*"

Her mother had scoffed. "*Salim says this, Salim says that... Freya, you owe me a ceremony. You're my only daughter. Don't be crazy.*"

Freya sighed under the warm water, inhaling deeply as she performed her ablution, cleansing herself physically and spiritually.

Norwegian. American. Group member. Therapist. Agnostic. Muslim. Crazy. Sane.

She hated labels. Her mother had once mockingly called her "The Asylumist," suggesting Salim only wanted her for a green card. But Freya knew better.

She was not 'crazy'. Neither was Kaitlin, nor Merve. Society labeled women in pain far too conveniently. Suffering that could be circumvented, if not prevented, with a little love and understanding.

Finally, wrapped in a yellow towel that matched her cotton bathrobe, Freya returned to her journal, smiling as she found the exact passage she had been searching for.

"Jinn—beings of fire mentioned in the Quran—are said to frequent those with mental ailments, otherwise keeping to their own realm apart from humans..."

I was not a good therapist, nor a good Muslim, for turning away someone in need. Just not a good person at all.

Freya had failed Merve. She had shunned her. But she wouldn't make the same mistake with Kaitlin.

She sighed, feeling the weight of her past. "I was an amateur then," she murmured. "I let my personal feelings cloud my profession."

"Freya, *meri jaan*? Are you sure you're alright?" Salim's voice was warm with concern.

She sighed again. He must have heard her. "Yes, just emotional over my client's story again. I'll be out soon."

His head peeked in, his dark eyes playful. "You could have waited for morning for your shower, baby. I'm not letting you sleep tonight. I'm extra horny today…"

Freya burst out laughing as he waggled his eyebrows suggestively. Despite his long hours at work and conservative demeanor, he still knew how to make her laugh.

"I don't mind showering again in the morning. I like my new shower gel. I'm almost done here. I'll be right out, baby."

Once Salim closed the door, she stared at the wall decorated with both his and her diplomas and certifications in their unique fields. Freya smiled. Everything happened for a reason. If she hadn't gone through the jinn trauma, she supposed she couldn't have been able to develop what it took to heal enough to advise people about it.

"My experiences," she muttered to herself. "They may at least have been more valuable than any diploma."

CHAPTER 29

CLICKING OFF THE VIDEO CALL WITH KAITLIN AND MALIN, PAUL wasn't satisfied. There had to be something he was missing—some way to fix all of this if he truly wanted to, though so far, he had found none.

How the hell can I get rid of this Finn once and for all? He had searched online for various ways to deal with a jinn, but none went beyond exorcisms (and Kaitlin wasn't 'possessed' as far as he knew), prayers, and protective amulets. Plus, Kaitlin had said Finn was now interested in having his little boy play with Malin in dog-form! There had to be something else—something connected directly to Kaitlin that needed to be addressed at its root.

Rummaging through Kaitlin's drawers, Paul had no luck. He wasn't sure what he was looking for, but he hoped he would recognize it once he found it. And, of course, she had taken her precious laptop.

The website! He could try looking through some of her older content. Scrolling through her page from his own tablet, he finally found something—an entry Kaitlin had posted during his time in jail. *Bingo.* Maybe it held some clue about what she had been up to.

November 24, 2014

"Tomorrow is my daughter's first birthday party, and I'm alone. Yet I wanted to thank those of you who've become members and supporting me online throughout my struggles not only as an outsider in a new country, but also as a married mother now forced

to fend for herself as a single parent due to the injustice my innocent husband, Paul, has been facing. I had been reluctant to share my story, fearing misjudgment, but I've been blessed with much kindness and understanding.

Update (edited): I thank everyone for the countless messages of support and responses to my posts— which I've now decided to archive in order to leave that negative chapter of our story behind and attempt to move forward..."

Archived? What had she deleted? Were there interested men who'd pursued her, under the guise of 'support'? *That Salim dude she talks with, perhaps?* His curiosity pressing, he typed in Kaitlin's password to her website and peeked at 'Archives'.

"Let's see," Paul muttered. He knew he'd have to login as Kaitlin herself in order to see such content—luckily, he could always guess her password. She had trouble remembering and had revealed it during a fight at one time when he'd been jealous about something. On her own free will. **Malin112513#.**

Jackpot! He found four to five archived blogs from the time of his brief stint in jail, and Paul's heart sank as he read through Kaitlin's words in each of them, as well as the responses and her replies in turn. One of them in particular touched his heart.

"I miss him… I *understand* him better now. I *appreciate* him. The very things that used to frustrate me during our arguments—those little quirks that once irked me—now seem *endearing* in retrospect. We can sometimes take for granted that the people who care for us will always be there. But the truth is, there are no guarantees—no promises of *tomorrow.* So, to those in marriages or long-term relationships: appreciate what you have, flaws and all. Because one day, you might look back and realize that raw imperfection and vulnerability was *love*—and by then, it could be too late."

Paul's eyes burned with tears. Had Kaitlin loved him more than he ever realized—despite his mistakes? Maybe even *because* of them? Did he have any guarantee it would have been different with anyone else?

He hadn't expected this. Kaitlin had *chosen* him—*declared* her love for him, publicly.

And what had he done?

Or rather—*what had he been forced to do?*

Finn.

Paul's jaw clenched, fury boiling in his veins. Had it been that jinn all along? Stirring up trouble? Keeping Kaitlin at a distance?

"*Du Feu!*" he roared, fists tightening as he spun around the living room. "Wherever the hell you are—come and face me! Man to man—jinn—whatever the hell you are!"

His voice shook with rage. "If you've got some unholy scheme, it runs through me first!"

Nothing—*no one*—was going to tear his family apart.

§

COULD NOISE BE HEARD IN AN EMPTY FOREST? THE old adage about the falling tree crossed his mind, making Paul chuckle. In the bitter cold of a very cloudy day, his laughter traversed through the crackling twigs, a feeble attempt to soothe his nerves. Turning in every direction, Paul barked into the relative darkness. "Come out and be a *man,* jinn-man! Man up, and face me, Du Feu!"

His breath curled in the frigid air. Somewhere, somehow, Finn had to be listening. From what Paul had gathered, Finn had apparently lured Malin toward these woods after her dance class. This was the only trail he knew.

"You and your damn dog have been showing my daughter around—why not me?" Paul spat, his voice rising. "Show yourself, like your kind did in my jail cell to screw with me! Appear before me if you have the balls to explain how you've kept my wife under your spell for so long! She calls you her 'friend'—fuck that, Du Feu, you're a jinn! And you crossed a damn line when you went near my daughter."

A shiver ran down his spine, but no one appeared. How in hell did one *summon* these beings exactly? How the heck did Kaitlin do it? He clenched his fists then forced them open again, trying to clear his head.

Was Finn simply not there? Paul's stomach twisted. Maybe Finn was busy in the United States. *Stalking Kaitlin.*

The thought sent ice through his veins. His voice dropped to a growl. "You better not be after them while they're visiting family abroad, Du Feu!"

§

STILL SHIVERING, PAUL ENTERED HIS APARTMENT, ARMS wrapped tightly around himself. He hadn't gotten a response in the woods, but prayed his message had gotten through to Finn, somehow. As he shut the door behind him, he dropped his keys onto the kitchen counter. The sharp *clack* echoed through the empty space.

A sudden ringing filled his ears, a piercing pain that made him twist in agony. Then, as if the sound had summoned him, Paul spotted a blond man lounging comfortably on his couch—wearing black pants, a loosely buttoned black shirt, and a smug expression.

"Finn," Paul muttered, forcing down the ball of fear rising in his stomach. He recognized him from a photograph Kaitlin had shown long ago of 'The Group'. He glanced around for something—*anything*—to use against the jinn. His wife had mentioned something about Finn's discomfort with metal while she was packing for her trip. "You heard my invitation after all."

"I didn't want to be rude, Maverick," Finn tilted his head with a grin. "I apologize for being indisposed when you visited my neck of the woods— for what I assume was some…tea?" His smirk widened.

"So—I thought I'd return the courtesy. What do you say we play a game? And *all shall be fair in love and war*, as the expression goes."

Paul barely had time to scoff before he noticed the chessboard, set-up neatly on the glass table.

"What is this, high school?" he sneered. "You seriously want to *play a game* with me? What's the prize—getting the *girl*? Are you out of your damn mind?"

"In the old days, your kind dueled with swords and shields," Finn smirked with a shrug. "I just supposed that'd be more your speed—that you'd be familiar with such patriarchal ways to get a woman's love."

"Don't you dare sit in my house and talk about things that aren't your business, you human-wannabe!" Paul growled, inching toward the heavy metal decoration in the corner of the living room. If things got ugly, he'd be ready.

"I'm not trying to *get* anybody, Paul Maverick. That's what you don't understand." Finn tapped his temple. "This is about *honor.* The honor of fighting for *real* love. Your ring on her finger means *nothing* if you don't fight for her."

"Oh, and I suppose a chess match will prove that?" Paul scoffed, exhaling sharply as he dropped onto the corner of the couch.

"Not the game itself," Finn said casually, smiling. "The *effort* will."

Paul rolled his eyes. "Alright, love guru. You're on."

Finn's expression didn't change, but his voice dropped as he set his eyes on the board. "Brother Tan used to cry with nostalgia, recalling the chess games he and Linette used to play." He shook his head. "Before *you* messed them up."

Paul stiffened. "You're not seriously bringing up those *disproven* charges against me? The bastard *himself* confessed to killing her before lethally-injecting his own body!"

"There are worse ways to kill someone than taking their life, Maverick," Finn's gaze burned through him. "You killed Tan's *belief* in love."

"Oh, give me a break." Paul let out a bitter laugh. "Okay, let's play, jinn. I played a little back in the day. Let's see what you've got! But remember— you have to play *fair* with me. No superpowers or whatever the hell it is you've been using to cloud my family's mind…"

"I'm always fair," Finn's smile was creeping Paul out more than his angry words. "No tricks. I'm black, you're white. Start the game."

As the minutes passed, the ticking wall clock echoed alongside Paul's heartbeat.

"It's a sad predicament to find that sometimes one's enemies are more reliable than some friends, isn't it, Maverick?" Finn mused, holding a pawn in his hand. "At least you can be ready for their next move…"

"Yeah, yeah, cult jinn, keep playing," Paul snickered. He was running through every strategy he could remember, opening with his knight, then advancing his pawns. To his surprise, Finn mirrored his moves. Piece by piece, they dismantled each other's armies, the game unfolding in a delicate balance of attack and defense.

Then—

"Checkmate."

Finn's voice slithered through the air, almost a whisper.

Paul's brows furrowed. "Wait… No, you *didn't* win. I might be rusty, but I *know* I'm not in check. Your knight can't touch my king—"

"You *can* move your king," Finn said, his grin widening. "But either way, he'll still be in check." He pointed to his remaining queen. "See?"

Paul's stomach twisted. "You *bastard!*" He lunged forward, swinging his fist at Finn's smug face—

But his hand passed straight through him.

As if he were punching at air.

"Where the hell did you go?!" Paul spun around, chest heaving.

Finn's voice drifted from across the room, calm and mocking. "Fighting *me* won't bring her love back."

Paul clenched his fists. "You made me play this damn game just to give me some *symbolic* speech?"

"I'll be leaving now, Paul Maverick." Finn's voice was melodic.

Is he seriously going to float out of here like a goddamn ghost? Paul gritted his teeth. If he couldn't fight, maybe he could *reason.* Maybe even let down his verbal artillery, for now, and beg. Sometimes, a man had to do what a man had to do.

"Kaitlin said she's upholding some promise to you—renting some place in Toronto." He exhaled, voice tight. "*Please.* Keep up *your* end. Leave her and Malin *be.*" His jaw clenched. "You can bet your *burning ass* I'll be keeping an eye on them back here, but there—I'm asking you to do the right thing, Finn. Have a conscience. *Please.*"

Finn reappeared by the door, scoffing. "I have more of a conscience than you could ever dream of, Maverick."

Paul swallowed hard. "Then *prove* it."

"Don't worry," Finn said smoothly. "I haven't seen them in a long time. And I will keep my promise—as I have for years. *Unless I am needed.*" He took a step forward. "Just remember…"

Paul's pulse pounded. "What?"

The air between them thickened, heat radiating from Finn's form, scorching against Paul's skin like the midday sun on burnt flesh. Could anger *manifest* in his kind?

"Just because she's away from *me,*" Finn said, voice dark and low, "…doesn't mean she's automatically closer to *you.* Love is *earned.*" Paul's body tensed.

"*Putain*!" he snarled, swinging another punch aimed at Finn's snickering face—only to find that he had vanished in an instant. The momentum sent him staggering forward, landing hard on the floor. His knuckles burned, as if he'd just placed his hand inside a blazing furnace.

Is that blood? He looked down at the shattered vase, the dried-up flowers Kaitlin had picked long ago now strewn across the floor. He had never thrown them away.

Finn's voice echoed one last time.

"Fighting won't help you, *man.* The only battle that can *earn* her love is the one against your pride and ego."

Paul, trembling with rage, slammed his foot against the door.

"Just *leave us alone!*" he screamed, voice hoarse, pressing his bleeding hand beneath his jacket.

CHAPTER 38

FIXING MALIN'S PONYTAIL—MUCH TO HER CHAGRIN, JUDGING BY her daughter's facial expression—Kaitlin smiled to try to keep her composure. "Grandma is a perfectionist, sweetheart. Trust me—it'll be more painful to hear from her later about the things we 'should' fix about our appearances."

"Okay," Malin obliged with an eyeroll.

"I hear the elevator door opening!" Kaitlin whispered to her daughter. "Stand up straight!"

Before Kaitlin could even see her mother, Linda Ramsay's signature perfume filled her nostrils. As Linda walked down the corridor, she locked eyes with them almost instantly. Kaitlin smiled. She was wearing a faux-fur black coat with checkered leggings tucked into flat winter boots. Kaitlin noticed her mother eyeing every nook and cranny of the hallway, then the entrance to the apartment. "Oh my, this place is huge!"

Malin jumped up and down. "Grandma! Welcome!"

"My baby!" Linda embraced her granddaughter, stepping inside. "You look like your mother when she was your age!"

"I've noticed that, too," Aidan said, walking from behind her with the luggage and closing the door.

"Welcome, Mom!" Kaitlin was surprised to find her eyes welling up.

"Kaity!" Linda looked up from her lingering embrace with Malin. "You look pale! You're not pregnant again, are you?"

"No, Mom," Kaitlin joined the hug, her emotions spilling over. Even her mother's idle chatter felt welcome that day, especially compared to the voice message she'd woken up to from Paul.

"Hi, *Chérie*. I hope New York is great. Has Momma Linda arrived yet? Give her my best, and kiss Malin for me, please. Tell her that Daddy—if you girls still remember him over there—is a bit hurt, but alright. Why is he hurt, you may be asking, my darling wife? Oh, it's nothing. I just had a little…run-in….with a little fiery friend of ours. That's right; the one whose last name matches his makeup. Your friend visited our home and challenged me to a game of chess! Of all things, can you believe it? He said some bullshit and then left—but not before I gave him a piece of my mind, and punched him! So, Kaitlin—I beg of you now…if he dares to show himself to you girls over there, and you don't tell me— you will be breaking more than just my heart. This is about our family. *Bisoux*."

"I can't believe it took Kaitlin and Malin visiting to get you to fly out, Mom," Aidan said, now relaxed on the couch next to Linda. "I told you—it's a short, comfortable flight!"

"Funny—I don't recall receiving a welcoming invitation from you, young man," Linda quipped, putting her forefingers to both cheeks in mock contemplation.

"Oh, come on—I always said you were welcome!" Aidan smiled, feigning offense.

"Yes, you've *said* it, Aidy, but it never sounded like you *meant* it!" Linda crossed her arms. "Kaity? Do you recall Aidan inviting me out here before you girls?"

The mention of her name brought Kaitlin back to the moment. "Hmm? Oh, yeah. Would you like another glass of water, *Maman*? Or something else, maybe? We'll be sitting down to eat soon."

"You two have plotted to team up against me, already?" Linda said, wagging her finger between Kaitlin and Aidan.

"Mommy made chicken!" Malin said excitedly before Kaitlin could protest. "From scratch, with sauce—not nuggets from the bag!"

"Oh, well, that's good to know," Linda chuckled, as did Kaitlin and Aidan.

Throughout dinner, Kaitlin appreciated the distraction of having her mother over. They'd already decided she'd go sightseeing a little before Kaitlin and Malin would fly back to Toronto with her.

"Why did Uncle Finn and Daddy fight, Grandma?" Malin's question came out of nowhere, between her first and second servings of chicken. Kaitlin's fork dropped, its sound the only thing audible in the ensuing silence.

"I didn't want to say anything—but I can't keep my mouth shut, Mommy!" Malin continued, shrugging. "Nanna Mila isn't here for me to ask, so… I don't know! I mean, *Daddy* knows me and Uncle Finn met, it's only fair Grandma knows the truth, too!"

"That's right, my sweet," Linda reached out to caress Malin's chin. "These two never respect your grandmother—you, don't be like them. You always tell me the truth, alright?" She leaned in closer to whisper. "What are they hiding?"

Kaitlin's heart skipped a beat. Did Malin know? About Finn and Paul's fight, of all things?

"Malin?" Kaitlin asked, her brow furrowing, chewing quickly on her bread. "What fight?"

"The fight over some girl when they were younger, Mommy!"

Kaitlin exhaled in relief. "Oh!" She pressed a hand to her chest. As much as it would suck explaining this to her mother, it was far easier than explaining the bizarre situation involving Paul and his punching Finn over a chess game.

"Uncle who?" Linda asked, stuffing another potato into her mouth and raising an eyebrow at Kaitlin. "Your mother introduced some man to you as an uncle? Aidan is the only uncle you have, sweetheart.

You only have aunts on your father's side."

"Finn is…like…a family friend, Mom," Kaitlin said, cutting her chicken. Aidan cleared his throat and exchanged a knowing look with Kaitlin, offering his silent support. "Someone Paul knows, too. It's a long story. Can someone pass the salad?"

"A family friend, eh?" Linda raised a brow, avoiding Malin's confused expression. She leaned closer to Kaitlin and whispered, "And why did she have to meet him as her 'uncle', Kaity? Was he your lover? And now you want me to lie to my granddaughter?"

Kaitlin sighed, trying to use subtle gestures to signal her mother to drop it without Malin noticing. She leaned in to whisper. "Mom, Malin believes Finn is her long-lost uncle, Paul's twin. Please, just play along for now... I beg you."

"Twin?" Linda fluttered her eyelashes. "You mean to tell me there's someone who resembles Paul enough to pass for his twin?"

"Yeah, crazy, right?" Kaitlin forced a chuckle. "Aidan, the salad, please!"

"Oh, right, sorry, here you go," Aidan winked as he passed her the bowl.

"Grandma?" Malin asked, peering up at Linda. "What's going on? You didn't know about Daddy's twin?"

Linda looked confused, glancing between Kaitlin and Aidan. Both of them shot her pleading looks. "Oh, well, it took me a minute to refresh my memory. But I think I do remember now, yes. But, Malin, siblings fight sometimes, sweetheart. Even your grandfather didn't talk to his brother, John, for years. Anyway, let's finish dinner so we can have that dessert I brought over."

"Pecan pie?" Aidan asked, licking his lips. Linda nodded.

"John?" Kaitlin wiped the corner of her mouth with a napkin, then stuffed it under her plate. "Oh, right. Aidan told me about the half-uncle. I'll help you with that pie in the kitchen, Mom, if you want."

"In the kitchen?" Linda asked.

"Yes, this way, Mom," Kaitlin said with a look that brooked no argument.

"Aidan, your sister's really taken over your place," Linda giggled.

"She's a natural," Aidan nodded with a soft laugh.

As Kaitlin led her mother into the kitchen, she motioned for her to sit on one of the stools and took her hand. "John was Dad's half-brother, right, Mom? Apparently from some extramarital affair Grandpa Robert had… or something like that? I don't need Malin to get more confused, though. I'm just offended you never told me so many things…"

"Kaity, I didn't know about the whole mental institution thing either at first!" Linda darted a glance at Aidan. "He only told me later. But who is this *Finn* that Malin believes is her uncle?"

"He's a friend Paul knows too, Mom, like I said," Kaitlin started, her voice quieter now. "He has a dog Malin plays with in Norway, so I've allowed a couple of playdates, but Paul doesn't like him. Anyway, it's just not going to be an issue anymore. No worries."

"Kaity, I wasn't born yesterday," Linda spoke softly but firmly, taking out the Tupperware she'd placed in the refrigerator earlier. "Why did Malin think this man was her father's twin brother?"

"Well, um, you guessed it," Kaitlin said, blushing, "he really does resemble Paul and had to pick her up from school one day when Paul and I were busy. We didn't want Malin's teacher to be confused, so we had to make up this story. So, about *John*…"

"Is there a picture of this fake uncle?" Linda asked, folding her arms. "And when is my poor angel going to be told the truth? Kaity, you do not want your daughter growing up thinking it's okay to lie."

"Oh, but harboring family secrets is okay, I suppose, right, Mom?" Kaitlin shot her mother an upset look.

"So anyway—about John," Linda continued, dismissing Kaitlin's jab. "Yes—John was Zachary's brother from a different mother," Linda began, taking a deep breath. "He and Zachary were never close, so he wasn't anyone who'd be an uncle figure to you and Aidan growing up, anyway. Without even Zachary around, it didn't occur to me to mention his half-brother to you kids."

Kaitlin nodded, feeling the weight of it all. How strange that Finn's fabricated story to Malin—about being her father's estranged brother—in fact contained truth… but from her own childhood. Half-blood or not, an uncle was still an uncle as far as she was concerned.

"Aidan filled me in on the drive here from the airport," Linda said, looking down at the floor. "You found out about the institution your father is in. I'm so sorry about all this."

"You really expect me to believe you didn't know until recently, Mom?" Kaitlin's eyes began to well up.

"It's the truth, Kaity!" Linda inched closer to her daughter. "Your brother found him, through John, coincidentally, of all means! Life is full of coincidences. You know I'd seen your father with that woman, but never again! How was I to know when he'd been admitted to that hellhole?"

"Well, I may want to visit that 'hellhole'," Kaitlin bit her lip, as she placed the pie in the oven. "It's kind of why I want to return to Toronto with you. Otherwise, this would have been enough for me to share with Malin, Mom. Her uncle and grandmother are here in New York. Toronto could have waited. But frankly—we don't know how much longer Dad has left on earth, and I think I *need* this."

"Baby," Linda reached out to hug her daughter as Kaitlin's voice stammered. "Meeting him may not be the Hollywood ideal you're fantasizing about. He may not treat you in a way that…"

"I don't care!" Kaitlin interrupted. "I don't want to avoid anything anymore. Can we meet this John, for example?" Kaitlin was also a little curious if she had any cousins she didn't know about. "John Ramsay, is his name, right? Let me look him up. I don't want to have to run everything by Aidan."

"Oh, no—not Ramsay, Kaity," her mother said. "Your grandmother, Mabel, divorced her husband after discovering the affair. Apparently, it was with some Arab woman in Beirut or something like that. A real looker. Lord knows where they would have met. I haven't met many Arabs in Canada. But I think your grandfather was doing a lot of business in the Middle East. He was a renowned engineer, my ex-father-in-law. Anyhow—she changed Zachary's last name to her own as a single mother afterward."

"Oh," Kaitlin murmured, her shoulders sagging in defeat.

"Yeah," Linda snickered. "Good thing, too. I like 'Ramsay.' Can you imagine if your dad had the same last name as his father, Robert? I heard his half-brother kept it… You kids would have had the last name 'Walker'."

Kaitlin almost dropped the ceramic cup in her hand. "*Walker*?"

"He would have been 'Zachary Walker,' like his brother, John Walker," Linda's eyes grew dreamy. "Your dad was so handsome when I met him. Sharp with his wits, too. Not like he is now, apparently. All that alcohol… and loose women. Oh, he did himself in…"

Kaitlin had long drowned out her mother's reminiscing about her youth with her father. An uncle named John Walker? A Canadian, but with an Arab mother? Her mind drifted back to when Paul's old boss, John Walker, had been at their house searching for Linette's killer.

"My mother and I are originally from Lebanon... half-Lebanese. She'd talk to me exclusively in Arabic, before I moved out to stay with my Canadian father..."

Could John Walker have been her uncle? What were the odds? Which would have made Linette… her late cousin! She supposed it could technically have been someone else. John was a common enough first name, after all. And Walker—a common last name. But with everything happening in her life, Kaitlin had learned not to believe in coincidences.

"Kaity?" her mother broke in, louder this time. "You're being rude. Excuse me, are you even paying attention to me? Or am I talking to the walls again?"

Oh. Mon. Dieu. Kaitlin snapped out of her thoughts. "I'm listening, Mom. I'm just realizing John Walker sounds familiar. Paul's boss from Quebec had the same name. He visited us in Norway on a trip."

"Sounds like him, alright," Linda shrugged. "He *is* from Quebec, from what I recall. Oh my goodness, Kaity, you had to see your paternal grandmother—how passionate she was! I wish Mabel could have been alive today. She stood up for herself so well in front of that mistress to your grandfather. Now, there was a 'feminist' if I ever met one. She left that man and never looked back! *'I curse you, Robert,'* she said. *'I curse you and everyone connected to you!'*"

A grueling feeling settled in the pit of Kaitlin's stomach. She placed trembling hands over her mouth. "Mom—she must have cursed her son, too, then, unknowingly… and therefore me and Aidan too, as his children! And John Walker… as Robert's other child, and God knows who else!"

"Oh, gibberish, Kaity, those are just words in anger," Linda chuckled nervously. "If that's the case, she would have *cursed* me, too, as Zachary's wife—and look at how great I am! Although a bit lonely…okay, *quite* lonely back in Toronto. But it's all circumstantial. The woman could have had no such power, don't be silly!"

But the look in her mother's eyes as it met Kaitlin's were asking—*Could she?*

CHAPTER 31

WHISTLING AS HE WALKED DOWN THE CROWDED STREET mostly unseen, Finn found himself singing a tune he'd known since his youth. "I'm an alien….I'm a legal alien….I'm an Englishman in New York."

It hadn't been necessary to manifest in this way—he could have sped to Freya's office much easier in his light energy form or even his feline one—but Finn wanted to have a little fun. *I deserve it,* he thought, smiling at the occasional persons able to see him, hands in his pockets.

He was still amused by how much he had enjoyed the little chess game with Paul Maverick. Though, he had to admit, messing with the man had taken a toll on his mental well-being a bit. *I can't believe Maverick finally had the balls to confront me.*

Finn stopped and looked up at the building he had been searching for. *Not everything in my world can revolve around the Ramsays and Mavericks.* Right now he had another matter to attend to. Rolling his eyes, he mentally checked in with Meredith. *All good with you and Bo?*

It took about a minute, but she relayed that they were fine, and inquired about New York. Assuring Meredith that all was 'swell' and that he'd be back in Stavanger soon, Finn's lips twisted into a smile at the sight of the now familiar security guard. Here was where he had to revert to his natural energy form in order to be able to get into the building.

Once at Freya's suite, Finn quickly flashed inside, waiting in the corner by the window until she sensed him. The flowing fair locks he remembered were now invisible, tucked beneath a purple headscarf. A sharp pain near his heart took him by surprise. Had Freya placed additional protective objects around the place—sources known to cause discomfort to his kind? The *Ayat-ul-Kursi* prayer on the door was still there, he had noticed it the last time he'd been there. *What else is it this time that's ailing me deeper?* Inching closer to Freya, the pain in his heart sharpened. *She's placed something on her body!* He had to be quick.

"Freya, hi," he called softly. Her posture on the swivel chair—alert, eyes scanning her surroundings—told him she had become aware of his presence. "Please…I just want to talk to you very briefly."

"Step back, Finn," Freya spoke toward the window, her voice steady. "Go away."

Finn's stomach sank as he heard her begin muttering the Islamic *duas* of protection from evil. *She thinks I'm evil.*

"Freya…dearest Norse goddess," he began, forcing himself to manifest in human flesh despite the discomfort. "Do I have no value at all from our good times together? Come on, just hear me out! It's your profession now, isn't it? Hearing people out…"

"*People*, Finn!" Freya's icy eyes met his emerald ones. "You are not of my kind. Please stop continuing to confuse me. I beg you. I thought I'd gotten rid of you for good. I didn't call for you. How are you able to show yourself before me again?"

"These prayers are meant for strict segregation of our kinds," Finn explained, attempting a smile. "They are not necessary when I come in peace, and am needed."

"And yet I can see you're in pain," Freya said, crossing her arms, a grin forming on her face.

"Do you *like* that I'm in pain?" Finn shook his head. "You should know I mean you no harm. Quite the opposite, in fact…"

"Oh, so, you admit you meant harm back then…" Freya lifted her chin.

"No," Finn spoke, eyes narrowing in disbelief. "I can't believe you think so ill of me. Despite the mission bestowed upon me by Lar and Amir—I let you escape, Freya! How easily you forget, or deny, what I did for you! I could have let Lar know where you were—I even convinced Amir to leave you be, assuring them both you wouldn't be spreading libel about 'The Group' from here in the United States."

"I'm sorry," Freya whispered, her voice thick with tears. "I know you've done good for me, too, and I am grateful, Finn. I wish you well. I really do. I just… I worked so hard for this, Finn! You have no idea. I came here for a fresh start—adopted this faith, found peace… formed a family."

"*That's* what I'm here to warn you about, Freya," Finn cut in. "Salim is a joke! He speaks of religion but acts worse than I ever could. Do you not see how he flirts with other women?"

Freya frowned. "My relationship is none of your concern!"

"You're only getting older, Freya," Finn pressed, stepping closer to Freya as she took a step back. "One day, you'll be home, sooner than you think—and he'll come back with a second or third wife. I just wanted to warn you, as I only want what's best for you."

"Oh, please!" Freya bellowed. "How would you know?"

"Freya?" A knock on the door interrupted them. "Is everything alright"

"Everything is okay, Nina, thank you," Freya called out to her receptionist, her gaze never leaving Finn. "I'm just on the phone!"

"I had to keep my promise to Kaitlin to stay away during this trip, but Amir has been keeping an eye on things instead," Finn continued. "She was on some professional meeting with Salim in Bryant Park—he helps with her cookie business, as you know. It was relayed to me that he began flirting with some jewelry seller there, and they've begun meeting in private."

"I didn't know he was helping Kaitlin with her business," Freya admitted, her hand covering her mouth. "I mean, I know he has several international clients, but I never inquired as to who…."

"Oh, Freya," Finn tilted his head, watching her closely.

"Does he flirt with Kaitlin, too?" she asked, her voice breaking.

"No," Finn lied. "Kaitlin isn't a threat to your marriage. Salim himself is. You're worth so much more than him. You've come so far, and I'm proud of you."

Freya wiped her tears and smiled weakly. "Thank you."

Finn looked at his extended hands, barely visible now with his slowly disappearing manifested-flesh causing him excruciating pain. He managed to open his eyes—lids heavy as mountains—to see Freya's eyes closed, her lips murmuring to herself under her breath. *Her prayers are too strong.*

"Please halt the verses at least until we're done with our conversation, Freya. You don't always need to get so defensive and worked up!"

"I will not be working with Kaitlin anymore as a patient so that's why I wanted to ask you," Freya said with a heavy sigh.

"Is it because she's found out about us?" Finn took a deep breath. "She's done nothing wrong. It's that other woman you should concern yourself with, in regards to Salim…"

"I know," Freya nodded. "It's all just too much, the coincidence of your connection with Kaitlin. It was easy for me to feign ignorance when your name was mentioned, but she's caught on now…"

"What does she ask about me?" Finn asked with a grin.

"Wouldn't you like to know?" Freya scoffed. "You'd better not have listened to our conversations!"

"I respect your profession, and have not!" Finn held his hands up in defense. He grinned. "The headscarf suits you, by the way. Brings out your eyes. Interestingly enough, you look more beautiful than ever."

Freya chuckled, shaking her head. "You're complimenting me even as I'm crying?"

"It's a shame for you to look even more beautiful when you cry," Finn smiled. "I'm just glad I'm not the cause of those tears anymore."

"Well, thanks for the compliment," Freya said. "I'll take it. But that's not why I wear it. I cover for my beliefs..."

"You used to *not* cover much of your body from what I recall," Finn bobbed his light brown eyebrows up and down.

"Finn," Freya steamed. "Don't remind me about my past. Allah forgives all. It'll only grow me colder from you, and remind me of your messing me up, please. And don't belittle my attempts to heal."

"I know, I'm just playing, relax," Finn held out his barely manifested hands again. *Ow!* The pain had spread through his legs now!

"It wasn't me that catalyzed your *situation* Freya. When I dated you, you were already a prominent sister in 'The Group', as you know. You of all people should practice what you preach to your patients."

"I know, Finn," Freya nodded, smiling at him. "Don't worry. I know I can't blame everything on you."

"Good—I'll be going now, then," Finn spoke, slowly disintegrating into his energy form. "I just wanted to share what I found out with you—you do with the information what you will. Take care of yourself, alright? And I know you won't, but just know I'm always here for you to call out to me if you need me."

"Thank you," Freya replied to the now invisible voice before her. She wrapped her arms tightly around her body, bringing up her hand to wave 'goodbye' as she whispered farewell. "*Ha det bra.*"

§

FREYA CALLED OUT HER HUSBAND'S NAME, BUT ALL SHE COULD HEAR was the sound of some materials ruffling into the speaker. She smiled.

Her husband had done this before, as well: 'butt-dialing' mistakenly on his walks.

"I told you it'd be gorgeous here!" a woman's voice speaking slightly-accented English suddenly became audible.

"You're gorgeous," Freya heard Salim respond to the woman, making her blood begin to boil.

"Salim," Freya could make out the teasing tone in the woman's voice. *"Our connection has been, surprisingly nice, but we're both married. Come on, now."*

"I'm happy to hear you like our connection, Luba," Salim answered the woman. *"It's more than just physical chemistry, I agree."*

Oh, damn, so they got physical. Freya's heart felt as if it had begun to pump a mile a minute. *This must be the woman Finn warned me about.*

"How's this going to work, handsome?" Luba asked.

How close to him she must be, Freya thought with anger. She could hear her voice clearly through his phone so it was likely in the chest area of his shirt or jacket pocket.

"I'm not saying let's leave our spouses, and run off into the sunset, beautiful," Salim was now telling her. *"I'm proposing a realistic, discreet time in each other's company. No expectations. No pressures. Fun, in fact."*

Freya held her breath, as a lull in their conversation ensued, with only Luba's giggles cutting through the silence. She couldn't take it anymore and clicked off the call, flinging the phone across the room. She gritted her teeth at the sound it made on the floor tiles. *Argh!* How was it possible she had conversed with Finn after all that time, fearing for the longest that it'd mess her up—and yet ultimately, it ended up being her partner, Salim, who'd done the actual damage to her that day?

What am I going to do? Tears rolled down Freya's cheeks as she stood up to retrieve her phone again. The screen hadn't cracked, as she feared. Going through her Directory, her fingers scrolled between her receptionist and friend, Nina, as well as her mother.

She'd heard all she needed to on the phone. There was no way in Hell she could reside with Salim for another day.

§

WITH THE SOUND OF SALIM'S VOICE CALLING HER NAME, THE TEARS she'd dried threatened to pour out of Freya's eyes again. How she would have liked to keep up the bliss of her ignorance, welcoming him at the door with an embrace as usual. Instead, she lingered on her bed. Silent.

Salim knocked on the open door before asking. "What's going on *Habibti*?"

"Drop it, Salim," Freya said dully.

"*Habibti*, why are you laying down?" Salim came and sat on the edge of the bed next to her, stroking her hair. "Are you feeling ill or something?"

"No," Freya said casually, eyes still not meeting Salim's. "I'm just watching the ceiling…it's more interesting than enduring this torture."

"What in God's name are you talking about?" Salim asked, retracting his hand.

Freya snickered. "Dust floats faster in the air than the stuttering lies from your tongue."

"What lies?" Salim asked softly.

"I heard you!" Freya finally turned to face Salim. She sat up straighter in bed, leaning closer only for a short moment to sniff him. "Flirting with a woman!"

"Where?" Salim stammered. "How? What are you talking about?"

Freya crossed her arms across her chest. "You butt-dialed me again, only this time I think you must have pressed me as your last call with your hand on your chest pocket. Or maybe it was *Luba's* hand on your chest—oh God, the idea is making me sick."

"Freya, baby, I think you've misunderstood some things," Salim attempted a chuckle.

"God allowed me to overhear," Freya said, heaving as she scratched hives developing between her neck and chest.

"Luba is this woman I met through work. I offered to help market her business, too—she could barely make a sale! But I think she's misinterpreted, and came on to me and…"

It was Freya's turn to chuckle. "I would say, save it for the divorce judge, but luckily we're not even legally married here, are we? Goodbye, Salim!"

"You're kicking me out?" Salim scoffed. "We share the rent. Let's talk this out, and decide with our brains and not emotions, *Habibti*."

"Oh, no, you can stay," Freya said with a shrug. "I'll just be sharing rent with a girl friend of mine. I've taken most of my stuff over to her place, while you were frolicking with Luba. You can do whatever you want with this place. Sneak around with that married girl easier, if you two sinners wish."

"Baby," Freya heard Salim begin to say, but she'd already stormed out of her room to splash some water on her face.

Nina was looking to share rent in a new place she'd moved to nearby, and Freya hadn't seen the place yet but knew it would be better than sharing housing with this lowlife of a man! Salim had been there for her and had loved her at one time—she knew it. But it had begun to fade, and they were both no good for each other any longer.

Am I a sucker for manipulative men? How far she'd liked to have thought she had come along since 'The Group'. *Lar Iktar.* Their leader. The only name that stirred more wrath inside of Freya's soul than Finn or Salim. The original instigator of her pain and anguish as an impressionable young woman. She cursed the day she'd attended his lecture.

How the others worshipped him. The others— some of them fellow schoolmates, as well as jinn like Finn she would discover upon her initiation. Freya supposed now, in retrospect, their deferential awe of him could have actually been due to fear—alongside their lack of a way out once they'd been sucked so far in.

"It's alright, Freya," Lar had said, eyeing her nude reflection in the mirror whilst her heart had been beating what had felt like thousands of beats per minute.

"Your beautiful body is your vessel, and will please the brethren. As long as you stay within 'The Group', it will not be considered adultery. Those outside clients? They'll only think they have a chance with you— while you trap them with your honey. We need their finances to keep our mission going."

She was not going to allow herself to succumb to the whims of any man ever again.

CHAPTER 32

WOULD IT BE TOO MUCH OUT OF FASHION IF WHITE PANTS ARE worn after Labor Day? Merve glanced her reflection in the mirror, and took in a deep breath. Her white suit fit her curves in all the right places, while still looking 'classy' in meeting her husband's family. She'd blown out her wavy, blonde-highlighted brown hair at the local salon.

Merve and Aidan had planned to wait, but apparently, they'd been discovered! She'd packed her clothes and accessories—it had taken four suitcases, but she'd done it! Yet how could she have forgotten their papers back in the apartment? Merve giggled when she thought of the pink tin box Aidan had asked her about.

She had spoken with Kaitlin on the phone earlier, and they'd arranged a coffee date, but things had come up, and now it seemed fated that she would meet both her sister- and mother-in-law on the same day! At least she got to talk to Kaitlin alone first, before dinner tonight. A head start on making good impressions.

Kaitlin had even insisted she should move back into the apartment, offering for her and her daughter to stay with one of her girlfriends again. *How sweet*, Merve thought, though she'd politely turned it down, saying the hotel was comfortable for now. "I'll move back when you girls go up to Toronto with your mother soon."

If only I had a sister like Kaitlin.

She had once considered Sibel Pak from work a sister figure. Sibel hadn't wronged her, but ultimately, she had learned too much, and Merve simply couldn't keep in touch with her anymore. If she had, she knew Sibel would want to continue being her goody-two-shoes self, reporting her whereabouts to her parents in the States. And that therapist she'd thought could be a friend—Freya? *Forget it!*

Merve couldn't believe how far she and Aidan had come. Her husband. She still blushed thinking about it. She'd gotten butterflies the moment she'd first laid eyes on him at work but had always thought him out of her league. And now, here he was—her legal husband. Who cared if they'd said their vows in secret? She was now meeting his sister, and she knew his mother would be next.

Would her own parents ever forgive her for leaving them to escape to the States? They had to understand, right? And forgive her. She had forgiven Aidan, after all, after everything. Yes, it was Emir who'd raped her using his body as a vessel. She'd recognized his flaming eyes—a darker shade from Aidan's. But regardless of not raping her, Aidan hadn't exactly treated her kindly. Flashbacks of how it used to be crossed her mind as Merve smoothed her dress.

"You want this job or not, Turkish girl?" Aidan's speech was slurred, his eyes roaming all over Merve's body. "What's the matter? You don't look like the uptight, prissy religious type? You're in the West now baby, it's okay…I'll make you feel good. Come here…"

"Mr. Ramsay…. You're drunk," Merve held out her arms in front of her. "Someone will see. Please just go…Or I'll…"

"You'll what?" he asked with a grin. "Call the cops? And tell them what? That you've absolutely…maddeningly seduced your boss? You blush every time you see me, Turkish girl. You know I could have any woman I want, right? Yet why the hell has *your* cute face gotten stuck in my mind. Huh? Tell me? Have you done a spell on me or something?"

He used to be such a pig—arrogant and even racist! Yet she'd domesticated Aidan. Merve smiled. The grin on her face fell as flashbacks of his ensuing entry into her body now crossed her mind, but she quickly shook them away. *It wasn't him,* she reminded herself. Emir had done it.

The shock of the pregnancy brought a tear to her eye.

"There's something I've been meaning to talk to you about, Aidan," Merve said, staying behind after work.

"Well, I'm glad we've graduated away from Mr. Ramsay, at least. What is it?" Aidan asked.

"I think…you're going to feel really bad when I tell you this," Merve started, biting her lip.

"Oh, no…I hope it's not one of your jealous ramblings again about my clients…That last time…"

"I'm pregnant!" Merve cut in, shutting her eyes and exhaling a long-held breath.

Aidan dropped the pen in his hand onto the floor. "What?"

"And…yes, I'm sure," Merve smiled and let out a big sigh. "I've already taken two tests."

She had taken an additional pregnancy test in front of him, and Aidan had softened. He'd actually taken her out on proper dates afterward—albeit in secret—and later proposed. Yet the curse had returned as they were set to say their vows, with only two other witnesses present— her aunt Helin and her husband.

The miscarriage. A tear escaped Merve's eye as she remembered what she had gone through shortly after their ceremony. Emir had caused it, *that jealous jinn bastard*—she just knew it. Luckily, Aunt Helin had been there for her at that time. Without her parents back in Türkiye to talk to, she'd felt so alone.

No more, Merve thought, fixing her hair and clearing her throat. Now she had Aidan, and he had finally revealed their relationship to his sister and mother. *And niece, too,* Merve thought with a smile. Maybe she could finally feel like a part of a bigger family again.

A knock on her hotel suite door indicated her sister-in-law had arrived. Taking in a deep breath, Merve opened the door, welcoming Kaitlin in. She was holding a bouquet of red and white flowers.

"Kaitlin, hi!" *She looks even prettier than her photographs*, Merve thought, placing the floral arrangement onto a small counter by the door. "Thank you for these—they're lovely."

"It's nice to finally meet you, Merve," Kaitlin said, wrapping her arms around Merve for a welcoming hug. She pulled back and looked Merve up-and-down. "Let me look at the woman who's settled down my brother. You are absolutely charming!"

"Thank you, Kaitlin," Merve smiled. "Come in, come in! Have a seat! Would you like something to drink? Tea? Coffee? Juice? I can have them bring up some Turkish coffee, if you'd like."

"Oh, juice will be enough for me, thank you," Kaitlin said with a smile, taking a seat on the leather arm chair by a stylish desk. "My friend Sandy keeps me caffeinated too much!"

"Little Malin couldn't come with you?"Merve asked, taking out a carton of orange juice from the mid-sized refrigerator.

"Aidan took her to work today," Kaitlin chuckled. "I hear you guys will slowly be making an official debut there, too?"

"Oh, right, right, I forgot," Merve said, brushing her hair with her fingers. "I'll let him show off his niece for now. They've gotten used to me working remotely, and I'm just not sure how they'll react. I think revealing us to you guys is making him feel brave, but I'm not sure if it'll be good for his position. We'll see."

"You're a smart woman," Kaitlin said with a wink. "I don't know his colleagues—you know them best. I'll tell him to listen to a woman's intuition."

"Good thinking," Merve said with a wink. Her expression quickly changed. "Do you think Momma Linda will like me?"

"She'd be crazy not to like the woman who's gotten her son to settle down—with such exquisite taste around the apartment, too!"

"Thank you—Aidan tells me you've gotten used to living in Norway?" Merve asked, pouring some orange juice into Kaitlin's glass.

"Oh, yes, it wasn't easy at first but Norway has....grown on me," Kaitlin said with a chuckle. "I've made rather interesting memories there. And the nature is amazing. It's a safe, civilized place to raise Malin."

"And yet you still wanted her to see New York, and even her roots in Canada, soon," Merve said softly with a smile.

"Yes," Kaitlin sighed. "I've come to believe we can't blossom without tending to our roots first."

"I know about your father," Merve's voice took on a melancholy tone. "I'm so sorry. I can't imagine what finding that out must have been like. I haven't even seen my parents since I left Istanbul."

Kaitlin put down her glass and leaned in. "Would you like to talk about that part in particular? Aidan's sort of told me how we have something in common…regarding our experiences with *them*."

"Oh, I'm not sure if it's a good idea to bring that energy into today," Merve spoke quickly, scratching the back of her head. "The last time I did— it didn't end well."

"You mean confiding in Aidan?" Kaitlin asked, raising an eyebrow. Merve smiled. *She's being a protective sister.*

"No, no, Aidan's been very supportive," Merve said assuredly. "We've…overcome what we have, together. No, I just meant, like— I mentioned it in therapy when I first arrived here. And my therapist used to sympathize with me…until she didn't. You know? People can be so judgmental, and turn on you when you wouldn't expect."

"Therapist?" Kaitlin gulped down her entire glass.

She must be parched, Merve thought. "Would you like some more juice, or….?"

"No, no," Kaitlin waved her hand. "I'm good. Please, go on.... about this therapist."

"*Um*, yes, some woman with a Midtown office close to here, actually," Merve continued. "We didn't exactly part on good terms, and I've been so scared of running into her. Thank God I haven't! I read somewhere that once someone's energy falls out with a person, they can live on the same block and never run into each other! Good riddance! You know?"

Kaitlin's face darkened. "Merve—was your therapist, Freya Olsdotter?"

No way. Merve leaned in close to Kaitlin. "You know her, too?"

"C'est trop bizarre!" Kaitlin laughed as she shook her head. "Yet another strange 'coincidence', I cannot believe this! Yes, Merve, she was my therapist, too. A good one, I can't complain. But things got weird because of our... *jinn* connection, as I believe happened with you guys as well."

"I'm surprised she's still in practice," Merve sat back, folding her arms across her chest. "She was so rude to me—suggesting all these psychiatric treatments as if I were suddenly nutty like a pistachio! As if she hadn't been empathizing with me up until that time! All of a sudden, she decides she wants to get her 'life in order', get some license, or whatever—and she sacrifices me! When I just wanted to talk to her. It had been freeing and healing for me, you know? She was so selfish!"

"She regrets it, Merve," Kaitlin rubbed Merve's hand. "She's told me about her one regret in life with regards to a patient she lost touch with. Believe me. You've left quite an impression on her! Just know that. As closure."

"I don't need closure to know I did the right thing," Merve scoffed, turning her face to look outside the window. "Finally seeing her for who she really was."

She glanced back to see Kaitlin still smiling at her.

"Thank you, though," Merve said, cheeks pink.

"How was it like for you to go to a new land all on your own?" Kaitlin asked, leaning back in the sofa. "I mean, I don't know how I could have survived in Norway if Paul hadn't been there."

"I came here secretly, and so fast, without thinking, Kaitlin!" Merve recalled. "Because of the....jinn thing, Aidan's told you about, yes. My jinn was following me and somehow I thought I could lose his trace here."

"Have you been able to?" Kaitlin asked, twisting her face. "Keep the jinn away?"

"Gratefully, prayers have helped," Merve nodded. Her eyes welled up. "And improving my mental well-being. Without Aidan's love and support in my life, I don't know where I would have been today. Little by little, I was able to free myself."

"I'm so happy for you two," Kaitlin cooed. "You're an amazingly strong woman, Merve. You started life from scratch in a new land."

"Hey, look who's talking?" Merve asked, smiling. "You should know I'm a fan, already. I signed up for your newsletter!"

"Thanks," Kaitlin blushed, tucking her wavy auburn hair behind her ear.

"Besides, I had some help, luckily," Merve continued. "My aunt Helin— she pronounces it *Helen* in Canada— has a husband, John, who does business in New York, too. They helped me find a place to stay. And what were the odds? One day he ended up being a client for Aidan! Lo and behold, he helped Aidan discover his father...and they turned out to be family! I used to call her *Helin Teyze* as a little girl. What a small world, right? They were witnesses in our ceremony!"

Kaitlin's dropped jaw and ensuing quiet took Merve by surprise.

"Are you alright?" Merve asked.

"Yeah, it's just....Aidan didn't mention our half-uncle was in your ceremony!" Kaitlin was stumbling through her words.

"Oh, well, yeah— Aunt Helin has always seen me like the daughter she was never able to have," Merve began to explain, twisting her face. "I didn't want to exclude her, and of course her husband came along and it worked out so he could be a witness for Aidan. My aunt has suffered for years, the poor thing—so many fertility treatments, to no avail…"

§

HOW WAS IT POSSIBLE THAT HER WORLD WAS GROWING SMALLER AND smaller lately? Kaitlin chuckled to herself, trying to ease the pounding inside her chest. Her mind wandered back to what her mother had said, about her grandmother Mabel 'cursing' her husband and his mistress for their affair. The curse, if it existed, may have extended to Merve, too, she realized, with regards to the jinn experience she'd gone through. After all, she was 'connected' to Grandpa Robert through her aunt Helen—married to Robert's illegitimate son, John, and who apparently suffered with infertility. John—as that mistress' son— who lost his daughter!

Linette, Kaitlin thought as a chill ran down her spine. *As John's daughter from a Norwegian ex-girlfriend, she literally suffered the most—paying with her life.*

Kaitlin shook her head. Now she'd have to expand her research into generational curses, in addition to all the studies she'd conducted on jinn over the years. *Is this why both Aidan and I were affected by the jinn? The damn curse?*

Or perhaps it was their mental state, inherited from Zachary. *"Prayers have helped,"* Merve had just told her about how she'd gotten through it all, in addition to Aidan's love and 'improving' her 'mental well-being'.

Dialing the number Freya had handed her with a heavy sigh,

Kaitlin spoke into the receiver. "Hi, Freya."

"Hi, Kaitlin," Freya answered with hesitation audible in her voice. It was bizarre to talk to her on the phone and not in a virtual meeting; it felt final, somehow, that they were no longer mentor and patient. What was this their new dynamic? Friends, maybe? No, it didn't feel like that either to Kaitlin. Allies, perhaps? Fellow survivors?

"I just wanted to let you know I've met Merve Turan," Kaitlin continued. "She's Merve Turan Ramsay, now. What a 'coincidence', though we both know it probably isn't, Freya—but she's married my brother, Aidan! And she's happy. I know you'd been worried for her. I just wanted to give you that closure."

"Thank you, Kaitlin," Freya's voice sounded shaky. "So, you've met…Merve. And she's alright? Married to your brother? Wow!"

"Yes," Kaitlin said with a snicker. "*Wow* is right…."

"I'm glad she's happy, I suppose," Freya said. "Are *you* okay? Will you be heading to Canada?"

"Yeah," Kaitlin answered. "I may see my father after all. Malin might stay behind with her grandmother, but we'll see."

"I'm glad," Freya said. "I know you worry about your daughter. But I just thought of something! How old was she when you noticed her symptoms, you know, the ones you described as 'worrisome'— like talking to herself and the OCD rituals?"

Kaitlin pursed her lips, glancing up at the ceiling. "She must have been around five or six, because I remember she was in the first grade."

With the silence that ensued, Kaitlin tilted her head. "Am I missing something?"

"Weren't *you* around that age when you said your father left you?" Freya asked, her voice gentle.

Mon Dieu! "Do you suppose there's a correlation, Freya?" Kaitlin asked, her heart pounding.

"It's hard to know for certain, but I know anxiety *can* be genetically-inherited," Freya explained. "It often originates in our family histories, where certain inherent triggers can cause us to react in certain ways similar to our parents or grandparents. I cannot say for certain since I don't specialize in children, and I haven't met Malin, but based on the case studies I've reviewed, I think Malin may have started reacting to a subconscious fear of being abandoned."

"What can I do about this?" Kaitlin was still in shock.

"You can talk to her," Freya said. "Assure Malin that you'll always be there for her, and so will her father, no matter what happens."

"Thank you, Freya," Kaitlin smiled, feeling a bit of relief. Freya's advice sounded like a solid place to start helping her daughter, regardless of what may have triggered her anxiety. "I still can't believe all these coincidences."

Freya chuckled. "Well, speaking of which— I'll let you know that Finn has visited me. To warn me about my husband, whom you apparently know, by the way— Salim."

Kaitlin couldn't respond immediately. *Salim? What the hell?* "Freya—I honestly don't know what to say anymore. I mean—I swear at this rate, the next person I meet at some grocery store is going to turn out to be your…I don't know….sister? Father? Heck, can you send me your entire family tree, so I can be prepared?"

"You're funny," Freya giggled. "In another life, I think we could have been friends."

"I agree," Kaitlin said. *In another life.* "I don't know what Finn has told you about him, by the way, but Salim is great at what he does. He's helped me tremendously with my website."

"He's just not the best husband," Freya said with a sigh. "I've known that for a while. I just couldn't admit it to myself until Finn showed me the truth."

"Finn…can interestingly be helpful sometimes, can't he?" Kaitlin asked with a chuckle.

"Yeah," Freya agreed. "That's why I wanted to share this with you. To let you know he's been in New York, and visited me. But he hasn't bothered you, right?"

Kaitlin nodded. "He's kept his word, I suppose, even as he visited this region—I never felt him around me. Though I did see that curious black bird…"

"Amir was keeping an eye on Salim, apparently," Freya smirked. "Maybe he owed Finn some favor? Oh, I don't know."

Oh, boy. Kaitlin took in a deep breath. "You know, these jinn—sometimes, I swear they're out to ruin us. But at other times, it almost feels like they're looking out for us. Do you get that sense, too, Freya?"

"I do," Freya said. "Anyway, thanks for letting me know that Merve is good. I don't want to bother her, if she even wants to hear from me, that is."

Kaitlin just bit her lip, unable to respond.

"I got the message," Freya said with a giggle. "She doesn't want to hear from me. No problem. But, hey—I just wanted you to know that Finn kept his word, in turn for you letting me know about Merve."

"I appreciate it," Kaitlin said. "I just have to focus on being a good mother now. You know what I mean?"

"You have to focus on *your* well-being first in order to be a good mother, Kaitlin," Freya reminded her.

CHAPTER 33

Ontario

THE GLIMMER OF SUNLIGHT FROM THE TINY WINDOW surrounded his visage, appearing like a halo on her father's head, though dark shadows took precedence. Kaitlin was certain Zachary had heard her sitting across the white, plastic table, despite his eyes remaining fixed on some mysterious object somewhere behind her. Something on the wall, perhaps? Whatever it was, Zachary's eyes and facial expressions responded to the sound of her voice, as if traversing time to recognize something familiar.

'Daddy?' Kaitlin asked again. "Daddy, it's me… Kaitlin… Kaity…"

"Miss, you may want to come back another time, if you'd like?" The nurse suggested but Kaitlin dismissed her with a wave of her hand. She turned around to face her for a polite smile. Aidan had beaten her to it, standing next to the nurse and nodding reassuringly, as if saying '*it'll be okay*'.

"Kaity?" Zachary whimpered meekly, still unable to meet Kaitlin's eyes.

"Yes…"

"Mountain air, Kaity?"

Kaitlin could no longer hold back the tears she hadn't even realized she'd been holding in. Her father still refused to meet her gaze, so she reached across the table, gently placing her hands in his.

"*Um*, Kaitlin, you may not want to touch him…" Aidan started.

"It's *alright*, Aidan," she enunciated, turning to shoot her brother a consoling look.

"Yes, Daddy. Mountain air. It's always refreshing, isn't it?"

Zachary's eyes traveled to their interlocked hands before slowly looking up, his eyes just as tearful as hers. "Kaity. It's you. You've grown. You're so beautiful."

"Thanks, Daddy," Kaitlin said through wet lips. "Yes, I've grown."

"Everybody, look!" Zachary suddenly pounded the table with glee. Only two additional nurses stood by the other corner of the room, with some patients seen strolling through the hallways of the visitation area.

"Yes, it's a blessed day, Zachary. She is here," the nurse called to him, stepping away from Aidan and moving closer to the table. She bent down, whispering in Kaitlin's ear. "He can get overexcited, and unintentionally violent with his pent-up emotions. Let us know if you're still okay with…?"

"Yes, yes, it's okay," Kaitlin whispered back, nodding. The nurse sighed and walked back to Aidan's side.

"I miss the lake, Kaity. I miss it … I miss it all," Zachary met her eyes, and Kaitlin swore she saw a recognition there as he reached out his quivering, callused hands and placed them on her cheeks. She inched her face closer to his, letting his grasp tighten with affection. Tears welled up in the corners of his dark eyes.

"I miss it all too, Daddy."

"What happened?" Zachary whimpered. "We've missed so much… *too* much. It's my fault. I'm so sorry for everything."

"I only just found out about you, Daddy," Kaitlin responded, leaning closer and adding in a whisper. "Mom and Aidan thought they were protecting me. I'm so angry with them."

"Don't be, Kaity," Zachary smiled into her eyes. "I chose this life. I dove into my work—and then the bottles—to escape reality. And then they dove into me… driving a wedge between me and my family. I neglected your mother, and even your brother."

As Zachary's face turned toward Aidan, he motioned him over with his hand. "He's a good kid."

"He's made mistakes," Kaitlin spoke softly, smiling at her brother as he took two steps closer to them. "So have I."

"Which one of us hasn't, in our own ways?" Zachary chuckled. "Our mistakes, like our sweeter eccentricities and quirks, are too unique to each and every one of us… The world is messy, but there's beauty in chaos—and meaning, too. The only thing inevitable in life is death, and survival is the exception. Even the mere existence of a human being is dependent on the low-chance survival of a particular sperm and egg."

Kaitlin smiled, feeling uneasy and restless as birds during uncharacteristic seasonal changes. She realized she hadn't remembered her father's speech and mannerisms in years. He sounded remarkably eloquent for someone who'd spent so much time in rehabilitation and mental health centers.

"Why're you smiling, my beautiful girl?" Zachary's eyes appeared curious.

"I never would've taken my father for an existentialist," she chuckled.

The nurse began to chuckle softly. "Oh, Mr. Ramsay entertains us with his wonderful sayings sometimes. Don't you, Zachary?"

Kaitlin overheard the nurse adding in a whisper to Aidan, "When he's well, he's quite fabulous to be around. But on other days…"

Aidan bit his lip and nodded with understanding.

"Oh, I got my education, before getting caught up out there," Zachary beamed. "I've been reading all I can in here, too. But whatever it takes to see you smile. Your smile is the same as when you were little… how old were you when I last…?"

"Five, Daddy," Kaitlin found herself recalling her recent conversation with Freya about Malin, who'd also been five when her anxiety symptoms had started. "I was five…"

"Five years…" Zachary nodded, biting his lower lip. "Damn. That's all life allowed me to be your father. But I prayed for you. For whatever the prayer of a man like me would be worth—to the Man upstairs… but I prayed for you…"

"I know you loved me in the only way you knew how…" Kaitlin tried to reassure him. Or maybe it was for herself.

"I knew you'd grow up better without me around…" Zachary went on, sniffing his nose. "Not influenced by an unsuccessful loser like me… I wanted you to grow up happier… I didn't want you to see me like this."

"Dad, I didn't care about seeing you successful," Kaitlin reached out for his hands again. "I just cared about seeing *you.* And knowing you wanted to see me. But you didn't. What good are our intentions if our actions—or inactions—hurt the ones we claim to love?"

Zachary sighed, pounding his fist softly onto the table, leaning back in the plastic chair that was too small for his wider frame.

He doesn't seem illogical, Kaitlin thought. She wondered why doctors had evaluated him as needing to stay cooped up here for so long.

"I wonder why, too…" Zachary said, his voice low.

Kaitlin felt shivers sweep through her as the hairs on her neck stood up. Had she spoken that last thought out loud?

"I heard you think it, Kaity," Zachary winked at her. "You didn't speak it…"

No way! Kaitlin's hands clenched so hard on the corner of the table that her knuckles hurt. She pushed her chair back, taking a deep breath. "Dad? Are you telling me you can read my thoughts?"

A million new thoughts swirled in Kaitlin's brain. Finn and his jinn kind—reading her thoughts, manifesting themselves before her, and eventually before Paul and Malin. Toying with whatever family she had left, while simultaneously being there for her and Malin in a bizarre marriage of good and evil, as far as she could deduce from her instincts.

A tingling sensation permeated her body. Surely her dad couldn't be a…?

"Don't worry, I'm not one of *them*, Kaity. But I *do* have telepathic abilities, yes," Zachary raised an eyebrow and leaned his head back, intrigued. "You've met *them*, too, haven't you?"

Kaitlin nodded, reaching out to pat her father's arm. "You're not alone. I've befriended one, but there's no harm. I'm alright. It's okay."

"Run, Kaity!" Zachary raised his voice, his breath quickening. "Get away from me, and get away from *them!* I love you. Just know that. And sometimes love requires sacrifice. For protection. You're better off…"

"Daddy!" Kaitlin gasped. "What are you saying? I've just finally been able to come face to face with you, so no, don't worry. I don't need to run. I'm not afraid."

"You don't understand," Zachary squealed. "I'm afraid. Of what it can do…when it does this. It…activates."

Zachary leaned in closer to his daughter and whispered. "*The curse*. It's *in* me…."

Kaitlin's knuckles tore into the table as she gripped it, witnessing her father's crying eyes transform into blazing, angry ones, with a honey-colored tinge.

She let out a scream, and the nurse quickly came to lead her out of her chair by the shoulders. "Ma'am? This way…"

As the nurse and Aidan wrapped her in their arms and led her away, Kaitlin stopped for a moment to glance back at her father. She squinted, trying to make out his eyes again. They were on her and dark green once more. Smiling.

Aidan waved at him. "Dad—I think your visitation time has ended. You need your rest now."

Zachary nodded, in tears, with his eyes still fixed on Kaitlin.

"I love you, Daddy," she whimpered. "I'll see you next time, okay?"

"Go, Kaity," Zachary's voice was meek as he nodded. "Thank you so much for coming, my angel. I love you."

§

BACK IN HER CHILDHOOD ROOM IN TORONTO, KAITLIN REMAINED distracted in thought, gazing outside the window.

"Weren't the waterfalls lovelier from the Canadian side?" she heard her mother ask Malin, who eagerly agreed.

"Mom, she hasn't *seen* them from the New York side!" Kaitlin rolled her eyes with a smile. "She can't compare."

"Oh, nonsense," Linda dismissed. "New York just has its popular name…Are you girls packed and ready to head back to Norway? You leave everything for the last minute, Kaity…."

"Yeah, yeah," Kaitlin smiled and nodded without turning her head to face her mother.

"That tower was so cool!" Malin exclaimed. "It had a revolving restaurant like the one Uncle Aidan took us to in New York. Spinny restaurants are more fun than waterfalls!"

"See?" Linda shook her head. "Your daughter is unappreciative of more important sights being shown to her. She's going to grow up spoiled like you, Kaity, I'm telling you."

"Okayyyyy, Mom, let's get some lunch," Kaitlin rolled her eyes, chuckling at the memory of her daughter amusing herself running around the CN Tower.

Linda stood still for a moment in front of Kaitlin. "By the way—I didn't ask too much, but you know I'm waiting to hear you talk about it to me when you're ready, Kaity."

"Talk about what, Mom?" Kaitlin began to ask, though she knew exactly what her mother meant. "How it was like seeing Dad?"

Linda nodded, her eyes filled with sadness.

"It was…okay," Kaitlin said with a shrug. "I needed to see him, and I'm glad I did. I don't feel any particular way toward him anymore. Certainly not anger. It has subsided somehow, replaced perhaps with sympathy? I'm not sure how, but I've let go of any anger, seeing how he's been suffering."

"Maybe this trip to Toronto has been better for you than you'd have thought," Linda said with a wink.

Kaitlin smiled at her mother, remembering her first night back in her childhood home with Malin. The warm hug they'd all shared over hot cocoa. Her eyes had filled with tears as they'd placed the luggage on the floor of her childhood bedroom.

"Wow, who's that?" Malin had asked, pointing at her poster of Nick Carter from *The Backstreet Boys*. Kaitlin had chuckled, immediately taking down the poster. She couldn't throw it out, but had folded it carefully and placed it on one of her old shelves.

The mystery series she'd read over and over again as a teenager, despite knowing the ending. Her photo albums from her student years tucked under the bed—from which several photos had been displayed, up until Paul entered her life and suddenly it didn't feel cool to have her prom photo out. She'd been proud to exhibit how she'd looked in her apricot dress— not necessarily being with her prom date, who had been a friend she'd never see again.

And the box. The one still on her old desk, covered with rose stickers. Kaitlin knew she'd show most of it to Malin—and she did. It contained letters and first photos of her and Paul when they were dating.

The pictures of them embracing brought tears to her eyes. Paul would forever be the link to her youth, she realized, and perhaps she would always be the link for him to his.

They had accumulated so many life experiences together, Kaitlin realized, that it would always bind them. No matter what had happened between them or how imperfect their relationship had been, their love had always been dependable and real. Kaitlin felt it in her heart more than ever now.

One of his greeting cards stood out to her, and reading it made her throw herself on her bed, wrapping herself under her old covers. Thankfully, they smelled of fresh laundry detergent rather than musty. Her husband's first greeting card to her from Valentine's Day—his least favorite holiday, but not hers.

Being yours has given my life meaning, and I can't wait to grow old with you. I'm the luckiest man in the world for being able to call you mine, my Kaitlin...

"Mommy, Grandma says lunch is ready!" Malin called from the kitchen, returning her to the present moment. Kaitlin giggled; being in her old room made it feel like the roles had reversed between her and her daughter.

Rummaging through her bag, Kaitlin smiled at the photograph the nurse had taken of her standing behind her father at the institution, before she'd taken her seat across him. "Thank you, Daddy." She kissed the photo and tucked it back into her passport wallet. Her and Malin still had a couple of days left before their return to Norway, but she wanted to make sure everything was in place.

Her fingers jingled through the keys of the fifth-floor suite she'd rented out for 'The Group', as promised to Finn—who had, surely enough, provided the exact amount needed in her debit account.

Kaitlin sighed, smiling as she placed the Valentine's Day card from Paul, next to the photograph with her father. Somehow, she knew just what she had to do back in Norway.

CHAPTER 34

Dubai
2021
(present day)

THE MUEZZIN'S HAUNTING CALL TO PRAYER FROM THE HIGH minaret of the mosque echoed through the streets as Lar paced his way closer to his childhood block. *Beautiful,* he thought, already filled with immense emotion.

Throughout his flight from Oslo, Nora's words resonated in his mind. *They have awakened, my little cubs, from hibernation.*

He looked around for signs of any cats still following him. *Good old, Stig,* Lar thought, laughing to himself, having recognized him earlier. *Going to all these lengths for his girlfriend.*

Lar supposed he should still be bothered by the conversation he had with his favorite female disciple before leaving for the airport. Yet somehow being here in Dubai again had made him forget the sting.

"No, *you* listen, Master...*Mister* Iktar!" Nora bellowed." I've had it! I know you've packed all our passports, the humans. And we saw you take our hidden files with you on your trip. You were afraid we'd find out all the dirt you were keeping on us while you were away, weren't you? You always claimed to want to help us, yet you *thrived* on us feeling trapped, didn't you? Didn't you?"

Lar couldn't believe what he was hearing. "No, no, no...You've got it all wrong, my precious one, dear Nora. I've always welcomed those who were lost. You, like the others, have come and remained of your own *free will.* What in Satan's name are you now screaming to me about?"

"You were keeping them behind the damn painting. We found them!"

"We?" Lar asked.

"Meredith, Anja, Stig and I."

"Nora, that's enough my girl," Lar interjected, motioning with his fingers to the outside view from the window. "You're wrongly judging what I've simply saved as personal souvenirs of my disciples and my business. I just wanted to make sure they didn't get into the wrong hands."

"Yeah, right," Nora scoffed.

"Go on— head outside to *Svartdalsparken*," Lar continued, patting Nora on the back. "Complete your weekly nature requirement. Calm your foggy mind, and judgement, and we can discuss this in a more civilized and appropriate manner…"

Nora was adamant. "I will not be walking it out in the park, Sir, I'm sorry."

It hurt his heart a little to hear that word. "Sir?"

Nora gulped with a glimpse directly into the anger ablaze in Lar Iktar's eyes. "Master. I'm sorry. You know how grateful I've been for everything. I've gained a lot here in the brethren, yes, but lost just as much, if not more!"

"I always held you in a special regard, dear Nora," Lar softly touched her hair, from which Nora turned her face away. "Which is why I cannot believe this filth coming out of your mouth….And Meredith's been helping you, too? That ungrateful jinn. I allowed her to stay and live abundantly, even with her son. I even managed to forgive her for catalyzing Tan's depression. Banning him out of the cabin, as if she had that authority…."

"Lover or not she could not allow him to have such free reign as someone capable of murder," Nora defended. "How could *you* allow it? That was the beginning of my loss of trust in 'The Group'. In the Maxims I once held so dear along with you…."

"Nora you practically grew up under my very nose. Say no more of this foolishness. I said go on into the woods and clear your head already! At once!"

"I will leave….when I am done," Nora crossed her arms.

The silence that ensued hurt Lar more than he thought could be possible from something non-physical.

"Where do you think you're going to go, Nora?" Lar steamed as he followed Nora into her room. "Huh? To your brother— for him to keep abusing you?"

"Stop it!" Nora shouted over her shoulder, flinging open her closet door to take out her luggage.

Lar continued in after her. "Or, to Mommy? What do you think your precious mother will say when she sees your videos from our rituals, with all the brethren taking their turns on the bed with you?"

Nora's nails dug deeper into her palm and almost cut through, with her clenched fists. "You wouldn't….you're going to blackmail me, too? Like a client?"

"I don't want to," Lar explained, lowering his tone. "I care for you like a daughter, you know that! But if that's the only way to bring some sense into your head, and keep you here where you belong, then…"

"You jerk! You claimed to free us from the misery of our familial issues. Yet you only managed to further trap us here! Enslave us! And condemn all of us to your own hell on earth! Children weren't allowed. Only jinn and non-jinn relations were encouraged….Why? So, we couldn't create families naturally, just because you couldn't do so yourself, as a homosexual man, didn't you?"

"Nora, you're crossing a line!" Lar said through flared nostrils.

"But natural or not, you always ignored love!" Nora continued, tossing clothes into her luggage. "And how two people could raise a child- whether biologically a product of their own physical union or not- and create a family with love! Even you could have done so yourself, Master. Many homosexuals around the world do. They adopt! They use surrogates! We're not in the Middle East."

"You think this is about children?" Lar asked, darting his eyes to the ceiling in thought.

"You claimed to show us the love we were all desperately seeking- but could have chosen an actual loving path- rather than all these

additional burdens," Nora went on. "When so many children are left without love in the world. Couples of all kinds. What happened to you when you were younger- why couldn't you deal with all your garbage on your own? Why did *we* have to carry your burdens along with you?"

"I provided all my disciples with acceptance...and love!" Lar insisted.

"And what do you know of love?" Nora cried. "I can't believe how blind I've been...how blind we've all been...taking your life advice...living under your rules as if you'd had all the answers! When you'd preached about 'true love' being 'family', yet you allowed for murder to take place, for your supposed love for Tan. To whom you couldn't even remain loyal in your heart, as soon as John resurfaced!"

"That's enough!" Lar slapped her across the face. "Leave!"

"I already have," Nora deadpanned in a quiet voice, holding her cheek. "My mom knows everything, and she's welcoming me. She'll understand after her anger subsides. So I don't care what sexual images you're threatening me with!"

"The police..." Lar said, clenching his fists.

"The police?" Nora laughed. "Oh, poor, dear Master Iktar....Don't you know if you go down that route- you'll be throwing yourself into the core of the pit? You should know we've created a file on you, too! We can get ourselves off the hook as your fellow victims—we have proof that *you* have been the mastermind."

"I'm no mastermind," Lar shook his head, looking at his feet. "You've been told of Amir. He's been behind it all."

"You know?" Nora crossed her arms. "You blame that jinn-bird whenever it's convenient, yet it's funny—*you* have always taken credit for all the wealth and success 'The Group' accumulated! Wasn't that, technically, then, through *him* as well? What good are *you* on your own?"

"If I'm so terrible...." Lar looked up at her with doleful eyes. "Why are you still here? Yelling at me. Go!"

"We're all done," Nora scoffed softly. "You despicable, miserable excuse for a human being."

"Stig!" Lar cried out, spinning around. "Stig! Appear at once. I need a witness!"

"He's not here, and he's on our side too!" Nora said with a grin. "He'll accompany you on your little trip to visit to Dubai, keep an eye on you. Go. Say your goodbyes to your family. Let's see who you'll have left when you return. This ends now."

"You've been here all alone with me, without jinn protection?" Lar smiled, creeping close to her face. "You haven't been afraid I'd hurt you?"

To his surprise, tears began streaming down Nora's face. She quickly wiped them off. "No. I haven't been afraid."

Tilting his head, Lar caressed her cheek. "Then, good girl. See? You *have* learned something at least with your time here. You have evolved. It couldn't have been all bad."

A cat meowed at Lar's feet as he walked, bringing him back to the present moment. He paused. "Stig?"

But the cat looked up at him with a completely dumbstruck expression, causing Lar to laugh and pet its head. "You must be just a hungry stray. I'm hungry too, actually."

He paused at the corner of a familiar candy store and walked inside.

"*As-salamu alaykum*," he greeted the store owner, his voice thick with emotion as he took in the sight of the small shop packed with a variety of sweets. "I can't believe this place is still here."

"*Wa-alaykumu salaam*," replied the man behind the counter, an older man with a full white beard, wearing jeans and a Nike sweatshirt. Despite his appearance, he seemed to be around Lar's age. "Yes, I inherited this place from my father, *Habibi*. It's been around since the 1960s!"

Lar smiled as he walked around, his hands clasped behind his back, admiring the boxes of nutty desserts. He never thought he could miss the routine exchanges of greetings on a typical suburban street as much as he did right now.

"Are you alright, *Habibi*?" the store owner asked, dangling a cigarette from the corner of his mouth.

"I've just been abroad for too long," Lar replied, continuing in Arabic. His eyes scanned the cigars behind the counter, searching for his favorite luxury brand—but to no avail.

I must repress all cravings, he thought to himself.

"My sister's in the Netherlands, so I get it," the man nodded with a smile. "She's working on her PhD and lives in a beautiful house by a lake there. But she visits every summer, you know? She could vacation anywhere, but the motherland always pulls her back."

"Yes, it does," Lar nodded, patting the man on the back as he glanced out the window. His eyes landed on the familiar, cream-colored, worn-down apartment building with laundry hanging from balconies.

"The name's Ahmad, by the way," the man extended his hand.

"Oh—Aresh," Lar said, shaking it.

"Where are you visiting from, Aresh?" Ahmad chuckled, taking a puff of his cigarette before resting it on the ashtray next to the cash register. "What do you do?"

"I teach in Oslo, Norway," Lar answered matter-of-factly, adding a stern look to warn Ahmad to drop any further interrogation. *Oh, fuck my alter ego,* he thought with a snicker. *I'm just Aresh Jahan.*

"Can I have two kilos of baklava, please? I'm visiting my mother."

With a heavy heart, Aresh paid Ahmad and exchanged a friendly pat on the back, telling him to 'keep the change' for the extra Emirati dirhams before heading out to the apartment building of his youth. He took in a deep breath and rolled his shoulders back, glancing at the familiar windows.

The parking spots next to the building were mostly empty now. Were the neighbors even home? Did they still live here? What would

Kareem do if he saw Aresh had returned? Would he knock him out immediately? Call his cop buddies to have him arrested for homosexuality, that hypocrite? Or worse—would he shoot him again?

A group of black birds startled Aresh. *Amir?* He prayed constantly that Amir hadn't accompanied him on this trip. He needed to get away from it all—on so many levels. Amir wouldn't understand his desire to see his mother and brother, especially not after how he'd gotten him away from them in the first place.

He stepped closer to the birds, noticing their dark eyes and fully black wings. *No. These are crows. Not related to grackles like Amir likes to become.* Crows were mentioned in the Holy Quran. They were to be respected—loyal creatures, protective of those who helped them. They buried their dead and even taught an early human, Cain, how to do the same for the brother he'd murdered—Abel.

Bismillahirahmirahim. Ringing the doorbell, Aresh silently prayed for the second time that day—once to keep Amir away, and once more for good luck.

Here I go.

A little girl with black curls and an adorable toothy grin opened the door. "And you must be little Fatima," he said, kneeling down to meet her eyes. He snickered as he spoke her name. Their voluptuous neighbor had long married a wealthy merchant and moved away, but Aresh suspected Muhiddin would always relive her memory by naming his daughter after her.

"I'm your Aresh *Amo*, princess," he spoke gently, kneeling to her level.

"I know!" the girl responded excitedly, her deep brown eyes wide. "*Jadti* has your photos!"

"She does?" Aresh asked, raising his eyebrows in playful disbelief.

"Yeah! Is it true you moved to Europe and became some famous author? *Jadti* says you run a famous paper business!"

Aresh chuckled. "Something like that…"

His eyes began to fill with tears—happy ones, much to his surprise. His mother bragged about his successes to her grandchild? He couldn't believe it.

"She's resting now," Fatima continued. "But my parents are inside. Shall I call them?"

"Yes, please," Aresh smiled at her.

"*Maas'Allah,*" Muhiddin walked in after a minute or so, his stomach fuller then Aresh remembered, and his hair completely gray. But his face looked almost exactly the same.

"Look who finally decided to grace our humble abode with his presence…" Muhiddin smirked, pinching his brother's cheek. "Is it really you? The Sultan of Europe? I can't believe my eyes."

"I left to allow you to reign here, *akhi,* don't forget!" Aresh joked, punching his brother lightly on the shoulder. He was surprised at the warmth between them, as they hadn't exactly parted on the best of terms. It was funny what time—and perhaps his fame as 'Lar Iktar'—could wash over. *He's my blood, after all.* "Let me look at you!"

As the two men hugged, Fatima approached, holding the hand of a woman adjusting her headscarf. Aresh could tell she had just thrown it across her hair and shoulders.

"Mina! You haven't aged a bit! You're as beautiful as ever! My brother's a lucky man!"

"*Sekra, naseeb* Aresh," Mina blushed, shaking his hand. "Come inside, sit. We have freshly brewed tea."

§

BACK IN HIS OLD ROOM, NOW CONVERTED INTO A GUEST ROOM, Aresh cleared his throat and adjusted his shirt in front of the mirror.

"*Umi*?" he practiced addressing his mother, lowering his voice one more level. He didn't want her to think his manner of speaking had become too 'feminine,' as she had screamed at him once, among other insults, just before he'd left for Norway.

He cleared his throat again. "*As-salamu alaykum.* It's me... Aresh." If his tears could be contained, they would fill rivers at that moment.

"Your… unsatisfied... dreamful... feminine, demonized..." Aresh gathered all his strength to keep from choking on the words that wanted to burst through his trembling lips. "…homosexual... son!"

"Amo?"

"Oh, sorry, Fatima, dear," Aresh wiped his tears, noticing that the girl had brought him a glass of water. "I didn't see you come in. I'm just practicing a speech for, *um*, work, and…"

"What's ho—mooo-tekshual?"

"Oh," Aresh said, scratching his head. "You heard that. It means... different. I'm a... different kind of son for grandmother. You know... because I don't live here, like your father. So, yeah... go back to sleep."

"What's wrong with being different, *amo*?" Fatima shrugged.

How innocent she was. And how right. Aresh wiped a falling tear from his cheek, caressing hers.

"Nothing at all, my sweet. Nothing at all."

Aresh had been told their mother's pills made her sleep longer, so he hadn't faced her yet. He knew he wouldn't get any sleep that night, not before seeing his mother the next day. That was for sure.

The following morning, Aresh found his mother stirring in bed, her eyes still closed. Her face had become more wrinkled over time, but she still wore that angelic, smiling expression on her tanned skin that Aresh remembered.

"Wake up, Mother. It's me—Aresh. Forgive me," Aresh whispered at her bedside.

"Forgive me, *Umi*," he repeated, his voice thick with emotion.

"Aresh?" Her whisper was feeble as her eyes finally met his. "Is it really you? Come closer. Let me look at you. Take that mask off…"

"Mother, your immune system is compromised, and I'm not vaccinated against this damn global virus. I've only had some seasonal sneezes, but I don't want to risk hurting you if I'm carrying something," Aresh explained.

Reaching out a shaky hand and rubbing his face, his mother sniffed his aftershave. She took off the medical mask across his mouth. "I actually think I prefer your soft skin to Muhiddin's scratchy beard." She snickered softly.

Aresh smiled, taking her hand and kissing it.

"I'm not afraid of some virus, *abni,* nor of death. Especially now that you're here. I can see one last time with earthly eyes…" Her voice trailed off as she started coughing.

"Aresh," Muhiddin stuck his head in the door. "Can I speak with you for a minute, brother?"

Aresh looked at his mother. She was glancing back and forth between the two men with a joyful smile. He nodded.

"I'll be right back, *Umi*," he kissed her again.

"You should've come earlier…" Muhiddin's tone shifted once they were alone in the corridor.

"Let bygones be bygones, my brother," Aresh said softly. "We're family. And she's happy to see us getting along, don't you see?"

"Yes," Muhiddin sighed. "But through the years, Mother's needed you. I needed you…"

"She wouldn't have accepted me back then," Aresh replied, biting his lip. "She always knew I was different, even as a child… You were always more of an 'expected' son than I was. I needed to pave my own path."

"You gave up on her!" Muhiddin's voice rose, though he struggled to keep it down.

"It was easier for you to avoid the confrontation about your sexuality and just escape! Yes, she may not have loved it at first, but eventually, things could have worked out. You accuse her of not having empathy, but have *you* shown her the same? We're here, Aresh! We're not in the West! We stay in our homeland. I travel, but this—this culture is all she's ever known. You could've shown more understanding, more compassion for her..."

"You don't know the whole story," Aresh said, shaking his head, his voice thick with tears. "I didn't just leave to avoid judgment from you two. There was more to it than that."

"Oh, please, I read your book!" Muhiddin scoffed. "Blaming us for everything—your twisted take on science, philosophy, and religion to manipulate the youth, gaining their sympathy with your sob stories..."

"I never mentioned you or Mother by name," Aresh shot back, shaking his head. "It was a brief, generalized passage about 'not being accepted by family,' encouraging others to 'look elsewhere.' That's where my organization came in. I helped a lot of people."

"You helped your followers," Muhiddin sneered, "but at the expense of how many misled others, brother?"

"You don't know what you're talking about," Aresh scoffed, scratching his head. "Am I here now, at least, to help take care of Mother, or not? Let's leave the past behind us."

"You never had to leave..." Muhiddin said softly, biting his lower lip. "You could've studied here, in the Emirates, if you wanted to become some big shot. You didn't have to run away, Aresh Jahan."

"I didn't run!" Aresh insisted. "You know I went to Norway for medical help."

Muhiddin raised a thick, dark eyebrow at him.

"I didn't run!" Aresh repeated, his voice tinged with frustration.

He had only wanted to escape the harassment he faced for his sexuality, hadn't he? Amir had helped him. The jinn who had saved his life.

"Okay," Muhiddin crossed his arms. "Let's say you left for other reasons, as you say. Medical, or whatnot. What about 'Lar Iktar'?"

"Oh, and you secretly loved it all, didn't you?" Aresh scoffed. "In comparison to me, you always seemed like the 'good' son, despite your own imperfections, didn't you?"

Muhiddin smirked. "I'm not the one who changed my name and denied my heritage, my brother."

"I did what I had to do to survive, trust me," Aresh shut his eyes, taking a deep breath. When he opened them, he was pleased to see his brother smiling at him.

"So what yearning has brought you back here to your roots, Mighty Lar Iktar?" Muhiddin chuckled, playfully punching Aresh's arm.

Aresh grinned. "I've simply been yearning for a homeland."

§

THE REFLECTION OF THE FULL MOON ON THE WINDOW HAD ARESH'S attention, though not his mental focus. *Stig?* He felt the presence of his closest jinn disciple ever since Finn had strayed, though he couldn't be certain.

He lowered his gaze to Kareem's window, taken aback to see the curtain snap shut abruptly in the room where he'd once frequented as a young man, making eye contact with Aresh. Had Kareem seen him? Was he still there? Aresh considered asking Amir, but he didn't want to get him involved in this trip—not after everything. He had to do this by himself, for himself.

The hairs on the back of his neck prickled, and Aresh straightened in his bed. "Please... I know you're here with me, Stig. Nora's told me everything. I'm not angry. I need your help, actually. Please manifest."

"Master," came the voice. "I am embarrassed. I only followed you here to please Nora. I don't mean any disrespect."

Aresh smiled toward his right, where the voice seemed to emanate from. "You can read my thoughts, Lad. You should know I don't mean any harm. I know you love her. And it's okay."

"The maxims…" Stig began, gradually manifesting in human form, with his eyes lowered to the ground.

"What good have my maxims ultimately been if 'The Group' hasn't been able to provide its members with somewhere they wanted to belong to in the long run?" Aresh sighed. "I've made a decision, Lad."

"You have?" Stig asked softly, looking into Aresh's eyes.

"I do not wish to be arrested in Norway," Aresh continued, patting Stig on the back. "I don't want to be somewhere my family cannot visit, if they desire to. Nor do I need to be arrested *here* for some bullshit 'crime' about my homosexuality my neighbor might throw my way—which he'd threatened to do long ago, and which I don't deserve. No, Lad. If I'm to pay penance, and free my soul from my burdens, I will do so for my business dealings. Nora is right. Please, release whatever you have on me to the local police."

"Master, I cannot do that to you…" Stig shook his head in disbelief. "I don't know how much you understand, but Nora's leading a revolution among the brethren right now! You're wanted on several counts with what she's released. Charges like… let's see…" He hesitated after making a mental list, but went on anyway. "Brainwashing, drugging, invasion of privacy, and sexual extortion in recruiting underage members... These are charges bad enough in Norway—I can't even begin to imagine what they would give you here…"

"I want you to help me turn myself in here," Aresh insisted, his voice firm. "I'm *begging* you, in fact. I've seen my mother and brother. Even my little niece. I feel ready. I need this. I could confess, but they'll think I'm mad. You have the evidence. Just put it on the table for the chief of police. They'll come for me. I'm sure they'll coordinate with the Norwegians, although I know there isn't an extradition treaty between the two countries. So I doubt I'll be sent to Norway. I'll be kept here..."

Aresh took in a deep breath and added. "…and I'll belong."

§

"THIS HAS BEEN THE BEST BREAKFAST OF MY LIFE, UMI", ARESH SAID with a smile as his mother caressed his cheek.

"Me too, *abni*," she replied, as Aresh popped another olive into his mouth. "I have both my boys here with me again, finally, and my little princess."

"*Ahem,*" Mina cleared her throat, bringing in a bowl of fresh figs.

"And my amazing daughter-in-law, of course!" Her mother-in-law caressing her arms as she said so caused Mina to smile.

"If I don't see you guys again, please know I've always loved you, and carried you with me," Aresh spoke through falling tears. "Despite all my mistakes—I've always carried you. And will always do."

Placing his hand on his heart, Aresh spoke. "*El aileh lel abd.*"

"*Family forever,*" Muhiddin repeated, smiling back. "What's with the 'goodbyes' already?"

"You're going back to Norway, *amo*?" Fatima's big black eyes looked up at him.

"I'm not sure, princess," he patted her head.

"I think your uncle needs more tea," Muhiddin winked, pouring him another glass, just as the sound of running feet could be heard. They stopped right outside their door.

"Open up! It's the police!"

"Muhiddin, what's happening?" Mina stood up in alarm.

"I don't know, but take Fatima into *Umi*'s room. *Umi*—you go with them. Leave this to the men."

"I will not leave my sons at the hands of whatever these officers want!" his mother said with anger, struggling to sit up straighter.

"*Umi*, please, it'll be okay, trust me!" Aresh insisted with a smile.

"Open up or we'll have to kick the doors! We are looking for Aresh Jahan, in connection to his operations under the name…Lar Iktar."

As the officer chuckled at his name, Aresh released a sigh of relief. *Thank you,* he sent a thought Stig's way, just in case he'd been near to hear his thoughts. *Best of luck to you and the others.*

"Muhiddin, it's okay, I'll go with them peacefully," Aresh placed his hands on his brother's arm.

"Why in God's name do they want you, and how do they know you're here?" Muhiddin's face was frozen in shock.

"I allowed one of my disciples to lead them to me," Aresh said with an acceptant smile. "I thought they'd come tomorrow when Fatima is in school. They came early. It's about some….discrepancies in my operations back in Norway. I'm sorry she's had to see."

"Brother…*why*?" Tears were streaming down Muhiddin's face.

Aresh smiled at him. "I couldn't do it abroad. I wanted to be pay my dues to society here, in my homeland. Close to you all."

"Alright we're kicking the door in one…."

"Open the door," Aresh nodded at Muhiddin, who reluctantly did so.

"Don't shoot!" Aresh Jahan smiled at two cops through his tears, noting both of them pointing the gun at him and Muhiddin.

"Which one of you is 'Lar Iktar'?" the taller one asked.

"I am," Aresh said with a smile, raising his hands above his head.

"My family here has nothing to do with my dealings in Norway. I surrender."

As he got handcuffed and taken outside, where he was shoved into the police car, Aresh Jahan continued to smile. Prison? Death penalty? He didn't mind. He knew whatever he was to face, it would be for a reason. And he needed ablution.

I'm ready for whatever divine punishment necessary to be purified, so I could finally be free in Jannah—Heaven—inshaAllah. Perhaps I can see Tan again there, after Judgement day, of course. Or even Jaan one day.

Aresh sighed. Maybe it didn't even matter. Maybe some people were never meant to have met the love of their lives on earth, meant for other joys and contributions instead. If that was the case, would he find love in the afterlife? Would God allow for that? Allah, after all, was said to be ever forgiving for those who repented for their sins.

He gazed out the window to see his brother crying, covering his daughter's eyes at the scene. Mina was hugging her mother-in-law, consoling her.

I have a family, no matter how much water has passed through that bridge, and they love me. It felt reassuring, somehow.

"It's okay," he mouthed to them through the police car window. And he believed it. Somehow, someway—it'd all be okay.

"You idiot!" he heard Amir crow at him in his grackle form, following along in flight as the car started on the road.

Aresh rolled his eyes. He'd forgotten about *him.* He who had once saved him, but at the cost of so much more.

"It's okay, Amir," he spoke. "My soul will be free at last. I don't need *you.*"

Maybe I never did.

CHAPTER 35

Sandnes

WATCHING MALIN PLAY 'TAG' WITH BO, LOOKING LIKE COTTON candy in a poofy pink jacket he hadn't seen before warmed Finn's heart. He could just picture her on some shopping spree in the big city with her mother. *If only things could have been different*, Finn thought with a heavy heart. If only he could have joined them. "How was your big trip, Malin?"

"It was really cool!" Malin exclaimed. "The buildings were so tall in New York City, and there was some similar ones in Toronto, too!

"Sounds amazing," Finn smiled.

"Uncle Finn? Can I ask you a question?"

"I don't know…*can* you?" Finn winked at Malin, taking a playful swipe at her full cheeks, rosy from the winter chill. As he did so, Bo jumped onto Malin's leg for attention.

"Down boy…" Bo did as he was told by Finn, albeit nuzzling his nose closer to Malin's leg.

"My teacher uses that cheesy line all the time when we ask if we 'can' go to the bathroom," Malin chuckled. "So, alright— *may* I ask a question then?"

"Of course," Finn giggled. "Anything."

"When you and my dad were little…"

"Okay anything *except* the past with your father," Finn interrupted, turning his face from her. "I told you— and your mother agrees—it's too painful to talk about. We'll explain when you're old enough to understand, perhaps…"

"My grandmother and Uncle Aidan also acted strange about it, Uncle Finn," Malin twisted her lips, shrugging. "I can't wait to grow up so people can actually tell me interesting stuff!"

"Oh, Malin," Finn chuckled. *They've had an entire Canadian family discussion about me apparently. Yikes!*

"But don't worry, Uncle Finn," Malin continued, her face serious. "My question wasn't about family secrets or anything like that, anyway. It was just about…being an actual twin….no 'family drama' or anything. I promise…"

"Oh?" Finn folded his arms across his black coat, intrigued.

"Yes," Malin nodded. "I've always been curious about being a twin. Do you feel any…special connection to yours? I mean, I can't ask Dad about this stuff, so I really wish you could tell me. Could you ever sense how he was feeling or what he was thinking? Can you still do so?"

Kaitlin—my twin flame. Finn smiled. *Many people spend their entire lives searching for the way in which we make each other feel alive.* He considered for a second whether he'd be able to feel such a bond with an actual twin sibling, had he truly had one.

"Sometimes," he fibbed. "Sure."

A bark from Bo interrupted them, causing Finn to erupt in forced laughter. It felt good to have the distraction.

"Sorry, Bo!" Malin went over to pet him. "Come, let's walk a little bit before I have to go. Hey, is Bob around?"

As Bo made pleading eye contact with him, Finn insisted he calm himself. *"No, Bo, you can't,"* he communicated mentally. *"Not now."*

"He's helping out his Mom, today," Finn said, scratching the back of his head. "It's his birthday, you know?"

"Oh, tell Bob Happy Birthday for me!" Malin said excitedly. "I still have the drawing he made for me on mine. Oh, darnety darn! I wish I could draw something for him, too!"

Bo nuzzled his nose into Malin's leg, causing Finn to giggle.

"Don't worry, I'm sure he'll be just as happy when I tell him you wished him well."

Malin petted Bo again, her voice turning dolorous. "Uncle Finn says we may not be able to meet as much anymore, Bo. Mommy and Daddy have taken me out of my extra activities to focus on my schoolwork. I'm going to miss you. You've already gotten so big since I've been gone."

Bo whimpered and nuzzled his face into her arms, bringing a pesky tear to Finn's eye that stung.

The cake is ready, he heard Meredith mentally relay to him. It was their boy's birthday, and he was expected home. Finn chuckled. *I have to be the responsible husband, like Paul damn Maverick.*

His face soured, and Finn took in a deep breath. *Keep calm. It's all for the best.*

"Hey, Malin?" he called out, catching up with Malin and Bo. He placed one hand on her arm while the other ruffled the fur on Bo's tan-colored head.

"If I don't see you for a while, I just want you to know, my dearest, that it's been my pleasure spending this time with you. You've been …like the daughter I never had. And Bo has enjoyed himself as well."

"Oh, Uncle Finn," Malin hugged him through tearful eyes.

"You're loved more than you know, and you are never alone," Finn buried his head into the soft hair underneath her winter hat. "You're a very special spirit, Malin. Don't ever forget that. Always have faith in yourself, even if it feels like the world has lost faith in you."

§

DRYING THE DISHES WITH THE CHECKERED TOWEL IN HIS HAND, PAUL darted a quick glance in Kaitlin's direction. She was handing him the freshly washed dinnerware.

"I can't believe you didn't share everything you found out about your dad earlier, and about John Walker being your half-uncle," Paul said.

"I think I felt safer keeping it inside until I was more certain about the whole situation, babe," Kaitlin shrugged.

"You can be as secretive as your family members, it seems," Paul raised an eyebrow.

"We ultimately learn how to love from our parents…" Kaitlin smirked. "Speaking of being secretive, Mr. Maverick, have you hung out with Jeanette while I was gone?"

"Neither her nor Tim, no, not outside of work," Paul said, shaking his head. He threw in a smile. "Mrs. Maverick."

"Hmm," Kaitlin rolled her eyes. "She didn't bring over cookies or anything? Maybe she'll visit when your mom comes soon. They know each other from back in the day, don't they?"

"Here we go again with the baking!" Paul threw his hands in the air. "Why do you look down on domestic women, Kaitlin? I'm especially surprised as you're making a living off of, ironically—cookies! And Jeanette works."

"Ouch, touché," Kaitlin bit her lip. "You're right. She works at the same company as you. She doesn't have a child to tend to at home, after all!"

"Baby," Paul shook her head. "Why are you always doing this? It's not a competition. You're a working mother, and I'm proud of you more than anyone. You don't need to criticize others."

"I am not!" Kaitlin softened her tone after his compliment. "I just believe we're *equals*— that's all I'm trying to say. That's all I've *been* trying to show you, Paul! No one type of woman can, in fairness, be categorized as better or more 'right' than another. What I think you don't recognize is, *you* have been looking down on *me*, Paul—simply because I don't necessarily share the same dreams as *they* do!"

"Why would I have wanted to marry you if I had been looking down on you, Kaitlin?" Paul asked. He took what felt like an entire minute to respond, folding his arms before reacting softly to Kaitlin's frustrated exclamation.

He's trying to make me look like the bad one, Kaitlin thought, feeling the whole act was purposely contrived.

Or was it all just in her head? Her ego? Kaitlin closed her eyes, inhaling deeply for four seconds, holding it for seven, and finally letting the air out for eight. Sibel had insisted she practice the technique during moments of stress.

As Paul took a deep breath and flopped onto the couch, still shaking his head in frustration, Kaitlin found herself pouting and swaying, hoping her silence would eventually grab Paul's attention.

Am I more turned on by the drama? Kaitlin had been journaling about their fights as Freya had suggested, noticing a pattern. Were she and Paul only able to find their way back to each other after fighting? Did it stimulate her emotions whereas, at other times, she felt numb?

"I wish I could have been your hero, Kaitlin," Paul's eyes met hers, his hands firmly planted in his jean pockets.

"And I wish I could have been yours," Kaitlin shut her eyes as a tear escaped. She placed her face in her hands. "Although I admit it scared the hell out of me, *Superman*, that you confronted him— I was also impressed!"

"That jinn better maintain his focus on his own life with his own kind from now on!" Paul steamed.

As an image of Finn with Meredith crossed Kaitlin's mind, she quickly shook it off, nodding in agreement.

"I've always known we were of two different mindsets about what we were hoping to gain from marriage, Paulie. But you were so heartbroken when I met you, and I wanted to heal your heart and confidence. I know you liked being older than me, and feeling like you could provide for me in many ways…and over time…I think you maybe fell out of love with me when I no longer needed you as much."

"I never fell out of love, Kaitlin," Paul shook his head, twisting his face. "The intense passion expressed at the beginning of all relationships naturally fizzles out for everyone, babe—it doesn't mean the love goes away, just changes form. I just expressed my love for you more when it seemed you needed it most. You've been speaking of family influences since your trip—so think about that from my perspective now, if you can."

As Paul kneeled down next to her and caressed her knees, Kaitlin took in a deep breath and gazed back into his eyes. "I'm listening."

"Baby, I'm used to being in protector mode as the eldest child in my family."

"Yes, I see your point," Kaitlin remarked. "But I'm not your child or sibling, Paulie. I'm your *wife*. We are supposed to act as *partners* in life. Equals, keeping each other in balance. I think I didn't feel, for a long time, like you viewed me in that way…like I was your priority."

Kaitlin remembered one of the last things Freya had told her.

"Just because you could not get his full attention, you believed you didn't have Paul's heart, Kaitlin... and tried to fill in the void left by your need for your father with any attention you could get, immediately mistaking it for love—even when it may not have been..."

Paul finally spoke, clasping his hands together. "Kaitlin, I truly regret not having made you feel my sincerity. You and Malin have been my top priority, though not the only ones. I've had to tend to my other family members, job, and friends. That may have been my shortcoming, I guess. The way I expressed myself, or couldn't, regarding all this."

Kaitlin nodded, licking her lips. *He's trying*, she thought. And perhaps he always had been.

"I showed Malin a box of our stuff back in Toronto," Kaitlin said, blushing. As Paul raised a curious eyebrow, she continued. "Our first pictures, notes to each other before getting hitched….your words about growing old together—it was all so romantic."

"I meant it then, and I still mean it now," Paul said, his tears rolling freely. "You've made me a proud husband—and Malin, a proud father."

"And you've grounded me when my head was in the clouds," Kaitlin smiled. "I think it's made me stronger."

She reached out and gently wiped the tears from Paul's cheek, her own eyes welling up as she struggled to hold back the emotions threatening to spill over.

"I just want to know that I'm enough for you, Paul," Kaitlin whispered, her voice barely audible. "That I don't need to be constantly fighting for your heart."

"You are enough," Paul said quickly, his voice urgent. "You always have been. I know I haven't always shown it, but you mean everything to me. I just—I've been so focused on trying to fix everything, trying to protect everyone, that sometimes I forget to just be here, to be present with you. I'm sorry for that."

Kaitlin shook her head, letting out a soft, bittersweet laugh. "It's not just about being present, Paul. It's about feeling like you're really here, that you're not just... physically here but emotionally, too. I want to feel like I matter to you in the way I need to."

Paul's gaze softened, and he reached for her hands, holding them gently in his. "You matter more than anything, Kaitlin. I promise you that. I don't always express it the right way, but I'm working on it. I never meant to make you feel like you weren't important."

Kaitlin studied him for a moment, searching his face for sincerity. The years they had spent together, the love they had built, didn't feel like it was all lost, but there were scars, silent wounds that neither of them had fully addressed.

"I think we've both been so caught up in what we *think* the other needs, that we've forgotten to *ask* each other what we *really* need," Kaitlin said softly.

Paul nodded slowly. "You're right. I need to learn to listen better, rather than assume…I need to understand you more. I know I've been too wrapped up in my own stuff. I'm sorry for that."

Kaitlin smiled faintly, feeling the smallest weight lift from her chest. "It's okay. I'm not perfect either, Paul. I've got my own baggage, my own fears. We just need to find a way to be... *us* again. Not just me, not just you, but both of us."

Paul leaned in, pressing his forehead gently against hers. "We'll find our way. I believe in us, Kaitlin. I always have."

She closed her eyes, letting herself relax into the moment. There was still work to be done, still pain to heal, but for the first time in a while, she felt a flicker of hope. Maybe, just maybe, they could rebuild what had been broken, piece by piece.

The silence between them was comfortable now, no longer charged with the tension that had gripped them before. Kaitlin felt a small sense of peace settle over her, knowing that they were still fighting for each other.

"I guess we'll have to take things one step at a time," Kaitlin said, a soft smile curling at the corners of her lips.

Paul chuckled, his hand brushing her cheek. "One step at a time. Together."

Kaitlin leaned in, pressing her lips to his in a gentle kiss. As they pulled away, Kaitlin gazed into his eyes, seeing the sincerity there. They still had a long way to go, but for the first time in a long time, she felt a glimmer of confidence in their future. They would make it through this. They had to.

"Did we… actually have a conversation without fighting?" Kaitlin chuckled. Paul grinned, kissing the tip of her nose as he grinned.

Odd, just as it feels like we may be past mending—we're actually mending.

Later that night, after making sure both Malin and Paul were sound asleep, Kaitlin pulled out her laptop. She glanced at the clock—2:12 AM. Quietly, she tiptoed to the living room, laptop in hand, eager to open it up. When inspiration struck like this, she knew she had to follow it.

why is it
that the beautiful sun
peeks out
from the clouds
just as the day
is ending?

why is it
that the hurtful lover
with the shout
only succumbs
to softness
just as the relationship
is past mending?

why is this
human nature?
can we redeem ourselves
to enjoy what we can
while we are able?
let's ponder
and enjoy the sun, not thunder

Stretching her arms in front of her before lifting them overhead, Kaitlin took a deep breath, rolling her shoulders back. Creatively, she was on a roll. Her mind drifted to New York and the things Freya had shared about Amir, even managing to control someone like Lar Iktar from his bird form. She pondered humanity—and all beings, both human and beyond.

nature always beckons louder than whimsical calls
of benefiting folk

encircling you

like the hawk
that focuses on its prey
tricks and reckons

nature's call is defiant
not compliant
yet nonetheless reliant

nature embraces the weary
when fellow kind feel more scary

Kaitlin leaned back against the leather sofa, grabbing the orange throw from the corner and draping it around her shoulders. She'd just close her eyes for a few minutes... she couldn't possibly fall asleep, could she?

Suddenly jolting awake with a start, Kaitlin sat up straight, her eyes drawn to the brightening sky outside the window. A small bird perched nearby, eyeing her curiously, and her smile made it flutter away. She quickly flipped open her laptop, which had been shut. 4:58. Shit! She'd actually fallen asleep!

Thankfully, the laptop still had charge, and she sighed in relief when she saw that her Word document had saved her progress.

She checked the last thing she'd written and shook her head with a chuckle. What a crazy trip this had been. Just then, an email alert from her Google account grabbed her attention—it was from Salim, talking about another shipment. Kaitlin grinned. If he could act like nothing strange had happened between them, so could she. For the sake of her business. For Freya. For her own dignity. She didn't need any more chaos in her life—especially not one she *could* control.

Wiggling her fingers in front of her, Kaitlin blinked a few times, stifling a yawn before switching back to her Word document.

'I'm tired...
though at least I've t.r.i.e.d'
dear bird:
unique one
piquing my interest this celebrated morning
with your slender tail
and proud beak,
shapely head

I wonder...
are you reflective, too,
as this, yet another dusk into dawn
nears another day's conclusion?

have you, too, tried to flock
and provide
for others of your kind,
seeking inclusion?

...worked endlessly,
relying on the feed provided daily,
knowing one day it can stop,
inexplicably?

have you, as well,
welcomed
seeking solace in the affection of a friend,
whilst they saw you as means
to a different sort of end?

dear nestling
at least
I've tried, have you?
at last
I seek only peace now,
I'm tired, and you?

The sound of a man's voice caught Kaitlin's attention. Was someone smoking by the doors again before heading to work? Closing her eyes—almost as if it would heighten her sense of hearing—she quickly discerned that it was Paul on the phone.

Shutting the lid of her laptop with a sigh, Kaitlin tiptoed toward Malin's room, peeking through the cracked door to make sure she was still sound asleep. Paul's voice was still audible from their bedroom.

"Mom, you're being unfair, right now!"

He's talking to Momma Mila! Kaitlin rolled her eyes, walking to their room. It was past 11 pm back in Quebec—what was the woman doing up? Curious, she stayed out of his sight, leaning against the corridor wall as she listened.

"Mom, Kaitlin was dealing with so much over there! I'm sorry but you have no right to be angry at her for not visiting Quebec!"

Kaitlin heart swelled with emotion. Was Paul actually *defending* her to his family?

There's my man. Not needing to hear more, she slipped into the bathroom, splashed her face with water and ran her fingers through her hair, smoothing out her slightly wrinkled nightgown. She couldn't wait to slide into bed with him before Malin woke up. Spraying on a hint of body mist, she stepped out and inched toward their bedroom.

Pushing the door open all the way, she locked eyes with Paul, making sure he saw her before she leaned suggestively against the wall, gyrating her body. A sly grin played on her lips.

"Okay, *Maman*, I, *um,* have to get ready for work now, alright? We'll talk later?"

The seductive smile he shot back let her know he'd caught her message loud and clear.

"Did you mean what you told your mom?" she cooed as he hung up the phone.

"You were eavesdropping?" Paul snickered. "Silly goose. Where were you?"

"In the living room," Kaitlin shrugged, smiling. "The writing inspiration hit. But now I think we both need another kind of…hit."

"Oh, yeah?" Paul pursed his lips, brooding playfully. "And, of course I meant what I told her, baby. You are my priority. The poor woman got the time difference mixed up again…"

"I meant…" Kaitlin began, sashaying closer to him and ruffling his hair. "About going to work. Do you really want to…*go to work right away*, so soon, Paulie?"

"Not *at all*," Paul whispered, standing up. Sticking his head out the door to check for Malin, he swiftly pulled Kaitlin inside, closing the door behind them. Pinning her against the wall, their lips met hungrily before tumbling onto the bed.

§

KAITLIN WOKE UP A COUPLE OF HOURS LATER WITH A GRIN ON HER face, still grateful for the intimate connection she and Paul had just shared— their first since their anniversary. She stretched, then slid closer to him on the bed. He'd already let his boss know he'd be late, making up an excuse. She knew what she had to do once he left for work. It wouldn't be easy, but it was necessary—she had been shown this by the universe and God, through various vessels.

It gutted something in her heart, but Kaitlin knew she had to face Finn with her truth one last time. He deserved that much. And so did she, after everything.

Once Paul had left for work and Malin's bus had picked her up, Kaitlin made herself an extra cup of coffee, playing relaxing music in the background to set the mood. When she felt ready, she did it.

Finn. I need to talk to you. Are you available?

After several minutes, the familiar sensation hit—the hairs on the back of her neck standing on end, the rush of energy flowing past her. And soon enough, there he was. Finn appeared in the living room, his presence both comforting and unsettling, as always.

"Ms. Kaitlin?" he asked, his voice laced with uncertainty. Kaitlin tried to grin at him. He must have sensed that something was different.

"Hi," she said softly.

"Hi..." Finn returned the grin, though his eyes were filled more with emotion than flirtation.

"Thank you for coming," Kaitlin said. "And for everything... since my trip and my return."

"You're welcome," Finn cleared his throat, shifting on his feet. His eyes were locked on her, as if urging her to get to the point.

"Was everything okay with the Toronto suite?" Kaitlin asked, picking up her mug and taking a sip of her now-cold coffee. "I left the keys by my mailbox, as promised."

"Yup— thanks," Finn said, biting his lip. "You didn't want to see me in person to hand them over. I've gotten the message."

"Finn, yeah, about that…"

"Okay, fine, we'll talk," Finn interrupted, closing his eyes and taking a deep breath. "But before we do, I've been meaning to share something I wrote with you. May I? I've kept busy while you were away."

"Oh, yeah?" Kaitlin raised an eyebrow, a playful glint in her eyes as she crossed her arms over her chest.

"Yes, I've been…*inspired* by you," Finn said, raising his eyebrows with a mischievous grin. "By one of our last meetings."

"Okay, Shakespeare, go ahead… let's hear it," Kaitlin teased. A part of her felt relieved that he wasn't holding her decision to keep her distance against her.

"Don't laugh…" Finn flashed his trademark bashful smile.

"Oh, I don't think I can promise *that*," Kaitlin shot back with a grin.

"Hey, I've been reading your practical worship of those CBD-infused cookies that blew up your blog… and never once laughed at your written art form, Ms. Kaitlin. Come on now! This is actual artistic expression—a poem," he said, pouting with his lips slightly pursed and pink.

"I infuse poetry into my articles too, you know," Kaitlin replied, folding her arms and holding her head high. Would his lips still sizzle with the same heat, as she remembered?

Why did I just think of that right now? Argh! Kaitlin cleared her throat. "Marketing is simply my field. And you liked my cookies—be fair…"

"Oh, I loved your cookie…" Finn scratched the back of his neck, his eyes cast downward as he bit the corner of his lip.

"Finn!" Kaitlin blushed, clearing her throat and motioning with her hand for him to move on. She could swear that sometimes the fiery intensity of his being had rubbed off on her, the way impure thoughts of them together left her with scorching sensations. She quickly pushed the thought away. "The *poem*…"

"Alright, yes… here goes…" Finn began, after taking another deep breath.

I saw my beloved today
and all my blues went away,
yay!

the clouds parted once again
in the company of my special friend

the sun shone happy and gay
when there was a will, there was a way

With shut eyelids, Finn exhaled slowly, then glancing at Kaitlin to gauge her reaction. "Well?"

"Oh! That was... cute," Kaitlin covered her mouth with her slender hand, unable to suppress her chuckle for much longer. "Did Malin help you write that?"

"What?" Finn interjected, joining her in laughter. "Can't adults like rhymes?"

"There are rhymes, and there are r*hymes*, Mr. Du Feu," Kaitlin replied with a teasing grin. "Oh, I'm just messing with you! I'm not used to you writing anything... It really was cute. Not bad, not bad."

"Okay, I'll admit that was just something I made up on the spot," Finn's tone turned serious. "I actually have the real one jotted down."

"Oh, you do, do you now?" Kaitlin watched as Finn took out a folded piece of paper from his jacket pocket. "You wrote it down and everything... I'm already impressed. Is 'The Group' branching out into literary work these days, following Lar's footsteps?"

"I don't think I can read it now in front of you..." Finn ignored her question. "Here... you can have this. You should read it after I leave..."

Kaitlin reached out, meeting Finn's outstretched hand, feeling the sizzling spark of energy as her fingers brushed the cream-colored sheet, which looked like it had been torn from a journal. Finn pulled his hand back and raised an eyebrow, offering a solemn smile before she could take the paper. "Are you sure this is a good idea?"

"Writing is art, and I respect art," Kaitlin encouraged, her voice trembling slightly. "It's cool. I won't judge. I promise. I'm curious. Please. Go ahead."

"It's not about my... art. I'm worried you'll judge me," Finn said, holding the paper close to his face. "This isn't exactly my thing. It's just... something that came to me naturally. Maybe reading your writing's inspired me, not sure. I don't want to confuse you or anything. But all right. It's just a poem. Here goes..."

I saw my beloved today
and the clouds
up to then drenching me with dolorous rain that almost extinguished me
finally parted to reveal the sun

her smile...
not only sparkling around the corner of her bow-shaped lips,
but brightening the darkness with the hazel in her pupils...
lightening my heavy load...

I saw my beloved
and all logic stopped, replaced by wiser instinct-
and all I knew with certainty in that subsequent moment
where I had to part from her presence again was that
I'd never miss the rain again-
unless I could be comforted afterward by her sun

...that I'd only tolerate it upon assurance of her rainbow-
her gaze brightening my sorrow...
burning into my soul,
her eyes—
both my mirror
and window

"It's…exquisite," Kaitlin said, holding back tears. "Truly. Like everything was. Like everything has been. I'm honored if I was your muse for that."

"You are," Finn said with a smile. *He's blushing like a boy,* Kaitlin thought. She cleared her throat. She couldn't let herself get carried away again. The decision was made. It was done.

"Did you write poems for Freya, too?" Kaitlin asked, her voice tentative. She still felt asking about Meredith—now his wife—was too strange and painful. Freya felt safer, somehow.

Finn smiled at her. "I can imagine you've been curious since meeting her…Freya used to attend university in Norway. Bjorn and I met her, along with several others, to discuss how we could strengthen human-jinn connections to aid Lar Iktar's mission, and…"

"Were you two in love?" Kaitlin cut in.

"Yes, we eventually became paired," Finn replied nonchalantly. "You should know by now it's normal practice in 'The Group' to…"

"Okay, okay, forget it—I don't think I really want to know."

Kaitlin placed her face in her hands. "I can't believe I've been so stupid! I've been talking to someone about my private feelings—mentioning your name so casually, thinking it would just be another stranger's name to my therapist…"

"You couldn't have known," Finn assured her. "Kaitlin—you have to believe me when I tell you I had no part to play in Freya becoming your therapist! Trust me, the last person I'd want treating someone currently in my life would be my ex-girlfriend! Especially since we never exactly broke it off on the best of terms."

Can I believe him? Kaitlin wasn't so sure. But what other choice did she have? Besides, she had to admit she was utterly curious.

Finn paced, his gaze focused on the ground for a minute or so before he stopped and faced Kaitlin. "She left for New York City. I was persuaded it was for her studies and even supported her at first. That is, until I saw her with someone I initially thought was just a 'friend.' Then she moved in with that guy… Salim."

"Yeah, and we both know how that worked out," Kaitlin scoffed. "I'll be fair to Salim, though. He's good at his job."

"You still need to be careful with him, you hear?" Finn's tone turned serious.

"I will," Kaitlin smiled.

"Anyway," Finn continued. "I guess I always thought I had to hold on to love for as long as I could, not stopping to think about whether the other person was happy—or even if I was happy."

"You've... been very patient," Kaitlin grinned. "With me, anyway. Patience is a virtue... which *I* hadn't even attempted to cultivate until now."

"Now I see I have to let you go *because* I love you as deeply as I do," Finn went on. "Life is too short, Kaitlin, and I don't want you to ever second-guess whether you're in the right place in your life with me. If you're always second-guessing *us*, then letting you go isn't selfish—holding on is."

"Did you... did a part of you know why I've called you out here today?" Kaitlin asked, biting her trembling lip.

"I had a strong hunch, especially with our connection," Finn grinned. "But one can never truly know—even a jinn like me. We live in a world where anyone can do anything at any time. Some have a higher probability of certain things, true, but there's still a possibility for anything."

"Finn... I need to focus on raising Malin and creating a stable life for my daughter," Kaitlin started, taking in a deep breath. "That means keeping you at arm's length. I need to start setting better boundaries in my life."

"I see," Finn's eyes shot to the floor. "It's a shame our earthly circumstances couldn't allow for this, I suppose. I tried."

"I tried, too," Kaitlin nodded.

"*Have* you, really?" Finn raised an eyebrow.

You can do this. Kaitlin took in a deep breath. "Finn, please.... I need to prioritize my motherhood. Malin needs me to be strong. A life with you would require me to give up so much more than you ever would. I mean, think about it—could you ever give up 'The Group'?"

Finn's shoulders caved, and he folded in on himself. "I'd love to, but I can't. My soul is tied with them. And now, with Meredith and Bo,

I have to do the right thing, be responsible. Regardless, you don't want a jinn husband anyway. Don't kid yourself, Kaitlin. It's okay."

"I would have to give up so much *more* just to live with you openly, can't you see?" Kaitlin implored. "Can you imagine when Malin becomes a teenager, and soon afterward, a young woman? She needs to lead a healthy life—not one with the risks that a jinn's presence poses to her. My daughter's safety and well-being must come first."

"Please tell me at least you've seen by now that I've never been a source of harm for her," Finn stated, averting his eyes. "The opposite, in fact."

"I know, I know," Kaitlin closed her eyes.

"Let me get this out, too," Finn began. "We should at least ensure our children don't suffer for us. Neither Malin nor Bo should have to pay for our mistakes, just because we may or may not be paying for our own families'…"

"You're saying little nestlings need to be free of their chains," Kaitlin began, "before they grow and fly…"

Finn smiled. "Yes, bird lover. It's for our little ones, who need to feel our wings covering them. The little things in life are bigger than we think when we're younger. We must fight like eagles, however, for our nestlings."

Kaitlin nodded, smiling back.

"I will always put her well-being first," Finn took a step closer.

"I know—and thank you, truly," Kaitlin blushed. "But not all of your kind are like you. The Amir creature…and maybe others down the line….I just can't risk exposing her. I've seen how my father is still affected."

"Yes," Finn nodded, eyes downcast. "I could see he was, too. I wanted you to see everything for yourself."

"What's haunting my father, Finn?" Kaitlin asked, her shoulders slumping. "He said something about a 'curse'. And my mother told me something about my late paternal grandmother, Mabel, potentially 'cursing' my Grandpa Robert for cheating on her—he went on to spend his last days in an institution. I just can't have my father… I mean, I don't know…"

"Kaitlin, Kaitlin," Finn comforted her, his hand gently resting on her trembling shoulders. "Curses are real, yes. But they can't be activated unless it's willed and fated. Your father… he's heeded his own dark companion, rather than the light. We all exist with dualities from birth."

Kaitlin shook her head, her mouth agape. "Right, okay, so how can I help him? Can *you* help him? Ask one of your kind, or… or, I don't know…"

"I'm afraid that's something every creature on earth has to figure out for themselves," Finn bit his lip, his expression serious. "But I feel your visit has been healing for him on some level. Let that comfort you. When it's his time, it will be his time. And rest assured, there's nothing either I or you can do."

"I see," Kaitlin murmured, casting her eyes to the ground as tears began to well up. "Then I will do whatever I *can* do. I will need…to keep you away. Will you…be alright?"

"You're seriously not going to read the Ayat—are you?" Finn asked, raising both eyebrows. But they quickly lowered, replaced by a slick smile. Kaitlin's expression, and the way she pulled the thick burgundy book from her bag on the couch, showed she meant business. "That's the Quran. It's in Arabic."

"Yes, it is," Kaitlin replied, inhaling deeply.

"I know you like languages, polyglot, but you don't read Arabic," Finn snickered.

"I've memorized the prayer instead," Kaitlin spoke softly. She was surprised at how calm he seemed.

"I'm sure your voice will be angelic as you recite it, regardless," Finn said quietly, gazing into her eyes.

"I have to do this," Kaitlin said, lowering her gaze. "For Malin. For me. I'll always be grateful to you, care for you, and pray for you, but…"

A sudden flow of tears interrupted her words. Her lips tasted the salt.

§

SHE SAYS GOODBYE LIKE HOW OUR LOVE HAS BEEN, Finn thought—*elongated, doomed, and painful, yet perhaps more beautiful because of it.*

"Hey, it's okay," he said, stepping forward and reaching his hand out to her. He grinned, though his heart was breaking. Finn had to be the mature one now. He'd let go of love before, and he could do it again, if it meant her happiness—and her safety, too. *I'm too involved, but they must be safe from 'The Group.'*

"May I?" Finn's hands hovered close to Kaitlin's trembling shoulders. "Hug you one last time, Ms. Kaitlin?"

"Oh, Finn," Kaitlin smiled through her tears and nodded. The embrace was so tight it lifted her feet off the ground along with him, both of them spinning slowly.

She kisses me like she talks, Finn thought as their lips met briefly. *Hesitant, but sweet.*

"I know this separation wouldn't have been your heart's first choice," he whispered to her soul. "I know if we *could* have been, we *would* have been. Knowing that is love, and more real than what many married couples share. That's enough for me."

"I…" Kaitlin started, blushing, but couldn't finish her sentence.

Finn smiled at her. "It's alright. Though you haven't stated it in words, you have—*for what it's worth*—loved me. I know."

§

IT FELT LIKE THEY WERE TWO PLANETS ROTATING, WITH volcanoes erupting in different spots of their physical forms. His embrace was beautiful; yet the heat radiating from his touch wasn't as sizzling as Kaitlin remembered. It was almost as if his presence was slowly fading.

Was it the religious text she held in her hand? Or was it her purposeful severing of their connection this time? Kaitlin didn't dare ask. She just hoped he'd answer her anyway, having read her mind.

She took a step back from his face, and allowed herself to get lost in his emerald forest eyes one last time. "You're wonderful, Finn. You don't need me. You're so damned special, and I hope you always know that."

"*Merci beaucoup*," Finn chuckled, beginning to cry himself. He quickly wiped the tear away. "You're a great writer, good with words. You don't have to flatter me, it's alright."

"It's true," Kaitlin smiled. "If I'm a poet, you've been my muse, too. You've gotten me in my emotions again, and have always been there for me through all my craziness—and sometimes my downright selfishness. I'll always be grateful."

"Never forget someone out there loves you… for you," Finn spoke looking straight into her eyes. If the tears in both their eyes could merge, they'd form oceans.

"Don't worry, it's okay," Finn went on. "You were right earlier—my energy has already begun being affected by the verses separating us."

He darted his eyes toward the Quran. "Just get it over with already. The words. Whether you're reading them from there or not."

"Will it…*hurt* you?" Kaitlin's voice trembled. "It would pain me to have to hurt you."

"We don't get hurt by the Creator's words," Finn smiled. "Only enough to become distanced from your kind, when you want….when you're ready…"

"By the way— I've always wondered," Kaitlin began, crossing her arms. "What *does* hurt your kind? Beyond metal. Death-wise, I mean?"

To her surprise, Finn burst out laughing. "You want to straight-up *kill* me now?"

"Nooo," Kaitlin laughed, rolling her eyes. "Of course not. I'm just curious…."

"Relax," Finn continued, "I won't be able to connect with you, manifested like this, after the prayer. If at any moment you develop doubt, you can repeat the verses. Murder won't be necessary. It's not easy for a human to do, anyway. It takes a lot of steps. Don't concern yourself with it."

"I know, I know," Kaitlin shrugged. "But what if I meet…you know, another one of your kind…one who's not as nice as you, Finn?"

"I'll make sure that won't happen," Finn said, smiling into her soul. "For as long as I exist… I'll protect you from afar. No other jinn can cross your way, unless God wills it."

"Finn," Kaitlin muttered, tilting her head.

"Kaitlin, just open the Surah-Baqarah already, and get this over with, please!"

"Finn…" she repeated.

"I know…" Finn winked at her. "I love you, too… Now do it! You've catalyzed us both… and yet only I've paid the penance."

"That's not true," Kaitlin's voice quivered as tears rolled down her cheeks.

"Now—*do* it, Kaitlin!" Finn closed his eyes and took three steps backward.

She took a deep breath. With eyes shut, Kaitlin began.

In the Name of the God, the All-Merciful, the Most Pitying. Allah! There is no God worthy of worship except Him, the Immortal, All-Assisting. Neither drowsiness nor sleep overtakes Him. He owns whatever is in the heavens and whatever is on the earth. Who could negotiate with Him without His permission? He knows what is forth of them and what is beyond them, but no one can grasp any of His knowledge—except what He wills to reveal. His ultimate seat encloses all the heavens and the earth, and the preservation and care of both do not tire Him. For He is the Highest, the Greatest.

As Kaitlin slowly opened her eyes, she gasped to see that Finn had dissipated from her sight. She threw herself onto the ground in further tears, hitting the carpet with her fist.

She knew in her heart that she's made the right decision for herself and her daughter, but Kaitlin couldn't shake the feeling of loss that lingered in his absence. Her companion. Now gone.

Finn.

His name popped up in her mind again. But she somehow knew in her heart he'd gone for good. Deeper into his own realm. Farther from her. Somewhere where her thoughts couldn't reach him anymore.

Would she ever see him or even hear from him again? Kaitlin had no idea. But what had to be done, had to be done. She couldn't risk becoming like her father. Ostracized. Ashamed. Addicted. Alone. *I can't risk not being able to be there for my daughter as she grows up.*

She uttered his name aloud one more time. "Finn..."

Nope. There were no tingles in her neck, nor any goosebumps. Finally after so many years, it was over.

CHAPTER 36

HELEN CALLED OUT AGAIN TO HER DISTRACTED HUSBAND. "John—Merve called earlier. She wanted to ask *you* something."

"I'll get back to her…" John replied over his shoulder, unfolding the letter in his hand. It had arrived in the mail for his name, with a prison address from The United Arab Emirates.

"One second, Helen. I'll be right there, hold on."

Dear John Walker

That's right. As I do not wish to burden you further with anything reminiscent of our inconvenient love, I will not distract you from your new life. Our past will remain securely hidden only in my heart and memory. Therefore, I will not even refer to you by your birth name anymore, let alone our nicknames for each other.

Nor do I wish for my last letter to you in this lifetime to take too much of your time. I just wanted you to know; I love you. I always have, and I still do. I love you with all my heart.

Not '*loved*', in the past tense. Nor '*will love*', as if I can have any way of knowing the future- especially my uncertain one, most likely rotting in prison for the remainder of whatever lifespan Allah Almighty has willed for me. But I *do.* Actively. Wholeheartedly. Heck, sometimes I think I may have even created this whole business, written my books, and done everything I could in order to get your attention. Hoping to reach you,

when you would not allow me any other way of communication.

Gathering lost souls—the jinn and our humankind— in unison to find a bigger purpose in their lives...I made that my mission, a mission I took very seriously. Remember *Robin Hood*, the tale from our youth? So what, I thought, if we sometimes took from the already wealthy? Heck, they didn't even miss it. The people in those companies had so much. I gave back so much more with that money in return. I gave my members a reason to live. When their families and loved ones had turned their backs on them, I welcomed them. Just like I myself have always wanted someone to do to me, after first my mother and brother—then you— had all, for different reasons, turned your backs on me.

I was always an inconvenience. I couldn't be the 'traditional' and therefore safe son to show off. Nor could I be a convenient lover. No. My mere existence in your lives had become burdensome.

So, I relieved your burdens and ran. I ran and created an entire new world from scratch. I wrote. I recruited, I commanded....I became respected. If I could not be loved for who I was, I thought, at least I could be admired.

John Walker, I sincerely am deeply sorry for your daughter, Linette. The young woman did not deserve to die. No more excuses. I hope you can forgive Tan, too, one day. He was a kind, but very lost soul. I know he cared a lot for your daughter, and we were both led astray by our jealousies. We must forgive the dead— no matter how much wrong they may have done, and heal their penance in the afterlife. And, in doing so—heal ourselves. Unload ourselves of that burden.

Forgive Tan, but forgive me, too. I led him to think it would all be justified. I was selfish. But I was in love. Mostly with the idea of what could have been, the love we might have shared—if our circles, for varied reasons, hadn't pulled us apart.

Some things may have been beautiful—and even more beautiful in nostalgic reverie. Yet that does not mean they should be revisited later on— especially if it'll cause more pain and suffering. We were beautiful that summer, and that is frozen in time, preserved in my memory. I let that go now, for holding on to it this long has only caused disservice- mostly to my own self.

By the way— remember that jinn friend since my youth I told you about? Amir? He caused all this. He was the mastermind behind 'The Group'. The business I created. The members, the wealth, and even the slight fame I garnered—everything. He started it all. He once saved my life when I was a young man, and in turn, I pretty much sold my soul to him. I justified it all, as I've said—by convincing myself I was doing something good with my life.

Don't worry about me, though. I've made peace with my brother and mother here, and it's helped me a lot. I don't get visited by Amir anymore. Not even in his bird form. I'm in solitary at the moment, but I'm not alone. I have a little crow friend who visits my barred window almost every day. I watch him. He watches me. I feel accompanied. Gratefully he doesn't talk to me, so I know he's a genuine animal.

My dearest: I know they vet the letters, and I pray the people here in this prison have it in their hearts to allow this to be sent to you. I hope they can have mercy.

As I let you free- energy and soul wise- just promise me one thing. Be happy. Thrive. Pick up my words from time to time, eh, my half-Canadian? Remember me. Please. Allow me to live free still on this earth, through my *words, works.* Freer than I was ever able to in my real world, in my physical shell.

Finally: yes, you may have wondered how, if my love was so strong for you, I cared so much for Tan. I did. But it was you, behind even that love. I was

always searching for you, and for the memory of us from our youth. You. My fire. My igniter. My catalyst.

Don't forget me.

Yours always,

Aresh

John crumpled the paper in and punched the wall as he burst into tears. Taking a deep breath, he straightened the two sheets of paper again, folding them neatly this time, before kissing them. A deep breath swept through him, like the tide coming in.

Aresh Jahan's last request echoed in his mind, as he knew it always would.

He picked up his daughter's copy of Lar's book, which he'd kept for himself. He kissed it.

Never, boy. I promise. No matter what happens. To you, or to me. You will live inside me, in each and every one of my days.

EPILOGUE

Istanbul
2031

THE STRING MELODIES SOUNDED BEAUTIFULLY IN SYNC WITH the view of the ships passing by their hilltop venue, yet Merve's stomach still twisted in knots.

"What if we're always haunted, Aidan?" she whispered to her husband, biting her bottom lip. "What if it never lets us free completely?"

"We're experienced by now, baby, and prepared for anything life may throw our way," Aidan kissed the top of his wife's head.

Merve had felt silly wearing a veil, having been a married woman for years already, but her mother had insisted on something on her head for their social circle. So, she'd settled on a bridal fascinator that looked like a pillbox hat with a small tulle.

"Well, I hope it doesn't," Merve held on to her hair as it blew in the Bosporus Strait breeze. "I hope life finally gives us a break!"

"I think it already has," Aidan winked at her. "Look how far we've come. We've got a new life here, and everyone is behind us."

"You're sure you're okay living in Istanbul now, right? Merve snuggled next to him as they thanked the waiter who passed by with another appetizer. On her official big day, she couldn't bring herself to ask the other more troubling question in her head: *are you also sure you're okay with the fact that we haven't been able to again conceive a child together since the miscarriage?*

"I'm sure, *güzelim*," he said, kissing her forehead with the Turkish word for 'my beauty'. "I'm happy with you. I'll take the easy with the difficult—as long as I get to spend my life with this amazing woman right here. It's enough for me."

"I'm just glad my mother-in-law likes me," Aidan continued with a smile, raising his glass as he gazed at the older lady with silver hair braided across the hors-d'oeuvres tables. She smiled and raised her glass back at him. "I think."

"My mother was just relieved to hear I've been married all this time instead of living in 'sin' with different American guys every six months!" Merve giggled. "I'm just playing. You know she adores you."

A tear fell across Aidan's cheek, tickling Merve's palm as she caressed it. She adored the emotional side of her husband, and had known his feelings to be sincere from the start, despite how much he tried to deny them at work. With anyone else, she might have listened to her mother's warnings after they had reconciled—that he may be a 'gold-digger,' only with her for the wealth left behind by her late father.

Initially, they weren't going to have a ceremony, but her father's recent death had them all thinking differently. Her mother had taken over her father's company but had soon entrusted enough in her son-in-law to make him a partner.

"I haven't exactly… been the ideal man you dreamed of marrying," Aidan said with a heavy sigh.

"We all have our demons, Aidan," Merve shrugged, adjusting her short veil. "Some of us just learn to overcome them… I believe life is giving us both another chance."

"Now I'm going to cry," Aidan chuckled, making Merve giggle along. He cleared his throat. "I'm sorry your father couldn't be here. I would have liked to meet my father-in-law. *Kayınpederim*. Let's visit his resting place again soon."

Merve smiled and nodded at his correct use of the Turkish word for "father-in-law." His Turkish had improved remarkably in a short time. Aidan had made such efforts for her that it felt only natural for her to move mountains for him as well. She only wished her father could have been there at the wedding. *I wish I could have made things right with him.*

"I was too late, Aidan. I can only take comfort in what my mother's been telling me—that *Baba* knew I was alright, thanks to your sister sharing our secret marriage with Sibel and then Sibel calling my mother. I never thought I'd be glad for a friend not keeping her mouth shut! Speaking of which... where *is* that maid-of-honor of mine?"

"Isn't that her?" Aidan squeezed Merve's waist for reassurance, tilting his head toward the brunette approaching them, wearing a lavender A-line gown.

"*Cok güzel olmuşsun*," Sibel said, walking up to Merve, eyes teared as she complimented the bride with a hug.

"*Sağol canım*," Merve thanked her. *Nereden nereye*, she thought. From one corner of the earth and across the ocean—what a friendship her former colleague in Istanbul and her would have. She was so glad the unfounded cases against her husband had been dropped, and that they'd both returned to Türkiye.

"I'm going to go over to Engin," Aidan stated. "I'll let you ladies talk."

"I'll join you soon, baby," Merve agreed as they kissed.

"Everyone's having a wonderful time," Sibel said, patting Merve reassuringly on the shoulder once Aidan strolled off. "The view from up here is exquisite! I'm so happy for you. You deserve this. Truly."

"You deserve to be happy, too," Merve said with a grin. She added with a sigh. "And our country is indeed beautiful, Sibel, but there are some ridiculous things here. Did you hear about that woman found murdered by her husband last night?"

"Argh—I know, don't remind me," Sibel said, making a disgusted face. "The sad music on the news last night played flashbacks of her life. Apparently, she was discovered to be pregnant when her body was found! I also heard she'd tried to get a restraining order against her estranged husband to no avail! They still haven't been able to catch the guy!"

Merve shook her head in disappointment. "It's strange—people can mourn here for days or even weeks with sad music and dedications all over the TV when someone dies unexpectedly… yet they're never supported while they're alive."

"I know," Sibel agreed, her heart heavy. "But this is your official wedding. Let's talk about happier things!"

"Istanbul always brings out the melancholy in us, it's in our blood," Merve snickered. "Sorry!"

"Where did Kaitlin go??" Sibel's eyes scanned the crowd, sighing. "We should get a group photo with the photographer."

Merve turned her head in all directions with worry, offering small smiles to everyone who made eye contact. "Come to think of it, both Kaitlin and Malin wandered off."

"I'm sure Malin's chatting with one of those flirty, cute Turkish guys," Sibel rolled her eyes. "But Kaitlin?"

"Oh, come on, Sibel," Merve chuckled. "You've known her longer than I've known her as my sister-in-law. She's all about playing it safe lately. She probably just went to follow Malin!"

"Exactly—I've known her longer, and she has plenty of suitors, but you're right—she's been focusing more on her health and well-being lately."

"Do you think the therapy's been helping her and Paul?" Merve asked, pursing her lips. *I wonder if Aidan and I will ever get to that point, beyond just a couple of little arguments here and there.*

"It would have been cool of him to at least accompany her at the wedding. He gave Aidan some sickness excuse."

"Maybe it's better he's not here— Kaitlin is a great dancer, you saw her out there!" Sibel snickered. "Paul would have surely given her a hard time about attracting attention. He's worse than Engin sometimes."

"They're still technically married though estranged, right?" Merve asked.

"There must be a reason neither of them has signed any divorce papers, despite it all," Sibel said with a shrug. "Malin's no longer an excuse—she's old enough if they'd truly wanted to seek greener pastures."

"I think after everything they've been through, they're both just trying to water where they are instead," Merve chuckled. "Forgiveness is key. Life is too short already."

Sibel faced her friend. "Look at you, Merve! I'm proud of you. I mean, sometimes I can't help but think—maybe me and Kaitlin even becoming friends in Norway was somehow meant to lead me to you."

"You helped me make things right with my roots here, Sibel," Merve smiled. "I'm grateful. I could definitely have reached out to my father sooner, but I for one will never regret my mistakes overall. They somehow led me to where I am today—and to Aidan."

§

MALIN MAVERICK WAS LOST. THE TALL EVERGREEN SPRUCES surprised her in this new Turkish climate, but the outdoor wedding venue in a forested area of Istanbul's European side absolutely mesmerized her. After all, growing up divided between Canada and Norway— being outdoorsy was more familiar territory to her. If this was an escape from the idle, fake conversation she had to endure back at the wedding reception—she'd gladly relish it a little longer!

"Lucky I'm not wearing some long gown to trip over," she snickered, inhaling the pine aroma as she wandered on, wrapping her arms around her glittering pastel dress, feeling the slight chill in the wind. She'd chosen white, designer-sneakers, too—unlike her mother in her red gown and high heels. Aunty Sandy had already commented on her social media post, saying she approved of the unique look. *She's so cute and sporty*, Malin thought with a smile. She was glad her mother's best friend was happy, with a successful acting career. Settled down with an amazing man. A tall military guy. Devin.

Mom wears more sweats and sneakers now but still couldn't bring herself to wear flats or sneakers under a gown. Malin smiled despite rolling her eyes. Of course her mother was trying to look her best, in the way she knew how. Her father would see the photos, after all, and Malin knew he'd soon be visiting family in Canada again—just in time to visit her and her mother in Toronto, too, after they'd have returned from the wedding.

She had sent a selfie of the two of them with the Marmara Sea glimmering behind them— to which her father had responded "Enjoy, my beauties!"

Malin knew they still loved each other in their own way, as much as both had tried to move on. And it truly felt like any day now they'd be finding their way back together.

Love. Would Malin's new life as an adult mean complicated relationships for her, too? She sighed, recalling how she'd confided in her mother about *him*—Bo. And what he'd turned out to be. And who, in relation, 'Uncle Finn' had turned out to be.

"I think I may love him already, Mom, but I don't think I can lead the type of life he wants to live with me." Malin had cried on her mother's lap after the heartbreaking 'prom' incident. She shook her head. She didn't even want to remember the prom. How embarrassed Bo had

allowed her to be in front of her senior class, and how he'd dismissed her emotional reaction!

"This path we're on is difficult enough, Malin," her mother had told her affectionately, stroking her hand through her hair. *"Life is difficult enough, sweety, that you don't need someone's 'conditions' met to feel loved. Just keep walking. No matter how many times you fall. Just get back up and keep going. I can't have you reliving my mistakes. But some things are unavoidable, I know by now. Regardless—it's all experience, and your disappointments will only make you stronger. No matter what— I've got your back."*

Wiping a fallen tear from her eye—and cursing the blue mascara that had run and stained her fingers— Malin drew in a deep breath as she gazed at her surroundings.

"Now where the hell was that turn I made?" Running her hands through flora in all shades, Malin hummed along to the Beethoven melody as she strutted forward. She smiled. It had been good to see her uncle and Merve—despite being married on paper for years—actually have a large public ceremony. Sure, it was mostly for Merve to appease the family she'd only recently reconnected with in her home country, but Malin didn't mind. It felt refreshing to have physical distance from the emotional bombs the Toronto and Sandnes streets often reminded her of.

The appetizers had already been eaten, and pictures were posed for. Hopefully, no one would notice her temporary absence. Somewhere to the left of her, the subtle sound of violins playing classical music drifted with the breeze, and Malin sighed in relief. She couldn't have strayed too far. She checked her phone again—still no signal.

"Oh, come on," Malin mumbled under her breath. She at least wanted to check her social media account and add more snaps of the breathtaking views she'd taken with her phone. She posed for another selfie, making a peace sign for the camera in front of a particularly dense group of flowers. She'd just post it later.

A sudden cracking sound behind her stopped Malin in her tracks.

"H-hello?" she stammered, spinning around fast—twice, unable to spot anyone. Had Aunty Sibel been right to warn her before she went on this walk? Had that flirty Turkish waiter followed her? She really had to be more careful!

"Malin..." The sound of Bo's voice was ever so close to her ear, sending tingles throughout her body, accompanied by the very familiar heat. *Oh no.* How was all this possible? He had come here, too!

"Malin, please... we have to talk," Bo insisted, his wavy hair blowing in the wind. "You can't avoid me forever."

The shade from the trees made the air cooler than the heated path on the track adjacent to the dog-walk trail. Malin hated how it made her shiver more than she already was at the sight of him. She hugged her torso closer.

"What's there to talk about? You lied to me, Bo! I was made a fool in front of everyone at my prom!" she snapped.

"I... I couldn't control my manifestation powers, Malin!" Bo's face expressed genuine sympathy. "I told you! I didn't disappear on purpose to make you *look crazy in front of your friends*, as you claim!"

"Well, you did!" Malin fumed, clenching and unclenching her fists. "I knew something was off about you after we met, but I ignored my instincts. I was so desperate to make prom a 'cool' experience that I was blind to your true nature!"

"If anyone should be hurt, Malin—it's me," Bo crossed his arms across his chest, scoffing. "You ran off on me. You couldn't accept me in my natural form. Your friends Lucinda and Robert at least saw me as I am in my manifested human form. Why couldn't you just tell them I'm a jinn? If we'd just started dating and I was making you happy, what was the big deal?"

"I couldn't do that, Bo," Malin exclaimed. "And you refused to understand why I had to run. I just want a normal life!"

"You're already going off to university soon," Bo said softly now, shaking his head. "You don't need to see those people from your stupid prom ever again! You're applying to schools in Norway, aren't you?"

"I haven't decided yet," Malin said, holding her hands in front of her, trying to inhale deeply. "Please—we're here for my uncle's big day. I just need to be alone right now."

"I was going to tell you everything right after the dance," Bo swore. "I fell in love with you. You know that."

"Can't you understand that love isn't the issue, Bo?" Malin begged with her eyes. "Feasibility is! My mom had this happen to her—with a jinn. I can't! I know how it goes! I just can't do it!"

"It's all my fault!" Bo stomped on the ground, breaking off some twigs. "I've been so used to my *canine* form that I didn't rehearse my *human* form enough! I didn't mean to disappear on you."

"Canine form?" Malin inquired. "You mean you can… as a jinn… manifest as a dog, too?"

"Whatever," Malin shook her head slowly as Bo nodded. "Those who couldn't see you still wouldn't have been able to. You should have just told me who you really were before letting me be seen with you at such a major event!"

"I didn't think logically, Malin," Bo admitted, blushing. "I just wanted to dance with you. Our actions—and, to some extent, even our thoughts—we can control, but not our emotions. That is both the beauty and burden of being human."

"Lucky for you, then," Malin challenged Bo, gazing straight into his eyes. "…that you're not human."

"Maybe I'm more human than you know," Bo raised his brow. "Or more than other guys you may meet who try to lure you with empty promises."

"What the heck are you talking about?" Malin folded her arms across her chest. "It's chilly here—I need to get back."

"You came here for a reason, Malin! Your spirit led you to this wooded area. You subconsciously felt my presence. Another fellow human, perhaps."

As Bo winked at her, Malin's mouth fell agape.

"Are you going to finally tell me what this is about? The wedding will be over soon."

"I asked Master Lar one time," Bo cut in, beginning to explain. "I asked him why we had to live in the woods. He said it was to protect us from unkind humans, who wouldn't understand why the non-jinn among us were seemingly talking to themselves while communicating with the jinn brothers and sisters. He told me about one particular human member named Tan…"

"Bo, I don't want to hear this," Malin dismissed. "I have to go."

"Wait!" Bo interrupted, smiling. "You're so impatient. Okay—I'll get straight to it. You should know that my birth father could have been a human—Tan. When I asked my mother where this 'Tan' Master had told me about was, she told me about their jinn/human relationship and how he died before I could get to know him."

"Okay, and…?" Malin motioned with her hand for him to go on.

"I could be half-human, girl," Bo teased, adding a wink. "Tan may have been my father. That would make me a more suitable match, no?"

"Meh, I guess it could give you a slight advantage, I suppose… a bit more potential for me at least," Malin smiled and blushed, swinging playfully side to side.

Watching her more relaxed stance, Bo grinned. "Malin, I want to be fully honest with you. I need you to trust me again. So—I'll show you something. Don't be scared. Just… *remember*."

"Remember… what?" Malin asked hesitantly, taking two steps backward.

"When I said that I fell in love with you," Bo started. "I didn't mean on our first date, before your prom. I meant… when we were both kids."

"Oh my God," Malin placed her palms over her mouth as Bo kneeled and transformed into the canine form he'd mentioned earlier. Her hands began to tremble, her tears mixing with the sweat on her palms.

"It's….*you*." Her dog friend from childhood. Their playdates in the Norwegian woods, with her 'fake uncle' Finn—whom her mother had told her about after the prom incident. Was this, then, also the boy with the snowflakes grazing his lips? The one who'd drawn her and gifted it as a birthday present? *The drawing I still keep.*

"You can also call me… *Bob*," Bo nodded with a wink, his voice remaining the same even coming from his dog form. "But Bo is my real name, yes."

"This is all too surreal," Malin swayed in disbelief, her palms still on her face. *Mom's told me about this*. "You can read my mind, can't you?"

"I simply know we were meant to be," Bo shrugged, transforming back into his form in human flesh. "And, yes, I can."

He inched closer to her. "Look, I'm not going to try to fool you, or myself, into thinking this will be easy. Maybe we'll never have biological children. Maybe you'll be uncomfortable walking with me in public, unsure how people will look at us. Maybe we won't have the stable life my dad was too scared to sacrifice…"

As was my mom, Malin closed her eyes, nodding.

She cleared her throat. "Don't you think you're getting a little ahead of yourself, Mister? We've only had a couple of dates! So what if we were childhood sweethearts? Well, *sort* of…"

Bo met her gaze, and they both erupted in laughter.

"We can take it as slowly as you want," Bo went on. "If you

decide to go to college in Norway, you can stay with me in my cabin. You've heard that Master Lar isn't with us anymore, right? 'The Group' doesn't officially exist anymore…"

"That guy's in jail now, yeah," Malin scoffed. "I know how he nearly ruined my parents' lives and even had my dad imprisoned for a time!"

"Right, well, Mom and I still have the cabin," Bo continued. "It won't be easy, but if you stay with us, there's a secondary cabin for just us two, if you prefer!"

"Your mother," Malin started, eyeing Bo up and down. "My mom mentioned her name is Meredith, correct? Making your other potential father… my fake 'uncle' Finn?"

"Yes," Bo sighed deeply. "It's a bit complicated, I know, but…"

"I'm sorry, but this is all too much, too sudden, Bo," Malin stammered, spinning around in a full circle. "I need to focus on finding the best educational opportunity for me. One that doesn't depend on potentially cohabitating with some jinn/human—whatever—boyfriend or sweetheart!"

"We can always forge our own path…" Bo said. "I can make it official on paper if you want, manifest as best I can. If you want kids one day, we can adopt… No half-breeding necessary. When there's a will, there's always a way."

"Why would I ever want to just run off into the woods with you?" Malin snickered, adding a smile. She had to admit, despite everything, she still liked him and didn't want to offend him.

"This has been my life for as long as I remember," Bo shrugged. "I enjoy logging, I genuinely enjoy working out here. And it's not because of Lar's philosophy. I know the world sees him as someone who trapped folks like my parents in a twisted, sexualized pyramid scheme, ruining their lives. But he was actually pretty good to me. He treated me well. And, hey—no matter how it happened, at least life brought me to you."

"Why would you think things could work out for us, when they didn't for my mom, or your dad—if it's Finn… or even that 'Tan' you mentioned?" Malin asked.

"All I know," Bo said, placing his hands on her shivering shoulders, warming her from head to toe, "is that you and I can create our own paths. We might be young, maybe even naïve, but we're not anyone's slaves, Malin."

"I know, Bo…" Malin nodded, smiling as she encouraged him to inch closer. His forehead pressed against hers, sending a tingling warmth through her skin.

"Let's take it slow, okay?" Malin asked, to which Bo nodded.

"Can you try to stay in your human form for me?" she added. "If I promise to try, too, at least as much as possible?"

"I love you, Malin," Bo replied softly. "I'll do anything. Please, do me the honor of being my friend… girlfriend… wife… life partner—whatever you want to call us. All I ask is that you let there be an 'us.' I don't care what label anyone puts on us. I just want to coexist with you. Okay?"

Malin Du Feu. She couldn't help but smile at how natural it felt to even fantasize about her name with his. Despite the complications, the idea of their unconventional union somehow felt right. Maybe Bo was just feeling the romance of the wedding. But something in her heart told her he meant every word.

Malin kissed him. "Okay," she whispered, closing her eyes as their lips met. At first, it was slow, but then they both grew hungry for each other's touch, as if their souls were starved and needed to connect.

Bo slowly pulled back, his brown eyes gazing off into the distance. "Isn't that your mom?"

"Oh, *putain*!" Malin cursed. "What's she doing out here? *Argh*—

she must be worried about me. I have to get back to the ceremony."

"I understand," Bo said, placing his hands in his pockets. "Go."

"I'll see you?" Malin asked, turning back to face him. "And how will I do that?" she added.

"I'll call you," Bo said, winking.

"You promise?" she asked, smiling.

"I'm a being of my word," Bo replied, blowing her a kiss.

Waving goodbye, Malin smiled as she spotted her mother in her red coat over her gown. It was old, but vintage was always in style. As she walked closer, Malin noticed an animal around her mother's feet. *Shit, is that a raccoon? Do they have those here in Türkiye?*

"Mom, I'm here! I'm coming!" Malin called out.

As she neared her mother, Malin sighed in relief. It wasn't a raccoon after all—it was just a black cat, circling her mother's legs as she gently pet its head.

§

KAITLIN WAS LOST. IT'D FELT LIKE A PECULIAR KIND OF HOME TO unexpectedly find herself in a forested area in urban Istanbul, but now, a million questions swirled inside her worried mind. "Malin?" Where had her daughter walked off to? She checked her phone. Still no service.

"*Merde*!" Her heel sank into a muddy patch, and Kaitlin hoped to God it wasn't actual excrement from some animal! "Yuck!"

Oh, bloody hell. Kaitlin removed her heels and held them in her hand. She'd had wet wipes in her purse- she'd deal with her dirty feet later, in the ladies' room. Right now, she had more pressing matters—like just being able to walk to look for her daughter without risking her health!

"Malin?" she called out again. She could have sworn she'd heard her daughter's voice a moment ago. Was she hanging out with someone here?

What's that? Something white, lean, and rectangular in shape, was sticking out of the soil among the bushes. Kaitlin hiked up her gown to her knees for leverage and kneeled down for a closer look.

Mon Dieu! She'd recognized it right away. It was a pregnancy test! She took out a wet wipe and grabbed it.

"Eww!" The soiled half buried under the soul had become discolored.

Wait a minute. It was more of a dark red than brown or black. Was that—blood? The result displayed was 'positive'!

Her mind raced a mile a minute. Why would someone throw a pregnancy stick out here in the middle of the woods?

A chill ran down Kaitlin's spine. She'd thought she'd left all the drama of the last decade behind her, particularly after her father passed away. She was grateful that God had allowed for them to meet—and for him to meet his granddaughter, too, upon his insistence, during a later trip, before he passed on.

But there was 'no such thing as coincidence', was there?

She looked around. Kaitlin couldn't see anyone for miles. She had an inkling she was somehow meant to find this. But why?

Where could this pregnant woman have been now? And why was there blood on the pregnancy test? Had some poor woman shown it to her lover, only to have the lover find the pregnancy inconvenient—maybe even hurt her? Was the woman okay?

Kaitlin giggled to herself, the sound echoing among the spruces.

I'm nuts. For all she knew, the woman had long since given birth, forgetting the test in her bag. Maybe it had fallen out when she tripped and hurt her knee after a nature walk.

But something told her there was more to it. The positive result seemed fresh, after all.

And so, instinctively, she called out to *him* again, wishing he could hear her again, like the old days.

Would he? She wasn't sure. For the longest time, ever since her special prayer to finally ward him off, Finn had seemed to leave for good. She could feel it—the connection was no longer palpable in energy form between them.

Yet, now, she called to him. Hope had become a lifeline to cling to, in a world full of mysteries.

Just maybe, some of those mysteries could have miracles.

Perhaps he could hear her after all—the only one who wouldn't think her crazy for whatever random thought or question had popped into her head. The only one who, no matter what they were—or weren't—would make her feel welcomed. Make her feel grateful to be alive. To exist on this earth as her authentic self, with all her flaws and shortcomings. Maybe, just maybe, they could co-exist. Perhaps he could even age with her. She could convince him to appear in an older human form so she wouldn't feel strange next to him. She could picture it now. Could he do that?

Kaitlin laughed to herself. Or maybe they could just be friends again and solve even more of life's mysteries together. Like this one. They could help the police. Be of use on this planet—just two people, with souls at peace simply in each other's company, no labels necessary. A team.

She knew he'd reassure her, as always, and help lead her to her daughter. *Meow.* Kaitlin looked down—and sure enough, there he was. She petted his furry black head. His green eyes, heavily-lidded and wise, gazed up at her, smiling into her soul.

Finn.

THE END

ACKNOWLEDGEMENTS

Dear reader,

I want to express my heartfelt gratitude to you for accompanying me on this 'catalyst' of a journey through these three books—the latter two of which were originally unplanned but ended up being deeply cathartic for me.

In writing these stories, I've not only drawn inspiration from people I've known (including, yes, brief experiences witnessing jinn), but I've also discovered parts of myself within my characters. Some experiences, like Kaitlin meeting her father before his passing, reflect my personal 'wish fulfillment'—a moment I longed for but never got with my own birth father, who left when I was young (though, unlike Kaitlin's father, who was in a mental institution, mine battled a terminal illness).

I've often found it easier to express myself through poetry, so I felt compelled to interweave some poems into some of the characters' journeys in this final book. I hope these verses have added depth to their stories, and that the variety of characters has resonated with you in some way.

I'm forever grateful to the 'catalysts' in my life, starting with my daughter, and to everyone who has supported me along this writing path.

As I write this in early 2025, I hold hope that by 2031—hopefully even much sooner—justice for the wrongly imprisoned in my homeland, Türkiye, will be realized, just as it was for Sibel and Engin in the novel. Though I was fortunate to grow up with a wonderful stepfather, my 'Malin' still deserves the reunion with our 'Paul' in real life.

Dear reader— may you never have to face certain 'demons' to appreciate the 'heaven' in your life. But if you do, may you recognize that light while you're alive, and always find your way toward it.

Blessings.

XOXO,

Selin Senol-Akın

SELIN SENOL-AKIN is a political scientist and adjunct language instructor aside from her creative writing and featured spoken/published poetry.

The Catalyst, an award winner which reached the online new release charts at #1 during the pandemic, has been re-released as a reader-requested trilogy; with *The Penance* and *The Nestlings*, respectively.

Her acclaimed and top-released multi-modal compilation, **'The Elemental Collection'**, features four books consisting of poetry, a coming-of-age memoir, short stories as well as a play.

-Write Out Your DROPS
-Set Free Your FLOW
-Earth Up Your ROOTS
-Fire Up Your FLIGHT

She lives in New York with her young daughter and family.

Visit selinsenolakin.com for updates.

BOOK CLUB QUESTIONS TO CONSIDER

- Across the three books- particularly in *The Nestlings*- the concept of closure and things coming 'full circle' across generations runs deep. What are some examples of this?
- Since Book One, we've seen Paul's pragmatic, sometimes aloof and traditional-minded personality contrast with Kaitlin's more emotional and spontaneous nature. How do you think this dynamic influences their relationship and the overall story?
- In the trilogy, we often see the opulence and grand beauty of both natural and urban settings contrast with the characters' inner turmoil. How does this juxtaposition affect the tone of the story?
- Younger Aresh mentions the Islamic belief that one angel and one jinn are assigned to each person from birth, with Amir appearing to him as his jinn throughout his life. Given Finn's inexplicable closeness to Malin, do you think he may have been her assigned jinn without realizing it?
- The theme of moral ambiguity runs throughout the trilogy, with examples of both exemplary and negative behavior found in humans and jinn alike. What are some instances that stand out to you in the different characters?

the good.... whispers;
the bad, lies and screams for attention.
the conscience.....whimpers;
torn between the wrong,
for fleeting affection
and the right,
for truth and salvation.

'Bo', by Dalya Akin

www.ingramcontent.com/pod-product-compliance
Lightning Source LLC
Chambersburg PA
CBHW010356050826
48979CB00052B/2822/J

* 9 7 8 1 7 3 4 6 5 6 3 6 7 *